Cold talons pinched his skin

"Dean..." someone said, and he couldn't believe how much it sounded like Krysty.

Something shimmered into being on his right. It was impossibly close, near enough to reach out and touch him. He'd have seen anyone or anything that had come that close to him.

Then he saw the face, made out the features. She was indistinct, as if he were seeing her through a heavy fog.

"Krysty?" Dean said, not believing it.

"Your father is coming for you. Look for him." The words sounded as if they were coming from a long distance, then she was gone.

Before the boy could puzzle over her appearance and what it meant, the door burst open. Framed in it was a nightmare figure Dean remembered well: a giant mutie pig, its beady, merciless eyes nearly buried in wrinkles of scarred gristle.

Before he could draw the Browning, the beast started for him, squealing shrilly in anticipation of an easy kill.

Other titles in the Deathlands saga:

JAMES AXLER

DEATH LANDS®

The Mars Arena

A GOLD EAGLE BOOK FROM
WORLDWIDE®

TORONTO • NEW YORK • LONDON
AMSTERDAM • PARIS • SYDNEY • HAMBURG
STOCKHOLM • ATHENS • TOKYO • MILAN
MADRID • WARSAW • BUDAPEST • AUCKLAND

First edition August 1997

ISBN 0-373-62538-3

THE MARS ARENA

Some say that men love games
Some say that war's a game
And from the Roman days
The red god sets the pace

Mars, it's always Mars
With Venus in his arms

Don't they know the real arena
She draws blood to stoke her love
And the Reaper shows his bones
Shedding kindness like a cloak

Mars, his nights of bliss
Venus and her blood-red kiss

——from the Liar cycle
the rock group Polo Heads

THE DEATHLANDS SAGA

This world is their legacy, a world born in the violent nuclear spasm of 2001 that was the bitter outcome of a struggle for global dominance.

There is no real escape from this shockscape where life always hangs in the balance, vulnerable to newly demonic nature, barbarism, lawlessness.

But they are the warrior survivalists, and they endure—in the way of the lion, the hawk and the tiger, true to nature's heart despite its ruination.

Ryan Cawdor: The privileged son of an East Coast baron. Acquainted with betrayal from a tender age, he is a master of the hard realities.

Krysty Wroth: Harmony ville's own Titian-haired beauty, a woman with the strength of tempered steel. Her premonitions and Gaia powers have been fostered by her Mother Sonja.

J. B. Dix, the Armorer: Weapons master and Ryan's close ally, he, too, honed his skills traversing the Deathlands with the legendary Trader.

Doctor Theophilus Tanner: Torn from his family and a gentler life in 1896, Doc has been thrown into a future he couldn't have imagined.

Dr. Mildred Wyeth: Her father was killed by the Ku Klux Klan, but her fate is not much lighter. Restored from predark cryogenic suspension, she brings twentieth-century healing skills to a nightmare.

Jak Lauren: A true child of the wastelands, reared on adversity, loss and danger, the albino teenager is a fierce fighter and loyal friend.

Dean Cawdor: Ryan's young son by Sharona accepts the only world he knows, and yet he is the seedling bearing the promise of tomorrow.

In a world where all was lost, they are humanity's last hope....

Chapter One

It was the moon that gave the brushwooders away, hanging against the sable sky, as white and bright as a man's skull just carved clean.

Ryan Cawdor stifled a curse as he moved through the shadows and silence of the forest, quiet himself so the stalkers wouldn't know he was among them. The Steyr rifle that had seen him out of so many tight spots across Deathlands was hard and sure in his hands.

Jak Lauren had noticed the brushwooders first, even before the sun had dropped like a burst heart against the leaden evening sky. But Ryan's combat sense had been prickling the back of his neck an hour before that.

Ryan held his breath as he watched the brushwooders, not wanting the thin gray fog to give away his position. The pursuers had broken into at least two groups that he could identify, and walked up the broken terrain in a staggered line. It was a pincer movement, as old as war itself.

The one-eyed warrior had used it a few times himself, and he knew it would be deadly effective. He and his companions were outnumbered at least seven to one.

The sky was clear at the moment, but against the mountains the weather could change in an instant. The wind came out of the north and carried a wolf's bite. Ryan had dressed warmly, wearing a heavy coat he'd found after he and his companions had raided deserted houses along their trek in from the gateway among the Western Islands. But he'd had to shed the coat to double back on their would-be attackers because the material was too light colored.

He felt as if he were freezing on the outside, but inside his survival instinct was burning him up. He was a tall man, a couple inches over six feet, broad shouldered and clean limbed. His dark curling hair held a frosting of snow from the flurries that appeared suddenly over the Sierra Nevada along the Cific Ocean.

Most women would have called him handsome, if not for the black leather patch that covered his left eye, and the cruel, puckered scar that ran from the corner of his right eye, down his cheek to just above his jawbone.

Two pointmen, one the head of each group of the pincer arms, met and knelt to examine the ground in the light of the full moon. Ryan knew they were following footsteps his group had left in the damp earth underneath the crust of snow. Given the weather conditions, it was hard to pass unnoticed even as practiced as his people were.

They'd seen the brushwooders earlier in the day without being seen themselves, not many hours after they'd made the jump through the mat-trans into the area. It had taken Ryan only a few minutes of observation to figure them for the raiding parties he'd been told about. The companions had encountered a group of farmers in the early evening and learned that brushwooders had fired several farmhouses and killed a dozen people. It was part of a spree of violence that had been going on for days.

Violence was nothing new in Deathlands, or to the companions. The fleeing group of farmers had also warned Ryan that the weapons they carried would be highly prized by the brushwooders. Their leader had designs on consolidating his hold on the area and killing anyone who stood to oppose him. Adding to his armament was necessary to achieve his goal.

Ryan had kept his people clear of the roving hands of brushwooders, but their search for a pass through the mountains had brought them here, and within sight of one of the brushwooder patrols. Now they were running through the darkness for their lives.

Rising, his nose tilted up and forward as if he were taking in the air like a hunting hound, the pointman nearer to Ryan turned to his group and pointed toward the east, where the terrain grew steeper. He moved on, moonlight glinting from the blaster in his hands. He'd torn branches off trees and stuck them inside his clothing for camouflage, as well as down the neck of his coat and in the sleeves. Other branches were pinned against his chest and shoulders.

Footfalls crunched into the snow behind Ryan. He whirled, bringing up the Steyr to cover the lone shadow twenty feet away.

"Me," J. B. Dix whispered.

"How many?" Ryan asked.

"I counted forty-two," J.B. replied, closing the distance between them without being spotted, "then I gave up. It's bastard cold out here, and I'm not happy about them not being sociable enough to fall for our little trick back at the other camp."

When they'd found out they were being followed, Ryan had kept his group moving, ready to defend themselves. Once he'd seen the brushwooders were willing to wait, he'd guessed they were waiting to ambush the travelers while they were sleeping rather than risking an all-out confrontation. Tense minutes had passed before they acted as if they were making camp not more than three miles back.

"Could be they did," Ryan replied. "Mebbe they waited until the camp fire we left died a bit, then crept down to where we left those rocks piled up under blankets and realized we'd already gone."

"Didn't have any trouble picking up our trail," J.B. observed, taking off his steel-rimmed glasses for a moment to clean them. When he put them back into place, he reached up and gave his battered fedora a tug, making sure it was settled into place.

"I figure Krysty and the others are a hundred yards ahead of the pack," Ryan said.

"Yeah." J.B. glanced at his wrist chron. "It's been long enough."

"This bunch of coldhearts have got their noses opened up for the chilling they're expecting to dish out," Ryan said, nodding at the rear of the two pincer movements. "They aren't going to expect us to come up on them from behind."

"We want to introduce ourselves fast or slow?"

"Slow," Ryan answered. "They aren't interested in moving quick, and they're getting spread out. If we put a few of them down, it'll only add to the confusion when they start running into their own dead backtracking us after the wheels come off."

J.B. looked up at the dark sky. "The way this snow is picking up and sticking so quick to what's already here, we could buy a few minutes. By the time they get themselves regrouped, the footsteps going up that mountainside will have disappeared."

"Mebbe we'll have disappeared right alongside them." Ryan flashed his old friend a grim smile. "I got the left."

J.B. nodded, then faded into the shadows.

Ryan went in the other direction.

WITH THE STEYR slung over one shoulder, Ryan slipped the panga free of its sheath. The eighteen-inch weapon sported a wicked blade that he kept honed to razor sharpness.

He crept up on the man walking drag on the left pincer movement, moving easily and quietly. The brushwooder had stopped briefly to adjust his pack.

Ryan stepped forward without hesitation, the panga pointed up from his fist. He clapped a hand over the brushwooder's mouth, then sliced the edged steel across the man's exposed neck.

The blade bit deeper than Ryan thought it should have, then hung up for just a second. The man jumped in his grasp as the wound spewed hot blood over Ryan's arms. The brushwooder tried to force a scream past the hand over his mouth, then drew in another breath through his nose to try again, letting Ryan know the windpipe hadn't been severed.

Glancing down, Ryan saw the man had evidently been scratching at his bearded throat when he'd raked the panga across. The blade had sliced off three of the man's fingers, the stubs shooting blood into the air, but the panga had gotten trapped in the middle joint of the index finger.

Ryan changed his leverage and pulled more forcefully on the panga. The blade separated the last finger a heartbeat before opening a wound in the man's neck. He held the kicking, dying man until only spasmodic quivers were left, then shoved the corpse into a stand of brush. He took the man's coat, glancing over his shoulder to make sure he hadn't been seen.

In the moonlight, and supported in the brush, the dead man looked as if he were about to commit an ambush. As a final touch, Ryan propped up one of the corpse's arms and leveled the man's blaster in front of him. Both dead eyes remained open, catching the moonlight reflected up from the patches of snow around them.

Ryan knew it would be enough to fool most folks.

RYAN FELL IN behind the pincer movement again, pulling on the dead man's coat as he ran. The garment was snug across the shoulders, too small to be properly closed. But the stains from his bloody hands blended right in with the accumulated dirt that soiled the coat.

The sounds of his footsteps were lost among the shushing and tramping the brushwooders made. Marked by muddied snow, their trail was easy to track. The next two men in line were together, their heads close as they talked.

Ryan closed the distances then. He held his pace, gazing ahead of the two and spotting the man in front of them. He couldn't act yet, but a dip in the terrain was coming up. If he could move fast enough, he could take them both out before anyone saw. He tightened his grip on the panga.

The dip arrived, and Ryan lunged between his two targets and knocked them off balance. He thrust the panga through the first brushwooder's throat, the point skidding along the vertebrae for an instant, then plunging through the other side.

The brushwooder dropped to his knees, hands seizing the panga impaling his throat. Strained gurgling bubbled from his mutilated throat.

The second one turned, leveling a blaster at Ryan's chest. The brushwooder's face was pale, unravaged by time or circumstance as yet—and feminine.

Ryan swung an arm out, chopping at the wrist behind the blaster. There was enough time for him to draw his 9 mm P-226 pistol and shoot, but the noise would have alerted her companions.

His arm connected with the wrist solidly, and the blaster went spinning away.

Her mouth opened for a scream, and she tried to step away and rake his face with a handful of jagged nails at the same time.

Ryan slapped the arm away, then stepped in and punched her in the stomach. Only a wheeze of pain escaped her lips. Moving into her again, he used his greater weight and size to tackle her and send them both crashing to the ground.

Grabbing the woman's shoulder and maneuvering his weight, Ryan landed on top, keeping his face and eye just out of her reach as he put a hand over her mouth.

Her lips smeared wetly against his palm as she tried to sink her teeth into him. Angry tears brimmed in her pale eyes, then slid down her face.

Ryan had no real mercy in him for hostile strangers, and none at all for people intent on making sure he caught the last train West. But for a moment, looking down into her face and feeling her struggle for life, he paused. He didn't feel anything for her. She was just a predator who'd taken on a bigger and more efficient predator. Her death was a natural progression.

Something in her face reminded him of Dean. Not a resemblance, because he'd marked his son with his own features most, despite Sharona's contribution to the gene pool. Though this was a young woman, clearly no more a child, she possessed that same spark of vitality, the same brash disbelief that anything could ever harm her.

Dean was the reason the companions had come to the Western Islands. Over the past few weeks, the nightmares about the boy had wakened Krysty from sleep a handful of times and left her shaking with dread. Thinking of his son, Ryan let out a slow breath that became a gray cloud, mixing with the air escaping through the girl's nose.

The girl moved quickly, taking advantage of her respite. She shook her arm, and a long-bladed throwing knife popped into her hand from a spring-loaded sleeve sheath.

Only Ryan's quick reflexes, honed by a lifetime in the courtship of sudden death, saved his life. He shifted to one side and felt the stinging kiss of the blade as it slithered along his ribs, unable to find real purchase. The folds of the heavy coat prevented the girl from drawing the knife back and using it again immediately.

Closing his hand more tightly over her mouth and lower jaw, Ryan grabbed a fistful of hair at the back of her head. She kicked under him, trying to dislodge his weight. He rode out her efforts, then twisted her head in his hands just as she managed to work the knife free again.

Vertebrae shattered in her neck as her skull popped free of her spine. The damage robbed her immediately of her motor skills. The knife fell from nerveless fingers.

Her eyes were already dimming when Ryan released her. He forced himself to his feet and ran a hand inside his coat. His fingers came away covered with bright scarlet from the wound along his side, but his touch revealed its clean edges, only a couple inches long and not bleeding seriously.

"What the fuck is going on here?" a man's deep voice demanded.

Ryan was already in motion, his legs driving him. His peripheral vision revealed the man standing at the top of the hill that had cut off the violent business from the rest of the brushwooder attack teams.

Instead of breaking and trying to run away from the man, Ryan raced straight at him, his hand grabbing the throwing knife that still had his blood on it.

The brushwooder hesitated for a moment, stunned by Ryan's apparent suicidal play. He raised his rifle when the one-eyed man was less than fifteen feet away and closing fast.

Chapter Two

Ryan drew back his arm and let the knife fly. Jak Lauren was by far the best hand with a blade Ryan had ever seen, but working for the Trader had provided an all-around education in the arts of death. The knife sailed like a steel dart, barely passing above the muzzle of the leveled rifle.

Ryan dived to one side as soon as the knife left his fingerprints. He hit the ground on his wounded side and stifled a cry of pain from the impact. He rolled at once, clawing the P-226 from its holster.

Coming up on his knees, the blaster before him, Ryan watched as the brushwooder struggled to remain on his feet. The rifle remained unfired. His mouth was open, the haft of the knife jutting from between his lips.

Ryan kept the SIG-Sauer trained on his adversary as he approached the man.

Harsh gagging croaks issued from the man's bloody lips, cut up by the passage of the sharp blade. He tried to bring the rifle around, but Ryan grabbed the barrel and yanked it away. He then pulled up the knife, bringing the man's face toward his own.

The brushwooder tried to scream, but the sound came out his nasal passages as a drawn-out whine that announced his death.

Holding on to the haft, Ryan kicked the corpse free. He cleaned the blade on the man's clothes, then noticed the case over his back. Inside, neatly stored, was a fiberglass

bow in three pieces that screwed together, and a quiver of
arrows.

Ryan drew out one of the shafts and studied the big,
triangular hunting arrowhead at its end. It showed signs of
use, like the bow, but appeared in good shape.

He tossed the case to one side, then maneuvered the dead
man into the trees. It took only a few minutes more to
retrieve and clean the panga, and to arrange the other two
bodies.

Moving at a trot, warm now from his exertions and from
the adrenaline pumping through his system, Ryan adjusted
the case containing the bow and arrows and followed the
brushwooders.

KRYSTY WROTH PUT the thought of the pursuing brushwooders as far out of her mind as she could, concentrating
instead on the broken terrain. The full moon was both a
blessing and a curse.

Without it, they'd have been dead for sure. Chasms
opened up unexpectedly, covered by shadows.

"No torches, no muzzle-flashes," Mildred Wyeth said
beside her. "And that's the good news. The bad news is
that Ryan and J.B. could already be chilled and we just
don't know it yet."

"No," Krysty said. "If Ryan was dead, I'd know."

Pressing on, the red-haired beauty followed the narrow
path that Jak had taken only minutes ago. The ledge was
only a couple feet wide, and wisps of snow trying to cover
its surface made walking only a little tricky. She thanked
Gaia, the Earth Mother, that the wind was too cold to let
the flurries cling to the stone. Conditions could have been
much worse.

Krysty felt her hair coil tightly against her scalp. Her
hair was deep crimson and prehensile, products of her mu-

tie blood. She was a couple inches short of six feet, with generous curves and emerald green eyes. The dark blue Western boots she wore weren't made for hard climbing, but they were what she was used to, and anything else would have made it even harder.

Navigating another area of loose rock, she concentrated for a moment, trying to *feel* her lover's presence. Besides the sentient hair, her mutie heritage bequeathed her other things. The limited prescience she sometimes experienced had been working overtime of late, mostly about Dean. And maybe only then because the boy was so much a part of Ryan.

Mildred nearly slipped, and Krysty watched as the woman righted herself and pressed against the stone face of the mountain. Her coat whipped around her.

"Damn wind," the black woman said. "Caught me by surprise. I'm not as aerodynamically correct as you are."

Of medium height, Mildred was stocky. Her face was almost covered by the hood she wore, but a few of the beaded plaits of her hair hung out on either side of her chin. A Czech-made ZKR 551 .38 target revolver was in one of her gloved hands. She'd learned to shoot more than a hundred years ago, and her skills had been good enough to win her a few medals.

Born on December 17, 1964, Mildred was still in her thirties. Three days before 2001 had been rung in, she'd gone to a hospital in her hometown of Lincoln, Nebraska. The operation was supposed to be somewhat boring to those in the medical field: exploratory abdominal surgery, nothing life-threatening at all.

Instead, she'd had a reaction to the anesthetic and gone into a coma. In order to save her, the surgeons had placed her in cryogenic sleep. She'd slept on for a hundred years, through the death of the world and of everyone she knew. Ryan Cawdor and his companions had rescued her.

"Usually I rather enjoy a brisk walk in cool weather. And mayhap a little adventure, as well. However, as we come to the end of this injurious little excursion, I shall be vexed to end up without a cup of tea to cap off a rather exciting evening."

"Doc," Mildred said, "as long as you're flapping your lips the way you are, I know you aren't too put out."

"My dear Dr. Wyeth," Theophilus Algernon Tanner said, "your erudition is beyond reproach. However, the skill you exhibit in expressing yourself can be a tad bit lacking for one of the medical calling."

Mildred had been a medical doctor in her day, specializing—ironically—in cryogenic research and development.

Like her, Doc Tanner had been displaced in time, though his removal from the century he'd been born into had been achieved by means Krysty understood even less than cryogenics.

Doc was tall and thin, which gave his long arms and legs even greater reach. His silver hair normally fell to his shoulders, but was now whipped into a frenzy by the wind. He'd thrust his ebony walking stick through his belt, the silver lion's-head handle protruding through the part in his coat. The collar of his stained and faded frock coat was visible above the collar of the thermal jacket he wore over it.

Born in a small hamlet in Vermont in 1868, Doc had been hauled into the twentieth century by the white coats of Operation Chronos. He had proved ungracious and difficult by his own reckoning, and had been dead set on returning to his beloved wife and children. As a result of his rebellious actions on several occasions, the powers behind Operation Chronos had shoved him a hundred years into the future, into the sprawl of savagery that had become Deathlands.

"Blow it out your ass, Doc," Mildred said.

"Indeed," the old man replied. "Your words ill become you, dear lady."

Krysty ignored the bantering. Camaraderie took many forms. Some were more noisy than others.

The ledge turned right at nearly ninety degrees. She took it gingerly, keeping her weight toward the stone face.

The snow flurries swirled into her face now, making it hard to see. She blinked stinging tears from her eyes. Her hands felt numb, and she had to wonder how much longer she could trust them.

"Are you sure about the pass, Doc?" she called back over her shoulder.

"My dear Krysty," Doc said, a smile framing the shocking white perfection of his teeth, "my certitude is based wholly on the fact that I trust John Barrymore's skills with that minisextant of his, even though we're operating on knowledge gleaned from an exercise in cartography that is only a modest hundred or so years old and did not enjoy the opportunity of conforming to a vastly violated topography in this region."

"You're making my head hurt," Mildred complained.

"You have," Doc said in simpler words, "my best guess. Admittedly we appear to be betwixt a rock and a hard place."

Krysty silently agreed and went on. The ledge ended abruptly. Without pause, it vanished right into the side of what looked like a sheer rise of fifteen feet or more.

She scoured the wall in front of her and on the right. Nothing was there.

"What's wrong?" Mildred asked.

"Dead end," Krysty replied. She looked over the ledge

to her left, feeling the pull of vertigo. The flying snow vanished into the shadows that lay stretched against the mountainside. She couldn't see the bottom.

"What about Jak?" Mildred asked.

Krysty shook her head, not feeling the albino teenager anywhere. "I don't see him."

Mildred scraped a foot across the stone ledge. "Awful damn slippery here."

Doc came up beside them, one hand on the mountain behind as he balanced and peered over the edge. "Oh, dear," he said in a quiet voice. "The poor lad."

Chapter Three

Catching the lower limbs of an oak tree, Ryan climbed ten feet up. The branches shook, littering the ground with snow that fell from the green leaves, but none of the brushwooders took notice. Despite the wintry feel of the night and the snow, it was only early fall. The nukecaust had screwed up Nature's rhythms a hundred years earlier, and the earthquakes and the active volcanoes in the area affected the weather, as well, seeding the air from dozens of radioactive hot spots.

Trader had talked about the strange atmospheric conditions hovering over the region. Ryan knew for a fact that farther north the land had turned to frozen ruin, and the volcanoes stretched in between, with some of them way to the south. With the volcanoes spouting rad-blasted waste into the air on a regular basis, anything could come falling out of the sky and he wouldn't have been surprised. He'd stopped really smelling the sulphur stink hours ago, but he remained aware of it.

He nestled in among the boughs, gauging the strength of the pincer movement spread out around him with a trained eye.

His and J.B.'s efforts hadn't gone unrewarded. The steady advance of the brushwooders had been broken, and a few milled around waiting for the rearguard to catch up. Word was evidently spreading up the line that a number of them weren't coming. Ryan could see even the pointmen were holding their position some 120 yards away at the foothills that led to the steep mountain trail where Krysty and the others had gone.

Clouds scudded over the bright moon, laying patches of darkness over the broken land. But against the growing white islands of drifting snow, the brushwooders stood out as good targets.

Ryan didn't intend to miss the opportunity to add to the confusion. He opened the case containing the bow and quiver of arrows. The three sections easily screwed into one another. Fitting the string was tricky while standing in the tree, but he managed.

Voices reached his ears now, letting him know the brushwooders were abandoning the stealthy approach.

The arrows felt heavy enough for proper chilling. He was more at home with a handblaster or the panga, which was an old friend, tried, trusted and true. But he knew his way around a bow. His father, Baron Titus Cawdor, had seen to the education of all his sons. The barony at Front Royal hadn't been easily won, nor easily held. A knowledge of weapons had been necessary.

He nocked an arrow, drew it back to his ear and sighted through the opening between the branches. Releasing half a breath, he let it fly. As the arrow jumped from the bow the string twanged, but not loud enough to be heard from more than a few paces.

Less than forty yards distant, the arrow pierced a man's inner thigh, and a primal cry of pain suddenly rent the chill air.

The man stumbled, bent double and hovered over the fletched end of the arrow. The other brushwooders stood frozen, wondering how one among them could have been wounded without sign or sound of an attack.

"Fireblast," Ryan cursed. Shooting one of the men and

dropping him dead in his tracks had been the plan. Maybe he'd have been lucky enough to down another one or two before they'd have even known he was among them. Wounding the man and letting him scream spun events into the sudden rush of near death.

He sighted on another target, reminding himself to aim higher with the bow because the trajectory had proved wrong on the first shot. He let out half a breath, then released the three-fingered hold he had on the string.

This time the feathered missile flew true, biting deeply into the chest of a brushwooder taking cover behind a lightning-blasted tree at the wrong angle. The man went backward, hands wrapping around the shaft as he was driven by the impact, and stretched out across a patch of snow that quickly turned dark.

Blasters roared, muzzle-flashes visible among the trees in a semicircle of fire.

None of the bullets came close to Ryan. He drew back another arrow and released it, leading a figure sprinting across an open space. Though he'd aimed at the center of the body, the shaft went low, taking the brushwooder in the thighs from the side, fixing them together. The man fell headlong to the ground.

Bullets whacked into the oak tree, ripping leaves and branches free. A collective cry rose up from the brushwooders as more and more of them spotted the source of the arrows.

Ryan abandoned the bow, letting it drop through the branches below, and reached down to grab the barrel of the Steyr. Slipping the sling from his shoulder, he brought the rifle on target as three men broke cover and streaked for the tree.

His finger stroked the trigger, two shots per man. Three

corpses dropped in a tangled sprawl before the last one could break away.

"He's in the tree!" a woman yelled.

"Over here!"

"Get him!" someone yelled. "Blow the son of a bitch out of the tree!"

Ryan emptied the Steyr's clip rapidly. He knew he brought down three more men scattered beneath the trees, and one of them for sure wouldn't be getting back up again.

A bullet cut through Ryan's sleeve as he worked his way into a clear area between the branches on the rear side of the tree. He stepped out over the ten-foot drop and let go.

He bent his knees to get himself loose for the hard landing. At the bottom of the fall, he let his weight go with the pull of gravity, then pushed himself back up.

Out of the corner of his eye, he noticed the shadow along the bole of the tree that didn't fit. It was man-shaped and held a blaster.

"FUCKER'S REALLY PUT his foot up the ass of Satan this time."

As he gazed through his Starlight binoculars at the one-eyed man in the oak tree calmly fitting another arrow to the bowstring, Hayden LeMarck said, "I'll give you five to two that he comes out of it alive."

"I'll take your jack," Wallis Thoroughgood replied, "and be man enough to stand you a beer at Dripping Sal's when we get back to Jakestown." He was a blocky man, crowding sixty if he was a day. Dressed in a coat and insulated coveralls, only the man's round face showed, the features resembling those of a demented cherub.

The rattle of bridles and the creak of saddle leather sounded behind LeMarck. "Keep those damn horses still.

You don't, and we could still end up hip deep in goddamn brushwooders.''

"Yes, sir," someone replied.

As one of the head sec men for Baron Sparning Hardcoe, LeMarck got respect. He was a tall, lean man with fair hair and muttonchop whiskers that ran deep auburn. A hawk's bill of a nose jutted over a thin-lipped mouth.

The brushwooders had raided some of the outer farms around the little ville of Angeltears less than a week earlier. Representatives from the ville had sailed north to Jakestown ville, the biggest community in the seven villes under the control of the Five Barons, and talked with Baron Hardcoe himself. Hardcoe had made it LeMarck's job to track down the brushwooders and punish them, and assigned twenty men to go with him.

Angeltears was the smallest of the seven villes. As such, it was the least productive and the least developed. Any of the other four barons would have ignored it and let the people in Angeltears work out their own problems.

Hardcoe cherished every bit of his temporary empire, though. Even if he had to relinquish it to one of the other barons at the end of the Big Game in eight days.

In the day and a half he'd been tracking the brushwooders, LeMarck had found out the group had grown to nearly a hundred strong. He'd gotten his information from three brushwooders he'd tortured the previous night. The different groups had united under a man named James Ball Daugherty, who'd blown in from somewhere across the big desert if the stories were to be believed. No one had known how successful Daugherty had gotten at organizing the brushwooders until the raids on Angeltears had left so many dead farmers in burning fields. It was the biggest mob of them that had ever been seen in the history of the villes.

After learning how many enemy they were truly facing

and knowing they'd be taking them on in their turf, Le-Marck's team had wanted to pull back and call on Hardcoe for reinforcements. With all that the baron had going on in Jakestown, LeMarck had been reluctant to do that until he couldn't see any other way clear.

That was why he'd been tailing the brushwooders. If Daugherty was to get himself suddenly dead through an assassination attempt, LeMarck figured the big group of brushwooders would break back down into smaller, more-manageable units that could be exterminated at the proper time. Their threat would have been removed.

The sec man was in his late twenties, and his closest experience to a father figure had been Hardcoe. There wasn't anything LeMarck hadn't done or wouldn't do for the man. He knew Hardcoe was concerned about losing the seven villes to one of the other barons through the baronial charter, and LeMarck had been up late nights thinking about how to ensure Hardcoe retained control.

That was why he'd been playing with the idea of trying to take Daugherty alive after hearing about the man. Arriving in Angeltears the day before yesterday, though, he'd heard about the way Daugherty ran the brushwooders like barbarians. There was no finesse about the man, no real cunning. The only thing that stood out about him was that he had a genuine taste for blood.

Before, the brushwooders had scavenged from the out-lying farms, not killing unless someone tried to stop them. They were thieves, and a menace only to people who traveled among the seven villes. Of the Five Barons, Hardcoe was the only one who organized sec parties to ride shotgun on trade caravans. Of course, to get the protection, the caravans also had to fit in their schedules with Hardcoe's, which caused problems for those people selling perishable items.

Now LeMarck figured it was only a matter of time before

Daugherty got to thinking about taking one of the fat caravans in the next eight days. The people of the seven villes knew about the Big Game, too, and the fact that they might be changing barons again. And if Hardcoe did lose out, there would be no more caravans.

It would be Daugherty's last chance at a big score worth a lot of jack.

LeMarck had come into the forest with the intent of not letting that happen. But watching the one-eyed man work his team ahead of the brushwooders and double back on them, the sec boss got to considering his rejected plans for Daugherty.

The brushwooders' leader wasn't as cunning and smart as LeMarck had hoped. But the one-eyed man was a thriller on wheels, the kind of man Hardcoe could use for the Big Game. He'd like to give the baron some good news when he joined his sec men on the ride to Vegas.

Still, the brushwooders outnumbered the two men they were stalking. Just in case he had to tip the scales in the one-eyed man's favor, LeMarck reached for his rifle and kept a keen eye on the advancing brushwooders.

JAK LAUREN MOVED instinctively, rolling to his left, already wary since the blaster had erupted down the mountainside. He swiveled his head, trying to figure out what had attacked him. All he'd noticed on some subliminal level was an explosion of movement from the snowbank ahead of him.

Broken terrain ranged all around him. Some of it looked smoothed over by the drifting snow, but it was deceiving. A step on unsafe ground meant a twisted or broken ankle for an unwary traveler. Twice he'd found areas where the snow had covered cracks in the mountain big enough for a body to plummet through. The first one ended in a shattered death's-grin of rock thirty feet down. He never had seen the bottom to the second.

A sibilant hiss ripped through the air.

To Jak, it sounded like a man stropping a razor, working up a proper shaving edge. With the wind blowing, it was hard to tell exactly what direction it came from.

He wore a long coat over his regular clothes, but he shucked out of it. Even with the drop in the temperature and the howling wind, he knew he could stand the cold for a few minutes—especially if those minutes added to his life expectancy.

He drew the .357 Magnum Colt Python from his belt and a pair of his leaf-bladed throwing knives.

The hiss cut through the air again, followed by immediate movement. This time Jak got a better look at the creature.

It shot up from the ground as if fired from the mouth of a blaster. Diamond shaped and at least a foot and a half across from opposing corners, the beast sailed through the air straight at Jak's face.

The teenager ducked and spun, bringing up the .357.

From the brief glimpse he'd caught of the creature, Jak knew it was white and had two deep aquamarine eyes set close together. A thin, barbed tail almost four feet long trailed out behind it.

When it hit the snow, the beast vanished, blending in like a chameleon.

Jak fired three shots that ripped through the snow and hammered rocks into pieces. At first he'd figured the creature was albino, but the way it vanished into the landscape let him know it had control—at least to some degree—over its coloration.

Albinos he knew about. He himself was bone white and had ruby red eyes. His long hair was the color of fresh

milk. At something short of five and a half feet tall and
built whipcord lean, he didn't look like the deadly efficient
killer that he was. He'd been born and bred in Cajun country in the south of Deathlands, but he'd ranged far and
wide, going up against his share of predators.

With the sibilant cry, the creature rocketed at him again.
The tail whipped in readiness as it took to the air, and a
large, fanged mouth opened on its underside.

Considering the aerodynamics of the mutie beast, Jak
figured that it scooted along the snow until it built up
enough speed to get airborne. It didn't need much room or
time in the winds. And evidently it knew how to best use
those winds to its advantage.

The beast cut through the air, streaking for Jak's neck,
flipping sideways to lose altitude and change direction suddenly so it approached from an arc.

Instead of dodging this time, Jak took three running steps
toward the creature, which didn't break off its attack. The
tail whipped forward under its flat belly.

At the last moment, Jak leaped high into the air, using
his innate acrobatic abilities and spring-steel muscles to
their fullest. He put out a hand, and his fingertips lightly
grazed the slick, oily membrane of the animal's body.

The mutie beast shrieked in anger, flapping its sides to
change direction. With the wind against it, there was no
way it could turn, but it became a more challenging target.

Jak flipped over the creature, coming around with his feet
over his head and facing in the direction of the creature's
glide path. No more than five feet from his target, he pulled
the trigger through the remaining three rounds in the heavy
blaster. As he continued his flip, he twisted to land on his
feet facing the mutie beast.

Two of the hollowpoints slammed into the creature, ripping it apart. It collapsed to the ground, a bloody mass of meat.

The teenager put his knives away, then shook the empty casings from the Python and reloaded.

"Jak!" Krysty called.

"Here." The albino walked to the dead creature and picked it up by the barbed tail. He crossed to the edge of the cliff face he'd climbed.

Krysty, Mildred and Doc gazed up at him, worried looks on their cold-pinched faces.

"Dear lad," Doc said, "we thought you'd fallen to your demise."

Jak shook his head. "I fall, I'd scream. Let you know not safe."

"Of course you would. How foolish of me to think otherwise. Forgive the awkward ruminations of a man aged by experience."

"Sure." Jak shrugged. More weapons were being used down the mountainside. He saw the bright sparks leaping among the trees.

"What was the blasterfire?" Krysty asked, her attention divided between Jak and the action behind them.

The albino lifted the dead mutie beast, then dropped it onto the ledge among them. "This. See one, better chill quick. Otherwise, chill you."

"How'd you get up there?" Mildred asked.

Jak knelt and pointed, wanting to go back for his coat. But it would be better to wait, in case there was another of the gliding creatures. The next person up could cover his back.

"Step there," Jak said. "Careful. Skin knees, if go too sudden like. Then step there." He pointed again. "Get up this far, help pull you up."

Krysty went first, managing the climb with difficulty. "Did you find the pass?"

Jak shook his head. "Not yet. Mebbe out there. Not look everywhere yet. Shooting started, I got back here."

Krysty stood beside him, her pistol in her fist. Her attention shifted back to the forested lands farther down.

"Shooting good sign," Jak said as he reached for Mildred's hand. "Ryan and J.B. dead, nobody to shoot at."

Chapter Four

Ryan squeezed the Steyr's trigger before he had the rifle quite to his shoulder. When it fired, the recoil made the Steyr jump in his hands.

The bullet caught the brushwooder full in the chest and knocked him back. The man's blaster discharged into the ground more than a yard from Ryan, tearing up a fist-sized clod of snow-frosted earth. Already dying, with blood spitting up over his lips, the brushwooder stubbornly tried to bring his weapon to bear again.

Ryan shouldered the Steyr and aimed at the man's head. Before he could squeeze off another round, the familiar boom of J.B.'s Smith & Wesson M-4000 shotgun filled the clearing beneath the tree.

A nasty hornet's nest of the Remington fléchettes belched out by the 12-gauge shotgun tore into the man's face, shoulders and chest. The impact bared white breastbone and bounced him against the tree bole. The few fléchettes that had missed the man embedded in the tree and stuck out like steel spurs.

"Close one," the Armorer commented as he sought a new target.

"Been closer," Ryan answered. He pushed the dead man from the tree and used the trunk for cover.

J.B. stood fast and worked his way through the shotgun's magazine, spitting out death. The swarms of fléchettes chopped into the brushwooders and stripped them of their sudden courage. "You about ready to get out of here?"

"I'm done." Lifting the Steyr, Ryan quickly picked off two men who were within his range. "You take the lead, and I'll close the back door."

Renewed gunfire broke out behind them. Turning, his back to a boulder almost as big as a wag, Ryan glanced at the trees and brush where they'd left the dead brushwooders. The advancing brushwooders had gone to ground under his fire and were shooting at the corpses. Bullets hitting the dead brushwooders caused jerky movements, drawing even more intense fire.

"Hold your goddamn fire!" someone yelled. "Those people are dead!"

"That'll slow them for a minute. Let's get out of here," Ryan said.

The Armorer took point, moving in a broad semicircle that would bring them to the foot of the mountains.

Driving his legs hard against the muddy earth, Ryan hoped Krysty and the others had found the pass they'd been looking for. If the storm front kept moving in and trapped them in the mountains, it could mean their deaths.

"GREN!" J.B. called out.

Ryan went to ground at once, sliding in behind the thick trunk of a felled tree.

J.B. pulled the pin on the explosive and lobbed the bomb toward the small knot of brushwooders defending the foothills that led to the ledge climbing into the mountains. "A little something extra I took off one of the brushwooders while I was punching their tickets for the last train West."

Ryan hunkered down against the tree, both hands gripping the Steyr.

Someone tried to yell a warning, but the effort was torn

apart and lost in the detonation of the gren. Shrapnel sliced through the trees overhead, and the concussion hurled small rocks and gravel in all directions.

"Company's coming up from behind real fast," J.B. said into the silence that followed the blast.

Ryan spotted the shadows shifting through the trees behind them. No longer trying to keep their presence a secret, some of the brushwooders carried lanterns and torches.

"There's not going to be an easy way of doing this," Ryan called out.

"Then it'd be best to get it over with quick so we don't have time to obsess on it," J.B. replied without hesitation. "The coldhearts behind us know we're in a tight spot."

Already bullets were starting to clip branches from the trees overhead and slam into the bark on Ryan's side of the dead oak.

"On three, then," Ryan said, knowing the brushwooders nestled in the foothills could hear them. He drew the SIG-Sauer with his right hand and held the rifle in his left.

"On three," J.B. repeated.

"Three!" Ryan pushed himself up and into a run. There was a lull as the brushwooders were caught by surprise.

Spotting two men who shared cover behind a big squared-off rock that came up to their chests, he brought up the SIG-Sauer and snap-fired two rounds. Both 9 mm hollowpoints caught the man on the left in the chest over the heart and drove him backward. As he spun, bringing the blaster to bear on the second brushwooder, Ryan saw the other man's head jerk backward.

Ryan never broke stride. A second later he reached the rock in time to spot a hard-faced woman kneeling at the side of a tree. She had J.B. in her sights less than a dozen paces away.

Chapter Five

Ryan fired three rounds into the woman's belly, blowing her guts out. The woman started to scream, forcing more of her intestines outside her body.

Ryan left her to it. The screams might prove distracting and hold off the other brushwooders for a few seconds more.

J.B. finished up with the last man remaining in between them and the path leading to the ledge. Expertly he moved his Uzi subgun in a tight figure eight that chopped his target down.

Ricochets whined off the square-cut rock as Ryan knelt to examine the second brushwooder who'd been standing there. He kicked the man over onto his back, surprised there was no exit wound from whatever had hit him.

The silvery chill of moonlight bathed the dead man's face. A neat, round bullet hole was centered between his wide, staring eyes.

The gut-shot woman finally died, and all her painful shrieking died with her.

"Problem?" J.B. asked, ducking behind the rock.

"He's been chilled." Ryan dropped the head. "But I didn't chill him."

"It could have been an accidental shot, what with all these rounds flying."

"Square between the eyes like that?" Ryan shook his head, then raked his gaze over the ridges surrounding the forested valley. The distance was too great and the shadows drawn too deeply to allow him to see much. And getting more adventurous in looking wasn't a good plan; the brush-wooders were hitting the square-cut stone regularly now. "I don't think so."

"Me, neither," the Armorer stated. He leaned over and put his fingers on the dead man's face. "Big round. Thirty-aught-six mebbe. And for it not to penetrate the head, means it had to have been a subsonic round." He flinched from stone splinters driven from the rock by a fresh salvo of bullets. "Hanging around here has about run its course."

Ryan nodded, his mind still working at the man who lay before him. He didn't care for mysteries or puzzles. He broke for the path leading to the ledge.

"ANYTHING?"

Ryan shook his head, scanning their backtrail along the climb while they took a breather. "Brushwooders are coming up behind us, but they're losing ground."

"How many?"

"Thirty, mebbe."

Kneeling beside him, J.B. lifted his fedora and brushed an arm along his forehead. He grimaced at the sweat stains on his coat sleeve. "We keep moving like this, sweating this hard, we're due for a bad case of hypothermia."

Ryan nodded. Through the binoculars he could occasionally see the line of brushwooders winding around the turns. Sniping would get a few of them, but then they'd have his position, too, which might make it bad all the way around.

He pushed himself to his feet. "Let's go."

The cloud cover had wiped away the moon, dimmed the light they had to move by. If it wasn't for the reflective quality of the snow, they wouldn't have been able to see in the dark at all. Their progress had slowed considerably.

"The ones who don't fall and kill themselves on the climb, or we don't shoot if they come up on us, the storm may take," Ryan declared.

The wind had picked up, and it had turned colder.

"Their man isn't a leader," J.B. said. "He gets enough of them chilled tonight, they'll turn on him. They must be good and afraid of him to come this far."

Ryan kept a hand in contact with the stone wall at his side as he pressed forward. The snow flurries increased, burning cold into his face except where the scar tissue had robbed him of sensation. Though he couldn't feel his face so much anymore between the old injuries and the fanged cold, he couldn't keep his teeth from chattering like a desert rattler in full threat.

Without warning, his boot skidded out from under him. The edge of the abyss to his left yawned open suddenly. Wrapping around him like a demanding lover, the wind sucked at him, trying to pull him from the wall.

"Fireblast!" he swore, getting his balance back enough to fall against the wall behind him.

J.B. reached for him.

"Got it," Ryan said. The hunger and the cold had hollowed him out enough that he knew he was running on adrenaline. He pushed himself up, feeling the dark anger moving around inside him. Dying quiet, frozen to death on some mountain, had never been in the cards for him the way he had it figured. When he caught the last train West, it'd be with a blaster in his fist and his blood mixing with that of an enemy.

"We can rest," the Armorer said.

"We can rest when we're dead. Something here." Ryan scraped at the ground with his boot. Thin black liquid covered the stone in odd-shaped clots. As they tore under his boot, some of them turned red.

"Blood," J.B. commented.

Ryan nodded. "Somebody's." His eye lit on the awkward shape at the bottom of the sheer rise in front of him. The wall ahead bore one of Jak's signs, letting him know to keep going straight.

The shadow turned out to be a dead beast that had been blown apart by bullets. The eyes had dimmed, but there was no mistaking the deadly way the tail was barbed. One of Jak's leaf-bladed knives was thrust between the creature's eyes.

"You ever seen anything like this?" Ryan asked.

"No."

"Trader always said a man could live out his whole life in Deathlands just looking at what there is to see and never see it all. As soon as a man passed on, mutie genes tickled by all the radioactivity breezing across the Deathlands would make up something new."

"And more than likely it'd be something hungry," J.B. finished.

Ryan pulled the throwing knife from the dead mutie beast. "Guess Jak left this as a message."

J.B. grinned. "It isn't hard to understand. You see any of these, kill them quick."

Ryan slung the creature out over the abyss and let go. He never heard it hit bottom. He cleaned the knife with the snow and put it in his gear. "Step careful around the blood. I'll help you up first." He put the Steyr against the wall and made a stirrup of his hands.

J.B. stepped into Ryan's hands and scrambled up as he was pushed along. He reconned the top, then gave Ryan a thumb's-up. "Ace on the line. We're clear." He offered his hand down.

"In a minute," Ryan said, unbuckling his pants. "Got something to take care of." It was almost too bastard cold to piss, but he managed. His urine smoked as if it were on fire, splattering the ground in a wide puddle. When he finished, he buttoned up his pants again, then took the hand the Armorer extended.

At the top of the wall, Ryan looked back down on the puddle of piss. It was barely noticeable under the cover of shadows.

"A few minutes at this temperature," J.B. said, "that's going to freeze up real nice."

"Hope so. Be a nice surprise for the first brushwooder or two who happen up on it. If we get lucky, mebbe it'll take out the ramrod."

He found Jak's next mark, then turned his steps in that direction. Krysty and the others couldn't be much farther ahead.

Chapter Six

Krysty pushed herself against the wind as fast as she could, taking time only to make sure each footfall landed on solid ground. They were up in the crown of the mountains now, and the crevasses that had resulted from the quakes and the volcanic pressures cropped up more frequently.

Jak and Mildred had gone off in a northerly direction to check out another route open to them. She still had fifteen minutes before they were supposed to return to report their findings.

The valley between the gap-toothed peaks she was using as her compass points suddenly split into two again. She turned up the collar of her coat. The thought of Ryan out there unprotected against the elements didn't sit well.

"Gaia watch over him," she said, "because I've never loved anyone more." The wind whipped her words out of her mouth, battered them into nothing.

"What's that, my dear?" Doc asked from behind her.

"Wishful thinking."

The old man came up beside her, his head pulled down into his coat and his hands jammed into his pockets. He held his walking stick up under his arm. The butt of his .63 Le Mat blaster stuck out from between the buttons of the coat. "Not upon a star, though, I see. It comes to mind that with the seeming scarcity of the mercury's ability to hit the scarlet field at all upon this night, and with the stench of sulfur from the volcanoes so like brimstone, one could truly say it is as cold as hell upon this mountain.''

Krysty ignored the comment and considered the two options before her.

Both chasms led through the rock, angling down.

''Pardon, dear lady, I know your mind is not entertained a whit by my self-indulgent observations.''

''Not your fault, Doc. I'm just worried about Ryan.''

''Think not upon that. He'll be along in short order, I'm sure.''

Krysty knew Doc was trying to make her feel better, but he was also sincere. She let out a tense breath. ''I know. Mebbe I'm just more worried about us getting trapped up here.''

''We've options open to us yet that remain unexplored.'' Doc gestured at the narrow defiles standing dark and empty before them.

''So which way?''

Doc peered at the two trails. ''Neither of them appear to be heavily trod thoroughfares. But the one on the right beckons because it appears rather bleaker and even more deserted.''

''Let's get it done.'' Krysty pulled out her blaster. ''Double red, Doc. We haven't run into any more of those flying things Jak turned up, but that doesn't mean they're not around.''

''Sally forth, brave lass, and know that I stand at the ready in your service.''

Krysty headed forward, crunching her boots over loose, broken rock. She kept the .38's hammer eared back, and her eyes shifting back and forth to pick up any movement with her peripheral vision.

The mountain quivered unexpectedly, like an old dog

staving off its death throes one more night. But it was enough to knock Krysty from her feet.

"By the Three Kennedys!" Doc roared, tumbling to land on the stone.

Krysty threw herself to the ground and covered her head with her arms. Rocks rained all around her, some of them thudding painfully into her body.

As quickly as they came, the tremors stopped.

The woman raised her head, tasting blood inside her mouth from a split lip. Dust hovered in the air around them, dirtying the snow and mixing with the flurries. She was grateful to find that she hadn't lost her blaster in the confusion. She glanced at her companion.

The old man lay very still on the ground, partially covered with rock and dirt.

"Doc!" Krysty shoved her way up from the debris.

"I'm quite all right, my dear Krysty. I was just lying here, gathering my thoughts and making sure I remained yet anatomically correct. I do feel of a piece, but not the piece that I was. And I seem to hurt in every place near and dear to me, and a few that I'd not been aware of. I shall choose to view that as a good sign."

Krysty crossed over to him and took hold of his jacket in her free hand. She helped him to his feet, keeping watch over the two of them.

"Thank you for your concern, but I assure you I'm well enough to stand on my own." Fastidious as ever, Doc took a moment to brush at his clothing.

As Krysty shifted around, trying to peer through the haze filling the defile, rock rushed down the incline and shot through the fissure in the ground only two yards away. Evidently the quake had done some damage to the underlying strata, because the fissure was now three feet across when before it had only been inches.

Among the thuds and splats of rock and earth tumbling over the side, there was also a decidedly metallic sound.

"And how are you?" Doc asked, gazing at her with some worry.

"Shh," Krysty said, cocking her head to listen.

The sound repeated in a series of rapid basso beats.

Intrigued, Krysty crept closer, going down on her belly at the edge of the fissure. She peered down into it but could see nothing. "Did you hear that?"

"Indeed I did. These old ears are still sharp as a bat's." Doc went prone at her side, then stretched out a hand. "Do you feel it?"

Krysty stretched her hand out over the fissure, careful not to put it too close in case something predatory came roaring up with snapping fangs. The breeze coming up from the fissure wrapped itself around her fingers. "Warm air."

"Exactly." Doc peered down into the gloom, sticking his head in a little farther than Krysty felt was safe. "Mayhap the shivers we felt but moments ago opened up a new artery into the heart of the volcanic region that holds the roots of this mountain range." He extended both hands out. "Ah, and it's enough to warm an old man's bones."

His movements sent a fresh pile of rock and dirt cascading into the fissure. More bonging sounded.

"Something else is down there. Volcanoes don't make bonging sounds," Krysty argued.

"No, they do not."

Krysty pulled out one of the short torches she carried in her pack. Holding it only a little way inside the fissure, she set it on fire with a self-light. The oil caught slowly but spread fast, casting golden streamers of incandescence above and below.

The fissure hollowed out nearly three feet beneath the surface. The shattered stone understructure of the mountain held a chamber that showed signs of old growth; twisted, dead trees and bushes gathered against low spots where the rainwater runoff evidently flowed through into even lower recesses.

The warm air that pushed up into Krysty's face smelled of stringent sulfur and bacteria-laden loam. Her hair relaxed around her head, fanning out a little to better absorb the extra heat. She used her gift, trying to sort out any threats that lurked below. From the looks of things, she judged that nothing under the rocky crust lived.

"In past times, mayhap even stretching back as far as the nukecaust," Doc said, "that area below was once the top of this mountain."

"It isn't anymore." Krysty moved the torch, about ready to give up on the search. If the chamber did open up into the volcanic substrata, that definitely wasn't a course she wanted to pursue. Warm air would come in useful, though, if they had to stay on the mountaintop to ride out the storm.

"Wait," Doc said, "I thought I saw something."

"Moving?" Krysty brought her blaster forward.

"No. A vehicle possibly."

Krysty moved the torch again. The flames jumped and remained burning bright yellow in the steady supply of oxygen. The chamber was almost twenty feet across and thirty feet deep. Flaming bits of the torch dropped the intervening distance, and some of them landed on a metal surface halfway buried in the mountainside.

Canted on its side, the blue-and-white fuselage lay crusted over by boulders and dirt that had worked its way from the top of the mountain to the hidden chamber under the fissure. The rear propeller was missing, as was much of the tail section, and the main rotor held one bent blade stretching up. The others were buried somewhere under it. The Plexiglas bubble was almost covered, as well, but enough of it showed that the multiple fractures threading through it were apparent.

The facet of the craft that most interested Krysty was the word Rescue lettered on the door.

She looked around the fissure opening and thought she might be able to make the climb. "I'm going in," she told Doc.

The old man looked at her. "I don't wish to offend you, my dear Krysty, but the idea of you in that cave harbors no good thoughts in this weary old head despite the present temperature, which has undoubtedly slowed the flow of blood through my brain."

She handed him the torch and shrugged out of her backpack. "Good thoughts or not, that was evidently some kind of rescue airwag. There could be medicines and dressings inside that we can use."

"Then I beg of you, let me go there in your stead."

She gestured with the torch, pointing down as far as she could. The flames wrapped around her fingers for just an instant but not long enough to burn. "That's pretty steep. Do you think you could make it any better than me?"

"I would surely give it the effort," Doc replied.

"Doc," Krysty said, "I'm in better shape than you for this sort of thing. If anything happens down there, I'll need you up here."

The old man covered her hand with his and looked at her solemnly. "As you wish. I am yours but to command."

Krysty clambered into the fissure, her nasal passages and throat burning as she fought the gag reflex against the sulfur smell. Once inside, she fashioned a mask over her nose and mouth from a handkerchief, then took the torch from Doc and started down.

The grade tilted steeply. She took a tacking course, not heading straight for the helicopter, but rather making for

the other side of the flattest section of stone she could find
a few inches below her initial position. She made two more
angled passes before she got close enough to the aircraft to
touch it, scooting on her butt part of the way so she
wouldn't start sliding.

In the center of the chamber, the torch pretty well illuminated her surroundings. Craggy walls seemed to pulse in
on her with jagged teeth as the torchlight ebbed and flowed,
and a dark crack opened up beneath the helicopter.

Resting her hand on the craft gingerly, Krysty peered
into the crack under the helicopter. The blackness extended
a long way. She shoved the torch farther into it but still
couldn't see the bottom.

Shifting a rock with the toe of her boot, she nudged it
over the edge. The rock hit the sides of the crack as it
passed, making loud whanging noises as it dropped farther
away. She finally gave up on it when she realized her
breathing had gotten louder than the impacts.

"Are you all right?" Doc called down.

"Just eyeballing things before I go any farther," she replied. Still moving slowly, she went to the front of the
helicopter and peered inside.

A skeleton that had gone gray white in death sat strapped
into the pilot's seat, dressed in a red short-sleeved shirt and
gray slacks. The material hung in shreds, worried at by
insects and beasts, faded and ravaged by time. Layers of
dust and dirt caked the dead man and the inside of the
helicopter.

Krysty's hair tightened against her neck. Reminding herself of the potential booty that might lie inside the craft just
for her taking at a time when the companions might need
it, she thrust the torch forward.

Reflections of the flames danced in the webbed lines of
the Plexiglas. Shadows wavered around the corpse like dark

things that had been disturbed from their rest—or feeding. The hollow eye sockets seemed locked on Krysty as she took another step forward.

The door opened easily, creaking with the decades of disuse. A fresh shower of dirt and pebbles rolled down the incline in an earthen wave.

"Krysty!"

"I'm okay, Doc." She glanced up at the old man, peering anxiously into the gloom. "I'm going to take a look inside."

"Be careful. I do believe friend Ryan would be most vexed should I allow anything of ill nature occur to you."

Krysty turned her attention back to the aircraft. The helicopter had a low ceiling, which didn't give her enough room to stand. But it held seats for the dead man and one other, as well as space behind for cargo.

She pulled herself in through the door, pausing a moment as she felt the craft wobble under her. Metal shrieked in long, low notes, then it stopped. Evidently the helicopter was wedged firmly.

She held the torch as high as she could inside the cockpit. Upon closer inspection, she saw that the front of the dead man's skull was broken, smashed in completely along the right cheek and temple.

She grabbed the corpse's shirt and shook it. Dust and dirt fell away from the material, and a chunk of it came away in her fist. She smoothed it out on the empty seat, keeping the torch raised high. The pockets held an assortment of coins, a penknife and a few butterscotch candies in individual wrappers that had turned black.

Satisfied there was nothing of use in the cockpit, she went into the cargo area.

A stretcher clung to one wall, halfway covering a red fire extinguisher. Shallow metal racks covered the other wall, filled with narrow drawers that looked almost as big as bread loaves.

All of the drawers were marked with names. She knew only some of them, but they all had to do with pharmaceuticals or surgical equipment. She opened the drawers in succession, working quickly.

In minutes she had filled her pouch and pockets and every empty space on her person. It pained her to see that so much remained they could use. Once she got back with the others, they could arrange another raiding party.

She took up the torch from the fire-extinguisher mounting and headed back toward the cockpit. As she passed through, she felt something burn along the back of her hand. When she examined her hand, a long scratch dripped blood.

Using one of the packages of gauze she'd left in the supply bins, she wiped at the scratch to make sure it wasn't anything to worry about.

Her mutie ability kicked in with a force she'd seldom felt when not actually threatened with physical harm. Her senses swam, taking her into the bloody splotch on the back of her hand. It felt as though her heart had stilled.

Chapter Seven

The crimson smear expanded, drawing Krysty as if into a tunnel, eclipsing her surroundings. A magnetic force with unbelievable power pulled her inside.

Dean was in there with her. She felt him, then called out to him but he didn't answer. Shadows gathered around her, and she could almost see through them. Images changed and darted about, hinting at shapes or things she was familiar with.

Mother Sonja had mentioned experiences similar to the one she was having now. She'd seen trouble coming at times, and been able to warn the family members whom she saw in her visions.

But Mother Sonja had also said all her visions pertained to those who were related to her by blood.

Dean was Ryan's child, not Krysty's, born to another woman. Maybe that was why the vision was so unclear. That it existed at all was testimony to her love for Ryan.

Another deep breath, and clarity came to the vision.

She stood alone in a room that looked like a concrete bunker but felt like something else. Broken conduit pipes ran across the low ceiling overhead. Tables lay overturned in the center of the room, cards and multicolored disks spilling from them and littering the floor.

Corpses littered the room as well. Some hung over the chairs and tables, and others lay across the cards and disks. Many of them were years dead and missing parts from greedy insects and animals, but at least two of them still glistened with their own fresh blood. All of them had died violently.

A shadow lurched against the wall to her left and made hacking noises.

Krysty turned, her hand dropping automatically for the butt of her .38. But somehow she wasn't able to reach it. In her frustration she started to lose the vision.

"Concentrate," a woman's voice ordered. The words sounded nearly empty, as if the speaker had used her last dying gasp to deliver them. "You don't need a weapon here. You are not here. Find the boy. He must know what you have to say."

Krysty tried to ask who was talking to her.

"Do not waste this time. They will die if you do."

Going forward, Krysty stared hard at the shadow. Strangely colored lights caressed the high points of the young man's face and the armor that he wore. In the darkness, she believed the armor was a full-length bulletproof vest that covered the young man from his shoulders to his crotch.

He gasped, blood trickling from the corner of his mouth, and kept his handblaster pointed toward the door. The barrel wavered, taking all his flagging strength attempting to hold it level. Even in the darkness she could tell that he was blond and light eyed.

It wasn't Dean. Krysty felt relief wash over her.

"Wait," the woman's voice advised.

Watching the young man, Krysty saw the pattern of the colored lights change, winking and shifting to track across the dark skin. A shadow suddenly filled the doorway behind the young man, leaner but with a dangerous air of self-assurance.

The young man obviously heard some kind of noise and whirled to face the doorway. His blaster roared.

The shadow jumped out of the way as the bullet smacked into the door frame.

"Shit, Louis, put that blaster down before you hurt somebody you're not supposed to," a young man's voice directed.

Krysty recognized Dean at once. She tried to call out to him as he crossed the room to the wounded boy.

"Save your strength," the woman's voice said. "You'll get your chance to speak with him if you work with me. And you'll have to speak with him if you're going to save his life—or that of your mate."

"Who are you?" Krysty demanded. She tried to find the source of the voice, using her gift.

Abruptly Dean started to fade away.

"Concentrate!"

Krysty returned her attention to Dean.

The boy looked at Louis, then pulled at the straps holding the body armor. Blood smeared Dean's fingers as he worked.

Reluctantly the body armor separated with a sucking sound. Dean peered under the armor, his face wrinkling in fear and anger. He still looked like a little boy, not yet twelve, but Krysty felt the need to comfort him, too.

"Those shitters!" Dean yelled. "They shot you bad, Louis! They shot you real bad!"

Without saying a word, the taller boy suddenly slumped forward. His face went slack as crimson-stained spittle threaded from his mouth.

Dean went down under Louis's weight. "Louis, you can't die! You can't leave me here alone! Louis!"

The querulous snuffling of a large beast sounded outside

the room. Then it came closer. Split hooves rang on the concrete floor.

Dean heaved himself from under the dead boy. Blood, old and new, stained his green armored vest. He leveled his Browning Hi-Power before him, back against the wall.

"Talk to him!" the woman's voice urged.

"He can't hear me," Krysty said.

"Now," she stated, "now he can. Your mind will know the words."

Krysty stepped forward and reached out to touch Dean, who still gave no indication that he saw her. Her hand passed right through his shoulder, but for an instant there was the sensation of an electrical discharge.

The shuffling of the beast in the hallway sounded loud, letting her know it had to have been huge.

"Dean," she said, trying to talk normally.

His head swiveled in her direction, and he made an effort to focus. "Krysty?"

She wanted to tell him to run, that there was nothing he could do for his dead friend. Instead, she said, "Your father is coming for you. Look for him."

Before she could try again, the woman snapped, "Come, there is still much to do."

And Krysty's mind was overwhelmed by the darkness.

DEAN CAWDOR WAS on an adventure. It wasn't a grand adventure like the ones they talked about or read from books in his literature class. There was no Roland here, no Beowulf, no Tom Sawyer or Huck Finn.

But it was an adventure anyway.

"Dean!" Calgary Ventnor whispered. "Come on!"

The boy moved carefully, picking his way through the brush till he reached Calgary.

"Did you see anybody?" Calgary demanded, cutting his eyes in all directions.

"No," Dean replied.

The Nicholas Brody School hunkered on the gentle swell of land coming up from acres of vegetable gardens. Beyond the cultivated lands, the forest began again.

The school had its beginnings in an old stone farmhouse. Rooms and additions had been constructed with concrete blocks, then matted over with adobe bricks. Rifle slits were cut in along the walls, with thick steel shutters that could be pulled closed and bolted down inside.

"It's two-fifteen," Calgary said. "If we don't hurry, we're going to miss seeing it."

Dean laid a hand on the other boy's shoulder and held him back. "If we hurry too much, we're going to get caught. And then where will we be?"

Calgary made a face. He had fair hair, a squat, heavy build, some of the whitest skin Dean had ever seen aside from Jak Lauren's, and big ears that stuck out at right angles to his round head. He sucked at his teeth, a habit Dean had noticed in the other boy whenever he got nervous.

"Kicked out, that's for sure," Calgary said.

Dean figured that was about the size of it. But he couldn't resist the adventure that lay before them. He said her name just to build his courage: Phaedra Lemon.

"You keep talking like that, and the headmaster's night sec crew are going to catch us for certain."

"Is," Dean said automatically.

"What?"

"Is," Dean repeated. "The night sec crew *is* going to catch us."

Calgary's eyes widened. "You really think so?" He started to stand up. The brush was no more than waist high, and he would have been revealed at once.

At that moment the guard they'd been timing came around that side on the catwalk behind the wooden palisades built to withstand cannon fire, as well as the elements.

Dean tackled Calgary and dumped him to the ground, sliding a hand over his mouth. "Shh. And be still or I'm going to bop you one! I mean it!"

Calgary stopped struggling and stared hard at Dean.

Dean let him go once the guard had moved on.

"What the hell did you do that for?" Calgary asked angrily.

"You were going to give us away."

"You're the one who said we were going to get caught!"

Dean gave up. One thing he'd learned about Calgary Ventnor in the past few months was that the boy never admitted when he was wrong.

When it came to test grading and Calgary fell just a few points shy of a C, the boy would just naturally start arguing with the instructors. Dean had been amazed to see him in action. On the surface Calgary looked just like what he was: a preacher's kid getting a little bit bigger view of the world before going back to Leadville to take over his father's flock when the time came.

The thing that attracted Dean to Calgary was the fact the boy was good in his books. Something that escaped Dean in one of the classes, especially math, where the teachers put out word problems that sounded like something Doc would have rambled on about, Calgary just understood easily. Calgary refused to study, but he'd help Dean when asked.

Of course, Dean usually had to work some kind of trade-off and give Calgary something he wanted. Most of the time what Calgary wanted was easy enough, getting shown a wrestling hold he'd seen Dean use in phys ed, stories about some of the things Dean had seen while traveling with his dad, Krysty and the others and sometimes just to hold one of the knives Jak Lauren had left with him.

What Calgary had wanted for helping with the frog-dissection test had been different. At first the boy had been kind of cagey about telling Dean what he wanted. He'd helped Dean track frogs in the little creeks around the vegetable acreage, nail them to boards they salvaged from the carpentry shop, then cut them open and name all the parts.

Dean had seen the insides of lots of things, living and dead, but he'd never thought about naming what was in there. On a frog, as with most things, there were parts he'd eat and parts he wouldn't eat. Sometimes, when things had gotten really desperate for the group, there'd even been parts that he'd rather not have eaten but did anyway.

Almost a dozen slow and luckless frogs came and went, some in more pieces than others as Dean got better at naming the parts and got better at cutting really carefully, and Calgary still didn't say what he wanted in exchange.

Dean had even asked, as if he were just curious.

Calgary hadn't said.

Then the test came and went.

Dean asked again, telling him he didn't know why he was keeping all closemouthed about it.

Calgary said to wait.

Last week the test results had come in. And though Dean didn't figure himself a scholar, and biology wasn't all that interesting anyway, he'd made an A on the test. He was proud, but at the same time he knew Calgary would be figuring Dean owed him big.

Of course, Calgary had. And when he'd told Dean what he wanted, down in the root cellar of the school putting away canned vegetables on their rotation, Dean had had to ask him to repeat himself.

"Phaedra Lemon," Calgary had said, "sleeps in the

nude. I have it on good authority from some of the girls I know.''

Dean hadn't thought it was a big deal. Nudity was just something that happened to folks when they didn't have their clothes on. He couldn't see why Calgary would be so interested in seeing a naked girl.

"Because," Calgary had informed him in a strained voice, "I've never seen one."

"Oh," Dean had said. Evidently Mr. Ventnor was really strict, because Leadville had gaudies where a woman could be seen naked for very little jack.

Since the quest to discover whether Phaedra Lemon really slept in the altogether involved some subterfuge and breaking of school rules, Dean's interest had been piqued. And he'd made the plan that had brought them here tonight.

"Keep your head down," Dean admonished the boy, "and follow me."

Calgary grabbed Dean's ankle. "I've changed my mind."

Dean couldn't believe it. "What?"

"I don't want to go." Calgary sucked on his teeth and couldn't meet Dean's eyes.

"It's all you've talked about for a week."

"I no longer think this is a good idea."

Dean had noticed whenever Calgary got stubborn, his diction improved. "Fine. Suit yourself. Now that I'm out here, I think I'm going to go have a peek."

Calgary grabbed his arm. "You can't do that!"

"Why not?"

For a moment the boy seemed stumped. "Why, because I don't wish for you to."

Dean shook his head. "I'll be double-damned for a mutie stupe if I've made this trip all for nothing."

"You just want to look at her," Calgary accused.

"No." But Dean knew it might be true. In order to set up tonight's little foray, he'd had to find out which one of the girls' dormitories Phaedra Lemon was in, which part of that building she bunked in and—finally—what she actually looked like. It wouldn't have been good at all to go creeping around in the wrong girl's bedroom.

And he especially didn't want to end up in Edna Royerer's bedroom by ill luck. The old dormitory supervisor, it was said, had a habit of sleeping on a shotgun loaded with salt rock.

As the days had gone by, though, he'd discovered the adventure had taken on some aspects that he hadn't quite counted on. Phaedra Lemon, for some unknown reason, had become more beautiful during the past week than any girl he'd seen at Nicholas Brody School or before. The past couple of nights had passed by probably as uncomfortably for him as they had for Calgary. He just couldn't help wondering if Phaedra really did sleep naked.

Dean grew more irritable. "Cal, look. You have some choices here. You can stay out here tonight and sleep on the cold, wet ground and slip back into the school when the gardening shift comes out. Or you can join me in climbing those walls with this rope—" he held up the coils of hemp "—sneak by Phaedra Lemon's room long enough to find out if those stories are true and then get the rest of the night's sleep in your own warm bed."

Calgary sucked on his teeth and glanced up at the timber wall.

"Now, what's it going to be?" Dean asked.

Chapter Eight

Ryan and J.B. found Jak and Mildred just after the teenager started to pull the dead man from the collapsed overhang of snow and rock. Mildred lowered her pistol when she recognized them.

"How'd you happen on him?" Ryan asked. Keeping the Steyr in one numbed hand, he wrapped his arms around himself in an attempt to hold in his escaping body heat.

"Didn't chill him," Jak said. "Found him. Arm sticking out. Saw it."

The man wore a long coat, high boots and a thermal cap so furry the dead eyes under the bill looked like a taxidermist's glassy marbles. A backpack remained strapped on his shoulders. Ryan guessed that the man was probably in his late fifties and had been in robust health, judging from the broad shoulders and leaned-out build.

A cottony pallor had set up under his skin, washing it of most of the pigmentation. When Ryan moved the man's arm with his boot, just testing what he'd seen when Jak was moving the corpse, the limb moved fairly easily.

"Fresh dead," Jak announced, squatting next to the deceased. "Broke neck." He pulled down the man's collar and exhibited the bruised throat, then twisted the head from side to side.

Ryan knelt, hopeful that the coat might fit, and started to pull the dead man from it. He noticed the curious tattoo on the inside of the man's left forearm near the inner elbow.

A big dark blue dot was in the middle, echoed by concentric rings in lighter blue that got bigger and bigger around it, like the ripples made from a stone dropped into a pool. A double strand of orange bars and lines ran through it.

"Did you find the pass?" the Armorer asked as he put on his coat. Mildred had been carrying it for him.

"No," Mildred said. "The ridge Jak and I were following petered out into a drop-off that we'd need climbing gear to get down."

Chilled to the bone, Ryan shrugged into the coat, which cut some of the wind. When he spoke, his teeth still chattered. "Where's Krysty and Doc?"

"Split up," Jak answered. "Thought mebbe better chance two directions. Ain't heard, though."

"Are they supposed to meet you anywhere?"

"Back along the way you and J.B. probably come," Mildred replied. "If they were there, you'd have seen them or they'd have seen you." She stood close to the Armorer, one of her gloved hands in his. Though they were somewhat reticent about showing their relationship because of their respective taciturn natures, the commitment between them was deep.

Ryan turned up the coat collar. He thought he'd never be warm again. "When?"

"Overdue." Jak flicked out one of his leaf-bladed knives and sliced through the backpack's shoulder straps, then yanked it out from under the dead man.

"How long?"

"Eight minutes." Jak opened the backpack and pulled out a largish bundle of foil-colored material. He turned it over in his hands, inspecting it.

"What do you have, Jak?" Ryan asked.

"Therm tent." The albino shoved the bundle at Ryan, tapping the instructions printed on the foil surface. "Good for heat, good for cold. Got snap-together poles." He flexed his hands around the material hard enough to show the skeletal rods. "Got self-heats, ring-pulls and maps in here, too."

"The man came prepared for some hard living," Ryan said. "Take the food, water and the tent. Let's see the maps."

Jak passed them over, then started transferring items to his pack. There wasn't much, but it added to the small stores they had.

"Mildred," Ryan said, unfolding one of the maps, "take a look at the tattoo on the inside of this guy's arm. Tell me what you think."

Mildred hunkered down beside the dead man while J.B. took up guard.

Ryan unfolded the map carefully because it was old. Long strips of plaster tape held it together and repaired tears in different areas. Purple marker, looking almost black in the thin light reflected by the snow, stained the map, tracing routes across California, Oregon, Idaho and Montana.

Ryan passed the map to the Armorer. "Can't tell if he was coming or going."

J.B. took the map and looked it over.

"The dot," Ryan said to Mildred, referring to the tattoo, "I figure is the sun. The concentric rings around it are the solar system." He'd seen pictures in astronomy books he'd found in different places around Deathlands. "The cork-screwed ladder I don't know. Seen it on some doors in a few of the redoubts we've been inside."

"I think it's supposed to be a representation of DNA," the black woman replied, "building blocks of the universe. But why it would be overlapping the solar system like this so intentionally, I have no idea."

Ryan picked up one of the corpse's limp hands, cold as

the stone around it, and felt the fingers and palm. "He didn't do much honest work. Hands are too soft. No calluses. Big man like him, he'd be showing something of his life in his hands if he did anything physical. You have to wonder what brought him out here."

"I'm guessing," J.B. said, "but I think this guy come down from Montana."

"What makes you think that?" Ryan looked up at his friend. He felt a little warmer in the coat now. Thoughts of Krysty and her welfare kept tumbling through his mind. The dead man was proof of the dangers that waited on the mountain. Ryan was ready to move, but what he learned here might help them all, so he made himself be patient.

"This place—" J.B. touched the map just east of their present position "—is marked with one asterisk. There's a plotted line that leads down to it."

"That map is well drawn," Ryan commented. "Whoever did it took the time to make it neat. But the coastline's wrong. We know that from our trip up."

"Yeah, but it's bastard old. Paper's even gone yellow with age. Mebbe when it was first drawn, it was more accurate. Things could have changed along the Western Islands. Hell, they're changing now."

Light suddenly flared in Jak's hands, bright white and concentrated in a narrow beam. "Flashlight."

The light didn't have the finished machine look of some of those that Ryan had seen in the past.

"Homemade," Jak stated.

"Let me borrow it," J.B. told him. He took the flashlight when Jak passed it over, then shone it over the map. "Here."

Ryan stood up to look, joined by Mildred and Jak.

The Armorer traced the purple line north with his forefinger, careful to keep his arm out of the light. The line

ended at a point lettered Heimdall Point in the lower south-
west quadrant of Montana. "This is where he must have
started out."

"I've never heard of Heimdall Point," Ryan said.

Neither had anyone else.

"Norse mythology mentions a guy named Heimdall,"
Mildred said. "Guarded Bifrost."

Jak looked the question at her.

"Bifrost was a bridge," Mildred explained. "Supposed
to be made of fire, water and air and colored like a rainbow.
Asgard was the home of the Norse gods. Bifrost stretched
from Asgard to other parts of the world, or worlds depending on your interpretation of how things were. Way the
story's told, Heimdall had gold teeth and ears so sharp they
could hear grass growing."

"Sec man to gods," the albino said.

"Pretty much sums it up. Heimdall carried a trumpet and
blew it every time the gods came or went." Mildred's brow
knitted. "The stories also mention that Heimdall was supposed to blow that horn the loudest to announce the end of
the world. A time they called Ragnarok."

"The end of the world's come and gone," Ryan said,
"unless these people got something more planned. Or know
something we don't."

"A DNA strand overlaying a picture of the solar system," the black woman mused. "That doesn't sound like
they're preparing for the end, or even believe that it is."

Ryan looked at the dead man. "However it was, his story
died with him."

"There's probably still people out here who were with
him," J.B. countered.

"Does he have a weapon?" Ryan asked Jak.

The albino held up an empty holster. "Did. Gone. Mebbe
lost in snow when tremors come."

"No long blaster?" Ryan was wondering if the dead man might offer part of a solution to the subsonic rifle shot that had maybe saved his life.

Jak shrugged. "Mebbe lost, too."

"There's a pair of asterisks here," J.B. said, tapping an area beyond the pass they were looking for. It was south and east of Carson City. "I'm betting this guy was headed there next."

"Does it say what's there?" Ryan asked.

"This notation's new, marked on top of a piece of tape so nothing's lost underneath." J.B. squinted at it through his glasses. "Shostakovich's Anvil. Sounds Russian."

"Could be some kind of Russian settlement there, come drifting down out of the north."

Ryan didn't like not knowing what the man had been doing there, and how come he ended up with his neck broken. "And these people found out about it and were going to visit?"

"Way past asking," Jak said.

"Yeah, but it's an ace on the line this man wasn't out here on his own." Ryan headed off in the direction Jak had said Krysty had taken. They needed to be moving off the mountain if they could, or take shelter from the storm if they couldn't.

KRYSTY OPENED her eyes and found herself in a hallway that stank of death. Ahead of her Ryan—clad in a scarlet armored vest—moved through shifting shadows and a cloud of dust.

Her lover carried the Steyr rifle in his hands. The knuckles of his left hand were skinned; blood trickled between his fingers, spattering the floor beneath his steps. His beard growth looked days old, and his eyes had dark hollows under them.

"Ryan!" she called out.

As with Dean, though, the big man didn't hear her. Before she could move to one side of the hallway or the other, he walked right through her.

"Where's Ryan?" she asked, following along her lover's backtrail.

"It's not time for you to know," came the older woman's voice.

"This isn't happening now?"

"No."

Krysty felt the world shift around her, opening up slightly, and she suddenly realized she couldn't feel the rocks beneath her feet. "When?"

"Concentrate," the older woman snapped. "If you lose him, then I lose him, and it could be that you'll lose him for all time. Do you want that?"

"No." Krysty focused on Ryan, abruptly noticing she was no longer able to hear his footsteps against the rock-strewn floor. Even his edges had grown indistinct.

"Follow him."

Krysty started forward, surprised at how hard it was to move now. His long stride outdistanced hers. She put more effort into her steps, wishing she could run.

"You grow tired," the woman's voice said. "It's not your fault. This is very demanding. Especially for you, the focus point."

Ryan hesitated at the next door, letting the Steyr lead him around the corner. It gave Krysty almost enough time to catch him. She reached out to touch him, expecting her hand to go through his back, and it did. It looked as if her hand had been amputated at the wrist and thrust inside Ryan's back. When her lover took a step forward again, her hand reappeared as if by magic.

Ryan walked up a short flight of stairs. At the top a small

doorway let into a room that held splintered shards of the same multicolored light Krysty had seen during her visit with Dean.

"Close enough," the woman said. "Get ready to talk to him."

Krysty moved closer as Ryan stepped into the room. A lumpy shadow tore itself free of the ceiling only a few feet in front of him, then came hurtling down. She tried to cry out a warning, knowing it was already too late.

Ryan moved fast. Ducking under the lumpy pile of multi-legged flesh, he brought the Steyr's butt around in a wicked arc. The splat of the impact filled the small room.

The creature shrilled in pain and went scuttling away, hiding under the dilapidated bed. A broken mirror across from it held dozens of images.

Ryan drew the SIG-Sauer and pumped three rounds into the bed, searching for the mutie creature.

The whining it made became even more shrill and pained. Without a sign of its movements, it shot out from under the bed, its legs clawing for Ryan.

"Fireblast!" the one-eyed man snarled, but the word sounded out of sync to Krysty, slow and ringing. He pushed the blaster into the creature's face and pulled the trigger.

Momentum kept the mutie beast flying at him even after he'd killed it. Blood and ripped pieces of flesh thudded against him. Some of it stuck to the armored vest. The main portion of the creature's corpse dropped in a twisted heap at his boots.

"Now," the woman urged.

"Ryan," Krysty called.

He turned toward her, raising the blaster automatically until it centered on her face. His knuckle was whitening on the trigger before he squinted, then his eye widened in startled recognition.

"Krysty," he said. His voice was choked, thick with emotion. "I thought they chilled you." He reached a hand out to her, but it passed through.

"I'm not really here, lover," she said, then tried to explain what she was experiencing. But the words wouldn't leave her mouth. Instead, she said something else. "Dean's here with you. Find him."

"Dean?" He shook his head and called to her.

She tried to reach back for him even though her fingers would surely have passed through his anyway. Almost, they touched.

Her eyelids closed.

"You've done well," the woman said. "Now it is up to them, up to the chain of events you've helped set into motion. Destiny is written in the stars, but sometimes we can nudge them a bit in one direction or the other. Hopefully this will be enough."

"Enough for what?" Krysty tried to open her eyes but couldn't.

"Enough to let both father and son live." The woman's voice faded. "You must look to your own needs, my child. Your path remains rocky yet, as well. Take care. And do not tell Ryan, no matter how much you might wish to."

WHEN SHE OPENED her eyes, Krysty discovered she was still in the helicopter, leaning heavily against the empty copilot's seat. All she wanted to do was sleep; she didn't care where. Somehow she had managed to hang on to the torch, which was dying down rapidly now. Smoke filled the interior of the aircraft, stinging her eyes and making her throat burn.

Then she could hear Doc bellowing for her.

She pushed herself up, trying to find a more comfortable place on her shoulders for her bulging pack. She stepped outside the helicopter and waved the torch. "I'm here, Doc."

Her companion waved down from the open fissure. "So you are, my dear, so you are. I was on the verge of becoming greatly concerned when I saw your torch stop moving about. I thought perhaps you were having some kind of problem and had been incapacitated by something. Believe me, an overactive imagination is a curse of considerable magnitude."

"What about the others?"

"They have not as yet joined us. Perhaps they ran into Ryan and John Barrymore, and are even now plotting our course from these dire straits."

Poised on one knee, still a little down and forward of the helicopter, Krysty felt the beginnings of another tremor. At first she thought it might be her imagination, maybe her stomach jumping around because she was so done in.

When pebbles started skittering and falling down the incline, bouncing all over her in their rush to fall into the fissure behind her, she knew it wasn't her imagination.

Metal creaked as the helicopter slipped free of its grave. In a moment it was loose and sliding at her.

Chapter Nine

After throwing the knotted rope they'd swiped and prepared over the garrison wall, Dean went up it as quick as a monkey. Calgary struggled behind, huffing and puffing.

"Keep your head down!" Dean told Calgary in a hoarse whisper. "If we get caught, it'll probably go bad for us, but it'll go bad for the people pulling sec rotation, too."

Chastised and afraid, Calgary dropped his head to the hard wooden surface and watched Dean.

Sitting there in the darkness, contemplating the area he needed to cross to get to the girls' dormitory, Dean couldn't help wondering how his dad was doing. Only a few minutes ago, he'd felt really close to Krysty—almost as if he could just reach out and touch her. Once he'd even thought he'd heard her voice.

"Dean," Calgary whispered, "are you just going to sit there?"

"Until the guard makes the corner, stupe." Dean watched the distant shadow. "Get ready."

"I think I hurt my leg."

Dean heaved a sigh. "Calgary, you wanted to see a naked girl tonight. Or at least find out if she is naked. Now get up off your ass."

As the guard hit the corner, Dean moved off at once, staying low. He felt the vibration of Calgary's heavier steps echo along the wooden timbers.

At the end of the catwalk, the rooftop of the girls' dormitory they sought was only a seven-foot jump out, almost on the same level. Probably the original buildings hadn't been that close to the perimeter walls, but the school had grown over the years and the walls hadn't. Dean took the jump in stride.

Calgary hesitated, freezing on the catwalk like one of the gargoyles Dean had seen in a history book. He waved to the boy. "Come on."

Eyes closed, which Dean considered to be triple stupe of the first order, Calgary jumped. He made the distance with no problem, but tried immediately to remain standing straight up. The incline of the roof threw him off.

"Oh, shit!" Calgary said, waving his arms wildly.

Dean grabbed him by the shirt and helped him find his balance. "You hit this rooftop like a sack of guts hitting the butcher's floor," he whispered, pulling the boy down to the roof. "You better hope everybody in this damn building is a sound sleeper."

That was one thing that Dean had found true; people inside the school's heavy walls slept more soundly than he'd have ever thought about doing when he was with his dad. At school, it was a totally different way of living. He threw an arm around Calgary's shoulders and held him down until the sec guard passed.

"We're pretty close to her, aren't we?" Calgary said.

"Ever notice that vanilla scent she wears?" Dean asked.

Calgary hesitated a moment, then shook his head. "I've never been that close."

"Trust me," Dean said, "she wears it. Get your nose open a little bit, and you'll probably be smelling it in the next few minutes. Then we'll find out if vanilla scent is the only thing she wears at night." He grinned. Finding Phaedra was no longer just for Calgary and the thrill of doing something he wasn't supposed to. There were mysteries to be solved that he hadn't even known he was interested in.

Dean led the way across a third of the rooftop, staying below the ridged top so the sec people wouldn't see him. Calgary trailed at his heels, complaining that they were moving too fast, until Dean told him to shut his mouth or he'd make Calgary carry his own shoes between his teeth.

Leaning over the eaves, Dean counted windows. When he found the fifth one, he scooted across the rooftop on his stomach, using his fingers and toes. With his head lower than the rest of his body, the blood rushed to fill his brain and face, making it feel that it would explode. His heart hammered inside his chest, too.

"Is that her room?" Calgary asked.

"It's her room." Hauling himself over the edge, Dean looked into Phaedra Lemon's bedroom.

The room was small, holding only two beds, a chest of drawers and a trunk at the foot of each bed. Boys slept four to a room in bunks, but the girls only doubled up and had single beds. There were fewer girls, and Mr. Brody had mentioned that at one time only boys were allowed at the school.

In the moonlight slanting through the window, Phaedra Lemon's long hair shone like spun gold, spread out on her pillow. She slept with a blanket pulled to her shoulder and her fist under her chin. At fifteen, she had curves under that blanket.

She also had her mouth open, innocent like. That one detail almost made Dean feel guilty enough to shuck the whole adventure and go back to his room.

"Can you see anything?" Calgary asked.

Dean swiveled his head, finding the other boy hanging off the eaves almost as far as he was. Calgary's face was so suffused with blood it looked like a melon about to burst.

"I see that she's sleeping under a blanket," Dean replied.

"But is she naked under it?"

"Stay here." Dean handled his weight on his arms, gripping the eaves with his hands as he turned himself over. The ledge out in front of the window was no more than three or four inches, barely enough for him to put the ends of his shoes on. He managed and soon found it would hold his weight.

"What are you doing?" Calgary asked in a frightened whisper. "You're going to get caught!"

"Only if you don't shut your mouth." Quiet as he could be, Dean pressed his fingers against the windowpane and pushed up.

The window slid easily, only having a few rough spots. Nicholas Brody made sure craftsmanship went into every aspect of his school. Thinking about the old headmaster was troubling to Dean, because it was sort of betraying the trust the man had placed in him by accepting his enrollment. Of course, his dad had also placed a lot of jack in Mr. Brody's hands along with responsibility for his son's tutelage.

But Dean wasn't exactly thinking things through that night. Somehow he wasn't able to. Seeing Phaedra lying there under that blanket, all curvy and unaware, had numbed the guilty pangs.

Light-footed as a cat and just as sure, he crept into the room. He glanced at the other bed and saw the girl sleeping there, her head thrown back, snoring softly. He knew her, too, but he couldn't remember her name. He didn't even care.

He moved closer to Phaedra's bed, eyes running along the womanly body under the lightweight lavender blanket.

At least, it looked lavender in the moonlight. She smelled of vanilla, too, just as he knew she would.

He'd always known women had different shapes than men. Rona had been beautiful and he'd bathed with her, and Dean was aware of the stares Krysty got whenever they were around men.

The time was magical for Dean in ways that he knew he'd never be able to put into words. It was one of those pictures he knew he'd carry around in his head forever. Except for the sight of Calgary Ventnor's head hanging down in view of the window like some ugly fruit, it was perfect. The boy motioned for Dean to hurry.

Gently Dean reached out for the edge of the blanket, took it between his finger and thumb and began to pull it down. He hadn't done more than reveal one bare shoulder when he noticed that Phaedra Lemon's eyes were open and she was staring right at him.

The girl's mouth started to round out, opening, and she took a deeper breath.

Figuring she was going to scream, Dean dropped a hand to her face and covered her mouth, wondering what had driven him to be stupe enough to get caught in her bedroom.

Chapter Ten

Ryan spotted Doc leaning down into a hole in the ground. Then he heard the old man shouting Krysty's name. Another big tremor hit, nearly knocking Ryan from his feet as he redoubled his efforts. He skidded across a boulder, shaving skin from both palms.

In five more long strides over the wobbling ground, he was beside Doc. "Where's Krysty?"

"There!" The old man pointed.

Squinting his eye, Ryan peered into the fissure. It was dark inside, but he could just make out the dying embers of a torch as it skittered over the side of another, widening crack in the earth. For an instant the torch flared to new life, no longer battered by the stones it rolled across.

In the sudden light, Ryan saw Krysty as the wreckage of a helicopter emerged from the cracking stone wall above her, disgorging its trapped prize like a heifer giving birth. Krysty was struggling to maintain a grip, but Ryan knew the falling helicopter would rake her from her precarious perch the instant it ripped free of its earthen womb.

Then the torch disappeared into the yawning abyss below, not scattering in all directions from an impact. It simply kept falling, drawing farther away. Everything went dark. The scream of tortured metal continued, letting him know the helicopter was still in motion even though he couldn't see it.

Ryan glanced over his shoulder and saw that J.B. was

already tying a rope around an outcrop nearly six feet from the lip of the fissure.

"I volunteered to go down in her stead," Doc said, his face pale and drawn. He didn't move from the edge of the fissure. He gazed back down into the dark hole. "I truly did, but she would have none of it. I am very sorry, friend Ryan."

"She's not dead yet, Doc."

Ryan grabbed the free end of the rope. "Jak, get that light shining into that hole. I need to see."

The albino quickly moved into position. The flashlight came on with a burst of incandescence as he pointed it into the fissure. "Help's coming," he yelled down to Krysty. He couldn't throw her the rope; she was using both hands to hang on.

"How much rope are you going to need?" the Armorer asked.

Ryan peered into the hole, trying to gauge the distance from the fissure's mouth to Krysty's position. "Give me twenty-five, thirty feet beyond the lip."

"Fifty-foot rope," J.B. said. "I get you shored up good and proper, that's going to cut it close to what we've got to use."

Ryan nodded.

"Lover," Krysty called. Her voice was almost calm, but Ryan could hear the fear in her. "Give it up. I can't make it. There's no sense in losing both of us."

Working the end of the rope around his boots, Ryan watched Krysty as she scrambled along the moving incline and tried in vain to find purchase. She fell, and for a second he thought it might be the end of her. But she made it back up, just in time for the helicopter to take away another foot of precious space.

"Hold on, dammit!" Ryan shouted. He cinched the rope

around both boots, just above the ankle. There was no time to try a controlled hand-over-hand descent.

The tremors subsided for a moment, long enough for Ryan to think they'd quit completely. The helicopter kept sliding, breaking out bigger sections of the wall that had held it for so long.

"Ryan!" Krysty called.

He peered over the edge, then rolled down to hang from his hands. The rope dangled in a loose coil between his tied feet, looping back up and out of sight. He was still twenty feet from Krysty, another ten in horizontal distance.

"J.B."

"You're tied on," the Armorer said. He poked his head over the edge, face tense.

"I can't let you do it," Krysty told Ryan. "I'll jump off the edge myself before I let you get killed, too."

"You jump off," Ryan told her, smiling with a cockiness he definitely didn't feel, "hell, you'll only be making it harder, not stopping me."

"I don't want you to die, lover."

"I'm not going to die, and I'm not going to let you die, either."

PHAEDRA LEMON bit Dean's hand.

"Shit!" he whispered. "Don't be biting me!" He used his other hand, pulling at that gold hair from behind to turn her face up to his. The vanilla smell of her swarmed around him and clouded his mind. Most of the fear inside him went away as he realized he'd unconsciously covered her body with his.

She tried to bite him again, her saliva running across his palm. Twisting in the bed, she tried to escape him.

Dean was all too aware of the soft flesh just on the other

side of the lavender blanket, almost trapped in some tantalizing fashion beneath his body. "Hot pipe!" he croaked.

He threw a leg over her, trying to keep her from squirming off the bed. It was a miracle, he decided, how that blanket stayed in place.

Without warning, she brought a small hand out from under the blanket, curled it tight into a fist, then slammed him on the nose with it.

Dean stifled a curse and grabbed his nose. It hurt like hell. He held out his free hand to ward off another blow. He didn't know which hurt worse—his bitten hand or his nose.

"Stop!" he said in a forced whisper. "I'm sorry!" He was fully expecting the girl to bash him again and start to scream bloody murder.

Instead, she gripped the blanket with one hand and kept it tucked under her chin, maintained a fist poised to strike and scooted away from him. She looked at him, blinking, her nose flaring. "Dean?"

Looking at her face, Dean wondered why he'd never noticed what a cute nose she had. He took his hand away from his face and checked his fingers for blood. Only a few crimson stains colored his fingertips. "Damn, that hurt!" he said.

"Quiet!" Phaedra insisted in a whisper.

Dean blinked at her. "Quiet?"

"Yes, you jackass. You'll wake Bitha." She gave him a look that informed him he should have known that.

"I will?" Dean was confused.

"Whisper!"

He lowered his voice. "Sorry."

"That's better."

He looked at her, scrunched up against the headboard as

if she were afraid he was going to jump at her again. He felt bad about that. "Didn't mean to scare you."

"What did you think you were going to do creeping around in my room like that?"

"I—"

Across the room, Bitha rolled over in bed, talking in her sleep.

"Shh!" Phaedra hissed.

Bitha reached out to the small bedside table and took up a glass there. She drank deeply, then crumpled back into her pillow all without looking at them for an instant.

"She's a heavy sleeper," Phaedra whispered, "but she gets dry at night."

Since she was turned to face him, Dean knew Phaedra didn't see Calgary Ventnor hanging upside down from the eaves. He nodded, not knowing what else to do, wondering how the hell it was that he was having a conversation with the girl when she should have been yelling her head off. And there was still the mystery of what lay beneath the blanket. The heady aroma of vanilla surrounded him.

"Now," she whispered in a harder voice, "you were going to tell me what you're doing in my bedroom."

TEARS GLINTED in Krysty's eyes as she watched Ryan hang from the rocky lip above her. She wouldn't let him see her cry, not because she was afraid.

"J.B.," Ryan called out.

"You're tied on," the Armorer called back.

Krysty's arms shook from the effort of hanging on, the muscles burning as they writhed under her skin. Gaia, if she'd only fallen before Ryan had reached her, he wouldn't be here putting his life on the line.

"You look at me," Ryan ordered, putting steel in his voice.

She lifted her head and looked into the volcanic blue of his eye. The scars on his face were part of the man, not artificial things at all. She couldn't imagine him without them. He was the handsomest man she'd ever seen.

"We've been through too many things, me and you," he told her as he gripped his way around the fissure mouth for a more feasible purchase point, "for you to just give up on me now."

"You and I," she corrected automatically. The fissure behind her shook again, opening another three or four feet.

"You and me," he repeated. "That's how it's going to be. You and me getting out of here."

"What are you doing?" she asked.

Hardly before the words were out of her mouth, the helicopter finally shrugged itself free of its subterranean tomb and came skidding at her. There was nothing she could do to avoid it. The aircraft gained speed and grew larger, sparks jumping out from under it as the metal skin scraped across stone.

And Ryan leaped from his hold on the fissure's edge, falling.

"CAME TO SEE YOU," Dean answered.

"Me?" Phaedra's eyes lifted in surprise.

"Yeah."

"Why?"

"I don't know." He felt stupe saying that, but it sounded better than giving her the real reason.

"You don't know?" Her question became a challenge.

For some reason, knowing he shouldn't have but feeling it and giving in to the emotion all the same, Dean got angry. "That's right!"

"Shh!" Phaedra uncoiled her fist and put her forefinger to her lips.

They both glanced at Bitha, who slept on.

Dean swiveled his head back to Phaedra, gazing at her lips and wondering why he hadn't noticed how ripe and full they looked. He breathed in again, deep, but trying not to let her know what he was doing. The scent of vanilla filled his nostrils, and he knew he'd never forget it.

"Don't sit there smiling," Phaedra chastised.

"Was I smiling?" Dean put on a serious face.

"You still are."

Dean tried not to let his gaze linger too long on the rounded breast almost visible under the lavender blanket. He'd never known lavender could be so attractive, either. "I always look like this."

"Uh-uh." Phaedra shook her head, her gold locks flying. "Usually you've got a bored look on your face." She smiled, her eyes narrowing. "You don't look bored now."

"Getting punched in the nose kind of knocks the boredness right out of you." He moved his nose as if he were worried about it. In truth, he'd almost forgotten about it. Probably he would have, except for the occasional throb.

"So what brought you to my room?" Phaedra asked.

Guile was second nature to Dean, having been raised for so long by Rona to protect his father's identity and keep things about himself secret. "I didn't know this was your room."

She raised her eyebrows, the smile dimming only a little. "Oh, and who else's bedroom have you been prowling around in the dead of night?"

"I didn't say I'd been prowling around in anyone else's bedroom." Dean was feeling mad all over again because she was being so accusing about everything. Maybe it would have been better if Phaedra had just screamed. Talking to her wasn't something he really wanted to do. At least if the dorm sec people got hold of him, they'd ask him what the hell he thought he was doing and he could just say "I don't know," shrug and be done with it.

But then he'd have Nicholas Brody to contend with.

The prospect made him think maybe talking to Phaedra might not be as dire as he believed at the moment.

"You got in here by accident?" Phaedra's tone took on heavy sarcasm.

Lying, he sensed, would only have brought out the big blasters. "No," Dean said.

"Whisper!"

"I am."

"Then get better at it!"

Dean's face flushed and burned.

"If you didn't get here by accident," Phaedra said, "then you planned to be here."

But not caught, Dean wanted to say. He nodded. "I've got to go."

Phaedra frowned at him. "You just got here."

"This isn't exactly a visit," Dean said.

"Then why are you here?"

"Will you—?"

"Shh!" Phaedra's forefinger zipped to her lips, and the blanket slid down to reveal a bare shoulder.

Dean waited.

In her bed Bitha stretched, yawned and rolled over the other way.

"She gets restless," Phaedra explained in a whisper. "Usually when her period is coming on."

Dean also decided he could have done without that bit of information. "I've got to go."

"You can't go."

Dean smirked. "Look, you might have surprised me with that punch to the nose because I wasn't expecting it, but there's no way you can keep me from going." He stood.

Phaedra glared at him. "I can scream."

With the way the light was hitting her, Dean thought he could see the outline of one pointy nipple jutting out from her breast. That one little bump of flesh tonight intrigued him more than all the naked breasts he'd ever seen. "Why would you scream?"

"Why not?"

Frustrated, Dean sat on the edge of the bed. "You're confusing."

"I'm confusing?"

"Yes, and you're turning everything you say into a damn question. I feel like I'm in the middle of one of Coco Copeland's math exams."

"I'm confusing?" she repeated, irritation weaving through her voice as sure as a stickie had suckers on his butt.

Dean let his own irritation show. "Yes. First you're yelling at me for being here. Now you're threatening to yell at me if I leave. That's confusing."

"I'll let you go," she said, "if you'll tell me why you were here."

Dean took a deep breath, decided that he was doomed for sure, surer even than a triple-stupe mutie who'd wandered one time too many into a rad-blasted area following a vision. "I came to find out something."

"What?"

"Something about you." He couldn't just blurt it out. His face felt hot again, and the electricity was back squirming in his groin as he looked at that little nubbin of flesh poking at the lavender blanket. Glancing over Phaedra's shoulder, he looked at Calgary hanging there like some kind of stupe bat. Silently he wished the boy's head would explode. During the confusion of all the flying bloody matter and what little brains Calgary actually had, judging from tonight's little adventure, Dean was certain he could make an escape.

"What about me?"

"I heard that you slept naked." Dean watched her. There, he'd said it.

She looked at him, her mouth going open but no sounds coming out, as if she were a fish drowning in the air. She worked her jaw a few times.

Dean wondered if he had time to make a dash for the window before she started yelling. Or hitting.

Before he could move, she found her voice. "You came up here to look at me naked?"

That one he could dodge. "Actually just to find out if you were."

Her face went crimson, blushing dark in the shadows gathered in the room. Without her body moving enough to give a hint of what she was about to do, she punched at Dean again.

Before he could get away, the blow landed against his nose hard enough to start stars flashing behind his eyeballs.

RYAN FELL. Illuminated from above and behind by the flashlight Jak held, he skimmed across the hard rock leading down to Krysty.

Her face was turned from him, focusing on the approaching bulk of the wrecked helicopter.

The skeleton dressed in rags sitting in the cockpit jumped and jerked behind the controls, looking as though it had come to life and was piloting the wreckage of his craft with insane glee. The Plexiglas nose slid straight at Krysty.

Ryan hit the steep incline more than eight feet from her. His stomach lurched inside him when he knew he was going to reach her too late. Forgetting the rope around his ankles, he tried to push himself up and run. Unable to, he dug his boots in and leaped forward, skidding down the tilted rock, trying to navigate an interception path using his hands, ignoring the pain that was inflicted.

Rock and dirt came shooting after him, overtaking him, swirling up inside his mouth, nose and eye. He blinked, closing on Krysty.

But the helicopter was nearer. She put her hands out as if to hold it back, took a final look at him and went over the side, bulldozed by the helicopter.

Chapter Eleven

"Krysty!" Mildred yelled from above.

Ryan watched as Krysty fell, captured in the beam of the flash Jak held. Heaving himself over the side, Ryan plunged into the abyss after her. Hot sulfuric fumes pressed into his face, burning his nose and eye. He spotted Krysty ahead of him, on the other side of the helicopter. Her eyes were still focused on him.

Ryan prayed the rope wouldn't come up short.

In her desperation Krysty grabbed the helicopter as it tipped over the ledge. She got one hand around a helicopter skid. For a moment, despite the piles of rock and sand shoving up behind it, the aircraft teetered on the edge of the precipice.

Before it fell, Ryan was there. He wrapped his arms around Krysty, pulling her into him. The rope kept playing out, and they fell past the fissure's edge.

"Ryan!" Krysty screamed, taking his face in her hands. Her sentient hair coiled protectively around her scalp.

"It's okay," he said, reaching around her to hook his fingers in the thick leather belt at her back.

Just as he was beginning to think something had gone wrong and J.B. hadn't gotten his knots tight enough, the rope yanked up fast around Ryan's boots. The force bruised his ankles despite the leather and despite the elasticity of the nylon weave, and the rope felt as if it had cut into his flesh.

He came to a sudden stop.

While the rope held him, giving enough to keep his legs from popping out of his knee or hip joints, he was the only thing holding on to Krysty. He growled with the pain of it all. His legs, his back and his arms and shoulders suddenly felt as if they'd been subjected to the fiery kiss of an incendiary gren.

Before he could recover, the helicopter was on them, batting them aside like a piñata as it nose-dived into the abyss. An instant later they were slammed against the side of the fissure.

The rough rock bit into Ryan's back, but he didn't think there were any skin abrasions, since the dead man's coat provided padding. He bounced a couple of times, twisting along the rope's trajectories, swapping sides with Krysty, then came to a rest against the underside of the second fissure.

"Fireblast," Ryan said weakly as soon as he was able to draw a breath. He kept his arms locked tight. Krysty sagged in his arms, not quite limp. "Krysty?"

"Here, lover." With effort she lifted her head and met his gaze. "I'm right here."

"Don't let go," he warned. "Don't know how much I can trust my arms." They felt weak and numb all at the same time—a bad combination for a man needing his best from them.

"Ryan!" Jak called.

"We're here! Haul us in! Careful!"

Krysty shifted her grip, grabbing fistfuls of Ryan's coat and putting some of her weight on the garment instead of in his arms. "Thank you. I thought I was dead and done for, lover."

He shook his head, finding the unconscious movement

difficult under their present circumstances. "Not as long as there's a breath left in me and I see a way clear."

J.B., Doc, Mildred and Jak pulled them up, keeping the tension on the line steady, moving them along. Ryan and Krysty scraped along the fissure wall until they were raised above it. With the line unanchored, they twirled out of control until they reached the lip of the top fissure.

J.B. grabbed Krysty's arm and helped her onto solid ground. The echo of the tremors from the last wave of the quake still vibrated through the mountain.

"Truly, my dear Ryan," Doc said as he offered his hand, "that was one of the most outstanding exercises in courageous gallantry that these old eyes have ever beheld."

"Speak for yourself, Doc," Mildred said, flicking out a knife and cutting the rope from Ryan's ankles. The knots were drawn up too tight from the fall to ever untie. "I nearly wet my pants when I saw them both go over the edge."

Ryan kicked out of the cut rope, gritting his teeth against the pain in his ankles, legs and back. Everything still seemed to move when he wanted it to, which was a good sign.

"Thought lost for sure," Jak added. "Glad not."

"Me, too." Ryan took Jak's hand and forced himself to his feet.

A harsh, spitting bolt of snake-tongued lightning suddenly fried the sky above them, leaving the harsh, acrid smell of ozone behind.

Ryan glanced up just in time to watch a second jagged streak of lightning blaze across the sky. "Brushwooders'll probably hole up in this if they're smart."

J.B. nodded. "They'll probably be thinking we'll be doing the same thing."

Ryan bared a feral grin. "If we had a choice, we'd more

than likely do that. I think mebbe a little farther on, we could find a better place to set up that tent Jak found. Distance is a weapon we got right now, and we'd be better off using it.''

Mildred was the only one who voiced an objection. ''With the temperature dropping like it is, we're going to be risking exposure out here.''

''Exposure to hostile blasters and us without cover,'' Ryan replied, ''I figure that would kill us some quicker.'' He made decisions for the group, and they all knew it. And when they had something to say, they spoke their minds and he thought about it. Democracies didn't survive in Deathlands, because they took too long to react to changes in the given situation.

''You're right,'' Mildred said. ''I was just thinking maybe you and Krysty might take it easy after all you've been through.''

Krysty touched the woman's shoulder. ''I'll be okay. Ryan took the worst of it.''

Ryan shrugged on his pack, feeling the deeper pain of his ordeal hovering around him, warded off by the adrenaline still pumping through his system. ''I'm going to walk,'' he said, ''until I find a place safe enough or I can't walk anymore. Anything else would be double stupe, and put the rest of you in danger, as well.'' He turned to the albino. ''Jak, which way?''

The teenager pointed with his chin. ''Ahead.''

Turning up the collar of his coat, Ryan moved out. ''You got point, Jak.''

The albino nodded and vanished into the snow flurries within a half-dozen steps.

''J.B.,'' Ryan said, ''you're walking drag.''

The Armorer dropped out of the single-file line forming behind Ryan.

"Doc, you're the man next to him." He forced himself up the slight incline already covered with a layer of snow. He kept the Steyr in one hand and used the other to help balance himself as he went over the uneven terrain. He could no longer see Jak, but his combat senses allowed him to feel the teen's presence somewhere up in front of him.

Pain nagged every step Ryan made, but he knew it was nothing permanent. A good night's rest, possibly two if it could be managed, and he'd be as good as new. He pushed the accumulated aches and discomforts aside, falling into the easy rhythm of movement he'd become accustomed to.

"DAMMIT!" DEAN YELLED before he could stop himself. He was almost certain Phaedra had broken his nose this time. Red dots exploded in his vision. He put both hands in front of him to ward off another blow.

The bed shifted as Phaedra drew back her arm. "You triple-stupe mutie jackass! You bastard pervert! Your mother probably lay with the ugliest, foulest boar she could find to sire you!" She launched another blow.

Dean batted it aside, angry himself now, and fearful of taking another direct hit to the nose. Phaedra was three or four years older than he was, an inch or so taller and probably near the same weight because she carried a woman's figure instead of a girl's.

"Stop it!" he yelled at her.

She struck at him again.

Dean took the punch on the outside of his arm and moved it away.

Phaedra howled with frustration.

"They're going to hear you," Dean said, his voice not much above a strong whisper.

"I don't care! I hate you! I'm going to scratch your eyes out, then I'm going to stomp them into jelly, put them onto

pieces of sourdough bread and give them to the rats!'' She
flailed an open hand at him, and he caught it on his shoulder, the smack echoing in the room.

Dean grabbed her wrists out of self-defense. Over her
shoulder, Calgary Ventnor was waving frantically for him
to leave the room. ''Stop it!'' he told the girl. ''I thought
you weren't going to scream if I told you!''

''I lied!'' Her eyes blazed at him. ''You're insufferable!
I can't believe I let you sit on my bed!''

''You didn't let me,'' Dean said. ''I slipped in here and
let myself.'' The blanket had dropped even farther, to
where the material clung only by the nubbin of her nipple
to protect the last shreds of modesty. His breath felt thick
in his throat.

Calgary Ventnor mouthed Dean's name in wide panto-
mime. The boy slipped, a white look of terror crossing his
animated and blood-filled features.

For a moment Dean thought Calgary was going to fall
and had mixed feelings about the other boy's survival. He
kept his hands around Phaedra's wrists and forced her back
on the bed, where she couldn't gain enough leverage to
break free. One leg coiled around his waist in an effort to
move out from beneath him. With all the flesh showing,
Dean was suddenly and certainly sure that the girl wasn't
wearing panties, either. He was watching the expanse of
flesh increase, hypnotized, stopping just short of her sex,
but not short enough to keep the blond wisps of her pubic
hair hidden.

Dean swallowed hard, amazed at how all the air seemed
to have gone from the room.

Phaedra jammed a thumb in the corner of his eye.

''Dammit, dammit, dammit!'' Dean said, struggling to
keep his voice low despite the flash of pain. Blood swam
across his vision.

"Sick bastard!" Phaedra snarled.

Dean couldn't believe no one was coming to beat down the bedroom door. In a desperate move to shut up any more outbursts from the girl, he put his mouth over hers. It wasn't a kiss; it was just a seal of flesh against flesh.

Phaedra fought hard for a moment or two, wrapping her bedclothes around them. Then all the fight drained from her. Without warning, her lips sought Dean's.

Thinking maybe it was a ploy designed to win his confidence, Dean kept his mouth in place. The kiss happened without intention. Somehow he just wasn't able to keep his lips together. Then he wasn't able to keep his teeth together as Phaedra's tongue invaded his mouth.

He felt as if he were on fire, suddenly swollen up too big to fit inside his own skin. Not just in his crotch, but all over. He even felt light-headed. But he didn't for an instant believe he would be able to stick his tongue outside his own mouth without having it bitten off.

At length Phaedra broke off the kiss and lay quietly under him, her eyes closed. When she opened them, however, she said, "You're bleeding!"

Dean had noticed the liquid seeping from his eye, running down his face to moisten her cheek. He'd figured it was tears from his injured eye, but the injury hadn't seemed important at the time. Nor had the pain.

"Did I do that?" she asked, suddenly all innocence. She tried to pull her arms free.

Dean squinted the injured eye closed and tried to ignore the hurt again. It was definitely harder now, and the eye pained him badly, too. "I don't see anybody else who's been hitting me."

"I didn't mean to do that."

"You going to tell me you didn't mean to hit me in the nose, either?"

"I meant to do that."

"Oh."

"I didn't intend to hurt your eye." Pink strands of watered-down blood streamed from her cheek to her pillow.

Dean gazed down at her, letting his uninjured eye take in the sight of the creamy flesh open for his inspection. He looked at her breast, the nipple standing so proudly, flushed with blood and dark against the strawberry aureole. "You're pretty," he said before he had much time to think about it.

"Thank you."

He looked back into her face, noting that she didn't act embarrassed at all with his looking. "You kiss good, too."

"Thank you again. You kiss pretty good yourself."

He shifted on her, knowing she had to be noticing how excited he was against her leg, feeling kind of embarrassed about that himself. His dad had mentioned such things were natural; otherwise, what would bring men and women together long enough no matter what the hardship or circumstance to bring babies into the world? Of course, his dad had also said that bringing babies into the world generally wasn't on most people's minds at those times. But it was nothing to be ashamed of.

Still, Dean didn't feel comfortable.

"Have you been kissed before, Dean?" she asked.

"Sure." His response was automatic, defensive. He started to add that he'd been kissed lots of times even though that wasn't exactly true. Then he remembered that every time he tried to answer more than just the question on the table, he'd ended up in trouble. He wasn't stupe, so he kept his mouth shut.

She seemed happy enough about that. "Did you like it?"

"Yeah."

Her face darkened.

"But not as much as this time," he added.

"Why?"

He was confused. "Why what?" He was also aware of Calgary Ventnor struggling on the eaves of the house, either because he couldn't get his balance or because he was trying to better peer into the room.

"Why didn't you like it as much as this time?"

Dean wished he had more time to think. Hell, he wished he didn't feel so confused by everything his body was telling him that he *could* think. Telling her that he didn't know didn't sound like a good move.

"It was you," he said, hoping that was a safe statement. It also made clear that he thought all the responsibility, for good or evil, should be hers, which might be chancy.

She smiled at him. "You know, Dean Cawdor, looking at you all rawboned and unkempt sometimes, and hearing about how you fought so dirty out on the school ground, I didn't think you'd be such a romantic."

Dean raised his eyebrows, which made his bad eye hurt. He hoped Jak never heard about this, because he'd never live it down.

"If you'll let go of my wrists, maybe I can make your eye feel better. I can at least clean it up."

Gingerly Dean released her, pushing himself back.

Phaedra started to sit up, unmindful that the blanket had gathered at her waist, revealing her breasts to him. "Can't believe we didn't wake somebody up with all that noise," she said with a grin.

Dean couldn't, either. He was also aware that Calgary had edged down farther on the eaves. "Uh, mebbe you need to keep covered up." He didn't want the other boy to see.

"Why? You embarrassed? After all, it was you come stealing into my bedroom."

Dean watched Calgary suddenly come loose from the eaves over Phaedra's shoulder—and fall.

Chapter Twelve

Calgary screamed, loud and high-pitched like someone being torn apart by stampeding horses. A muffled thud ended it.

"Shit," Dean said, wondering if the boy had accidentally chilled himself. Bad enough to be caught in the girls' dorm, but triple bad if Calgary ended up dead. He pushed up from the bed, one hand clapped over his injured eye because the moon seemed too bright for him.

"What was that?" Phaedra demanded, yanking the lavender blanket around herself.

Dean stuck his head out the window and peered down. Calgary was squirming around, trying to suck in air like a man come near to drowning and finally back on dry land.

"That's Calgary Ventnor," Phaedra said, shoving through the window beside Dean.

"Yeah," Dean replied, wondering how the hell he was going to explain the other boy's presence. Telling Phaedra that the jaunt into her bedroom had been at Calgary's instigation seemed tantamount to slitting his wrists the long way. But he couldn't think, not the way his head was hurting and with the vanilla scent of Phaedra standing so close coming into his swollen nose with every breath.

She looked at him. "Calgary must have followed you up here."

Dean blinked his good eye at her, then didn't hesitate at all. "That's probably it."

"He's a pervert," Phaedra declared. "He's been caught two, three times peeking through glory holes he's carved through the girls' shower room."

"Phaedra?" a voice behind them said.

They turned together, Dean bumping his head on the window frame and creating a new onslaught of pain that nearly swept his senses away.

Bitha was sitting up in her bed. Her eyes widened as they locked on Dean. Then she screamed, an ear-piercing shriek that would have moved the dead.

Phaedra grabbed Dean's arm and pushed him at the window. "Get out!"

"What?" Before he knew it, she almost had him out the window.

"If they don't catch you, they won't know who you are," Phaedra said in a desperate whisper. "Bitha can't see shit without her glasses. If you don't get caught, neither one of us has to explain what you were doing in here."

"That's a long way down," Dean protested.

"Yes, well, Calgary Ventnor is still alive, isn't he?" Phaedra pushed again, shoving Dean through the window. "If he can make the jump, so can you."

Footsteps sounded at the door, and a man's voice demanded, "Are you girls all right in there?" A heavy hand beat against the door rapidly, shaking the heavy timbers.

Dean glanced at the door, one leg over the window frame and barely finding purchase on the narrow board below. Bitha was still screaming, the covers pulled over her head.

"Go!" Phaedra ordered impatiently. She put her shoulder against Dean with more force than he'd expected.

Off balance and hanging precariously, Dean had no chance to keep his grip. He plummeted, waving his arms wildly in an attempt not to land on Calgary. An instant before he hit the ground, he managed to get his feet under him. On impact he crumpled his legs and breathed the air out of his lungs, letting his body be its own cushioning system. He went forward into a roll and came up on his feet, none the worse for wear. The drop had been no big challenge, but it had looked bad because of the night shadows draping the landscape.

Peering up, he saw yellow light invade the bedroom behind Phaedra. Bitha was still screaming, and Dean couldn't believe the pitch she was getting, not to mention the lack of wear and tear apparent on her vocal cords. The girl should have been in choir.

"Sorry," Phaedra called down in an excited whisper, still holding the blanket over her breasts.

"Dean," Calgary said, "help me. I think I broke my leg." He reached a hand up, tears streaking his face.

"You're lucky you didn't break your bastard neck, you stupe." Dean took the other boy's hand, unwilling to leave him there.

"I think it was a pretty near thing." He hiccuped as he tried to suck in another breath.

A big arm swept Phaedra out of the window. She cursed and hit the man attached to it. The man shoved his flashlight outside and held it aloft to light up the grounds.

Dean knew they were drawing entirely too much unwanted attention. He moved Calgary by force, pulling the boy along behind him at almost a dead run.

He kept them moving, dodging between the girls' quarters and the stable. Horses whickered inside, woken by the shouts of alarm starting around the perimeter of the school.

Dean ran Calgary headlong into the corral fence, getting behind the other boy with just enough shoulder and strength to start him over the top rail.

Calgary wasn't happy about the turn of events at all, groaning as Dean muscled him over the railing and pulled him down into the tromped earth. It had rained a couple days earlier, so the ground was still soft in most places.

The flickering torchlight from one of the school's sec guards on the ground illuminated the rails but didn't reach far into the muddy areas beyond. Men yelled to one another, calling out clear areas.

There was no sound, no warning. Then a light but firm hand shoved against Dean's shoulder as he lay on the ground and watched two sec men go wandering by with flashlights in their hands.

Dean came around quick, curling up and ready to spring to his feet. As he made the effort, responding to the shadow leaning over him, the hand shifted from his shoulder to the center of his chest. A strong push sent Dean tumbling to his ass again.

"Don't," a man's voice warned. "Damn kid. You're already in it up to your neck."

Peering through the gloom, Dean recognized Jake. The sec man had been the first school resident Dean had met. "I'm sitting," the boy grumbled.

Jake glared down at him, then looked at Calgary and back again. He wore a sun-bleached and battered brimmed hat, a gray work shirt and blue jeans tucked into scarred work boots that had never seen an honest day of rest. The way he held the Browning 71 rifle in his hand, it looked as if flesh, bone and steel never parted company.

"That you up in the girls' dorm?" Jake asked.

"No," Calgary answered quickly.

Dean returned the man's penetrating gaze. "Yes, sir."

"He went in," Calgary said, pointing at Dean with one hand and trying to brush shit off with the other.

"You was just hanging around on the rooftop," Jake said, pinning the other boy with his gaze.

Calgary didn't have anything to say to that.

Jake canted the rifle over his shoulder and pushed his hat back with a gnarled thumb. He looked at Dean, his face stern but his eyes full of mischief. "I ain't gonna ask you what you was doing inside that dorm."

Dean felt relieved.

"But Brody, he's gonna want to know. You might want to think on that."

"Yes, sir," Dean said.

Jake nodded. "Let's go. You boys caused enough of a stir tonight."

Dean got up and followed the sec man, knowing he'd probably just blown every chance he had of finishing out the term at the school. He figured his dad was going to be real disappointed.

RYAN DIDN'T BOTHER checking his chron to find out how long the march took them to get to the pass. He stayed in the lower reaches of the narrow trail that twisted through the broken slabs of rock that had tumbled into their way, evidently from the latest earthquake.

Jak ranged ahead of them, a ghost on a field that looked beyond the pale.

Another few minutes saw them clear of most of the debris. When Jak turned, Ryan waved him to the north side of the pass near what appeared to be the entrance, or exit, depending on how a man was making his way through the mountains.

"I'm going up," Ryan said. "I'll take a look around above us and make sure there isn't any rock waiting to come tumbling down when we least expect it."

"Be careful, lover," Krysty said.

Ryan shouldered the Steyr, found some handholds and started up. Jak went with him. Below, J.B. and Doc started to set up the therm tent out of the wind in the protected areas afforded by the stone wall.

Arms aching, Ryan pulled himself up the final few feet and found himself on a small plateau that quickly fell away in all directions. Jak was at his side a heartbeat later.

Ryan shaded his eye against the swirling snowflakes and peered around. A carpet of white covered the land, interrupted in a lot of places by trees and treetops that made islands of green. There were no signs of fires or of the brushwooders in the areas open to him.

"Anything?" he asked Jak.

"No."

"Let's hope we're right."

THE TENT WAS IN PLACE when Jak and Ryan returned. Ryan smelled the aroma of a freshly opened self-heat even before they'd finished the descent. His stomach rumbled, reminding him how many hours it had been since he'd last had a meal.

J.B. sat hunkered down with his back against a wall a little up from the rounded dome of the tent. From his position he could see over the tent and all approach paths for at least fifty yards in any direction. The Armorer held a steaming self-heat in his hands, eating slow so he could savor the warmth of the container for a bit, too.

"Here, lover." Krysty handed him a self-heat when she emerged from the tent.

Ryan took the container gratefully. He figured his stomach might revolt later, but for now it put some warmth in him and got a good start on filling up all the hollow spaces.

"Go on inside the tent," J.B. said. "I got this watch."

Ryan nodded. "Wake me in an hour and a half. I'll take that one."

Ryan entered the tent, followed by Jak, Mildred and Krysty, who zipped the flap closed again.

"Not much room," Mildred said, sitting cross-legged in a corner, "but it does take a body out of that wind."

Ryan stretched out as much as he was able. The tent wasn't very big, so they were all touching one another. But that way they'd also be able to share the warmth. He finished the stew and put the container aside, laying his head on his arm. His eye drifted closed when he felt Krysty's hand on his brow. Her fingers felt soft across the areas that weren't nerve damaged from the injuries he'd taken over the years. Moments later he fell asleep.

Chapter Thirteen

"Wake up!"

Ryan cracked open his eye and closed his hand around the SIG-Sauer. Jak was nowhere in sight, but it had been the albino's voice. He got to his knees, feeling Krysty moving beside him. "Jak."

"Yeah."

"Trouble?"

Doc, Mildred and J.B. awakened, as well, all of them reaching for weapons.

"Burning daylight," Jak called back. He sounded irritated. "Figured you people up by now."

Ryan pushed through the tent flap, surprised by the brightness and warmth of the sun hanging low in a mass of purple clouds to the east. He left his coat open, knowing he wasn't going to need it for the slight chill that remained from the storm last night.

All around him was the sound of running water. Snow melted at an incredible rate, pouring down tracks already worn through the rock and soil. Steam curled up from the ground, rolling in gentle fogs across the countryside.

"I didn't expect this, lover." Krysty came up beside Ryan and put her hand in his.

"Don't see how you could have," Ryan replied.

"It probably has a lot to do with the underlying volcanic activity and the atmospheric conditions in regards to the debris that regularly shoots into the upper stratosphere,'' Doc stated, putting a hand to his forehead to shade his eyes.

"Feels like a cold sauna out here," Mildred said.

J.B. looked at the drenched ground. "There's a good chance we're going to leave a trail wherever we go."

Ryan nodded, surveying the terrain around them. "We stick to the rocks so we don't leave tracks."

"Yeah, but that's going to put us working the high ground. Better chance of the brushwooders seeing us."

"We get a few more miles behind us, they won't have a chance at all."

"Downhill," Jak said, "mebbe melting snow wash away all tracks." The albino teenager sat tending a slow cook fire nestled between a ring of rocks he'd evidently placed. He turned a long spit that held four animals that had roasted nicely.

"And mebbe we'll end up trying to cross some awfully flooded lands," Ryan added. "Up top we should be able to get a better lay of the terrain. Pick a good spot to cross at instead of being chased into a bad one."

"Where'd you get breakfast?" Mildred asked.

Jak waved an arm. "Little animals kept sticking heads up not far away. I pitched rocks. And I got these." He poured out a pouch that contained bright red cherry tomatoes and dark purple berries.

"Growing wild?" Ryan asked.

Jak nodded. "Have to look some. Color was pretty easy to see this morning against snow."

"By the Three Kennedys!" Doc hunkered down and picked up one of the tomatoes, which was about the size of his thumb. "Jak, lad, have I mentioned lately how valuable an asset I consider you to be?"

The albino just looked at Doc, then turned the spit another notch.

"I find myself constantly enthralled by the vagaries and mysteries of Mother Nature even in these godforsaken lands." Doc rolled the cherry tomato between his fingers, as if savoring the taste by touch. He tilted his head and glanced at Mildred. "Concerning all the volcanic activity and radiation residue, would it be wise to partake of this repast?"

"Those fruits could be holding in some radioactive waste," Mildred admitted.

"If do," Jak said, "can't be much." He waved at the roasting meat. "They eating it."

"Then let's eat," J.B. said. "Small as they are, if there was anything in them going to kill a body, they'd have died off."

Ryan squatted long enough to pull off a haunch. The animal looked like a ground squirrel of some type, but was the size of a chicken. Surprisingly there was a fair amount of meat on the bones.

He dropped the Steyr over his shoulder and took up a handful of tomatoes and berries. There appeared to be plenty of both. He walked to a nearby outcrop and unlocked his knees until he was in a squatting position that wouldn't allow him to be easily skylined against the mountain.

Krysty came up behind him, her hands as laden as his. Ryan looked at her, seeing the pinched worry lines over the bridge of her nose as she stared out beyond the pass. "Did you have any bad dreams about Dean?"

She hesitated, then shook her head. "I don't remember dreaming at all, I was so tired. I know I stood watch, stayed away during the whole time, but I don't remember that too clearly, either."

Ryan knew something was bothering his red-haired lover, but she also knew he wouldn't ask. When she was ready to talk about it, she would. It was how things were between them.

Scanning the eastern horizon, Ryan said, "It's been a long time. I need to see him again."

Krysty put an arm across his back and hugged him. "I know, lover. We've all missed him."

"I have to ask myself, though, if he's going to be ready to leave the friends he's made at that school and take up this hard traveling life of ours again."

DEAN WAS READY to be anywhere in all of Deathlands except where he was right at that moment. He sat in one of the straight-backed chairs outside Nicholas Brody's office, arms crossed over his chest and fidgeting. He couldn't seem to find a comfortable place to put his hands.

Jake sat across from him on the small desk where the secretary kept all the records and bits of school business intact and organized. A spray of dried flowers from one of the gardens filled a light green blown-glass vase from the art department.

The door opened, and Dean's heart leaped to the back of his throat.

Phaedra Lemon stepped into the outer office, wearing the light-colored blouse and denim skirt that were the school's uniform for its female students.

Dean's jaw almost dropped. He hadn't expected her there.

"My dear," Nicholas Brody said in that officious way of his, "I certainly appreciate your willingness to involve yourself in reporting this case of scandalous behavior on the part of these young men. Rest assured, then, that I will do my utmost to resolve these conflicts straightaway."

Phaedra started to say something.

Brody shushed her with an uplifted hand. "My dear, really. I've troubled you for enough of your time."

"Yes, sir." Phaedra dropped a short curtsy, then turned on her heel and walked to Dean. "I did my best to explain to Mr. Brody that you were only returning an earring of a friend's that I'd lost. I told him I thought it was a most gallant thing to do."

"Uh, okay." Dean gazed at her and blinked. Suddenly hot, he pulled at his shirt collar, thinking it had to have shrunk since he'd put it on that morning. He glanced at Brody.

The headmaster stood in the doorway, hands locked behind his back in a familiar pose. His broad face was unreadable.

Phaedra left without another word, her vanilla scent lingering after her.

"Mr. Cawdor," Brody said. "If you would, please." He stepped aside and waved inside his office.

Dean pushed himself out of the chair and swallowed hard. Muties or stickies, he thought, a dozen of them or two dozen, and him armed only with a pea shooter, that would be better than walking into that room.

But he went.

Chapter Fourteen

"Tracks," Ryan told J.B.

The Armorer walked forward, automatically unslinging the S&W M-4000 scattergun. Behind the round lenses, his hawk-sharp eyes surveyed the broken terrain. The sun blazed down, growing hotter and melting the snow even more rapidly.

Ryan touched the indentation of a boot that had slipped off a shelf of rock and made a J-shape in the soft earth. Then he pointed out the muddy impressions the boot had made along the rocky trail they were following.

"Fresh," J.B. said.

"Yeah." Ryan ran his fingers through the smear of mud. It was still damp. "Mebbe less than an hour old."

"We could find another way. Down there looks like mebbe we could cross without getting mired too bad."

Ryan studied the bowl-shaped valley nearly a hundred yards below. "That's a pretty wide stretch. If the brush-wooders come up on us suddenly, we could get royally fucked."

"We've got to be leaving them behind," J.B. said. "They'd have to be flat traveling to match the pace we've set."

Ryan flicked his eye over the rocky shelf. Here and there were other mud smears. "Whoever it was, he wasn't alone."

"No, but there couldn't be many of them."

"We'll keep on going the way we were." Ryan decided that partly because staying with the rise of stone seemed safest and the least traceable, and partly because he was curious. "Pass the word."

J.B. nodded and went back along the trail.

Carrion eaters circled lazily in the blue sky, their wings dead still. Ryan chose not to view that as an omen, because he wasn't a superstitious man.

"HAVE A SEAT, Mr. Cawdor." Nicholas Brody indicated one of the three straight-backed chairs in front of his desk.

"Yes, sir." Dean sat, dropping his hands into his lap.

Brody's brows drew together. "I await elucidation, Mr. Cawdor, with a calm demeanor yet a certain sense of purpose."

"Yes, sir." Dean had learned early on that when an instructor at the school spoke, it usually meant kitchen duty or mucking out the stables for not being prompt with an answer.

"Aren't you going to say anything?"

"Yes, sir." Dean let out his breath, maintaining eye contact with the older man with difficulty. "I'm sorry." He was bastard sorry he'd gotten caught.

"Your feelings in this regard are both noted and appreciated. But that in no way begins to clarify how you came to be on that structure."

"I climbed, sir."

"Of course you climbed," Brody snapped. "I know very well that you're incapable of sprouting wings like some Icarus. What I endeavor to comprehend is what motivated you to go up there in the first place."

Dean had been dreading that question, but he was prepared. "I don't know, sir."

"Did Miss Lemon invite you up?"

Suddenly Dean felt hot again, his mind preoccupied with the idea that maybe Phaedra was in the habit of asking other boys up to her room and he didn't know about it. That had to be why Brody asked. The possibility made him angry for reasons he wasn't certain of. Maybe her explanation of the earring was to clear herself and not him at all. Confusion followed closely on the heels of his anger.

"No, sir, she didn't," Dean answered truthfully.

"She didn't know you were coming?"

"No, sir." Now Dean wanted to know if Phaedra had asked other boys up to her room on different occasions. Maybe she'd even started the rumor of her sleeping naked herself, just to entice unsuspecting boys to her room so she could push them out windows. "Have I been the only one caught in her room, Mr. Brody?"

The headmaster scowled, not at Dean, but at the thought. "You mean there have been others?"

Dean's stomach rolled over. He was only making matters worse. Surely he would have heard about any others. Everyone had heard of him today. "No, sir."

"Do you know of any other boys who've visited Miss Lemon's room after lights-out?" Brody demanded.

"No, sir."

"Would you lie about that, Mr. Cawdor?"

Dean considered the question, thinking about the classes in philosophical reasoning he'd had. It hadn't been much, but it had given him a grasp of certain concepts. "Excuse me, sir, but if you have to ask that question, my answer's not going to be worth shit."

"I remind you about your use of bad language, Mr. Cawdor."

"Sorry, sir."

"I want to understand what took you up on that rooftop,'' Brody said. "This is a serious infraction of the rules of this school.''

"Yes, sir.''

Brody sighed. "Dean, I am in a hard way here. If your father was someone local, I could call upon him, seek his advice in this matter. At least have some avenue to pursue concerning your punishment. I would not want to see you ostracized from the student body and be rendered a virtual prisoner on these premises. Tell me, young Cawdor, in your own words, why it was that you scaled that building and transgressed into Miss Lemon's bedroom. Give me something upon which I might build a case for your defense, seeing as how you remain unable to defend your actions yourself.''

Dean tried, but the words just wouldn't come out. Just saying he went there because he wondered if Phaedra slept naked sounded totally stupe.

"Evidently Miss Lemon feels some allegiance for you,'' Brody stated. "Otherwise, she'd have been the first clamoring for your head on the proverbial pike. Instead, she marches herself into my office this morning in an effort to clear you. Her explanation of this missing earring is manifestly balderdash. I'm quite certain she realized I believed not a word of it, yet why would she defend you?''

Chapter Fifteen

Krysty fell into step beside Doc. "You and I have talked about my powers before."

"At length upon occasion," Doc replied. "As I recall, I have evidenced more real curiosity about your abilities than you yourself. You have always appeared predisposed to accept them on faith."

"That's true." She gazed ahead, spotting Ryan walking point, J.B. strung out behind him a hundred yards at right flank. Watching him, so far away from her if something happened, made a chill run down her spine.

"I assume you have not brought up the subject simply for the prospect of idle conversation."

"Everything I tell you, Doc, you can't tell Ryan."

"That man is savagely keen, dear lady. Mayhap he'll learn just as much from what I omit as he would from what I told him."

"That's the way it has to be," Krysty said. "To protect him. And mebbe Dean, as well."

"You're sure?" Doc's face showed he was troubled, as well as intrigued.

Krysty reached out and took Doc's hand briefly, squeezing it to reassure him as much as herself. Then she told him about the vision she'd had down in the chasm.

"You believe in my powers, don't you, Doc?"

"Believe in them, my dear, without a doubt. My ability to understand them is lacking. Though there were definite experimental studies being done within the Totality Concept, based loosely on scientific research. I never got too close to them. Speculation you cannot adequately quantify is something I never took to very much.''

"I have a theory."

"That, my dear Krysty, is a phrase every scientist loves to hear. For with the existence of such a hypothesis, a catalyst may be introduced whereby events may be suitably weighed and measured. Of course, it is possible that your theory will be disproved, putting you squarely back where you started.''

"I have to ask myself a couple of things. First I have to ask myself if seeing them mebbe kill each other in that place was the only event that vision really showed me.''

"What do you mean?"

"Suppose I saw them, but I couldn't do a thing about it. Couldn't stop it. Suppose my mind couldn't handle seeing such a thing and just created the parts where I went to them and talked to them.''

"Ah, my dear, you have truly twisted this puzzle. Was the whole event a fabrication, or were parts of it? If so, which parts?"

It sounded worse coming from Doc.

"So it could be that Ryan and Dean are going to face off against each other, the one never knowing the other was there, and mebbe kill one or both,'' Krysty said.

"Or possibly you have managed to intervene in some fashion,'' Doc said. "Or will.''

"It's just as possible, though,'' Krysty replied, "that the reason I won't be at Ryan's side when this happens later, is because I can't be.'' She turned and went farther up the mountain, avoiding the chasm Ryan had walked around. "It's just as possible that I could be chilled by then, and no help to him at all.''

"I shall make you a promise, my dear," Doc stated in a gentle voice. "As long as I yet live, nothing shall harm you until we see the truth of this vision. I shall become your shield and buckler, and may all that remains holy in this accursed land keep my strength unflagging."

Krysty looked at him. "You're a good friend, Doc."

"It is simple to be a good friend," he replied smiling, "when you're in the company of good friends."

When Ryan went down suddenly in front of her, Krysty at first thought her lover had fallen over a piece of the broken terrain. Then the sound of a blastershot rolled over her.

Chapter Sixteen

The only thing that warned Ryan the sniper had a bead on him was the glint of sunlight against glass. But it only amplified the feeling that something predatory was eyeing him. He went down to his right, throwing himself at a stand of grayish green rock jutting up from the broken earth.

The heavy bullet whizzed in, big enough to sound for an instant like incoming artillery. The round smashed a misshapen rock the size of a pumpkin into fragments where he'd been standing.

"Fireblast!" Ryan yelled as he slammed up against the outcrop. His back took the brunt of the impact, but his right ear bumped up against the stone surface hard enough to rip flesh. When he reached up to check it, he found the ear still in one piece but bleeding profusely. He rose to a kneeling position behind the rock.

The second bullet clipped a fist-sized chunk from Ryan's cover and sent stone slivers stinging into his face. He narrowed his eye instinctively. Sinking back behind the rock, he looked to his rear. "J.B., do you know where he's at?"

"Got a perch up there about four hundred yards away. At eleven o'clock."

Ryan checked back along the trail. "Anybody hit?"

They all answered back in short order, letting him know they were intact.

Slithering around the rock, Ryan went lower, staying on

his belly against the hot stone. Peering around the corner of his cover, he studied the horizon.

Another glint sparked like white fire nestled on the dark of the stone perch J.B. had to have seen. Ryan moved his head back an instant before another heavy bullet cracked against the rock with enough force to cause a vibration.

"Fireblast!" Ryan said. "Bastard must be up there with a damn cannon." He readied the Steyr, adjusting for the distance.

"Unless I miss my guess," the Armorer called up, "that's a Sharps .50-cal buffalo rifle."

Ryan was familiar with the weapon. In the hands of an expert, the Sharps was capable of making clean kills out to a thousand yards.

On the other side of his cover, the one-eyed man dropped the Steyr against his shoulder and squeezed off two quick rounds. Both of them hit the sniper's position, but he doubted either one hit the man. Still, it gave the shooter something to think about.

Ryan rolled behind cover again and looked back along the mountainside. Below and to his left nearly seventy yards, treetops scrubbed against the side of the defile. The drop might not kill them, but there was every chance someone could break a leg or an arm. Neither prospect would leave them in good shape to escape the brushwooders.

The mountain ridge to the right promised only more heights with not much in the way of protective cover. Every minute they were pinned down brought the brushwooders that much closer, as well. Ryan had no doubts that the shots had been heard.

Pushing himself up against the rock, Ryan yelled, "Stop shooting!"

"Fuck you!" a man's voice yelled back. "You didn't seem to have a problem shooting at us!"

Us meant more than one. Ryan wondered exactly how many more. "That's because you shot first! Wanted you to know we could do this the easy way or the hard way!"

"You people just hold your position! You will not be allowed to reach a greater proximity!"

"What the hell do you want us to do?" Ryan asked.

"Go back the way you came!" The voice echoed off the higher position, rolling across the mountainside.

"Can't do that!"

"That will be your preference, but I assure you that inclination will categorically lead only to your demise!"

"Talks like Doc," J.B. commented.

"Do you see him?" Ryan asked.

"No. He's got himself set in good. Got more sense than to move, either."

"You figure one guy?"

"Mebbe. Bullets come kind of slow. That Sharps is a breechloader. One round at a time at that."

"If we give him multiple targets, he's going to be hard up against it trying to get us all," Ryan said.

Ryan scanned the terrain for the albino teenager, who was nowhere to be seen. "Jak?"

A pebble thudded softly against Ryan's right arm. He turned in that direction and barely made out the youth lying like a second layer of dirt over the stone shelf little more than ten yards away.

"If I give them a target," Ryan said, "do you think you can get up in there behind them without being seen?"

"Daylight makes hard. Mebbe. Drop into trees, could get around."

"J.B."

"I heard you," the Armorer said.

"When I go left, you break right. You get somewhere safe, bang a couple rounds at them to let them know we're still knocking at the door.'' Ryan spared a last glance at Jak, then pushed himself up from the ground and ran.

He dived behind a low hill of fresh-broken earth, then kicked his feet, pushing up flush against the earthen ridge.

A bullet slammed into the ground and tore away a piece bigger than the palm of Ryan's hand. He pulled the Steyr to his shoulder and fired two rounds at the sniper's perch. Then he was running again, his mind automatically figuring the time it would take a man to jack another round into the Sharps buffalo rifle.

Jak had already disappeared.

Chapter Seventeen

"It wasn't Phaedra's fault we were there," Dean said, shifting in his chair and wishing his voice didn't shake the way it did. He hurried on before Brody could say anything. "Calgary come to me—came to me—a couple days ago. He'd done me a good turn, so I owed him. He wanted me to climb up in that dormitory with him, kind of help him along because he couldn't figure a way to do it himself."

"And Miss Lemon didn't invite yourself or young Ventnor into her room?" Brody asked.

"Mr. Brody," Dean said, looking at the headmaster, "you make a big deal here at the school about fair play and honesty. I'm being honest. I'm sorry I broke your rules, I truly am, especially if I'm gonna get kicked out over it. But if you're even thinking for a minute about blaming Phaedra for any of this, well, then, I don't think my dad knew exactly the place he was leaving me at. If Phaedra gets punished and her not guilty in any of this, I'll have to kick my own self out, because I don't want to be part of no place that does that."

Silence filled the room when Dean finished speaking. He couldn't believe he'd talked so much. If he hadn't been mad, he wouldn't have.

Brody broke the silence. "Thank you, Dean, for bringing my responsibility in this matter to the forefront of my mind. And for your forthrightness."

Dean shoved out of the chair and started for the door.

He was scared, but he kind of felt good all at the same time.

LESS THAN A MINUTE after they'd started their moves against the sniper's position, Ryan and J.B. worked out a rhythm. The Armorer would snap off a few rounds with his Uzi, splattering the rocks around the unseen gunman, and Ryan would bolt into motion. It took the sniper five or ten seconds to get up the courage to crank off a round. By that time Ryan had usually found his next bit of cover.

Flinging his hands in front of his face as he counted silently, Ryan threw himself forward. He hit the hard ground and slid behind a broken shelf of rock. A .50-caliber round dug into the earth only a few inches from his left boot, leaving a hole he could almost put his fist into.

The next bullet came before Ryan was ready for it, shattering a blocky stone in front of him and sending pieces of it thudding into his legs. He lost his balance and fell, rolling to the side to protect his rifle.

"Ryan!" the Armorer yelled.

"I'm okay." Ryan shoved himself to his feet and took shelter beside an outcrop from the ridge beside him. "Move up while I cover you." He shouldered the Steyr, putting the cross hairs over the sniper's perch. "Go!"

He squeezed off a half-dozen rounds as J.B. broke cover and ran. Even at 250 yards, the shots could have been centered on a pie plate when they struck the sniper's position.

J.B. came up beside him, breathing deep. "It'll work better if we leapfrog it. First me, then you."

Ryan nodded. He glanced back toward the area where Krysty, Doc and Mildred lay waiting. He'd told them to stay put. With too many targets taking the field, the sniper would have had a better chance to get one of them. "Ready?"

"As I ever was," J.B. replied.

"Do it."

The Armorer sidled up to the corner and burned another short burst toward the sniper, then broke cover and ran.

DOWN IN THE BAYOUS where he'd been born, there were stories told around camp fires that Jak Lauren could sneak up on mutie gators and take the teeth from their jaws before they knew he was among them. The albino had never contributed to the stories, except by doing things others were too afraid to do or weren't able to do. To Jak it had all been about survival.

And it was survival now that drove him from hiding into an assault up the narrow chimney of rock where the sniper hid. The climb through the tops of the trees at the edge of the cliff face had been simple compared to the vertical challenge in front of him.

The rock chimney stood almost forty feet up, looking like some kind of turret on a castle he'd once seen in a child's faded fairy-tale book. A trail curled around it like a dog's tail wrapped around itself.

The trail was tempting, but Jak knew it would leave him open to anyone keeping watch over it. The only other way to reach the sniper's perch was straight up.

The Sharps rifle banged loudly again, the report echoing in the narrow press of mountaintops surrounding the sniper's perch.

The albino slipped from the cliff's edge and sprinted across the fifteen yards separating him from the stone chimney. He stood at its base, listening intently, trying to hear the slightest scrabble overhead that would indicate he'd been seen or heard.

Satisfied he had escaped notice, he unlaced his boots and stepped out of them. He flexed his toes as he tested the

chimney for his first handhold, then took one of his leaf-
bladed throwing knives and placed it between his teeth.
Leaning into the rock and digging his fingers and toes into
the cracks and crevices, he started up.

"DO YOU SEE JAK?" Ryan asked, raking the sniper's position through the Steyr's scope. The cross hairs settled
comfortably between the albino's shoulder blades, thirty
feet up the sheer wall under the overhang.

"Yeah," J.B. replied, punching fresh bullets into the
Uzi's magazine. When he put the last one in and shoved
the clip home, he doffed his hat long enough to wipe his
brow on his shirtsleeve. "Going to have to be careful and
not hit him."

"If we stop coming in on the sniper, he's going to know
something's wrong."

J.B. nodded. "If Jak runs into trouble, we're not going
to do him much good way the hell out here."

Ryan squinted his eye and stared hard at the chimney
rock. "You see a trail behind that rock?"

"I was thinking mebbe," the Armorer said. "The distance and the dust, it's hard to make out."

"When he gets to the top of those rocks, I'm going to
make for that trail. If Jak has a real fight on his hands, you
take out whoever you see on that ridgeline and leave Jak
free."

"Sure."

Ryan readied himself, ignoring the cramp in his left calf
that came from the constant dodging and powering into
sprints. The chimney rock was still nearly 130 yards away.

The brushwooders had seriously cut their lead, though,
and were drawing closer by the minute.

"Go," J.B. said, opening up with the Uzi.

Even as the machine pistol belched an angry snarl of

death, Ryan shoved himself from behind cover and ran, counting.

CLINGING TO THE SIDE of the chimney rock, Jak saw the long barrel of the Sharps buffalo rifle stick out over the lip of the ledge. It was still beyond his reach.

Sweat from his efforts and the residual humidity in the air drenched his clothing. His arms and legs trembled slightly with the constant strain he'd expended crawling the past thirty-five feet.

He moved his left hand, prying for his next handhold, precariously balanced on his right foot and holding tight with his other hand. He pressed his left knee against the stone, finding enough of a grip to feel confident about searching for the new hold. Going down at this point would be harder than continuing up.

Shoving his fingers into the small crevice as hard as he could, he heard the definitive bang of the Sharps as the round was touched off. The hold he'd discovered was a good one. He eased his weight around, searching for a foothold and found it.

Jak shoved himself up, gaining nearly two feet this time. His right shoulder blade spasmed, and he nearly let out a foul curse before he caught himself.

The barrel of the Sharps nosed over the lip of rock above him.

Just as he was getting ready to shift his weight again, the irregular notch of stone he clasped in his left hand gave way. Bits of rock tumbled down the side of the stone chimney.

Swinging wildly for just a moment, Jak helplessly stared at the ground nearly forty feet below, hanging by his other hand as first one foot, then the other slid free. An effort of iron-willed determination kept the fingers of his right hand in place, supporting all his weight.

The big rifle banged again, and the echoes cracked against the open spaces where Ryan, J.B. and the others were pinned down.

Slowly, and in agony, Jak pulled himself back into place. Once his feet were on firm footing again, he pushed himself upward, not wanting to give his muscles a chance to cramp up. Fire burned through his limbs and back.

Bullets from Ryan's Steyr slammed into the rock beside the sniper's position, stone splinters raining in a sudden hail.

Jak narrowed his eyes against it and kept moving. When the Sharps thundered again, he was ready. As the big .50-caliber rifle pulled back and the breech opened, the albino shoved himself onto the ledge. He caught Ryan's sudden breakneck run from the corner of his eye.

Then Jak could see nothing but the bottom of the ledge as he pushed himself up with both hands. Saliva leaked down over his chin from carrying the knife, cool in the winds that rushed over the chimney top.

The man with the Sharps rifle spotted him first.

"Bernsen!" The man with the Sharps was a scraggly old man who looked as if he'd been worn whipcord tough by a hard, adventurous life. His gray beard was tangled, cut square at the bottom only a few inches below his chin. His silver hair was pulled back in a single stand that hung on his bony shoulder like the tail of a dead animal. He wore hiking boots, jeans and a black-and-red-checked flannel shirt that had the sleeves rolled up enough to reveal the same orange-and-blue tattoo on his inner forearm that had been on the dead man. He fumbled, trying to insert another cartridge into the Sharps.

"Get down, Hoyle!" Bernsen yelled. He was a few years

younger than his companion, broader built and softer by the look of him. A paunch settled gracelessly into his lap, and he didn't seem certain of the long-barreled Dan Wesson .41 Magnum blaster he held in both hands. However, he brought the weapon around quick enough.

Jak slipped the leaf-bladed knife from his teeth and flipped it at the man, deliberately missing the man's head only by inches. Ryan wanted them alive if it could be managed.

Bernsen ducked, rolling with a lack of coordination to another area behind his partner's position, and yelped in fear.

Still in motion, Jak leaped at Hoyle. The old man had the cartridge in the breech and was pulling the lever closed. Fisting another knife from the top of his boot, Jak batted away the barrel of the Sharps with his free arm. The rifle exploded as the hammer fell, sending the bullet ricocheting from the rock behind the ledge.

Closing on the man, Jak shouldered Hoyle in the stomach hard enough to knock him off balance. Before his opponent could recover, Jak stepped in behind him and seized his ponytail.

Bernsen tracked them with the .41 Magnum blaster. "Get down, Hoyle! You're in the way! Give me a clean shot!"

Hoyle struggled to get away, throwing his weight to one side and swinging back with the butt of the Sharps.

Already expecting the move, Jak shifted with the man, staying behind him and avoiding the rifle butt. Jak brought the knife to the man's throat, yanking back on the ponytail to bare it even further. The keen edge lay over the jugular.

Bernsen fired anyway, the bullet whizzing less than a foot from Jak's head. Awkwardly the heavy man thumbed back the hammer.

"Stop," Jak ordered in a harsh voice, "or die!" He nicked Hoyle's neck with the blade to emphasize his point. Three bloody tears wept from the small incision and trickled down the man's sweaty neck.

Instead, eyes wide and round with fear, Bernsen leveled the blaster to fire again.

Chapter Eighteen

Ryan found the trail behind the chimney rock and threw himself into an assault on the steep downgrade at the same time the big rifle roared from above. He didn't hear J.B.'s Uzi chatter into life, so he knew the Armorer hadn't had a shot.

Keeping the Steyr across his chest, his attention divided between the loose stones under his feet and the narrow corkscrew leading up into the chimney rock, he ran as hard as he could. Spots danced crazily in his vision.

A blaster—some large caliber—boomed only a few paces ahead of him.

Ryan came around the corner in time to see the heavy man taking up slack on the weapon's trigger a second time. Jak was covered by the man standing in front of him, the guy pressed into service by the knife blade held at his throat, but there was every possibility that the bullets would pass through the human shield and hit Jak.

Bringing up the rifle, Ryan fired four quick rounds, spacing them in an uneven line only inches above the blaster-wielder's head. The man ducked instinctively and brought around his weapon.

Ryan threw himself forward and chopped down with the Steyr's barrel, cracking the man viciously across the wrists as the blaster went off. The bullet sped by only inches from Ryan's head.

The man screamed in pain and dropped the heavy weapon. Before he could make an attempt to recover it, Ryan kicked it away, then booted the man in the side.

The man raised his hands in defense and buried his face in his arms. "Don't! Please don't hurt me any more!"

"Go ahead and kill us," the man Jak held said, "or leave him alone. He's not been out in this mean world overmuch. Not used to rough handling."

The man's words made Ryan curious about what had brought them to the Western Islands area, but not overly so. He picked up the revolver and stuck it inside his belt. Two backpacks with aluminum frames leaned against the stone wall, out of sight beyond the ledge.

"Stay away from those packs," Ryan growled.

Keeping his head buried, the man nodded.

Ryan looked at Jak.

"Hoyle," the teenager said, releasing his hold on the man's hair. "That one's Bernsen." He leaned down and picked up the Sharps.

Ryan stepped to the ledge overlooking the mountainside. Moving so he could be seen, he waved to Krysty, Doc and Mildred. Immediately the three began to move up.

The brushwooders weren't far behind, almost within rifle range, as a few of them proved by firing rounds that fell less than thirty yards behind Krysty's position. The companions had lost whatever edge mobility had given them in the long minutes they'd spent being pinned down by sniper fire.

"You got them?" Ryan asked Jak.

"Do now." Jak had his .357 Magnum blaster in hand as he waved Hoyle into place beside Bernsen.

Reluctantly, acting as though he was just waiting for an opportunity, the bearded man sat.

Ryan fixed both men with a harsh look. "Up to you now if you live or die." He reloaded the Steyr and slung it.

"Me, I don't much care. Easier to chill you than watch you." He glanced at Jak. "If they try anything, chill them both, then push them over the edge and let the vultures have them."

"Okay." Jak squatted, his pistol resting easily on one thigh.

"I'm going to take a look around and be back in a couple minutes." Ryan started up the grade at the back of the chimney rock. Simply outrunning the brushwooders was no longer an option. It remained to be seen what was left.

Chapter Nineteen

"Get down!" J.B. yelled.

Ryan stepped into the cave mouth he'd found at the back of the rock chimney an instant before the explosion shook the ground. He gazed down the long dark throat of the tunnel spearing out in front of him as debris slammed into the ground around him. He couldn't see the other end and had no inkling of what might lie in wait.

"Fireblast," he swore as small-arms fire opened up above. He turned and shoved his way back up the steep path that had led him to the cave.

The companions were spread across the crest of the chimney rock when he doubled back, seeking cover where they could find it. The Armorer had taken up the Sharps buffalo rifle.

Black smoke wafted up from somewhere below the edge of the rock, and a wave of heat washed over Ryan as he threw himself down beside J.B. and brought the Steyr forward.

"They've set up a mortar," the Armorer said, pulling the butt of the Sharps into his shoulder. The original peep sight had been replaced with a telescopic lens. J.B. fitted himself into the eyepiece. "Got close."

"We can't hold this position," Ryan said. "I found a cave back there."

J.B. coolly took up slack on the trigger. "Any idea where it goes?"

"I was figuring on asking our company."

The Sharps banged, slamming against the Armorer's shoulder. Immediately the wiry man levered the action and reached for a bullet in the bandolier they'd removed from the prisoners.

Down on the incline, one of the brushwooders manning the mortar yelped and went down clutching his thigh.

Ryan crept back to the prisoners, staying low, and stopped in front of Hoyle. Bernsen kept his arms wrapped over his head and mewled piteously. Doc kept cautious watch with his Le Mat blaster.

"The cave," Ryan prompted. "That's where you were headed."

Hoyle hesitated, his lower lip pinched tight against his teeth.

"They've got another one away," J.B. called.

Before the words trailed off, a second explosion rocked the vicinity, throwing up a fresh shower of pebbles and stone splinters. The detonation caused momentary deafness.

"Getting closer," J.B. warned. "Another round or two the way they're improving, they'll put one right on top of us."

"Talk," Ryan grated. "Either way it goes, we got no choice but that cave. If you hold back on me, I'll dangle you over the edge of this rock and drop you down to those brushwooders. If you get lucky, mebbe you'll connect with a mortar round before you hit bottom."

"We were going to the cave," Hoyle admitted grudgingly. "There's a river down below. Runs underground for a time."

"Then why try to chill us?"

"We checked earlier. River was too high to try. We were waiting for it to go down. We got a raft down there."

Ryan glanced at the rest of his group. "Jak, Krysty,"

Ryan said, "you two take point. Double yellow. I didn't hear anything, but that doesn't mean it's clear. Doc, give me a hand with the prisoners." He grabbed the shoulder of Hoyle's jacket and hoisted the man to his feet. "J.B., Mildred, you've got our backs."

Together the group moved toward the cave. Before they reached it, another mortar round impacted against the chimney rock nearly a dozen feet above their heads. A great tumble of split stone came slithering free, scattering across the rocky shelf under their feet, nearly knocking them to the ground.

"Get up and move," Ryan growled, yanking his prisoner to his feet. Hoyle had taken a stone ricochet to the side of his head. Streamers of twisting crimson ran down his temple and jaw, tracking across his neck before being staunched in his shirt collar.

Jak and Krysty vanished into the gaping maw of the cave. Bullets pocked the sides of the opening, spitting small shards that bit at Ryan's face. He hustled Hoyle inside the cave, moving the man forcibly. A blur of movement triggered instinctive reflex action on Ryan's part.

He shifted hands with the Steyr, then cleared leather with the SIG-Sauer. Snap-firing, he aimed the 9 mm blaster at the four men who'd climbed the trail up the side of the chimney rock and pulled off successive rounds as quickly as he could. He wasn't sure if he hit anything, but the bullets sent most of the brushwooders scurrying for cover.

One of the men leaned forward with a scattergun. Ryan lifted the SIG-Sauer, tracking on to his attacker. A heartbeat before his finger pulled through the trigger, bloody mist evacuated the side of the brushwooder's head, sucking away chunks of his skull and blobs of brain matter.

Ryan put another round through the man's left eye, yanking the head around almost 180 degrees. When he glanced to the side, he saw Mildred standing there, the Czech target weapon held securely in both her hands.

J.B. drew his lover into the crook of one arm and started her toward the cave. Bullets beat a deadly tattoo against the rock surfaces in their wake.

As the Armorer and Mildred raced across the open space, Ryan triggered a fusillade of bullets that ripped across the tops of the rocks the brushwooders were using for cover. Foul oaths cracked the air over the din of the blaster as the men ducked into hiding and remained there.

J.B. unbuckled the Smith & Wesson M-4000 scattergun from his back and tossed it to Ryan. "Close quarters like this, if those brushwooders try shoving into the cave, it'll be just like a gren going off in their faces."

Ryan readied the weapon and raked his vision across the dark inner recesses of the cave until he spotted Hoyle. Doc was moving Bernsen along at a fair clip. "Go," Ryan ordered.

Hoyle moved out at once.

The trail leading down into the cave was twisting and narrow. The heat rolled into the opening after them. In short order, though, the temperature started to drop rapidly. The perspiration that had settled under Ryan's clothing suddenly turned to mobile ice beads that tracked shivers along his skin.

"I hear running water," Mildred said.

Ryan heard it, too, a rapid splashing that sloshed wetly against stone. He blinked his eye in an effort to speed up the change to night vision. The rock floor split into a V, widening rapidly. In the mouth a raging torrent gushed from an underground schism and overfilled the space left between the legs of the V. Water twisted and spilled over the rock ledges on either side of the river, making the way chancy, its roar rendering conversation difficult.

The incline grew sharper, tilting down into the shadows that swallowed up the other end of the cave system. Debris choked the river in a handful of places, flotsam and jetsam from civilization in the form of timbers, chairs, bits of clothing and toys, all of it knitted together by clumps of weeds and tangles of branches, some of them still carrying leaves.

Ryan glanced over his shoulder and saw Mildred and J.B. working their way after him. "How much farther to the raft?" he asked Hoyle.

"Fifty yards mebbe. Hard to tell in this."

Gunfire flashed near the mouth of the cave. The men standing in front of it were skylined by the sunlight beyond, broken shadows against the darker and deeper silhouettes of rock. The positions of others were given away by muzzle-flashes.

J.B. cut loose with the Uzi and zipped a line of deadly demarcation in the middle of the group. There were at least six shadows, maybe more.

The next turn in the tunnel caught Ryan by surprise. One instant Hoyle was moving in front of him, light against the black rock, and in the next the man had disappeared.

The breaking wave of whitecaps smashing against the ledge gave Ryan an indication of where the turn was. He pressed in close against the rock and followed it. Water swirled up to his knees, fighting against the gravity and the insistence of the force spewing it out of the underground crevice.

"Lover."

Squinting, Ryan peered past Hoyle and spotted Krysty standing under a low overhang of rock. Jagged fangs thrust down from the rooftop, closing the cave up like a man dying of lockjaw. Scarcely four feet remained above the surface of the churning river.

The black water spread across thirty or forty feet of the cave opening, well out of the regular channel it had carved over decades. Judging from the way the white waves crashed against the walls with dulled roars, then swirled madly back in on themselves, the water level wasn't dropping. It was rising dramatically. The cave widened out at this spot, at the bottom of the incline. A bowl-shaped depression created by the regular fall of water over the years had left worn rings in the pale alabaster of the limestone. The shaft where the river continued was eight or ten feet across. The water roared into the spillway like a thing possessed.

"Dark night!" J.B. breathed.

"Hasn't gone down," Hoyle said. "Only a crazy fucker would try to go down that river in the shape it's in."

"Where's the raft?" Ryan demanded.

"You can't be serious." Hoyle stared at him wide-eyed. "We'd all die."

Krysty walked through the water with difficulty to join them.

"If we stay here," Ryan told him, "we're dead for sure. With a raft mebbe we got some kind of chance. That water's going somewhere, bastard quick."

"It goes underground."

Without warning, a large wave of water rolled forward, drenching them. A scream sounded behind them, then a brushwooder came hurtling over the fall, limbs flailing in the weak light as he shot out into empty space for an instant. The man hit the water and sank in the churning depths. A moment later he reappeared, yards from where he'd gone under, only long enough to suck in a breath as he was swept toward the bottleneck. Then he went under again and didn't come back up.

Hoyle stared with grim fascination at the bottleneck where the brushwooder had disappeared.

"The raft," Ryan repeated coldly. "Otherwise, I break both your knees with a rock and toss you in the river."

"Over here." Hoyle peered at the cave walls for a moment, then got his bearings. He made his way carefully along the ledge to a spot where a triangle of rocky spikes jutted from the wall. "I'll need some help." He put his hands on either side of the area around the three rocks and started to pull.

Ryan stepped forward and added his own muscle to the effort. The section of rock came out slowly, with a grating sound that ripped through the swish and swirl of the raging river and a vibration of friction that ran through Ryan's arms.

"Hiding place for emergency rations and our gear," Hoyle explained. "We've used this river before."

"You didn't come up it," Ryan said.

"No. Usually we use it to go down. Sometimes we can travel two, mebbe three days by river. A lot faster and easier than going overland."

The block of stone came out faster at the end, nearly tumbling Ryan off balance. Dropping the heavy weight into the water moving just below his ribs now, he reached out and caught a fistful of Hoyle's shirt as the man nearly slid back into the torrent threatening to pluck them from their perch.

Krysty reached into the opening and dragged out an olive oval of thick plastic and vinyl. She held on to it with difficulty as the river fiercely tried to take it away from her.

"I've got it," Hoyle said, closing his hands over the vinyl with Krysty's.

"Ryan," J.B. called.

Even as Ryan turned to look, bullets lanced into the

whirling caldron of water filling the basin. At least two men clung to the ledge above them, shooting blindly down into the water in an effort to take out their targets. J.B. triggered two 3-round bursts at the men, but they'd moved back into the rock and made difficult targets. They were also evidently wearing body armor of some type, because the Armorer's rounds knocked dust from their clothing.

Ryan raised the S&W shotgun to his shoulder and squeezed the trigger. At the distance, with the choke adjusted, the razor-edged fléchettes spread into almost a man-size pattern.

They slashed into the two brushwooders and sliced them from their position, cutting easily through whatever body armor the men might have scavenged. Their screams of pain ended suddenly when they dropped into the raging water.

When Ryan looked back at the raft, he saw that Jak had joined Krysty and Hoyle in trying to maneuver it above the water. The oval's size made it awkward; the footing made the efforts treacherous.

Hoyle reached into the center of the oval, snaking a hand through the folded wrinkles, then yanked. As he withdrew his hand, the oval started to unfold on its own with a prolonged hiss.

"Compressed air," Hoyle said. "It'll fill the raft. Scavenged this emergency raft and a couple like it over the years from ships and boats that went down around Vancouver a few years back when I was working on trade and barter for my next home-cooked meal. When I signed on with the Heimdall Foundation, I figured one of them might come in handy one day here." He shook his head. "I sure do hate being right when it comes to shit like this."

The raft continued to flop, and the dimensions became clear. It would be a tight fit, but Ryan thought they would all squeeze in. The way he figured it, if things got tight, the Heimdall Foundation men were ballast.

"What's this you were saying about the Heimdall Foundation?" Doc demanded over the roar of the river.

"Place I work for," Hoyle answered. "Bernsen knows more about it." The man struggled to hang on to the raft as the current tried to rip it from him, Krysty and Jak.

Doc turned his attention to the man he was keeping watch over. Bernsen had turned green in the dim light, his attention focused on the bottleneck of cave walls. Doc shook the man and began to question him.

Ryan ignored the conversation. The level of the water had risen, leaving precious little more than three feet beneath the cavern ceiling where it plunged through the orifice leading out of the basin. From the looks of things, the water was going to fill all the space within minutes.

Ryan took a length of rope from his pack and cut off a ten-foot piece with the panga.

"Watch it with that knife," Hoyle shouted. "You cut a hole in this raft, and we got no chance at all."

Working quickly, Ryan slid the panga back into its sheath, then tied one end of the section of rope to a loop on the raft. Checking the wall at his side, he found a notched rock that would allow him to tie the other end.

"When we start loading people into that raft," he explained, "we're not going to be able to hold it. This way we can keep it steady until we're prepared."

He cut another ten-foot length and passed it to Jak. "The side, not the other end. So we'll be able to cut it away."

Jak tied the rope on to the raft without comment, understanding at once.

In seconds the raft was as stable as they could make it. The vinyl craft jumped on the water, now at least a couple inches higher, and pulled at the tethers.

At Ryan's command, the companions loaded into the raft one at a time. The additional weight made it sink even more into the water, and the river's pull on it grew stronger.

Ryan pulled himself into the tangle and press of bodies. Krysty took hold of his clothing and aided his efforts. Even as Ryan tried to find a comfortable position, a small knot of brushwooders took up a line along the ledge leading down to the basin. A spark flared in the hands of one, then caught and became a miniature crimson star that threw off a spitting pink light to quickly fill the tidal cavern.

"Flare," Jak said.

Mildred raised her pistol and pulled through a round just as the brushwooders spotted the raft. With the way the raft bobbed and twisted, it was impossible to hit anything she aimed at. Her shot went well wide and high of its intended mark.

The brushwooders brought their weapons to bear.

Ryan ripped the panga from his hip and grabbed the forward lip of the raft, hauling himself over Hoyle. "Jak, cut away!"

The albino had one of the leaf-shaped throwing knives in his hand in an eye blink, the keen edge sliding through the stabilizing rope at the side of the raft. Immediately the craft jumped like a fish hitting the end of a line after a long run. Incredibly it lifted partially out of the water, threatening to turn crossways in the chop of the swirling currents.

Bullets plopped into the water from the brushwooders' guns, the sharp reports of the weapons punching through the steady roar of the rising river.

Ryan slashed with the panga. Off balance aboard the writhing raft, he parted the rope less than two inches from the vinyl air pocket forming the side. There was no time to brace himself against the sudden lunge the raft took. He felt Krysty's hands at his back, taking hold of his belt and adding her weight to his.

"Hold on, lover," she called.

The river took them, shoving them at the bottleneck at an unbelievable rate of speed. They missed the bottleneck opening by several feet and slammed into the wall. The raft rode the trapped current up out of the water, crashing the left side and a large portion of the bottom against the immovable rock.

Ryan grabbed one of the tie-downs and threw an arm across Krysty's shoulders, pulling her close to him. There was nothing else any of them could do. The river had them at its mercy, and it was a toss-up as to whether the raft would remain on top of the water or plummet into its black depths.

Chapter Twenty

Twisting suddenly, the raft came around, shifting ends and plunging down the dark throat of the tunnel. The light of the flare vanished behind them, though the brushwooders' bullets hammered into the sides of the tunnel for a few seconds more.

Ryan kept his arm tight around Krysty and took a quick head count before all light left them. Everyone had made it.

The dark water sucked away all vestiges of light from the flare and left them in darkness. Ryan hung on fiercely, riding out the fight the river was giving them so effortlessly. Though he tried not to consider it, he knew that it would only take one sharp rock to rip out the side of the raft.

Abruptly a light flared into life at the front of the raft, splashing against the cavern roof not more than two feet above their heads. In the forward end of the raft, Jak swung the flashlight he'd freed from his gear downriver.

Ryan shifted a little, rising but not getting too close to the low ceiling of rock. They were traveling fast; the way the water-worn limestone passed them above and on both sides told him that. The stone looked green in the yellow light of the flash, tracked in horizontal layers that showed years of formation. The rough edges announced the damage that had been done by the monster quakes and passage of water over the decades since skydark. It was possible that some of the cavern had been in existence even before the world had ended.

The raft continued to bob and jump, following the irregular path of the tunnel. Jak held the flashlight, shifting it to illuminate the way.

"How far before we slow down?" Ryan yelled to Hoyle.

"Don't know. I never got on the water when it was like this." Hoyle's gaze remained transfixed on the dark water before them.

The tunnel took another twist, almost falling back on itself and causing the raft to ride high enough up on the side to slam into the low ceiling. When Jak got the flashlight turned in the new direction, there was barely enough time for any of them to register the sudden drop-off facing them before they were shooting through it.

Ryan's stomach twisted in protest at the sudden feeling of weightlessness, then tried to pull through itself when the raft slammed back into the water.

"By the Three Kennedys," Doc exploded, "I should not like to be forced to endure that inauspicious travail again!"

Ryan silently agreed, but he could tell by the lurch of the raft that they were already picking up speed. He watched as Jak brought the light around. The raft swung sideways slowly in current, pulled faster still by the river. For a moment it looked as if the river channel was widening and deepening.

Then the blank wall rose before them without warning. The water smashed up against it, cresting six or seven feet to the broken stalactites above it. Bats fluttered in the beam of Jak's flashlight, bits and pieces of shadows startled from their resting places.

"Oh, shit!" Mildred exclaimed.

Then there was no more time. Ryan buried himself in the raft, drawing Krysty down with him. The water wasn't filling the chamber; it was being drawn away completely underground. But he had no way of knowing how far it went. He had one brief hope that the raft might somehow manage to stay afloat on the river without being drawn into the undertow. If it did, there was a possibility they could wait out the time it took to drain most of the floodwaters from the river.

The raft smashed into the wall hard enough to jar Ryan's teeth and his eyeball in its socket. He felt the pitch and yaw of the raft beneath him, then it overturned and started taking on water.

"Let go," Krysty told him.

Ryan released her, knowing she was right. There was no way to stay together in the deluge. He squeezed her hand, then released her. He had time to suck in most of one deep breath before the undertow reached out for them and yanked them under. There was no way to fight against the pull. Concentrating on survival, Ryan went with it.

The chill of the river coiled around him, filling his senses with a rush of confusion. He spotted Jak ahead of him, the albino highlighted by a nimbus of weak yellow light from the flashlight he still held. The youth's other hand was wrapped tightly in one of the equipment loops. Ryan didn't know if the albino was hanging on to the raft on purpose or if he'd been trapped by it.

With greater width and breadth, the raft acted like a kite caught in a strong wind, moving ahead of the rest of the companions quickly.

The bubble of light surrounding Jak faded with the distance, but held long enough to show the underwater exit for the river. Ryan watched the raft and Jake slide into the huge hole, then they disappeared.

He let himself go, riding out the current, remembering how the rest of the companions had been spaced out around him, all of them caught up in the river. The current pulled him deeper still, and even colder water ran rampant there, an ice wall that slammed him through the outlet. His left hand slapped into the edge of the opening with enough force to create a blaze of pain, followed almost immediately by numbness.

The water picked up speed, shooting him forward with greater intensity. He covered his head with his arms, hoping that he didn't go up against the tunnel's side. The impact would probably be enough to kill him. It would probably also be enough to kill any of the others. But they were all out of choices, and the ace was on the line.

GAZING THROUGH his binoculars, Hayden LeMarck watched the brushwooders walk away from the chimney rock. None of the outlanders appeared to be in their midst.

"Mebbe they got away," Wallis Thoroughgood said. "Even if they'd killed the outlanders, the brushwooders probably would have brought out the corpses."

LeMarck studied the brushwooders. All of them looked haggard and worn. None of them had any of the outlanders' weapons, giving him even more reason to believe the group had managed another escape. That possibility, however, was also daunting because this final escape might have taken them from him, as well.

"Don't appear to be as many of them as there was," the sec commander said.

"Three, four," Thoroughgood replied, "mebbe five of them are missing. Probably means they ran into the out-landers somewhere up in those rocks."

"And the outlanders got away." LeMarck dropped the binoculars into his pack. "Renstell, given that there's a point of entry to the river in those rocks, where do you figure they'd come out topside again?"

Renstell narrowed his eyes against the sun as he looked out across the broken landscape. "Four or five miles away. But they'd be fools to try that river now, sir."

"Why?"

"That blizzard last night, come this morning with the sun melting it all down the way it did, that river's gonna be raging. There're places in the tunnels where the river goes that fill up sudden when a man least expects it. They went into it, there's every chance they're going to drown like rats before they get through it."

The sec boss watched the brushwooders making their way across the land almost three hundred yards away. He wished he knew what was going on inside, hoping that Renstell was wrong about the outlanders' drowning.

LIGHT PENETRATED the water above Ryan's head. Weakened from lack of oxygen, battered by the river current and the stone channel it rushed through, he forced his body to work. He stroked for the surface, kicking as strong as he was able.

Long seconds later, stubbornly refusing to give in to the need to breathe, his head came up out of the water. He allowed himself two breaths, swiveling around to get his bearings.

The river was quieter here, but continued to exert a steady pull. It was also much wider, sixty or seventy feet at least. But it was still contained in a cavern. Stalactites lined the uneven rooftop nearly twenty feet above. Cracks opened the dome in places, allowing thin streamers of yellow light to pour in and give the cave a semblance of twilight at best.

He took another deep breath, then plunged under the water, angling down. There was enough light to see a few yards in all directions. Fish darted past him, some no longer than one of his fingers, and others greater than the length of his arms. Even though chilled by the cold river water, he still felt an arctic kiss thrill along his nape as he thought about what might be in the river with him.

When he surfaced, Ryan saw J.B. and Mildred less than twenty feet away. They managed on their own, hacking, coughing and spluttering up river water. Hoyle bobbed to the surface behind them.

"Dry land's over that way," Ryan called out, knowing it would take a few seconds for their eyes to adjust to the dim lighting. He pointed.

J.B. looked around, managing to hang on to his fedora while he floated. "Where's Doc, Jak and Krysty?"

"Don't know." Ryan went down again, kicking violently, knowing they were running out of time. He met Krysty, who was coming up, pulling the slack form of Doc after her, barely illuminated in the ghostly water.

Grabbing a shoulder of the old man's frock coat, Ryan helped Krysty swim to the surface. "Let me have him," Ryan said when they were up.

Krysty nodded, breaking away and treading water. She gasped, the sound echoing over the flat planes of the water and reverberating in the cave over the movement of the river current.

Ryan levered an arm under Doc's chin and started for shore.

Chapter Twenty-One

Dean lay on his back on his bed in the boys' dorm, his hands clasped behind his head. On the top bunk, he was almost lifted from the general hubbub from his roommates, and from the din oozing in from the hallway and the other rooms on that floor of the building.

He focused on a fly clinging to the ceiling. Maybe it wouldn't have been so bad to have been born a fly. And flies, Dean noted, seemed to be happiest when they were face deep in a pile of shit, which was exactly where he figured he was.

A heavy step trod on the wooden floor of the dorm, causing boards to creak.

"Uh-oh," someone said, signaling a mad dash that got all of them cleaning up their bunks. Paper swished as it was put away, and books made leaden thunks dropping into footlockers in front of the beds.

Dean didn't move. There wasn't any way he could get into more trouble.

"Boys," Nicholas Brody's deep voice rumbled, "I'd like to pass a few moments with Mr. Cawdor if I may."

Dean sat up on the bed, his bare feet dangling over the edge. He'd showered that morning, and his hair was still damp. He wore only the school-designated T-shirt and his underwear.

His three roommates moved back to their beds, looking

at Brody but trying desperately not to meet the man's glance.

"Alone," Brody said.

Immediately the three boys jumped up and herded out into the hallway, relief evident in the way they carried themselves.

Brody closed the door behind them, then reached into Dean's footlocker and brought out a pair of pants. He tossed them to Dean. "In proper decorum, if you please, Mr. Cawdor." He turned to face the window, hands locked behind his back as he stared out into the courtyard where the flag waved in the breeze from the pole.

"Didn't know you were coming," Dean said as he shoved one leg into the trousers, "or I'd have been ready." As much trouble as he was in, not getting dressed as asked would have been the least of his problems. But he had respect for Nicholas Brody.

"I really wish you had not ventured up onto that building, Mr. Cawdor," the headmaster said tiredly. "Really, I wish you had not."

"What's going to happen to me, sir? For what I did."

The headmaster grimaced. "That remains to be seen, lad. I am faced with a most difficult situation. Mr. Ventnor was summarily excused from the rest of his classes this year, over his father's insistent arguments and hostilities. He'll not be returning to this school without due attention in regards to this situation, nor without an official apology to this institution and to Miss Lemon. But that was due in part to his own licentious behavior and how he handled the whole affair, as well as his father's bullheadedness."

"Is that what's going to happen to me?" Dean felt his stomach lurch. He didn't realize how much he was going to miss the school, or how much the idea that he could get kicked out sickened him.

"I find myself in quite a quandary in regards to you." Brody's gaze was bright, direct. "You lied to me by omission, telling me you knew not what led you to stray to that building this morning. Surely the response of an irresponsible and churlish boy. Yet you stepped forward when Miss Lemon's integrity was in danger of becoming forfeit. An act of a young gentleman who knows there must be a recompense for actions foolishly taken, as well as the primacy of innocence being protected and a sense of fair play. Neither Mr. Ventnor nor his progenitor handled the situation with even a fraction of the courage you exhibited."

"Will I be allowed to stay?"

Brody shook his head. "I don't know, lad. I'll have to think on it. Punishment in these regards must be strictly adhered to, else the student body at this institution will run amok and even more stringent measures will need be applied to bring them into line once more. I set those standards, and I don't mean to see them broken."

"Yes, sir." Dean wished he could break eye contact, but found he couldn't.

"Keep your chin up, Mr. Cawdor. However it turns out, you've kept at least a portion of my respect today. A most important portion, I might add. And maybe earned self-respect in your own eyes that you will see once we are days past this present encumbrance. I shall try to get word to your father by the means I have open to me, and we shall see what must be done. Until then, you'll be confined to your quarters."

"Yes, sir."

Brody left.

As soon as the door closed, Dean tossed himself back onto his bed. He felt like crying, something he hadn't allowed himself to do in a long time. At the same time he felt like kicking down the walls of his room. Instead, he lay on his back and threw a forearm across his eyes to block out his vision.

"Cawdor."

For a moment Dean was unsure if he'd actually heard the voice or if it was his imagination.

"Dean Cawdor."

Dean unwrapped his arm from his eyes. He craned his head around and looked at the doorway.

Ethan Perry, tall and muscled, a blue-black undercoating of beard and mustache still showing through fresh-shaved chin, stood looking in at him.

"What do you want?" Dean asked.

Perry smiled. He had the easy confidence of the natural athlete. Some few months short of eighteen, Perry was the most gifted of those in the phys-ed class at the school. Whenever a game was played—football, baseball or dodge ball—everyone wanted to be on Perry's side.

"Heard about what happened this morning," Perry said. "I know Ventnor's too gutless to do something like that, so I figure it was you who put together the raid on the girls' dorm. Pretty clever."

Dean just looked at the other boy, hardly breathing. He and Perry had shared some differences out on the playing field. Perry had a group of ten boys that he ran roughshod over. They were the best the school had to offer when it came to sports. They ate together, slept in the same dorms and did their studying together. When one of them scored low on a test, the others pitched in to help him study harder so the group remained unbroken. No other team the school fielded was ever able to defeat Perry's team.

The reason Perry didn't like Dean was that in individual effort, Dean bested several if not all of the ten boys. Sometimes that included Perry himself.

Perry leaned against the door and stuck a toothpick in

his mouth. The other boys who belonged in the room stayed out in the hallway. "Me and my buddies are doing some exercises tonight with Mr. Solomon. Thought mebbe you'd like to join us."

Solomon was the new phys-ed teacher. At least, he was new by the school's standards. Payton Solomon had only been with Nicholas Brody's staff for the past seventeen months. During that time, the phys-ed teacher had helped mold Perry's group into the unit it was.

"Why me?" Dean asked.

Perry shrugged. "Mr. Solomon thought it might be a good idea. Me, I don't think we need you, but he was pretty insistent. Conover busted a rib this morning during one of our martial-arts sessions, and Mr. Solomon wanted you to fill in tonight."

"Doing what?"

Perry shrugged again. "Does it matter?"

Dean was silent. Really it didn't. It was a chance to get out and do something. "Does Mr. Solomon know I've been told to stay in my quarters?"

"Probably." Perry made a show of looking around. "Doesn't appear to be anybody gonna make sure that's what you do. So I guess whether you stay or go is mostly up to you."

A well of resentment opened up in Dean. He'd been more or less abandoned at the school by his dad, even after he'd voiced an objection to coming there. He'd minded most of the bigger rules, his mostly minor infractions more inconsiderate than rebellious. It wasn't until he'd gone to see Phaedra Lemon that things seemed to come apart.

And Phaedra hadn't appeared all that angry about his coming to see her.

So he couldn't understand how Brody had a real bone to pick with him.

"If I get caught, will Mr. Solomon talk to Mr. Brody for me?" Dean asked.

"Fuck that," Perry said. "None of us are gonna get caught." He smiled. "We'll even teach you to be more sly than you were this morning."

Listening to the other boy made Dean feel better. Maybe something good had come out of getting caught sneaking around after all. Of all the student body, Perry and his group seemed to be the most like Dean. They were fierce, hard, rough and feared throughout the school. They weren't pampered kids at all.

Used to being a loner, Dean hadn't tried overly hard to take up with the group. But he wouldn't have objected to an offer of friendship or interest on their behalf. Mr. Solomon had never before tried to pair any of Perry's group with him.

"So what's it gonna be?" Perry asked. "If you don't want to do it, I gotta ask somebody else."

"What time am I supposed to be there?" Dean asked.

Perry smiled. "I'll come get you when it's time. Mr. Solomon said it'd be after dark, and to try to sleep this afternoon if you could because we're gonna be out most all night."

"Okay," Dean said.

Perry left without another word.

Dean lay back on the bed, excited and scared at the same time, and wondering what Mr. Solomon had in mind. Skulking around in the dark, though, sounded good to him no matter what the excuse. He closed his eyes and, after a time, slept.

Chapter Twenty-Two

A pair of skikes came up out of the water in tandem, breaking the choppy gray surface, and streaked for Ryan. Hoyle had identified the creatures. Ryan moved to the side quickly, his blaster already in his hand. The five-foot wide section of graveled earth that formed a natural berm for the river didn't give him much room to work with.

The wedge-shaped bodies arced fluidly, bringing the barbed tails around into attack positions. There wasn't much air current in the cavern to allow the skikes to maneuver gracefully. Once they'd launched themselves from the river, they were more projectiles than fliers.

"Goddamn!" Hoyle shouted. The man went to ground, taking cover behind an outcrop, seizing two stones in his fists.

Ryan brought up the SIG-Sauer and cut loose two rounds at the lead skike. Only one round hit the mutie creature, but it punched through the skike's chest, blowing its heart and backbone through its dorsal surface.

The skike died with a shrill cry that ululated throughout the cavern. Writhing out its death throes, the creature plopped to the ground in front of Ryan, the barbed tail sticking out into the river.

The second skike hit the cavern wall over Ryan's head. The mutie creature seemed hardly dazed at all by the sudden impact against the wall. Flexing its sides, it scooted across the gravel, heading back to the river.

"Kill it!" Hoyle yelled. "Kill the bastard thing before it gets the chance to tell the others we're here! Those shitters hunt in packs."

Ryan kicked the dead skike out of his way as he pursued the live one. Shrilling now, the skike planed across the shallow water, obviously waiting until it reached a deeper part of the river before diving. Taking deliberate aim, Ryan squeezed the SIG-Sauer's trigger three times.

The skike possessed an uncanny skill for dodging while in the water, changing course a half-dozen times in an eye blink, rolling its membrane to feint in still other directions.

All three rounds missed the creature. Then Krysty's weapon boomed, too, throwing up geysers of water around the skike. Taking a double-handed grip on his weapon and wading into the cold water, Ryan fired in a steady roll, working a pattern around the skike that allowed for forward movement, as well as to either side. The water was the creature's element.

He'd almost run his clip dry when he scored his first hit. Ears ringing from the concussions of his weapon, he saw the plume of blood jet up from the creature's left side. The membrane curled in on itself slightly, trying to cover the hole near the bottom. The skike kept moving, pulling to the right and starting to go under.

Ryan fired his last two rounds. The slide blew back into the locked and empty position at the same time he spotted the sudden cloud of blood churn the water and erase the skike from view. He replaced the clip, storing the empty in his pocket.

He waited, tense. Krysty had a hand over Bernsen's mouth, and the man was only able to make small, plaintive noises. She prodded the back of his skull with the barrel of her weapon to freeze him.

"You got it," Hoyle said breathlessly.

Ryan glared the man into silence. A moment later the skike's dead and mutilated body surfaced in a diamond of bloody flesh. It floated upside down, blue-gray belly turned up against the ceiling of the cavern. Ryan waited a little longer, until he was sure nothing else was coming after them.

"HOW FAR ARE YOU GOING to go looking for the boy?" Hoyle asked.

Ryan had the lead, and Krysty covered his back. Neither of the two men had been allowed weapons. "As far as it takes," he answered.

"Him holding on to that raft like he was, he could be anywhere. Hell, if he drowned, he might not be stopped yet."

Ryan knew that was true. Linked to the raft, Jak had been at its full mercy. "I'll take that chance."

"Leaving your friends back there wasn't any too smart, either, if you ask me."

"Didn't ask."

"Those skikes will be all stirred up from the floods, swimming around all hot up from being in rut. They won't hesitate about attacking those people back there."

Ryan kept moving, ducking under an overhang of crooked, lichen-covered rock that jutted from the cavern wall. The cavern was continuing to widen slightly, allowing more light in from cracks across the ceiling. The river appeared to be moving slower, but still at a steady clip.

"They haven't been attacked," he said.

"How do you know?"

"J.B. would have blasted anything that tried," Ryan replied. "Would have heard that."

"What do you intend to do with us?" Bernsen asked.

"Depends," Ryan answered. Along the sides of the

river, trees and branches and other detritus had hung up in the scattered shallows, seining still more refuse from the current.

"'Depends'?" Bernsen echoed. "What kind of answer is that? My God, that's no answer at all."

"It's the only one I've got for you," Ryan said. "You and your friend here know this river, and I can use knowledge like that."

Ahead and to the right, a scarecrow figure in jeans and a green flannel shirt lay draped over a broken red-and-white-striped sawhorse that had seen its last good days years ago. Ryan approached it long enough to make sure the albino teenager wasn't covered over by the corpse.

He grabbed the corpse by the hair and lifted it. The woman was days-old dead, her throat cut straight across. Other cuts marred her face, showing she'd died hard and her killer hadn't been successful on the first try. Or had carried a grudge.

Jak was nowhere around.

Ryan dropped the woman's head back into the water, disturbing the small minnows that had been feeding on the soft parts of her face. In another few hours she wouldn't be recognizable at all. He walked back out of the water and kept on going.

"How far does the cave system go?"

"This one?" Hoyle responded.

"Yeah." Ryan kept his gaze moving. So far they hadn't been attacked by any more skikes, though they had seen a handful of the creatures skimming by underwater. There'd been no gunfire from farther back in the cave where they'd left J.B., Doc and Mildred, so it was a good bet they were still safe.

"This one goes on for a couple miles more. Then you have some daylight for another fifteen miles or so. Another cave system after that where you have to make a decision about where you want to go. The river forks in three directions and continues on for various distances.''

''As far as Colorado?'' Ryan asked.

Hoyle nodded, then asked, ''What's in Colorado?''

''My son,'' Ryan replied. And he gave the man that, just enough to let Hoyle know he wasn't going to brook any arguments later when answers were called for. ''Mebbe you want to tell me what you're doing up here.'' There was enough edge to Ryan's words that Hoyle would know taking a pass on the question wasn't a good idea.

''Working a job.''

''What job?''

''Guide.''

''For Bernsen?''

''And his friends.''

Ryan followed the turn of the river, going cautious, the SIG-Sauer blaster covering the terrain ahead of him in case there were any lurking skikes. Only parts of the cavern lay in shadow, and beams of sunlight from crevices in the ceiling glinted silver off the unsettled river. ''How many friends?''

Hoyle made the story short, saying that the men were scientists and all of them had been killed but Bernsen. Three of them had been chilled during an encounter with the brushwooders a couple days earlier. Two had died by skike poison after they'd gotten away from the brushwooders. And Mellelan had fallen to break his neck only the day before when they'd been hurrying through the mountains trying to beat out the approaching storm.

''Saw a tattoo on Mellelan,'' Ryan said when the man had finished. ''Spotted one on Bernsen, too. And you.''

Hoyle scratched the inside of his arm absentmindedly. ''They got a thing about identifying each other. In some places they ain't too welcome. Ten, fifteen years ago old David Napier tried telling a few folks up north to be on the lookout for certain things. Some of those folks took objection to what he was preaching, called him a heretic and strung him up. Made the other people of the Heimdall Foundation kind of shy about being noticed.''

"Heard mention of that Heimdall name, but what is it, this foundation?"

"You'd have to ask Bernsen to get the real particulars of that," Hoyle said. "Basically these people use telescopes and stare up at the sky all night long. They got books, vids and some comp progs that talk about all that stuff up there. Call it astronomy."

"All that looking, they got to be looking for something."

"Falling stars," Hoyle answered.

"That what brought you from Montana?"

Hoyle narrowed his eyes. "How do you know about Montana?"

"Mellelan had a map. Heimdall Point was marked on it."

"Now, that's a fool thing to do." Hoyle spit in disgust. "I hope you took up that map."

Ryan nodded.

"Don't need something like that falling into unfriendly hands. The Heimdall Foundation ain't set up proper to repel an attack." Hoyle shook his head. "These poor bastards, they been in their damn little towers too long looking up at the sky if you ask me."

"That's not what I asked you," Ryan said in a harder voice.

"Yeah, yeah. I've been guiding these assholes around a few places, going here and there for the last four years. Pay's good. I get some jack at the end of every trek successful or not, and I manage to steal enough predark stuff along the way to hock through some friends I got in a few places to keep myself living comfortable.''

"Get to it."

"Over the last few months they took a special interest in a star they started calling *Shostakovich's Anvil.*"

"Twisted name for a star."

"That's what I thought. But they don't ask me before they go naming them. And the way they talked, it sounded like somebody else had already named this one."

"Might not have such an easy job when you get back there," Ryan stated, "with a few scientists short."

"Hell, ain't none of us loose yet. I figure we won't be clear of the reach of the Five Barons for a while."

"Who're the Five Barons?"

"Now, that's a story," Hoyle said.

THE HISTORY Hoyle gave Ryan was concise but complete.

In the beginning there'd been a gathering of small villes along the Cific coast. Each had clung to ideals and traditions handed down from those who'd survived the nukecaust or had migrated there afterward to be near the ocean. The aquatic life in the area had been less harmed than the land-based creatures, and as Hoyle stated, a man had to eat.

The villes hadn't gotten along well together. Each had staked out territorial claims that had been disputed over the years. Several villes had split off from the original ville. One of those had died out from an epidemic that created a natural southern boundary.

After that, things remained peaceable—until the arrival of the barons.

"Any of them barons you ask about," Hoyle told Ryan, "you're going to hear a different story about how and why they came to be trapped out in the deserts the way they were. Only them and their Maker and a handful of their close sec people know the right of it.''

All of the barons, six of them at the time, had wandered in from the desert, drawn by tales they'd heard of the villes and how robbing was easy there because the people in the seven villes were too busy raising stuff to eat and fishing to worry about learning to fight.

When the barons got among the villes, greed had set in. The villes were too close to allow for expansion by each separate baron. They tried splitting them up, but none of them were men who wanted to share.

"They went to war with each other," Hoyle went on. "Fighting, killing and sabotaging, the like of which none of the people of the seven villes had ever seen before. Oh, they'd had their scraps over the years, but it wasn't nothing like what the barons could dish out against each other.

"But with the barons killing one another and reducing their manpower down to something that wouldn't allow them to stand firm against the mutie bands wandering in the desert if they had to return there, they struck a bargain.

"Only one of the barons could comfortably run the seven villes at one time," Hoyle said. "So they decided a competition was in order to figure out who was going to get control without killing each other. All of them were so aligned that if any one of them swore out a blood feud against another, the others would step in and stop it. A shift in the balance of power wasn't tolerated. Jink Masten, the old sixth baron, was the only man all five of the others couldn't stand. They killed him three years ago, and became known as the Five Barons.''

Ryan listened, knowing the savagery that had to have gone on between the barons. The history was a familiar story to him.

"They got together and created the Big Game," Hoyle

went on. "Found a place out in the desert, somewhere that held a lot of meaning to it at one time. A place where luck and chance came together, they tell me. I never seen it."

"What do they do there?"

"Choose up teams. Kidnap folk and use them to fight for them. Control of the seven villes for the next year goes to the baron whose team wins."

"What does the winning team get?" Ryan asked.

"Killed, mostly. Except for one man. Or woman. Or mutie. The barons ain't particular. They don't want anybody to get a chance at getting together an experienced team, you know."

"So why do those people fight?"

"Don't give them much choice at the time."

Ryan turned the story over in his head as he walked through inches-deep water where the river had completely filled the cavern. "Which baron is in charge now, and who's his sec boss?" Ryan asked.

"Baron Hardcoe," Hoyle answered. "LeMarck's his most loyal man, but not the only sec boss. Hardcoe probably has a half-dozen of them. Got a lot of men with him."

"And they've got control of the seven villes?" Ryan's mind flipped the details around, keeping them mentally accessible while he put everything together.

"For now. The Big Game will decide who's going to get control of the seven villes for the next year."

"That was LeMarck out there behind us?" Ryan was thinking of the mysterious rifle shot that had nailed one of the brushwooders before he and J.B. had caught up to their companions.

"Behind you and the brushwooders," Hoyle confirmed with a nod. "Spotted him through the telescopic sights of that Sharps."

"And you'd know him?"

"Met him last week. Sort of. Bernsen and his friends thought that star was going to drop somewhere near the seven villes. I explained to them that nothing went on in that area unless it was okayed by the barons, so they marched into Jakestown pretty as you please and asked Hardcoe for permission to stay for a couple days. I've always heard he was interested on predark learnings, and I guess it must be so, because he not only let them stay, but hell, he even put 'em up."

"Why would Hardcoe be up here?"

"The last I heard, Baron Hardcoe assigned LeMarck to bring in the brushwooder leader. Daugherty's been raiding some of the farmers in the villes, and Hardcoe takes his business serious."

"So he could have been after Daugherty?"

"Mebbe, but from what I saw, he seemed to be showing a lot of interest in you people."

Ryan didn't have an explanation for that, but he let it drift around in the back of his mind while they walked.

Nearly an hour later, they found Jak.

Ryan spotted the raft first, tucked up mostly out of sight behind and under some driftwood. Jak was just one shadow among myriad others, until he stepped out into view with a leaf-bladed throwing knife in one hand and his .357 Magnum in the other.

"Knew you come soon," Jak said, grinning a little. "Waited. Too damn hard pull raft back up river alone."

Chapter Twenty-Three

By the time they reached the part of the cavern where they'd left Doc, Mildred and J.B., Krysty ached all over. She hadn't rested well the night before, and she'd taken a turn at pulling the raft partway, which had started out easy then gotten to be serious work as they approached the faster-running water still pouring into the river.

Doc was sitting up when they arrived, drinking some soup from a self-heat, and his color looked better.

"Ah," the old man croaked in a voice that sounded more like him than his earlier weak whisper, "there they are now."

"Anything happen while we were gone?" Ryan asked J.B.

The Armorer adjusted his fedora and shook his head. "River seems to be slowing some. Saw no sign of anybody who was looking for us. Unless you count a body that come through about an hour ago. Looked like a brushwooder, but I didn't wade out to go check. Those damn skike were all over it. Things got bastard sharp teeth."

"We have another problem." Ryan squatted, waving at Jak to put the prisoners against the cavern wall almost ten feet away. He told the companions about Hoyle's sighting of Hayden LeMarck, the seven villes and the Five Barons. The picture Ryan painted of the villes was grim.

"Mebbe the brushwooders gave up," Ryan said at the end of it, "but mebbe LeMarck didn't."

"Didn't see him along trail," Jak said. "He there, I know."

"If he was tracking the brushwooders," Mildred said, "could be he found us then. We weren't able to take in everything going on behind us."

"But why get interested in us?" Krysty asked. "We've never even been through those villes."

"Don't know," Ryan said.

"Mebbe LeMarck and his sec men aren't looking for us at all," J.B. said. "Reckon they could have been on the trail of these two people just as much as they were after the brushwooders."

"Yeah, but why?" Ryan probed. "We found nothing in either one of those men's equipment that looked valuable."

"Perhaps their interest lies in the cartographic discovery we made in the dead man's pack," Doc said. "This Heimdall Foundation sounds intriguing. Mayhap Baron Hardcoe thought so, as well."

"In Montana?" Mildred asked. "That's way the hell out of his usual beat, sounds like to me."

"True," Doc said, "but follow my mental perambulations for a few moments if you will, while I digress. We've established from Mr. Hoyle's testimony that the Heimdall Foundation is without a standing army, yet has an abundance of foodstuffs and creature comforts that might sound desirable to Baron Hardcoe should he lose his bid at this Big Game a few days hence."

"You're saying instead of being turned back into the wastelands bordering the seven villes, mebbe Hardcoe has his eyes set on taking over the Heimdall Foundation?" J.B. asked.

"It would be," Doc argued, "a place to go."

"Makes sense," Krysty agreed.

"That does," Ryan said. "What doesn't is why Hardcoe

didn't just capture the Heimdall Foundation scientists when they were in his ville and be done with it.''

No one had an answer to that.

"Mebbe the falling star," Jak suggested.

"Mebbe." Ryan looked up at Bernsen. "Get over here."

"Me?" the man asked.

Ryan nodded.

Krysty knew part of Ryan's willingness to question Bernsen stemmed from her lover's own innate curiosity. Ryan Cawdor was a wanderer, a man who had to look beyond strange horizons.

Bernsen sidled over to the group, not looking happy about it at all.

"Tell me about *Shostakovich's Anvil*," Ryan ordered.

The scientist glared at Hoyle over his shoulder. "I don't have to answer you."

"No," Ryan said in a level voice. "Mebbe we'll see how the skike like you."

The man dragged a hand over his round face, sweating profusely from fear, exertion and the humidity trapped in the cavern. "*Shostakovich's Anvil* is—was—a Soviet space station. It was put up before the nukecaust and was supposed to collect data. And aside from the knowledge collected, it's also interesting if you remember the chaotic nature of the world at that time, nations aligning themselves with the two superpowers."

"Yes, it was a competition out there, too, just like on the planet," the Armorer said.

"Yes," Bernsen responded. "However, both the Americans and the Russians knew that forewarned meant being forearmed. Not everyone believed that aliens who came back to the planet would be friendly."

"As I recall," Doc said, "there were plenty of numbers

in either camp who believed aliens would be mankind's greatest friend, or its most loathsome enemy."

"Yes, all-out struggle for supremacy. And then bang! We almost encountered *the* end—but our ancestors survived the nukecaust," Bernsen said, "and they started the Heimdall Foundation. Most of the electronic equipment at that time was exposed to the electromagnetic pulse from the nuclear weapons. Nothing worked. They struggled together and managed to find enough telescopes and comps to survey the night sky and to record their findings. They also added to their treasure trove with books, comp progs, vids and buried government files."

"You've been tracking these falling satellites," Ryan said.

"When we could find them." Bernsen mopped his damp face with his shirtsleeve.

"If you were tracking them, what were you doing in the seven villes?"

"We've acquired conflicting data over the years," Bernsen said, "and even with the comps we've put together, we're in no way able to do the space monitoring they did in the predark times. Where the Soviet space station was going to land was open to conjecture. But we narrowed it down to two places."

"Jakestown," Ryan said.

The scientist nodded. "Depending on atmospheric conditions, which we're not too exact on."

"Where's the other place?" Ryan asked.

Bernsen seemed hesitant, but in the end he answered. "About forty miles north and slightly east of this position, there's a lake."

"Pyramid Lake," Hoyle cut in. "Should be on any maps you've got."

J.B. opened his map and traced the surface with a forefinger. "Got it."

"How did you plan on getting there?" Ryan asked.

"This river," Hoyle said, "goes most of the way. Got mebbe a twelve-mile hike over some rough country in Smoke Creek Desert."

"How rough?"

"Man's got no water, he's dead. Got no fire at night, he's dead. You burn to death during the day, and freeze your goddamn ass off at night."

"What about the water in the lake?"

"I'd purify it before I drank it. Drank it before and I'm still here."

"Any game along the way?"

"Precious little," Hoyle replied. "Country's still carrying a taint of rad-blasting from farther east."

Shifting his attention back to Bernsen, Ryan asked, "When's the space station going to come down?"

"Two days from now. An hour or two after nightfall."

"How sure are you?"

"I came out here to see it," Bernsen said. "Six other people from the foundation died getting this far. We're pretty certain."

"Everybody get your gear together," Ryan ordered. "We're leaving in five minutes."

"You're GOING after the space station, aren't you?" Krysty asked.

"Yeah," Ryan replied. "Only a day, mebbe two out of our way. Keeping the raft and staying with the river as much as we can, we should make the time up okay." He studied her.

Krysty knew the strain she was under showed to him. There weren't any real secrets between them anymore, ex-

cept the ones Ryan knew she didn't want to know about—
and the vision she'd had yesterday.

"You think we should do it another way?" he asked.

That he would ask rather than simply leading the companions let her know he was concerned about her. She
reached up and softly stroked his face. "Kind of thinking
about the people mebbe closing in on our backtrail bothers
me. It'll pass."

He nodded and started moving gear toward the raft.

Krysty picked up one of the backpacks they'd been for-
tunate enough to keep throughout the flood and started after
him. At least, with Ryan headed up to the site of the falling
space station—whether it landed there or not—it would
give him something to think about instead of why she was
being so quiet. It would also give her more time to figure
out what the vision actually meant. She hoped.

Chapter Twenty-Four

The moon was hidden behind a cloud bank when Dean joined up with the rest of Perry's group in the forest beyond the school's cultivated fields. Mr. Solomon, tall and angular, with a long, thick mustache that curled down from his upper lip, stood in front of them. He was dressed in black, as well, but had double pistol holsters with revolvers shoved into them.

"You're late, Mr. Perry," Solomon said in a low voice that carried.

"Won't happen again, sir."

Dean instantly rebelled against the man's military bearing as he fell into line with the other boys. Authority didn't suit him, and Solomon was more by-the-book than any of the teachers at the school. There were some rumors that Solomon had a background in sec work somewhere farther west, maybe even as far as the Cific Ocean coastline.

Solomon flicked his dead gaze on Dean. "Glad you could join us, Mr. Cawdor."

Dean nodded.

"I hadn't planned on the unfortunate incident that removed Mr. Conover from our midst this morning." Solomon crossed the space to stand in front of Dean. "Tonight's activities, though, required ten players. I've never seen you operate in the dark. How good are you?"

"Okay," Dean said.

"I guess we'll have the truth of that in short order."

Solomon walked back down the line, his hands clasped behind his back, his spine rigid and his shoulders squared. He met each boy's gaze in turn. "Tonight's exercise requires cunning and stealth. Follow me."

Dean went with the others and trailed after Solomon.

The phys-ed instructor came to a stop on a small promontory overlooking rugged terrain filled with trees, brush and hills. He pointed at five of the boys, then presented them with black handkerchiefs. "Put those in your belts, loose enough to pull out but not loose enough to fall out on their own."

The five boys tucked the handkerchiefs in their belts, testing them for tightness.

"The exercise works like this," Solomon said. "The five of you with the black flags will be given a minute head start. Your goal is the tree out there." He pointed.

Dean followed the phys-ed teacher's finger, spotting the tall Colorado blue spruce nearly a half mile away. A white banner fluttered near its top.

Solomon went on. "Then the others will follow. I want you to use stealth, not speed traversing that terrain. Some of you could run that distance in three, four minutes. Shadows are all over the place out there. One misstep and you could end up with a broken leg or a broken foot. Or worse. I don't want to get anyone hurt out there and screw up this team any more than it has been after this morning. Is that clear?"

"Yeah," Dean said, right along with the other boys.

"Those of you who are pursuing the flag bearers, your assignment is to take their flag," Solomon said. "By whatever means you have at your disposal."

"How physical can we get?" Perry asked.

"Short of permanent damage," the phys-ed teacher answered. "Bruises and small cuts I can explain. You do anything more than that, and this unit and its status will be in danger at this school.''

"What do we get for reaching the tree with our flag?" Hercules Moxen asked. He was close to six feet tall, almost a head taller than Dean, and had fiery red hair. Not all of his substantial weight was muscle, but there was enough to give most grown men pause. Coupled with the fact that Moxen loved to fight, he was a bad guy to have cross words with.

"You don't have to do the extra PT the others will for failing to catch you."

"What do we get if we catch them?" The question came from the other side of Dean.

Looking down the line, Dean saw the speaker was Louis McKenzie. Of all the boys in Perry's group, Dean liked Louis best. The boy always had a smile and a gentle way about him if he cared to show it. He was blond and had light green eyes that belonged on a cat, and he was a little taller than Dean but built in the same lanky fashion.

"Then they get extra PT," Solomon replied. "Some incentive both ways. After we do this once, we'll do it again, and the pursued will become the pursuers." He looked down the line of boys. "Everybody ready?"

"Yes, sir," they answered.

Solomon paired the boys off, giving each of them a target.

Dean got Hercules Moxen. The other boy smirked and shook his head as if he couldn't believe it.

"See you at the tree, small fry," Moxen said. "When you're doing the extra PT, think of me."

Dean didn't say anything. Talk was just talk; his dad had taught him that. He drew in deep breaths, pumping up his oxygen level. Despite Solomon's warning not to simply

head for the tree, Dean figured Moxen would try to reach
the tree as quick as he was able.

"Go!" Solomon said.

The first five boys launched themselves into the darkness,
feet swishing through the underbrush.

"Stand ready," Solomon ordered the other boys, checking his wrist chron.

Dean watched Moxen until the boy vanished behind a
triangular pine tree. He kept on breathing, waiting. The
minute passed slowly.

"Go," the phys-ed teacher finally said.

Dean bolted, already moving at top speed, trusting his
night vision and reflexes to keep him from serious damage.
He pumped his feet against the ground, swinging his arms
at his sides. It felt good to be out, testing himself against
someone else, deep in the wild where his primitive senses
could take care of him instead of social skills that he didn't
feel as confident about.

He ran, convinced he was closing the distance.

His breath sounded loud in his ears and burned along his
throat as he ran through the brush. He used every skill he'd
ever been taught, skirting plants, trees and bushes that
would have warned of his passage had he touched them.
He tried to listen for Hercules Moxen but couldn't hear the
boy.

The terrain was uneven and dangerous because the
cloud-covered moon cast no light. Still, he increased his
speed, not giving in. If the other boy had covered this much
ground, he would be tired when Dean caught up with him,
giving Dean an edge that he needed to overcome Moxen's
strength.

He was two steps up the rise before he knew it. Gravity
pulled at him, sucking him off balance. He put his hands
against the rough ground, slithering them through a painful

tangle of brush as thorns tore at his flesh. When he got to
the top of the ridge, the world opened up to him again,
letting him see the small valley on the other side of the
rise.

Moxen sprawled facedown at the bottom of it, arms flung
out to his sides, one leg twisted over the other.

"Shit," Dean said, continuing down into the valley. It
was just his luck. Remanded to his room, and here he was
finding Moxen probably dead.

He threw himself to the ground beside Moxen, not even
thinking for a moment that the bigger boy was just fooling
him. Moxen's legs were too twisted for that, and it had to
be painful. If nothing was broken, it had been a close call.

Dean grabbed the boy's shoulder, turning him gently,
wanting to make sure there was no chance Moxen would
smother with his face pressed against the earth like that.

The youth rolled over loosely, dirt smeared against his
pallid cheeks. The boy's eyes were halfway open, glinting
dully in the weak moonlight. Drool oozed out of one corner
of his mouth, mixing with the weak traces of blood. He
blew out white bubbles of spittle and moved one arm, struggling to speak.

Dean knew that if Moxen had been knocked out, he'd
have come to quicker than he was. And that white spit
looked like evidence of a bad reaction to something he ate.

"What's wrong?" Dean asked, leaning closer. Then he
spotted the small feathered dart stuck deep in Moxen's
neck. A chill slid down Dean's back. He tried not to act as
if he'd seen it. Then he heard the pad of a soft footfall
behind him.

Throwing himself to one side, Dean dived and rolled,
coming up on his feet so he could look back in the direction
he'd heard the footstep. He was breathing hard, his heart
hammering.

A dark figure, barely discernible in the black clothing and standing in the tree line less than forty feet away, took aim with a long-barreled blaster. A ruby dot appeared at the top of the pistol, sending a beam forward that stabbed into Dean's right eye.

Dean dropped, squatting and placing the palms of his hands against the ground. What sounded like two huge bugs whipped by over his head, missing him by inches. Shoving himself up again, he ran, heading back toward the starting area. Dean didn't recognize the man, but evidently he had been waiting for the boys to come breaking through the brush.

Or he'd come after them.

The new thought didn't sit well with Dean as he ran, making him more cautious. The sound of footsteps pursued him. His shoulders tightened up, expecting to feel one of the darts pierce his skin.

Yells from some of the other boys, scattered over the terrain, let Dean know the man hadn't come alone. He reached out for the slender bole of a pine tree and swung himself in a tight curve to point himself in an altered direction. While he had his hand on the tree, he felt a feathered dart sink into the rough bark between his fingers.

He stayed with the pine trees, knowing the branches would be heavy enough to deflect the darts. Then he was all out of trees, with the ridgeline leading back at the starting point seventy yards away. He zigzagged, risking a glance over his shoulder that showed his pursuer breaking out of the brush twenty yards behind him. His lungs burned from the sustained effort and fear, knowing the man following him could come faster simply by maintaining a straight line that Dean couldn't risk.

He made it to the top of the ridge and saw Mr. Solomon

standing there in the shadow of a tree and holding binoculars to his face.

"Mr. Solomon!" Dean gasped, sprinting toward the phys-ed teacher. "Something's gone wrong! There are men out there shooting us!"

Solomon turned his head, dropping the binoculars to his side. "I know."

Dean stopped his forward progress at once, reading the coldness in the teacher's answer. "You did it! You betrayed them, betrayed all of us!"

"Yeah," Solomon said. His fist came around suddenly, filled with one of the long-barreled pistols. The ruby light gleamed, splashing across Dean's chest.

Before Dean could move, a trio of whispered coughs sounded, followed immediately by three bursts of pain across his chest and stomach. Incredulous, he glanced down at himself. Three feathered darts stuck out from his body. He reached for them, feeling the pain already going away as a numbness spread throughout his torso. Then his legs wouldn't hold him anymore, and he fell to the ground.

A WAVE OF SUDDEN NAUSEA jerked Krysty upright in the raft. She clapped a hand over her mouth and swallowed a ball of bile that had risen to her throat.

"Krysty, my dear," Doc said, leaning forward to take her free arm, "are you all right?" His face showed concern, his brows pulled tight together.

The woman couldn't answer; her stomach still rolled. She kept her hand over her mouth as she struggled to the side of the raft. Trees lined the riverbanks on both sides. Jak and Ryan were scouting at the top of the nearby hill to get their bearings.

"Need some help?" Mildred asked.

Hoyle and Bernsen parted and made room for Krysty.

J.B. aimed the Uzi at them, just to let them know they didn't dare make a move on Krysty or try to take her weapon.

She kept her lips together until she had her head over the raft's side, then spit, trying to get everything out of her mouth that she could. She shivered, goose bumps pimpling her skin. She felt suddenly drained of strength.

"Krysty," Mildred said, slipping a hand over her forehead and wrapping an arm around her shoulders to help support her, "what's wrong?"

"Don't know."

"Something you ate?"

"Ate out of the same batch of self-heats as everyone else did. No one else seems sick."

"You don't have a fever."

"I don't feel hot," Krysty said. "Just sick. My head hurts, my vision's blurry and that ringing— Do you hear that ringing?" She wiped the back of her hand across her mouth again.

"No ringing. Do you feel dizzy?"

"Some." She reached into the brackish water, cupped a handful, then smeared it over her face. It cooled her a little, but not enough to take the real edge off the flush she felt.

Mildred continued to support her friend. Without the other woman's help, Krysty didn't think she could have stayed up at all. She felt boneless, totally lethargic.

"How's your hearing?" Mildred asked. She sounded very distant.

"I still hear ringing." Krysty shook her head to clear her ears but succeeded only in triggering another stomach spasm. She stopped and cupped a second handful of water to splash on her face. When she blinked the droplets from her eyes, she thought she saw something centered in the ripples spreading out from the raft.

Focusing her vision with effort, she breathed shallowly, trying not to put too much strain on her protesting stomach. The image cleared, riding the crest of the wave.

Even as it started to get lost in the distance and the darkness, Krysty recognized it: Dean. His face was slack, empty and pale. The boy's eyes shone dully, like the eyes on people Krysty had seen who had advanced cataracts.

"Oh, Gaia," Krysty said weakly. The sick feeling slammed into her stomach again, but there was nothing for it to purge. She tried to hang on to the vision, make it clearer so she could see where the boy was. From what she'd been able to glimpse, Dean didn't appear to be anywhere in the school. He was outside, surrounded by brush, long grass under his head.

"What is it, my dear?" Doc asked.

"It's Dean," Krysty said. "He looks dead. Gaia, Doc, he looks dead!"

Chapter Twenty-Five

As quick as it had come, the nausea left Krysty. All she felt now was cold and empty. She wrapped her arms around herself in an effort to keep warm, her teeth chattering.

Mildred took a blanket from one of the backpacks Hoyle and Bernsen had been carrying, then draped it around the woman's shoulders.

"Oh, Mildred, I saw him. Saw Dean dead," Krysty said, rocking slightly and trying to clear her head, trying to think.

"Maybe. Or maybe it was something else."

"What?" Krysty asked, looking at the woman.

"I don't know."

"Then you can't say that."

Mildred's face hardened. "You just get it together, girl. This is no place for someone who's lost her head."

"I know." Krysty dropped her chin onto her chest and closed her eyes. That was a mistake, because the image of Dean came swirling back into her head, all mixed up with the visions she'd had the day before. "But what else could it be, Mildred? Give me something I can believe in."

Mildred shook her head. "I can't do that. You're going to believe in whatever you want to believe in."

"If I may..." Doc interrupted.

Krysty looked at the old man, seeing him raise an eyebrow at Mildred.

"Go ahead," the doctor said.

Doc leaned in closer, his eyes locked on Krysty's. "Are you sure Dean was dead in your vision?"

"He looked that way."

"Then he could have just as well been asleep."

"Not asleep," Krysty argued. "I've seen him asleep. It wasn't anything like this. He was too pale, barely breathing. And he was outside somewhere."

"Then mayhap he was sick and you saw him at that time. It might not be something that is going on now at all."

Krysty wanted to believe that. At least it was something better than believing he was dead, a chance to get to Dean before it was too late.

"You might be able to find out," Doc said.

She looked at him, knowing what he was going to say. "I don't know if I can do that. I lost him, and I couldn't hang on to that image anymore."

"Don't try for an image," Doc said. "You yourself have said if anything happened to Ryan you would know. And you believe that tie goes beyond just yourself and Ryan."

Krysty nodded, not feeling so lost. It was a thought to hold on to.

Doc reached out and took one of her hands. "To allay your feelings and fears, you should try to reach out to Dean."

"But what if I can't feel him?"

"That's not the question you should be asking yourself," Doc admonished. "You should instead be asking yourself what if you *can* feel him."

She nodded, feeling her fear shove icy tendrils through her brain. "I know you're right, Doc, but I'm still afraid."

"The only thing to fear is the unknown," the old man said. "Not the truth. I know not what happened to my own family, and I would give anything to have that peace of knowing for sure. There comes a time when what you're supposed to do is lay down the burdens you've been carrying. And fear, dear lady, is a huge burden to bear. You've been given enough of them of late.''

Reluctantly Krysty closed her eyes and concentrated on Dean. She built his face in her mind, the way she'd seen it thousands of times, so like Ryan that she could see part of what her lover had to have been like as a child. Despite Ryan's irritation with Dean over behavior on occasion, there wasn't so much separating the father and son.

Electricity grazed her mind, sharp and insistent. Then Dean was there, his presence not as strong and as vibrant as it normally was, but that might have been because of the distance and her own fatigue. She reached out to him, felt his aliveness.

"Krysty," Doc said.

"It's okay, Doc." Feeling weak, Krysty wiped a shirtsleeve across her face to dry the fresh tears. "He's there."

"Alive?"

"Yes."

"And you're sure?"

"Yes. The only thing I really felt in him was tiredness and that he was afraid."

"Kind of sums up a normal day for a youngster if you ask me," J.B. commented.

Doc patted Krysty's hand. "Just you rest easy, dear lady. Ryan will return in a short while, and things will seem better."

"Guess so." Krysty pulled the blanket around her tighter, trying to stave off the chill still threatening to consume her. A headache dawned in the back of her head and lingered as a dull throb. She kept her gaze focused on the dark and forbidding forest around them, afraid to close her eyes because of what she might find there. "Gaia," she whispered, "stand by me. I don't know what you're trying to show me, don't know what it all means. But keep me strong enough to endure. And hold dear to you all that I hold dear, please."

"I CHECKED, Baron, and the boys appear to be all right. No permanent injuries, nothing that would keep them from being of service to you."

Full consciousness returned to Dean slowly, flickering in by dribs and drabs. His head hurt, and he could feel his heartbeat throbbing in his ears and his neck.

"All ten are there?" a deeper voice asked.

"Yes."

Dean slitted his eyes open. He could already tell he was lying on a hard surface—not the ground, though. As he let the dim yellow light filter into his vision, he opened his hand on his side opposite the one the men talked on. He splayed his fingers, sliding them across a smooth wooden surface that held only a few nicks and rough spots.

"You say this group has been trained together, Solomon?" the deep voice asked.

"For just short of ten months," Solomon answered.

"This one looks kind of skinny." Something hard pressed into Dean's side, and he closed his eyes, clamping his lips shut against a cry of pain.

"Don't worry about him, Baron," another man said. "Bastard kid there is quick as lightning. Had him in my sights, and he wheeled on me as I was squeezing the trigger. Disappeared like a fucking ghost and was gone before I could draw another bead."

"So he can run," the baron said. "Don't need a runner. Need a fighter."

"He can fight," Solomon said. "He's a chiller."

"Know that for a fact, do you?"

"If that boy had gotten his hands on a weapon, you

might not have all your men back out of the brush,'' Solomon replied. ''If he hadn't trusted me just long enough, I wouldn't have bagged him for you. And I think he was already figuring out that I wasn't on his side.''

Dean slitted his eyes open again. This time he saw the wall of bars separating him from the speakers. Solomon was talking to a gruff-looking man in road leathers, the right side of his face spiderwebbed with tattoos, a rifle resting easy in the crook of his arm.

''Moves like that, Baron,'' the gruff man said, ''you can't teach. Boy's been around some.''

Beyond the trio of men, another dozen were making final preparations on the wags that had formed a loose circle around the area.

''Give me that light,'' the baron ordered. He took a cylinder from the man beside him, switched it on and fanned the lens out into a broad cone.

With the extra light, Dean could see that he was in a wag of some type. The sides were covered by canvas over a rib cage of bars just like the ones covering the back end, converting the wag to a cage on wheels. Slavers used vehicles like these when they could.

His heartbeat sped up. Solomon had sold them out to slavers. The other boys were scattered around him. A few moved, struggling to throw off the effects of the trank dart they'd been hit with.

The baron strode to the end of the wag, then stepped up on a platform mounted there. The wag shifted as it took on the man's weight.

Framed in the light he directed at the top of the canvas-covered cage, the baron looked fierce. His face was scalpeled by hard living in mean times, scraped free of any softness or empathy. Long black hair framed his face and ran down past his shoulders. A mustache and goatee almost disguised the old knife scar that ran across his cruel lips. Another scar started from the bottom of the goatee and trailed down the side of his neck, showing how close he'd come to death.

He wore jeans with wraparound black chaps over them, a body-armor vest with a death's-head painted over his heart, a deep turquoise silk shirt with a high collar under that. Feathered earrings thatched with blue-jay quills hung from either side of his head. A cut-down Mossberg Bullpup 12 shotgun rode in a hand-tooled breakout holster that ran the length of the man's right thigh, the butt sawed off and replaced with a fold-out metal stock. He carried a Detonics .45 in shoulder leather.

"I'm Baron Vinge Connrad," the man declared. "That probably don't mean a thing to most of you."

It didn't mean anything to Dean. Scoping out the other boys without moving his head, he figured it didn't mean anything to anyone else, either.

"What does matter," Connrad continued, "is that I own you as of this minute. You can live or die right now." He slipped the Mossberg free of the thigh holster and held it in one hand. "What's it going to be?"

None of the boys said anything.

"I better damn sure get an answer," Connrad growled, leveling the Mossberg. "Otherwise, I'm going to shoot me some fish in a barrel."

"Live!" Ethan Perry said, blood tracking a split lip. The other boys took up the cry.

Dean, who'd said nothing, found himself being prodded with the shotgun muzzle. He thought about trying to grab the barrel but decided against it. Even if he managed to get it away from the man, there was nowhere to go.

"What about you, kid?" Connrad demanded.

"I want to live," Dean answered.

Connrad flashed him a cruel grin, eyes shadowed by the night's darkness. "Smart kid." He withdrew the Mossberg.

Dean sat up, sidling out of reach of an arm through the cage. "What do we have to do to live?"

"Chill a few people. Nothing big."

"Who?"

"Does it matter?" Connrad's gaze was direct and forceful.

Dean dropped his arms over his folded knees. "Not really."

Connrad looked over his shoulder at Solomon. "I like this kid, Payton."

Solomon nodded. "Knew you would. Like to talk about the jack you owe me for training these kids for you."

Connrad waved a dismissive hand, turning his gaze back to Dean. "You're kind of the runt of the litter, kid. Way you heard from Solomon, I paid him some good jack for finding ten of you here at the school and putting you together as a team. Promised him more when he delivered you." He grinned. "Been thinking about that, though. Saunders!"

Instantly the gruff man beside the phys-ed teacher put a gun to Solomon's head, then quickly relieved him of his weapons. "Put your hands up and keep them there," Saunders ordered.

"What the hell is going on?" Solomon demanded.

"Got to thinking about it," Connrad said. "You don't want to go to Vegas with us, and that leaves me kind of exposed. You might tell some of Brody's people about this transaction. Mebbe old Brody is an ornery enough cuss to send somebody looking for us. Can't have that."

"Wait a minute," Solomon said. "If I sell you out, I'm writing my own death sentence." Desperation filled his face. "Even if you didn't hunt me down, Brody or one of those townsfolk would."

"Mebbe. And mebbe you'd cut some kind of deal if you got caught getting out of this territory. Townsfolk get kind of soft, forget those hard roots that got them as far as they are. If you came with us, I'd know you got free of the situation. But you didn't want it that way."

"I'll go!" Solomon said in a strained voice. "I'll go with you! It's not that big of a deal!"

Connrad fixed Dean with his stare. "You believe him?"

Dean looked deep into the phys-ed teacher's eyes, thinking about the way Solomon had betrayed Nicholas Brody, the school and the nine other boys sitting in the cage behind him. "No."

Connrad smiled, honest pleasure showing. "Lad after my own heart. You figure ol' Solomon would up and split the first chance he got?"

"Yeah."

"So do I." The baron glanced at the teacher. Solomon was pale, shaky. "You think I should just shoot him and be done with it?"

"Up to you," Dean said.

Connrad abruptly passed the flashlight to another man, then worked the shotgun's slide to eject five shells. "Got one left in there. You hard enough to shoot Solomon for what he done?"

Dean returned the baron's flat gaze full measure. Nothing stirred inside him; it was all about survival now. "Yeah."

"Cawdor!" Ethan Perry exploded. "You can't do that! You coldhearted little son of a bitch!" The boy erupted from his seat and came at Dean.

Dean rose to his feet to defend himself.

"Sit down!" Connrad barked. He wielded the Detonics

in his other hand, pointing it directly at Perry's head. "Or I'll blow your bastard head off!"

Other boys, including Moxen and Louis McKenzie, reached up for Perry and pulled him back down. Perry put up a struggle, but it was mostly show. There wasn't any way he was going to go up against the baron's pistol.

Dean smelled the raw stink of fear filling the wag cage.

"Want to do it?" Connrad asked Dean.

"Up to you. You're in charge." Dean tried to play it the way his dad would, imagining his father in his shoes, willing himself to step into his dad's way of thinking. It was all about here and now, living to take one more breath and not regretting what he had to do to take it.

Connrad passed the Mossberg through the bars.

Dean took it, keeping his hand out of the trigger guard. The gun felt solid, dependable. He thought about the one round in the magazine, wondering if it was really there.

"Go ahead and do it," the baron urged, pointing the Detonics at Dean.

Slowly Dean brought the shotgun to bear on the baron's chest. He peered intently at the man over the barrel, neither of them backing off.

Chapter Twenty-Six

Dean continued to stare across the length of the shotgun at Baron Vinge Connrad, not letting himself feel anything. Several of the baron's sec men started forward, drawing their weapons. He ignored them; they would all be too late.

"Stay back!" Connrad ordered.

The men froze at once.

"What are you going to do, kid?" the baron asked.

"Depends."

"On what?" Connrad didn't seem afraid at all. The pistol stayed on target, not moving.

"Whether you're a slaver," Dean replied, struggling to keep his voice from breaking. "I got no wish to be a slave. Rather die. Guess we could find out who's faster."

"You'd be dead."

"And free."

"If you believe in any kind of life after this one," Connrad said. "Do you?"

"Don't know. Mebbe if I'm fast enough, we could go see together." Dean forced himself to keep from shaking. His finger stayed away from the trigger.

Connrad laughed. "God, but you're a mean kid. I could have sired you myself. I'm no slaver. Got some chilling work for you to do. After that you go free. My word on it."

"If I told you to open this door, would you?" Dean asked.

Connrad shook his head. "No. I didn't get where I am giving in to other people."

Dean nodded. "Didn't think so. But I wanted to make my point." He shifted the shotgun back to cover the phys-ed teacher. "Move your man back. Way you got this barrel chopped off, spread's going to get him, too."

Connrad waved Saunders off. The sec man stepped backward, but kept his pistol lined up on the phys-ed teacher's head.

Pulling the metal stock into his shoulder and thrusting the abbreviated muzzle through the bars, Dean covered Solomon. There was still some question whether the weapon was actually loaded. It might all be a setup to scare the phys-ed teacher. Dean prepared himself all the same, knowing he was willing to take the man's life for how he'd betrayed them.

He curled his finger around the trigger.

Solomon broke and tried to run.

Dean squeezed the trigger, riding out the recoil. The double-aught buckshot erupted from the muzzle and caught the man in midstride, knocking him flat at once, ripping his flesh to shreds.

"You killed him!" Ethan Perry screamed as Solomon kicked out his final few seconds of life. "You crazy bastard!"

Still in motion, Dean swung the shotgun on Connrad, catching the man by surprise. He squeezed the trigger, aiming directly at the man's head. The hammer fell with a click.

Connrad didn't even flinch. "Empty."

"See that," Dean said.

"Even if there'd been a shell in the chamber, you wouldn't have gotten out of the cage alive."

Dean made himself smile. "You said there was only one

round. Had to find out if your word is worth anything. If it wasn't, better to get the dying over with now."

Connrad shook his head and laughed. "You got balls, kid, I'll give you that. You and me are going to do just fine." He held out a hand for the shotgun.

Dean passed it across, glancing briefly at Solomon's corpse. He felt something, but he didn't let the feeling grow. He was going to have to stay hard, mean, if he wanted to live.

"You other boys," the baron said, "listen up."

Perry kept screaming angry curses.

"Shut up," Connrad ordered, "or I'm going to blast you through the mouth, see if that don't cut down on the noise."

Shooting Dean angry looks, Perry quieted.

"Better," Connrad said. "Got an announcement I want to make before we leave here." He pointed at Dean. "Anybody so much as lays a hand on this boy, that person's going to answer to me. Then that person's going to die. That's a promise. Any questions?"

There were none.

"Saunders, shut up this wag and make sure everything's secure." Connrad stepped off the platform behind the cage, already thumbing loads into the Mossberg.

Once the flaps had been dropped to cover the bars, Dean sank to his haunches and tried not to be sick. It was one thing to kill a man or mutie that was trying to kill him, or kill an animal for food, but it was another to shoot a man just standing there looking at him. His stomach rolled threateningly. His dad would have done it, though, and for just the same reasons he had.

"You feel better, you bastard?" Perry demanded. "Does killing an unarmed man get you off?"

Dean poked his fingers through the bars, finally able to

get his whole hand through. He reached for the edge of the tarp covering the cage, trying to separate it.

"Ease off on him," Louis McKenzie warned.

"Fuck you, too," Perry said. "If they put a gun in that bastard's hand and told him to chill us, what do you think he's going to do?"

"What the hell's wrong with you, Ethan?" Bobby Handley asked. "You have a soft spot for old Solomon? Seems you always was his favorite, and he liked looking at you in the shower."

Perry lunged up, hands reaching for Handley's throat. Several boys worked together to put Perry down, piling on top of him.

"That it, Ethan?" Jordie Ferguson asked. He was blond and blue eyed, his long hair spilling down his back. "Old Solomon feeding you sausage in the can?"

A cry of inarticulate rage split Perry's lips.

"Mebbe you already forgot how Solomon sold us out," Chanz Montoya said. "Me, I wasn't going to forget. Ever. If Dean hadn't killed Solomon, mebbe that man would have never got caught. Wouldn't have wanted to see that happen."

"I'd have killed him," Enrique Green stated.

Perry calmed down. "Dammit, let me go."

Louis fixed him with a hard gaze that Dean could read even in the darkness. "Word to the wise, Perry—don't try that again. Not to Bobby, not to Dean, not to any of us."

"And if I do?" Perry growled.

"Then we'll chill you ourselves," Louis stated.

Perry looked around the group. "You think you're talking for all of them?"

"Yeah."

His fingers on the edge of the tarp, Dean hesitated. Boots still showed at the back of the wag. He waited, not wanting to risk getting caught and catching someone's wrath. He turned his attention to the boys at the other end of the wag, watching the shift of power from Perry to Louis.

"He is," Moxen declared, quickly followed by the other boys.

Dean was surprised. Louis had always been the quietest and most pleasant of Perry's group. He hadn't seemed like leadership material.

"You okay with that, Dean?" Louis asked, not breaking eye contact with Perry.

"Yeah," Dean answered.

"I put this group together," Perry argued. "You're not going to just push me out like that."

"Solomon put this group together," Louis corrected, "and he named you leader." He gestured at the cage bars around them. "I, for one, am not too happy with where that has taken us."

"You're going to give me grief," Perry said in a disbelieving voice, "and Dean just chilled Solomon?"

"I did it for a reason," Dean said, feeling pressure to have his say. Some of it was so he could hear himself, maybe even convince himself.

"Why?" Perry demanded. "Revenge?"

"Works for me," Moxen said. Green echoed the sentiment.

"They took us down with those trank guns," Dean argued, "and didn't make any sound that carried. A shotgun blast might have been heard back at the school. Especially if Jake or Joel was on duty. Thought mebbe they might come looking."

"Then you should have missed Solomon," Perry snarled.

Dean gave him a cold look. "I didn't want to. Mebbe we aren't coming back from wherever they're taking us. I didn't want Solomon getting away with chilling all of us." He paused. "I had another reason, too. We're going to be noticed missing in the morning. Somebody'll come looking for us. If Connrad and his people leave Solomon's body where it is, it'll give whoever comes looking a chance to start searching in the right direction."

Louis looked at Dean, a slight grin on his lips. "Slick. I wouldn't have thought about that."

Dean parted the tarp after the boots moved away. All the boys except Perry crowded around him, peering through the tarp, as well.

Outside, a sec man held a lantern while two others lifted Solomon's body and threw it onto the wag.

"Guess they thought about it, too," Conor said glumly.

Dean let the tarp drop. "Mebbe. But there's the blood. Be harder to see, but they can't clean it all up. Not after what that shotgun did."

The wag lurched forward, banging the boys around. They spread out, everybody staying away from Perry.

Settling back against the side of the wag and getting as comfortable as he could, Dean forced himself to relax and not think about chilling Solomon.

"You think Brody'll send somebody?" Moxen asked Dean.

"I don't know. If Brody gets word to my dad," Dean said, "I know he'll be there as soon as he can be." And he hung on to that thought for comfort, not daring ask himself how far away his dad might be at that moment.

"WHAT ABOUT DEAN?" Krysty asked. She sat astride her lover on the riverbank behind a copse of trees, within shouting distance of the other companions as dawn colored the eastern sky rose and gold. Neither of them had any clothes on, pressing flesh against flesh, a blanket beneath them. Their weapons were within easy reach.

Ryan looked up at her, his hands kneading her full breasts, tweaking her nipples until they stood fully erect. "Can't lead these people to him. And that's assuming LeMarck doesn't overtake us. It's in our best interest to change courses."

While they'd been up on higher ground, he and Jak had spotted LeMarck. The seven villes sec commander had linked up with more troops.

Krysty loved the feel of her lover's hands on her, hot and insistent. She ran her own hands against his chest, pushing to roll her hips against his. His hard erection lay between the lips of her sex, not yet penetrating her. She had to make herself think, to keep the thread of conversation.

"I had a vision about Dean last night," she said, staring into Ryan's cobalt blue eye. It was red and bloodshot, mute testimony that he hadn't been getting enough rest. None of them had.

Ryan paused, waiting.

"In that vision Dean looked sick, out somewhere in the open so he couldn't be protected."

"Was he still at the school?"

"I don't know. Couldn't see that. I'm worried about him, though."

Ryan pulled her down to him and kissed her tenderly, then held her tight against him. "We'll get to him, Krysty. That's what we're all out here for. Just can't see a way clear to do it yet. The river goes on another fifteen, twenty miles before it switches back to the north and joins up with the Humboldt River according to Hoyle. It might take us the wrong direction, way the hell off the route we want to go."

"I know. I looked at the map, too, when you and J.B. were going over things. We could hole up somewhere and hope LeMarck and his baron miss us."

"We could," Ryan agreed. "But if we get caught out here, there's no defensible place we could hope to hold. Our best bet is movement. We'll catch a few hours' sleep here, then push on before noon. Hoyle says the impact area where the space station is coming down is about fifteen miles from here, according to J.B.'s minisextant. We can make that by nightfall, mebbe set up camp, see what we're left with next morning. Chron's ticking against Hardcoe and LeMarck. They got to be getting on to this Big Game of theirs. Once they do, we'll be left alone."

"We could be late getting to Dean," Krysty protested.

"I know." She saw the fear in him, then, and knew that no matter what he did, even though it looked as if he were directing the companions on a course that would take them far from his son, Ryan cared deeply about Dean. "But it's all I can think of to do."

She kissed him, feeling warmer toward him because of the softness she knew lurked in his savage heart. Ryan Cawdor was a true product of the Deathlands: hard, unrelenting and willing to spill any blood that wasn't his own or that he didn't want to look out for. But he intended to save Dean.

And that's all she could expect of him.

"To get to him any sooner without getting captured," Ryan said, "we'd need a mat-trans."

"I know." Krysty started moving on top of him, rubbing her slick sex back and forth across his erection, finally drawing it into herself with her vaginal muscles. She pushed all the insecurity and fear that the visions had seeded within her out of her mind, concentrating on the pleasure she was giving and receiving.

She felt Ryan hard and deep within her, his erection stabbing up into her belly, stretching her tight and making her feel so full. She pressed herself up again into a seated position, her hands shoving against his chest as she lifted her hips and slammed them back onto him, taking him even deeper.

His fingers burned hotly across her bare flesh as he seized her ass and cupped her into him, meeting her stroke for stroke. She let herself go with the pleasure, waves of it cresting inside her, building to something even bigger. She concentrated on the here and now, not thinking about the dangers that still faced them.

Chapter Twenty-Seven

Nicholas Brody sat behind his desk, staring across his steepled fingers at Jake. "You're sure someone was murdered?"

The sec man occupied one of the chairs in front of the desk, his hat in his hands. "Yes, sir. That much blood, had to be someone killed there."

"And what makes you so certain? That blood you found up in those hills could have been where someone shot an animal, hopeful to provision their larder."

Jake shook his head. "No." He opened a fist and displayed several bits of black fabric spotted with rust-colored blood. "That's from clothing, Mr. Brody. Shotgun pattern killed whoever was up on that ridge and tore bits of cloth from whatever he or she was wearing. We found pellets in the trees."

Brody glanced out the window at the school grounds. He couldn't believe something like this had happened. Never in all the years that his institution had been established had something so untoward occurred. "Was it school clothing? From one of the missing boys?"

"Hard to say."

Brody returned his gaze to the man. Jake had been out searching since that morning's roster showed the ten missing boys. "Your best guess, then."

"Sir, with all respect intended, ain't no way I can tell you that. What I can tell you is this—the wag tracks on top of that ridgeline are fresh. Still got green plants crushed up in the clods they turned out of the earth. I'm guessing, but mebbe there were as many as six or seven wags.''

"That sounds like more than someone would need to spirit away those boys," Brody said.

"Yes, sir. I'm thinking so, too. Got a feeling we don't know the half of it. All them wags, they got themselves a regular convoy.''

"Do you think the boys went with them willingly?'' Brody hated asking the question. It made him sound uncertain of himself.

Jake passed over a small object.

Brody took it, examining it carefully, noting its needle-shaped end and the feathers that were obviously there for guidance. "A dart?" He adjusted his glasses, looking toward the sec man for elucidation.

"Trank. Shoot someone with it, knocks them out for a while. Mebbe minutes, mebbe hours, depending on what it's carrying. Found that one in a tree around the blood site.''

"You're suggesting the boys were abducted.''

"Yes, sir. Come to find out that Mr. Solomon is missing from the ranks, as well.''

Brody didn't keep tabs on the staff as tightly as he did the students. If an instructor became remiss in his or her duties, that was duly noted and addressed. He referred to the list of the missing boys. "All of these boys were a part of Mr. Solomon's pet group, were they not?''

"Yes, sir.''

"Except for Mr. Cawdor.''

"Only kitten in a litter of skunks," Jake agreed.

"Have you talked to Mr. Conover? I believe he was hurt yesterday morning.''

"Talked to him. Told me Mr. Solomon was running some special maneuvers last night with his group."

"Without my authorization?"

"If you didn't authorize it, he did it without your authorization."

Brody placed his hands flat on the desk. "I didn't authorize it. Could you attempt to track these people down, Jake, and would you be willing?"

"Yes, sir," the sec man answered. "On both counts. But it's going to take considerable from the sec crew here, and I'll probably have to hire in some help from Leadville. Got some hardcases there do odd jobs when the jack's right."

Brody didn't like the idea of dealing with fiddle-footed ruffians, but circumstances had left him lacking in choices. "I'll defer to your esteemed judgment in that matter, Jake, and I'll place whatever amount of jack you need at your disposal whenever you say. As far as the sec around this institution, we'll limp along without you for the time it takes. Just bring those boys back safe and sound."

The sec man nodded and clapped on his hat. "I'll see it done, sir."

Brody watched the man go and tried not to think of what might be happening to the missing boys. God forbid that he should have to tell any of their parents that he'd failed to protect them as he'd promised. Especially Dean Cawdor's father. He'd heard numerous stories about the way the man had left Leadville after dropping off his son.

The man wasn't forgiving, Brody knew. Rather, Ryan Cawdor was the epitome of a mythological Greek warrior camouflaged in flesh and blood.

SUNDOWN HAD BEGUN in earnest as Ryan reached the foothills of the low mountains surrounding Honey Lake. The dry heat of the Smoke Creek Desert had sapped him all day long, drawing the moisture from his body. Now, with the long shadows of night coming on, the wind blew cold, erasing the desert's heat.

The sound of chanting off to his left, brought to his ears by the wind, sent him diving for cover. He waved the rest of the companions to cover behind rocks and boulders.

The chanting grew steadily louder, filled with ululating wails that seemed a cross between agony and ecstasy. Dozens of voices, male and female, young and old, took up the hue and cry.

Ryan took out his night glasses and trained them in the direction of the chanting. The land fell away from his position, settling into a bowl-shaped depression where a handful of camp fires burned embers against the night. Tens of dimly lit figures surrounded the fires, chanting, none of them really hitting a harmony or a tempo. All of them were gazing up at the starry sky.

"Muties, lover," Krysty said, crawling up on her elbows next to him.

Ryan nodded, trailing his night glasses over the rad-blasted stick figures clad in tatters of human clothing and animal pelts. Many of them were nearly bald or were patchy from the radiated lands they'd spent years in. None of them had any weapons beyond a club or a knife, though some wore cow and buffalo skulls on their heads as armor. A few others had worked rib bones into decorative chest protectors.

All of them were misshapen from leftover nuclear bombardment, covered with scabs and weeping, open sores that leaked vile green pus. Most of them looked to be scabbies, but there were a few stickies among them.

"Odd to see so many different kinds of muties gathered together in the middle of nowhere," Krysty whispered.

"Yeah," Ryan replied quietly. "And causing all this

noise seems out of place, too. Draw down the bigger predators on them in no time.'' He glanced back toward the
others and waved them forward, signaling to Jak and J.B.
that they were to come quietly.

In seconds the companions and the Heimdall Foundation
members were hiding behind the ridge overlooking the depression filled with muties. All of them kept their weapons
at the ready, and the two prisoners took time to pick up
stones to defend themselves.

''By the Three Kennedys!'' Doc exclaimed in a hush.
''They look like they are in the throes of some mystical
epiphany!''

''What's set them off like that?'' Ryan asked, his curiosity aroused. There'd been no sign of pursuit by Le-
Marck's group of raiders all during the day. With the muties gathered as they were in the area, that could work to
their advantage, as well. Where he and his group might
hope to slip through and escape notice, the wags would
definitely draw attention.

''I do not know, Ryan.'' The old man pointed. ''As you
can plainly see for yourself, they are not spending any time
communicating with one another. Rather, they seem to be
attempting to placate or seek acknowledgment from a being
higher than themselves.''

''Muties with religion?'' Jak shook his head. ''No such
thing, Doc.''

''That we have seen thus far, dear boy,'' the old man
corrected. ''And might I remind you that we have seen
many strange and wondrous things on our journeys.''

''Not religion,'' Krysty said, ''fear. They're afraid of
something, and they came here because they thought they
might be protected.''

''From what?'' J.B. asked.

Krysty shook her head. ''It's all mixed up. I don't have

an image. I'm not sure that they know what's driven them here.''

"The space station?'' Ryan asked. It was the only thing they knew that was going to make this night different from any others that had taken place in Smoke Creek Desert.

"I don't know, lover. Mebbe.''

"Primitive instinct,'' Mildred said.

"What do you mean?'' J.B. asked.

"Those muties live on an intellectual edge barely higher than most animals,'' the woman stated. "I think we can all agree on that.'' The declaration passed without objection. "Back in the twentieth century, before California was nuked and collapsed off the face of the planet, scientists had already been studying the effects of natural phenomena on animals.''

"Don't understand,'' Jak said.

Mildred turned to him slightly, but included all the companions in her conversation. "Earthquakes. Flood. Storms. Extrahard winters. The lack of game. All things that take place in Nature that humans have a hard time detecting, animals seem to know about ahead of time. Like they have an extra sense that humans forgot about or never developed.''

"This is true,'' Doc said. "Even after the invention of the seismograph, an observation of animals, especially their migratory habits, was maintained. Often the animals reacted to unknown stimuli that warned them sometimes as much as days before data-gathering devices would report activity.''

"You think those muties can sense the space station coming down out of the sky?'' Bernsen asked. He barked a short laugh. "That's preposterous. It took the teams at the Heimdall Foundation months to track *Shostakovich's Anvil.*''

"And you people got it wrong once already," Mildred said in a hard voice. "Or else you wouldn't have been up around the seven villes. I see these muties sitting here now, waiting for what you say is going to happen."

The fat scientist's face colored slightly.

"Would you then," Doc asked, "care to venture a hypothesis concerning the presence of the muties at this particular location at this precise time?"

"No," Bernsen admitted after a moment.

"How far are we from the area where it's supposed to come down?" Ryan asked.

J.B. took out his minisextant and did his calculations.

While the Armorer was busy, Ryan kept watch over the muties. They were growing more agitated, shifting individually and in small groups, not really noticing now when others encroached on their space. Some of them added more wood to their fires. Ryan knew that wood was scarce in the area. The companions had experienced some difficulty themselves in obtaining it in hopes of having a camp fire to warm themselves at some point in the night. The muties had come prepared with bundles of sticks, branches and driftwood tied by strings.

"About three hundred yards north and west of our position," the Armorer announced.

Ryan turned his night glasses away from the muties and looked toward Honey Lake. The body of water was much larger than indicated on the map they'd been working from. It glistened, dark and oily, in the distance, acting like a mirror for the stars and moon above. The reflection resembled a piece of sky that had fallen and taken root in the desert rock and sand.

Then a flare ignited, reflected on the lake's surface as it skipped between the stars like a rock skimming waves.

Ryan glanced back up, knowing what he was actually seeing was in the sky.

"There," Krysty said, taking him by the arm and pointing to the east.

Ryan stared at the orange-white burn streaking across the sky. It looked only inches long, but he knew what he was looking at was actually several miles in length.

"It's reentering the atmosphere," Bernsen said in a reverent voice.

"On fire?" Jak asked. "Be burned time gets here. Waste to come if does."

"Dear boy," Doc said, "the space station itself might not be burning up. What you're seeing is the friction of the station battering against the air."

"It could still burn up before it reaches the ground," Mildred stated. "Space stations weren't designed as reentry vehicles."

"No, not as a general rule," Bernsen said, his eyes glued to the action in the heavens, "but this one was built to withstand a hell of a beating—meteors, satellites and space weapons if it was ever under attack. There was so much the Russians hoped to gain from the recording equipment aboard it. They built it to last."

Below their position the muties were all pointing skyward. Their chanting and ululation had increased to almost deafening proportions even over the distance separating them from the companions. More wood dropped onto the camp fires, making the flames reach even higher.

Ryan watched, a thrill going through him. Looking at something no one had ever seen before was always exhilarating.

The space station, if that was what it truly was, fell quickly. The orange faded to yellow as the heat increased, then turned white. Streaking earthward, the space station's trajectory abruptly changed.

"It's breaking apart," Ryan said.

"No!" Bernsen screamed, almost starting over the ridge. J.B. grabbed the man by the shirt collar and hauled him back. "It can't break apart! It's not supposed to do that!"

"Stay put," the Armorer warned, "or you'll never get the chance to tell anyone you saw this. I'd sooner kill you than let the muties have a chance, because they'd take us right along with you."

Bernsen stuffed his fists against his mouth, shaking his head from side to side.

Ryan watched as the space station broke up into at least four pieces. He thought he might have seen a fifth go spinning away to the south, but whatever trail it might have made disappeared quickly against the harsh light of the reentry burn.

The light was so bright it reduced the night's shadows to pinpricks against the uneven ground, almost blinding in its intensity. The largest piece continued along its trajectory toward Honey Lake. The lake's surface blazed with white fire, shimmering across the surface, only a few pockets of darkness left where debris shoved up through the water.

"Dark night!" J.B. exclaimed as it got closer, approaching with increasing speed as bits and pieces of the space station were torn off or burned off and streamlined the craft. "Damn thing's so big it's going to fall on top of us!"

"Stand your ground," Ryan advised. "If we start moving, we could end up right under it, or the muties will see us."

The companions all dug into the ground, watching the falling space station's final approach. It slammed into the ground 150 yards from the mutie campsite, sundering the rock and scattering sand before it like an ocean wave. Tremors shook the earth.

The chanting broke as the sand washed over the muties, knocking dozens of them to the ground. A moment later the space-station wreckage rolled over them, pulping them against the desert floor. The closer ranks of muties broke and ran, coming up the grade toward the companions.

Behind them, red-hot and throwing off heat waves that could be felt even along the ridgeline, the chunk of space station skidded toward Honey Lake. In seconds it shot out over the black depths and sank, glowing eerily until it disappeared.

The screaming muties didn't stop their flight, moving on a direct course to overrun the companions' position.

"Move back!" Ryan roared, bringing the Steyr to his shoulder. He fired in quick succession, a rolling thunder of five shots that mowed down five muties, bullets driving deep through their chests and faces.

Corpses dropped in front of the charging crowd, but the other muties gave them little attention, trampling over them. The line broke only for a moment, the momentum unstoppable. Recognizing a threat they could deal with, the muties raised clubs and axs, bared blades and spears and continued to run.

J.B.'s Uzi snarled into angry life. The rounds cut a swath in the ranks of the muties. He ducked behind a boulder to change clips. "Ryan, we aren't going to be able to hold them back."

The one-eyed man silently agreed. The muties were a stampede of frightened flesh. Whatever had drawn them there, they'd been betrayed.

Sparing a glance over his shoulder, Ryan watched as Krysty guided Doc farther back into the broken landscape,

Bernsen at their heels. Jak was covering their backs, the
.357 Magnum pistol in his fist banging out death.

Hoyle was cut down in midstride less than fifteen yards
away. A hard-thrown spear took him in the back, sliding
into his heart, then burst through his chest. The Heimdall
Foundation guide halted his run, crumpling to his knees.
He grabbed the spearhead protruding from his chest in disbelief, then toppled forward.

His rifle reloaded, Ryan exchanged looks with J.B.
"Time to go."

"Ready," the Armorer replied as he pulled the shotgun
around. "Follow my lead?"

"Do it," Ryan said. He was no more than ten feet behind
J.B. when they broke into a run. The muties were almost
within clawing distance, and a spear sailed over Ryan's
shoulder, dropping point first into the inclined terrain ahead
of him.

Krysty was over the top of the next ridge, coming around
with her .38 in both hands as she took advantage of the
cover offered. She opened her mouth, screaming a warning.

Ryan couldn't read the words, but he knew the intent.
He cut hard left, his hearing only now starting to return
from the concussive force of the space station's impact. A
grinding groan echoed around him.

"Fireblast!" Ryan cursed as he saw the rectangular
shape of the wag crest the ridgeline to the left of Krysty's
position. He had no doubt to whom it belonged. "J.B.!"

"I see it!" the Armorer shouted back.

Heavy machine guns mounted on the wag started blasting away. Tracer rounds flared purple against the velvet
night. Fifty-caliber death drummed into the muties, spinning them, dumping them from their feet, knocking them

onto their backs. Then the withering fire whipped on, turning toward Ryan and J.B., smacking into the earth only inches behind them.

Chapter Twenty-Eight

Ryan went to ground behind an outcrop as the wag switched on its lights. He brought up the Steyr and put rounds through the driver's side of the windshield. One of them cratered the hood over the engine, ripping through the metal with a shriek and scattering sparks across the hood.

The driver turned away. If he was hurt, it wasn't enough to interfere with his driving. The wide bumper caught muties mercilessly, the tires rolling over them where they dropped.

Other wags joined the first, the wheels digging into the ground, throwing out huge rooster tails behind them. Their lights blazed over the sudden battleground.

One of the armored vehicles suddenly zipped out of the formation. As the headlights came around, Ryan spotted Mildred trying to outrun the wag. The driver must have recognized her, because he stayed with her without running her down.

"Millie!" J.B. shouted. He switched back to the Uzi and rattled a trio of short bursts across the front of the vehicle, the slugs hammering the metal but failing to penetrate. The autofire also failed to break off the wag's pursuit of Mildred.

For a moment Ryan lost sight of the action as more wags cut off the woman's escape route. He picked his targets, sighting carefully, then taking up the trigger slack. He put bullets through the heads of two men who swung free of the blocking wags and attempted to seize Mildred. The woman stood her ground fearlessly, willing to sell her life as dearly as possible. Every time her pistol cracked, a sec man or a mutie went down.

Abruptly the wag trailing her slewed sideways. Two men in back who'd been manning the machine guns whipped out a section of heavy netting equipped with weights. The net flew true, unfurling in midair until it dropped around Mildred.

She went down hard, trying to shake the empty brass from the Czech-made ZKR and struggle up from the folds of the net. Before she had a chance to finish the reload, at least six men pushed her back to the ground. When they cleared off her, she wasn't fighting anymore.

Ryan couldn't believe the woman was dead, but any kind of rescue was next to impossible. J.B. worked the Uzi calmly and dispassionately, raking short bursts across the wag personnel and the handful of muties who hadn't quit the area.

Ryan dropped one of the two men who'd thrown the net. The Steyr's round blasted the man backward over the side of the wag. Despite the supposed orders not to kill, the other machine gunner opened up on Ryan's position. Clods of dirt and rock ripped loose around him. He sank back into cover. Slinging the rifle, he drew the SIG-Sauer.

J.B. was already moving in on Mildred's position. Two 3-round bursts knocked down two of the men trying to lift the woman from the ground.

Ryan took that as a sign of hope. If they'd killed the woman, they'd have left her there. He broke cover, moving in from the other side, backing J.B.'s play. It was possible they could recover her if they got control of one of the wags and put the others out of commission.

He ran toward the nearest wag, the SIG-Sauer raised before him. The sec man on the passenger side noticed him first, yelling a warning to the men in front of him. Both had their hands full with muties determined to take their lives.

Ryan fired two rounds. Bright scarlet blood, illuminated by the lights from the other wags, splashed against the fractured windshield inside the wag's cab as a sec man dropped inside the vehicle. The driver had a chance for one quick, terrified glance at Ryan, then a bullet took him squarely between the eyes, snapping his head back.

Slipping his free hand onto the door latch, Ryan triggered it and started to yank it open. The sec man's body tumbled to the ground as a hail of bullets punched through the door.

Having no choice, Ryan abandoned his position. He dived toward the back of the truck, spotting one of the saddle tanks. He threw himself under the wag and unleathered his panga. Three quick thrusts opened holes in the gas tank. Liquid spilled out the holes, pooling rapidly in the sand.

The sec men cautiously approached the side of the wag.

Ryan scrambled through on the other side and saw J.B. cutting away at the net that held Mildred. The Armorer glanced in his direction once, hand sliding back for the Uzi. When J.B. saw who it was, he turned back to his task.

Rocks lay scattered across the ground. Ryan seized two that looked as if they had heavy mineral content. He hoped some of it was iron or flint. He tossed them underhanded toward the broad pool of gasoline beneath the wag. When they landed, he fired immediately.

The 9 mm rounds struck the rocks, knocking sparks from one of them. The sparks proved enough to ignite the gasoline. Flames spread across the pool, then started leaping up the torrents pouring from the ruptured gas tank.

"Cover her!" Ryan yelled at J.B. "There's going to be a blow!"

An instant later the gas tank under the wag exploded from the built-up vapor inside. The vehicle jumped in its tracks, the tank reduced to shrapnel that blasted in all directions. Several pieces ripped the sec men to shreds, and two of the wag's rear tires went flat.

Ryan pushed himself to his feet. Alerted by movement in his peripheral vision, he yelled a warning to J.B. just as a shadow stepped around the front of the wag that had come up behind Mildred.

The Armorer was deadly and quick, rounds from the Uzi chopping into the man standing there.

Ryan added two shots of his own, blasting the man's face apart. Then he watched as J.B. turned and fell to his knees. He dropped the Uzi before Ryan covered the distance.

Once he was close enough, Ryan saw the fletched darts buried deeply into the side of J.B.'s neck and cheek. "Fireblast!" he swore. Managing Mildred while unconscious would have been difficult enough even if they'd been able to commandeer a wag. With the Armorer out of the picture, the remotely possible had become decidedly impossible.

"Go!" J.B. whispered hoarsely, struggling to remain on his knees and failing by degrees. "They don't want us dead right now. Mebbe we got some time. As long as you and the others are free."

Ryan looked at his oldest friend. "If there's a way, J.B., I'll be there for you."

"Know you will." J.B was almost prone on the ground, his hand reaching for Mildred's. He almost made it before the drug in his system shut him down.

A bullet cut the air only inches from Ryan's eye, galvanizing him into action. He snapped off shots, emptying the SIG-Sauer's magazine. As he changed clips, he headed on a tangent that would take him across the fire burning the tarp from the back of the wag he'd left crippled. He knew that for a moment he'd be as clear a target as he could imagine, but after that, whoever had been watching him would lose their night vision.

It was a good plan, the best he could hope for under the circumstances. But he hadn't planned on the small wag that rocketed at him before his own vision could completely clear.

He glimpsed it for only a second, trying to pinpoint the sound. Then the wag was on him, skidding in the sand and the loose rock as the driver tried to avoid a head-on collision. Ryan's own footing was treacherous as he suddenly changed directions. His ankle turned under him painfully, costing him inches.

Unable to totally clear the vehicle, he twisted and put his hands out before him, cushioning the impact. When contact was made, it felt as if his arms were going to tear out of their sockets. The SIG-Sauer left his hand, lost from sight before it hit the ground.

He arced his body onto the wag's hood so he wouldn't go down under the four-wheel-drive, all-terrain tires. Out of control, he smashed up against the windshield, fracturing the glass with his bodyweight. He recognized Hayden Le-Marck's face on the other side of the spiderwebbed windshield, mouth moving as he shouted orders to the driver.

Breath knocked out of him from the impact, Ryan pushed himself from the hood as the wag came to a halt. His legs almost wouldn't hold him as he forced himself to stand. He managed only trembling steps. Angrily he ripped the panga free of its sheath as LeMarck climbed out of the halted wag.

Ryan went at the man full tilt, knowing if he could buy

himself only a few more seconds, he might be able to function better. His ribs ached and his ankle throbbed, but nothing seemed broken.

LeMarck was taken by surprise, but the sec boss's reflexes were quick enough to dodge the deadly panga.

Ryan drew back to try again, then felt the sharp bite of trank darts pinning him from his knees to his neck. Stubbornly he stayed awake to make one more slash at LeMarck, missing the sec boss by more than an inch. He didn't remain conscious long enough to feel the impact he made against the ground.

WHEN RYAN WENT DOWN less than sixty yards from her position, Krysty started for the top of the ridge, snapping the cylinder of her .38 closed after reloading. Her attention remained focused on her lover, and the man standing above him.

The mutie ranks had been broken, existing now only in retreating clumps. Some of them fought on from behind cover, directing their vengeance on the sec team. Snipers deployed at the sec commander's instruction and began to mop up the muties who chose to fight rather than flee.

Before Krysty reached the top of the ridge and was seen, Jak wrapped his strong arms around her. He clapped a hand over her mouth and put his face close to her ear so he could whisper without his voice carrying far.

"Do Ryan no good, go running out there," he said.

Krysty gave up the struggle almost at once, anchored in the harsh realities of the situation. It was almost too much for her: the visions, the not knowing if they really were the future or if they were just bad hallucinations, the secrets she was keeping from Ryan, and the suspense of what was happening with Dean. She pulled Jak's hand away and made herself exhale.

"It's okay," she said, going back to ground behind the ridgeline, "I'm not going out there."

"It would be a very brave thing to do," Doc said sincerely, putting a hand on her shoulder.

"It would be stupe," Krysty replied. "There'd only be one more person to rescue, and one less to help."

"Yes," the old man said quietly. "Dear Krysty, having a care toward our own freedom is how we may best serve our fallen companions."

Krysty knew that, but it didn't assuage any of the feelings of guilt that assailed her. She holstered her weapon. Below, sec men surrounded Ryan and carried him to the back of a wag. She watched until she couldn't see him anymore.

"Follow," Jak said. "Best make tracks away from here before they see us and come after. Then no one come rescue."

"We're going to find them," Krysty said so there'd be no mistake.

"Yes, dear lady," Doc agreed, "we shall. And it appears we have at least some time on our hands. The Big Game in Vegas is not until six more days."

But Krysty also knew transportation would be a problem. The wags could go much faster than they could. Crossing the desert on foot to Vegas would be almost impossible. Even if they made the distance, and on time, they'd be in no shape to help anyone.

"Gaia, help me find a way," Krysty prayed. She followed Doc, while Jak kept point, motioning to Bernsen to keep up with him. They weren't followed.

"GOT THREE OF THEM," Wallis Thoroughgood said, gazing into the back of the wag where the three captured outlanders lay caged and still unconscious.

LeMarck gazed around the battlefield. Everything was a flurry of activity as the sec teams secured their gear, tended to the few wounded and made what repairs were necessary to the wags. Two of the vehicles appeared destroyed. The first had been set on fire by the one-eyed man, and the resulting explosions had killed four men and burned the wag badly. He'd given the order to drain the surviving tank and leave the wag behind.

The second wag was lost when a group of muties had rolled a huge boulder at it while it had been going down the hillside. The boulder had smashed into the wag and buckled the vehicle's frame and drivetrain, flipping it onto its side. The driver's side had been buried in the sand, and it would have taken too much time to attempt a recovery of the saddle fuel tank on that side, so only the one on the passenger side had been tapped.

Both of the wags were being jettisoned. They didn't dare try to haul them across the desert because it would have reduced their top speed if they were attacked. And pulling them would have increased gas consumption, as well as announcing to the other barons that they'd undergone a hardship.

LeMarck looked at the three captured outlanders. "There are still three of them out there."

"I know it," Baron Hardcoe said, running a hand across his broad face. "But how many men is it going to cost us to try to dig them out?"

LeMarck nodded.

"Cut our losses here," Hardcoe said. "Three of them, from what I've seen, are going to tip the odds in our favor in the Big Game. Mebbe we ought to be satisfied with that much."

"All six would have been better," LeMarck remarked.

"I think so, too. But we got three. Let's work with that."

"Yes, sir."

"Get your men ready," Hardcoe instructed. "I want to shake the dust from this place in ten minutes or less."

LeMarck went to see that it was done, but he ordered men to keep an eye on the ridges around the area just in case. And he could always hope the other three would find a way to follow them. If they arrived in Vegas before the representing teams were dropped into the pit, they could be added. The thought gave him hope.

KRYSTY AND THE OTHERS waited almost an hour after the sec teams left before coming down out of the mountains. The muties had left, too, going back to wherever they'd come from.

They split up, reccing the area to see what the sec men had left behind. Bernsen went with Doc, since the two of them were more mechanically inclined.

Bodies lay everywhere, muties and sec men. Hardcoe and LeMarck hadn't bothered with their dead.

Krysty and Jak prowled through the interior of the overturned wag. She kept her mind occupied on what she could find and off what might be happening to Ryan, J.B. and Mildred.

"Got gas in outside tank," Jak said. "Slapped it. Sounded full. Got four tires still whole that side, too. Take lot of work to dig out."

Krysty found two boxes of .38 ammunition and a box of 9 mm in the sliding drawer under the driver's seat. Sand had spilled in through the open window, and she had to dig to get at it, then pry it open with a crowbar Jak dug out of the toolbox in the back.

"Got shovels," Jak said, holding up one of the folding trenching tools. "Some other things."

"Keep it in mind." Krysty put the ammo in her backpack. "Mebbe we'll find a use for them." Netting caught her attention, hanging from a hook above the door and disappearing under the mound of loose sand. She dug patiently, following the netting, getting to the bottom and finding a half-dozen self-heats in the bag. She took them out and stored them, too. They'd lost some of their food when Ryan and J.B. were taken. Mildred had been carrying half of the medicine Krysty had turned up in the helicopter.

"Krysty!" Doc bellowed.

Standing up awkwardly between the seats, Krysty looked through the shattered passenger-side window. Doc and Bernsen were under the raised hood of the burned wag. It had still been burning in places when the companions had arrived. They'd thrown handfuls of sand onto the flames until they died away.

"What's wrong, Doc?" she asked.

"Actually, my dear," the old man replied with a white-toothed grin, "things have the appearance of being very right." He turned to Bernsen. "Hit it."

The scientist leaned under the wag's raised hood with a screwdriver. Sparks flashed, then the wag's engine started with a throaty snort. It ran for only a few seconds before dying.

"The good news," Doc said, "is that this engine is capable of running in spite of the fire. The bad news is one tank was ruptured by an explosion and the other was drained of fuel."

"We've got fuel over here," Krysty replied. "It'll take some digging to get to it."

"By the Three Kennedys, then we shall give this the proverbial old college try. Repairs also necessitate replacing some of the fuel lines, but that appears possible, as well."

"Get on it," Krysty said. "Jak and I will get the fuel."

"Capital!"

She walked to the rear of the wag, sliding around the seat.

Jak waited for her, handing her one of the trenching tools he held. "Got can, too." He pointed at the empty jerrican in the back. "Looks usable. Get under tank, puncture mebbe with knife, drain into can and carry to Doc."

"Sounds like a plan." Krysty took the shovel and walked out the back of the wag. Rounding the vehicle, stepping over two muties who'd almost been eviscerated by heavy-caliber rounds, she scanned the ridges, wary of anyone who might be waiting.

"Nobody," Jak said. "Animals starting creep back into area. They feel safe, we feel safe."

Krysty took the youth's word for it. Her senses weren't as sharp as Jak's, but they registered no threats waiting in the shadows. She put her foot on the rolled shoulder of the shovel blade and rammed it deeply into the sand. The sand moved easily, but there was a lot of it. She kept working as Jak fell in beside her, concentrating on the effort, knowing every shovelful put her that much closer to Ryan.

Chapter Twenty-Nine

"Welcome to Las Vegas," Mildred said, pressing her face against the bars covering the sides and back of the wag. The sun was going down, setting in ocher and amber behind them as they traveled east.

Ryan roused himself from semislumber against the cab of the wag and joined Mildred. J.B. got on the other side. The wag continued on across the bumpy road, jarring the occupants as it rolled along at forty or fifty miles per hour.

The remains of the entertainment city lay like a dying neon rose in the parched sand of the desert. Dozens of colors sprayed across the broken buildings jutting from the landscape, and seemed to be centered in the heart of the city.

"Skydark was hard on this burg," Mildred said. "It used to be something to look at."

"Been here?" J.B. asked.

Mildred nodded, her gaze glued on the city as they came down off the long, sweeping hills surrounding Vegas. "A couple visits. First time was when I was a college freshman. Sort of to get the bridle in my teeth and prove I could do anything I wanted to do."

Ryan ran his eye over the wreckage of the city, which hadn't taken direct hits from nukes like some of the larger metropolitan areas during the war. But the nukes that had claimed nearby silo sites had created enough particle drift to kill off most vegetation and animal life in the days and

weeks that followed. Very little had crept back into the area
to begin the struggle against the desert and leftover rad
spots. The terrain so far had been dull, echoing a depressing
monotony.

The city was far more interesting. There were some tall
buildings among the shorter ones, but the majority of space
was taken on the horizontal rather than the vertical, not like
Lantic Ocean coastal villes. At some point decades past,
quakes had riven Vegas, splintering it and leaving huge,
gaping cracks in the streets. The tectonic pressures had also
tumbled down most of the taller buildings.

Ryan glanced at the line of wags ahead of them, then the
few that followed. In the six days they'd been traveling,
there'd been no sign of Krysty or the others. Not all of the
six days had been necessary to make the trip, but Hardcoe
and LeMarck had made certain they were used. There'd
also been limited interaction with LeMarck, and none at all
with the baron. The sec commander treated them like valuable livestock.

"How well do you think you remember your way around
the ville?" he asked Mildred.

"Depends on where we go. Vegas is built on a strip
where all the action stayed. Provided the pit is located
somewhere in that, and the landmarks weren't too screwed
up by the quakes and whatever scavengers there might have
been, I can find my way around."

"Gives us an edge," Ryan said.

"Mighty slim one," J.B. acknowledged.

Ryan nodded. "Going to have to work with what we
have." He stayed at the bars, studying the ville as the convoy drew closer. According to LeMarck and what Ryan had
learned from the Heimdall Foundation men, the chilling
was scheduled to begin at midnight. He'd wondered about
that at first, trying to understand how they'd be able to

wander around in the dark and tell who was chilling who. But seeing the way the neon lights lit up the ville's inner core resolved that mystery.

All that remained was the living and the dying.

"IS THAT THE WAG housing our companions, Krysty?" Doc asked.

From their vantage point up above the narrow road that led down into Vegas, the red-haired woman adjusted the magnification on her binoculars. She brought the first few wags into focus, not recognizing anyone.

The first wag slowed to cross a narrow wooden bridge that linked the cracked remnants of the highway on either side of a twelve- or fifteen-foot fissure that looked almost as deep. Twilight made it harder to judge distances.

She moved back, scanning each wag in turn. She knew LeMarck by sight. During the last three of the six days they'd spent pursuing the convoy, she'd marked the sec commander's face, knowing him from the description Ryan and Bernsen had provided, the latter confirming it visually on one occasion.

The initial three days of the pursuit, the companions had traveled hell-bent for leather, having to circle around a few times to pick up the convoy's trail. A map of the southwestern United States, found in the overturned wag, had helped them considerably, but had been misleading at times, as well. When they'd caught up with Hardcoe's convoy, they'd had to slow down, waiting for an opportunity to free Ryan, J.B. and Mildred. It hadn't happened. The baron's sec men had kept too tight a rein on things. So Krysty and the others had remained tantalizingly close, but had been given no opportunity to steal their friends away without getting captured in the process.

Jak had come the closest to breaking into the camp, but

even he had almost been found out before he could get within a hundred yards of the wags. Sec men in hiding had sprung their trap too early. Jak had gotten away, but the episode had let them know Hardcoe's men considered Ryan and the others as bait, as well as a prize.

A few wags farther down the convoy, Krysty found their captured companions. She focused the binoculars on Ryan, his face visible to her. By his features she knew he was plotting and planning. He hadn't given up at all.

"It's them," she announced to the others. She wished she could tell her lover that they were there, at the very least offer him some words of encouragement. She put those thoughts from her mind and turned to what she could do.

"Ville pretty with lights. Baron must have lots gas and generators," Jak said. "Not know only chilling waiting inside."

"Well, against yon walls and phantasmal faery illuminations," Doc said, "we shall test our mettle and discover if we should be found yet wanting in purpose and desire."

Jak nodded and looked at Krysty. "Sec tight on bridge. How we cross?"

Krysty put the binoculars away. "On foot. There's no other choice. We'll carry as much gear as we can. Darkness should cover us well enough."

"We're just going to get caught," Bernsen said gloomily.

Jak popped the hood on the wag and took the starter coil, pocketing it. Krysty understood enough about mechanics to know that the wag couldn't start without the coil.

"Leave you here," the teenager offered.

Bernsen's mouth opened, and his eyes looked dead. "No." He mopped his forehead with his sleeve. "No, I'm afraid that won't do at all."

Krysty gazed at Jak and Doc. "Strip down your gear. Keep the weapons and medication, anything that will help once we reach Ryan and the others. Everything else we leave here."

"You realize someone may find the wag," the scientist interjected.

"Mebbe," Krysty said. "And mebbe they won't find it until the Big Game is over and we have the others out. Have to take the chance."

"This is, I've heard," Doc said, gazing at the ville of lights spread out before them, "certainly the place for taking chances and hoping for long shots to come through."

The stripping completed, Krysty asked Jak to take point and Doc to keep Bernsen under guard. Then they moved off into the night.

INSIDE VEGAS, the wag carrying Ryan, J.B. and Mildred split off from the others and rolled down the cracked and crumbled streets. A contingent of pedestrian sec men fell into a jog beside the wag, their gear rattling as they moved. Most of the street signs were up, and Mildred read them off with growing confidence. Several of the streets were too cracked up to be passable by wag. Two-by-twelve boards lay across the cracks, supported by piles of rock and bricks that had been gathered from the debris left by the tumbledown buildings.

The wag slowed as it made its way across the makeshift bridges. The boards creaked under the weight.

"I know where we're at," Mildred said.

"Where?" Ryan peered forward. The brightness of the neon lights increased and the range of colors incredible.

"South Las Vegas Boulevard," Mildred replied. "Back in my day, they called it the Strip." She pointed. "See? Over there is the MGM Theme Park."

Ryan peered in that direction, barely making out the
framework of the building. As his eye grew used to the
darkness to their right, he spotted the massive statue of a
lion toppled over in the street in front of the structure. The
huge head had broken off and was separated from its body
by dozens of yards. A scar tracked its right cheek, deep
and irregular enough to have been caused by a mortar
round.

On the north side of the building, perhaps as much as
fifty feet of railing stuck out from the ground floor and
traveled due north. Weeds, trees and brush had scrambled
up between the cracks of the broken streets and structures,
filling the neon-lit ville with clumps of forest.

"What's the railing?" he asked.

"Monorail," Mildred answered. "Used to run people
from the MGM to Bally's and back again. They made
plenty of places for tourists to drop their money."

Ryan fell silent again, keeping watchful. Opportunities
for escape would present themselves if he remained patient.
There was no way to force it. He read the signs of the
places and streets they passed, listening to Mildred talk to
J.B. about the things she'd seen over a hundred years ago.

A huge building with a glittering entranceway stood on
the edge of a precipice. Neon lights announced the name
as Bally's. Ryan figured it was the one Mildred had been
talking about, especially after he saw part of the monorail
sticking out from the side.

The wag swerved off the street, following a path beaten
through the growing brush and over built-up patches filling
the cracks in the ground. Ryan shifted, holding on to the
bars with one hand as he watched a steel door in the wall
before the wag. The steel door wasn't part of the original
building. It had been added sometime later. Rust covered

the facade, blending the dents and tears into a rugged sameness.

With a rough rasping of chain links rolling over a drum, the steel door went up in jerks. The wag driver came to a near stop, then edged forward until the door cleared the top of the vehicle. Inside the parking area beyond, Hayden LeMarck had a full complement of sec men armed to the teeth.

Light came from fluorescent tubes on the high ceiling, supplemented by oil lanterns hanging on the walls and carried by some of the sec men. LeMarck rushed over to the wag, calling out to his men and gathering them around him.

A large, burly man with hair sprouting across his shoulders leaped onto the back of the wag. He fitted a key into the lock and removed it, then whipped the door back. "Out," he ordered. "And if you try anything, we'll gut shoot you and leave you to die while some of those rabid mutie animals we've got penned up eat you."

Ryan led the way out of the wag. The steel door came down with a rush of chain and a clanging thump against the remnants of royal purple carpet over the concrete foundations. He signaled to J.B. with his fingers, telling the Armorer to stand and observe.

LeMarck stopped in front of Ryan, remaining out of easy reach. "Are you ready?"

Somewhere beyond the concrete wall in front of them, the sound of drums beating echoed into the room, accompanied by wild yells and the sound of animal cries. There were also mechanical noises, groaning and hissing that Ryan couldn't recognize.

"I have a choice?" Ryan asked dryly.

LeMarck smiled, but it wasn't a confident effort. He turned to one of the other men. "Get them suited up."

LESS THAN TEN MINUTES later, Ryan had been outfitted with
a scarlet armored bodysuit that covered his chest, stomach
and groin. He also had his holster, though empty of the
SIG-Sauer P-226, and pouches and pockets for ammo and
other gear.

The guards took Ryan, J.B. and Mildred up three flights
of stairs and down two different hallways until they found
Hayden LeMarck. The room was large, a public meeting
place of some kind, lit by oil lanterns hanging on wall
hooks that left soot patterns on the decorative walls. Ryan
reckoned it had been a gaudy of some type at one time,
judging from the shelves, remnants of mirrors and free-
standing bar against the back wall.

LeMarck stood in front of the opposite wall, which had
taken heavy damage in the past. Sledges had been used to
knock out sections of it, and glass panes had been puttied
in, creating a ten-foot-wide and six-foot-tall window that
looked out over some of the worst carnage in Vegas.

It looked as though a giant had stomped a footprint into
the center of the ville just beyond Bally's. Keeping his
sense of direction even after he'd been brought into the
building had been second nature for Ryan. He knew they
were facing north.

The neon glare of the ville was strongest at this point,
teeming with dozens of colors of differing intensities. The
lights slammed against the windows, all of them offset from
the others, and created prism effects that spun out over
Ryan, J.B., Mildred and the nearest sec men. LeMarck
looked as if he were standing in front of a burst rainbow.

He addressed them with a military bearing, hands clasped
behind his back. "You people have been given a great
honor," he stated, "to be selected as Baron Hardcoe's
champions."

J.B. spit on the floor. The spittle splattered over the sec commander's boots.

Color rouged LeMarck's face, but he maintained his calm and ignored the act. "In a few minutes you're going to be released into that pit." He pointed through the glass wall. "Quakes dropped the center of this area years ago. The barons all worked together to build the restraining wall around the outside of the pit area and to rebuild some of the things inside. Like the neon lights."

Ryan could barely make out the metal wall created from pieced-together slabs of concrete and sections of metal.

"You can't get over it," LeMarck said. "It's forty-feet tall. Barbed wire strands circle the top another six feet over that. Concrete was poured on top of the wall beneath the wire, and glass, nails and shards of metal were mixed into it. Even if you found rope and a grappling hook, and could throw it that high, the rope would be cut by the glass and shards on top of the wall. Not to mention the fact that you'd be perfect targets for the snipers along the outer perimeter."

Staring back through the window, Ryan glimpsed two of the guards in the foreground, obviously walking predetermined areas.

"Whose guards?" Ryan asked.

LeMarck smiled, obviously pleased. "Thinking, are you? Good, I like that. Knew the survival instinct would kick in along the way." He glanced out the window. "The guards are from all the barons' camps, with overlapping fields of fire, on the pit fighters, as well as one another." He shifted his attention back to Ryan. "In years past one of the barons had the idea of using a couple of his wall guards as snipers. They had silenced weapons, thought they wouldn't be noticed. But they were. And they were shot. For every man they shot, one of that baron's men was shot. The two that were left over didn't last long."

"You said there'd be ten of us," Mildred stated.

LeMarck nodded. "And there will be. I wanted to talk to the three of you. You're used to working as a unit. Got a lot of hard miles on you, from the look of you. Saw how you went through those brushwooders. The other seven aren't going to be much help, I'm afraid. Unless you can convince them to listen to you."

Ryan didn't say anything.

"I figure it'd be a waste of time," the sec commander said. "They're going to be scared, not wanting to listen to anyone."

"What's in the pit," J.B. asked, "besides the other teams?"

"Muties—scabbies and stickies," LeMarck answered. "Animals, some of them mutie and some of them not. Four-legged. Snakes. Got some water traps in there with poisonous eels, piranha, anything nasty that could live and kill in that environment."

"If we win," Ryan asked, "we're going to be set free?"

LeMarck lied without hesitation, Ryan not seeing a flicker of guilt in the man's eyes. "Yes."

Chapter Thirty

"How much do you know about the Five Barons and the seven villes?" the sec commander asked. He checked his wrist chron.

"Man whose team wins this," Ryan said, "gets control of the seven villes for a year." He didn't give a damn about any of the history of the Big Game. Hoyle and Bernsen had provided enough of it. Once he stepped out into that pit, it was chill or be chilled.

"What about Baron Sparning Hardcoe?"

"I was told he's one of the more efficient chillers in the group," Ryan replied. "Runs second to Baron Connrad in numbers of his private army."

"There's more to Baron Hardcoe than that," LeMarck stated.

"Yeah," J.B. said. "I can see how he'd give folks that impression, what with the way he invites some of them to play this game for him."

The sec commander looked angry and defensive. "The baron is building docks and boats in the seven villes. Building up trade along the northern Cific coastline. People are moving into the villes now, instead of working to stay away from them. There's work there, homes, mebbe a future if they all pull together."

"And he's doing all of this out of the goodness of his soul," Mildred said sarcastically.

"I'm trying to give you something to fight for. What's

at stake is bigger than just the people in this room. I want you to see that."

Ryan fixed him with a harsh stare. "If you believe in what Hardcoe's doing so much, why don't you go get nine other people who can fight and believe in the baron as much as you, and you jokers take a dive into that pit tonight."

LeMarck's lips tightened as though he'd just bitten into a sour lemon. He didn't try to answer.

"Got plenty to fight for," J.B. added. "Our lives are on the line here. That's enough for us. And when you boil it down, that's what's good enough for most people. I don't give a rat's ass about docks or boats or trade. Hardcoe's planning on making plenty of jack out of the deal or he wouldn't be doing it. And it's the jack he's got a greedy eye turned to, not the people you say are going to benefit by it."

LeMarck's face hardened. "Move out. Only got a few minutes before they start releasing you people into the pit."

A SHORT WALK LATER, through musty hallways outside rooms that were filled with wrecked furniture, overturned gambling tables and skeletons that had died of rad-drift, Ryan stood in the center of a smaller room lined with metal walls.

LeMarck and his men left them there, bolting the door behind them.

The ceiling had been torn out, leaving an upper level where people could look down on them. A short railing covered with wrapped lengths of razor wire surrounded the opening. In a short time LeMarck was at the railing gazing at them.

A net was suspended from the ceiling above the sec boss,

a length of steel cable running through a pulley system holding it in place.

"Our weapons," J.B. said.

"That's right," LeMarck replied, raising his voice to manage the distance. "Figured you might give a better accounting of yourselves if you had the tools you were most familiar with. You'll find they've been well taken care of, and there's ample ammunition for all of them."

"What happens when we run out?" Mildred asked.

"Hopefully you'll be sparing with it and pick your targets," LeMarck told her. "Along the way you'll find you can pick up more from the other teams. Assuming that you've killed them. And there are caches where more ammunition has been placed."

Ryan stared at the double doors in front of him that undoubtedly led into the pit. He crossed the distance and pushed against them. Neither moved.

"Bring the rest of them in," LeMarck ordered.

A moment later seven men entered the room. All of them had a look of hardness, but it was the black giant, his hair tied with bits of cloth, who captured Ryan's attention.

The black man's eyes held yellow madness, like someone who had traveled too long in the rad-blasted lands. His hands were secured behind him. One of LeMarck's sec men moved in behind him and keyed open the cuffs. Giving no warning, the black giant turned and backhanded the sec man.

The man flew through the air and crumpled against the wall by the door, unconscious or dead. Blood trickled from his ears.

"Black Michael!" LeMarck yelled.

The giant ignored the sec commander and leaped to the door, trying to pry it open with his thick fingers. The other

six new arrivals quickly put distance between themselves
and the big man.

"Stop, you bastard, and move away from that door, or I
swear I'll chill you myself." LeMarck drew his side arm.

Black Michael growled insanely. "Do that and you'll be
a man short."

"Mebbe."

Ryan wasn't fooled. LeMarck meant his threat, but there
was some hesitation in the sec commander.

Black Michael barked laughter, but moved away from
the door just the same. He reached up to his shoulders and
started pulling on his armor's straps. The vest he wore
hadn't been intended for a man of his girth. The outfitters
had obviously had a hard time finding something he could
wear. The red paint looked fresh.

"Leave that on," LeMarck ordered.

"Fuck you," the giant roared. The straps gave with long
tearing noises, and the body armor dropped to the floor. His
naked chest, shoulders and abdomen rippled with sweat-
slick muscles. "If I'm gonna die, I'm gonna die my way.
Shirt makes too much color in the night. Like this, no one
see me."

LeMarck said nothing, stepping aside as five men moved
into view at the railing. One of them Ryan recognized as
Hardcoe. He guessed the others were barons, as well. All
of them had bands tied around their left biceps. Hardcoe's
was red. The other colors were purple, orange, green and
blue.

"I count nine in your color, Hardcoe," a baron with
green on his arm stated. Blue-jay feathers hung from his
earrings, and his face looked carved from angry stone.

"The tenth man refuses to wear his armor, Baron Connrad," LeMarck said.

"Rules say the champions are supposed to wear their

color," Connrad said. "Keep down confusion on who's who."

"No," Hardcoe said coolly, "the rules don't say that. As to confusion, take a look at this man. I don't think there'll be any confusion with him."

Connrad scowled but said nothing more. The group passed on.

LeMarck looked relieved. At his command two men stepped into the room and grabbed the man Black Michael had hit, pulling him out.

Grinning, the giant crossed the room to Mildred. "Black, like me," he said, looking down at her.

"Black," Mildred agreed, not backing away, "but not like you at all."

Black Michael raised a hand as if he were about to slap her.

"No," J.B. said, stepping forward into a combat stance, his hands loose and ready before him.

Laughing, Black Michael turned to face the Armorer. He dwarfed J.B. in height and in build. "You think you mean enough to take me, little man?"

"Up to you whether we find out," J.B. replied.

"Break you in half like a stick."

The Armorer didn't make a reply, slowly reaching out and moving Mildred behind him out of the big man's zone.

"This man something special to you?" Black Michael asked Mildred.

She didn't answer.

"You don't have to tell me," the giant said. "I can see in your eyes. Mebbe I'll catch up to you and him out there in the dark and those pretty lights. I twist his head, and you can hear how his neck cracks and see him jump when he dies." He laughed again, an evil sound that filled the small room.

J.B. continued guiding Mildred away from the man, never turning his back to Black Michael.

"Wait for me out in the dark, little man," the giant promised, "and I'll be there soon."

"Ryan," the Armorer called, wrapping an arm around Mildred. The woman shuddered against him.

"Extra baggage," Ryan said in a flat voice. "See no sense in taking it along."

J.B. nodded.

Black Michael ignored them.

Up above, LeMarck's sec team raised two sheets of see-through plas and braced it with four-by-four beams, booting them together in an L-shape.

"Lower the weapons," the sec commander ordered.

The cable creaked as it was fed through the pulley, and the net descended into the room. Ryan, J.B. and Mildred were the first to reach the net as it came within grasp. The other men came swiftly, shoving at one another to claim their weapons.

J.B. reached into the net and pulled his S&W scattergun from the collection. Black Michael surged forward, swatting men out of his way without a care. Moving quickly but without mistake, the Armorer opened the shotgun's receiver. Ryan spotted the red casing of the round sliding home as J.B. released it.

Ryan took up his own P-226 and worked the slide, stripping the first round into the chamber. As he watched, Black Michael picked up a huge revolver. From the size of it, Ryan guessed it was a remake of a .454 Casull, large by any standard, but looking small in the ebony giant's fist.

Without warning, J.B. shoved the shotgun's muzzle into Black Michael's face, and pulled the trigger.

The ebony giant's pistol hand had been moving toward the Armorer, but when the explosion of fléchettes slammed into his face and ripped away the flesh, diving in through the eye holes, the nasal cavity, and the mouth, emptying out his brain pan in a crimson-and-gray rush, the hand flopped lifelessly away. The Casull clanked as it hit the floor.

"What the hell are you doing?" LeMarck demanded.

The blast from J.B.'s shotgun was still echoing in the room.

Ryan fired two shots, aiming for LeMarck's heart. He wasn't surprised to see them leave splintered fractures across the surface of the plas but not penetrate.

Two sec men stepped around the edges of the plas, only exposing enough of themselves to aim their weapons into the room below.

"No!" LeMarck screamed, raising his weapon.

J.B. fired another round. A few of the fléchettes became embedded in the plas, but the majority of them caught the sec man in the shoulder and arm, spinning him, his flesh in tatters.

LeMarck blew out the back of the other sec man's head. Brain matter splattered across the plas in a red gush. Most of the remaining sec men appeared confused.

"Leave them alone!" the sec boss ordered. "Any man raises a weapon against them dies by my hand!"

The sec men calmed down grudgingly.

"What the hell do you think you're doing?" LeMarck demanded.

"Man wasn't going to work with us," Ryan said. "Figured we weren't going to let him work against us, either."

"You stupe son of a bitch!" LeMarck roared. "You've got one less man to fight for the baron!"

"Tell the baron he's always welcome to join in, fight for himself," Ryan replied. Then he turned to the other six men, ignoring the sec boss. "How many of you want to take a chance on getting out of here alive?"

Two of them answered immediately, while the other four remained silent. After a moment one of them asked, "Why the hell should we join up with you? Way I understand it, it's every man for himself out there."

"Mebbe," Ryan agreed, "but if you aren't working with me, then I'll put my sights on you when I see you. Work with me, mebbe we can find a way clear of here."

"Have you seen that wall?" the man asked. "Fuck, ain't no way we're going to climb that."

"In or out?" Ryan asked. Though he kept the barrel pointing down, he swiveled the SIG-Sauer in the man's direction.

"Don't give a feller much choice," the man stated.

"Choices ended the minute Hardcoe's people dropped you in this hellpit," Mildred said. Her own Czech target pistol was in her hand.

"Lady's right, Owen," one of the other undecided men admitted. "If we don't throw in with him, it mebbe means going up against him in the end. Seems to know his business all right. Mebbe with him we'll have a chance of getting clear of this once and for all with a whole skin."

Another man agreed after Owen nodded.

The fourth man said, "Fuck, that still leaves us going up against him in the end." He glanced around at his comrades. His words carried weight.

"Don't have to be that way," Ryan said.

"You see any other way for it?" the man asked.

"Yeah," Ryan said tightly. "All of us getting out of here."

"Mister, I don't know where you're from, and don't even give a fuck, but you got to know one thing from the get-go. Ain't nobody never escaped from the pit once they were shut up in it.''

Ryan regarded the man. "You mean, nobody yet."

"He's got brass, Fielding," Owen said. "Got to give him that." He turned to Ryan. "I'm Owen. This's Fielding. Two skinny jaspers in the back are Tyler and Taylor Thompson. Twins, if you ain't made that out yet. Heavy guy's Moosh Whandell. And that leaves Clingdon."

Ryan quickly introduced himself and the others.

"You people know each other?" he asked when he'd finished.

Owen shook his head. "The twins knew either other. The rest of us met on the wag. Knew Black Michael's name 'cause the sec guards were always having a hard time with him. Heard he bit a man's cock off in Jakestown before they put him on the wag and brought him out here. Bastard sick son of a bitch."

"Know what we're up against?"

"Some of it. Sec men liked trying to scare the shit out of us telling us stories."

"Start off figuring it's all gospel," Ryan said, "we'll find out the truth of it as we go along. We're going out there together. You move when I say move, where I say move, and you move damn fast."

"You know something we don't?" Fielding asked. "That why you were getting such special treatment?"

"Hell," Ryan said, "I'd never even heard of the villes or the Big Game little over a week ago."

"So this is all new to you," Fielding said. "Why should we listen to you?"

"This pit's new to me," Ryan said, "but chilling isn't." He made his voice hard, abrasive. The other men could be an advantage, and he wanted to win them over. "There's a certain safety in numbers."

A siren ripped through the cavernous upper floor, startling several of the sec men who'd been peering anxiously down into the lower floor.

"Open the doors!" LeMarck said. "It's time!"

Chains ratcheted in their housings as the wheels above were turned. The double metal doors drew apart by inches at a time. In short order the light from inside the room spilled onto the wreckage of buildings soaking up the neon glamour of the Five Barons' private killing ground.

Ryan stepped forward, the SIG-Sauer in his fist as he scanned the edges of the wall less than ten feet higher than his present position. Moonlight and neon reflected from the keen edges of the razor wire looped around the poles set on top of the wall surrounding the quake-sunk area. Other patches gleamed, as well. Upon closer inspection, Ryan identified them as glass and sharp bits of metal.

Even with the brief running start that was possible from the lip of the room jutting over the grounds below, Ryan knew he'd fall short of the wall, and not get the height he needed to grab the top. He glanced at the ground. The terrain had been shaped over the years, falling away as much as fifteen feet in a direct fall, then sloping away to the floor of the pit.

He raked his gaze around the pit and thought he could see two other groups making the jump into the battlezone to the west of them. He also spotted some bulky shapes moving casually through the dark, and some feline ones, as well. Something hungry snarled out its warning, building up its courage.

"Get outside!" LeMarck yelled.

"Fucker can't make us do that," Fielding said.

As if he'd heard the man, the sec commander made a show of pulling a pin on a gren, counting down, then dropping it into the room. It smacked against the concrete floor.

"Move!" Ryan ordered as he stepped off the edge of the building. He dropped fast, landing on spongy ground, his knees giving as he dealt with the sudden stop. Mildred and J.B. were on his heels. The other six men dropped only a heartbeat or two later.

Then the gren blew, spewing forth chunks of Black Michael that rained all over the terrain. Something in a pool of water only a few yards away reared up, seized one of the ebony giant's hands in its sharp teeth and pulled it into the mud-colored liquid.

Overhead the doors closed, cutting off any hope they might have had about using the room as an escape hatch later.

Ryan watched, waving his group back while the rectangle of light coming from the room closed off and disappeared. He looked at his friends, perspiration already making his skin slick under the armor.

"J.B.," he said, "you've got point. Mildred, you're behind him, leading these men." He made sure Fielding and the others heard. "I'm walking slack."

They all nodded.

"Weapons out," Ryan said. "Safeties on until I tell you otherwise. We're going to keep a low profile for as long as we can. Kill quick and kill silent if we get the chance. Those other teams can take each other out for a while. They do it proper and really work on it, mebbe they can cut down the odds for us."

When there were no questions, Ryan gave the order to move out. They sank into the shadows, listening to the first of the firefights break the natural rhythms of the night creatures gathered in the pit.

Chapter Thirty-One

Ryan stayed ten yards ahead of his group, panga in his right hand. Screams echoed all around him, punctuated by single shots and by short bursts from automatic weapons. Residual heat contained in the pit, whether from atmospheric conditions or from some other source, covered him with perspiration. His clothing stuck to his skin. Insects, including some of the largest mosquitoes he'd seen since his trek through Minnesota, swarmed him, darted at his eyes, danced on his exposed flesh and penetrated his clothing not covered by the armor.

Most of the neon lights were mounted on the buildings on either side of the cracked street twenty yards to their left. A few of the buildings were whole, but most of them were smashed. Whoever had put the lights back into operation had known something about electrical work. Fields of brightly colored illumination overlapped one another, creating even more tints, ripping away even the blackest shadows.

Glancing up at the wall forty feet above him, twenty feet above the nearest and tallest tree, Ryan saw the perimeter guards walking their assigned posts. Killing them from the distance was simple enough, especially with the Steyr slung over his back. But it didn't give them a way out.

He moved on, looping around a collection of busted and rusted wags. Something shifted inside, giving Ryan the only warning he received. He backed away a half step from the vehicle as a serpent's head shot out of the dark recesses.

The snake's mouth was open wide, jaws distended and fangs glistening bone white.

Ryan raked the panga through the thick neck behind the wedge-shaped head, decapitating it. Operating on nerve reflex, the rest of the snake's thirty-foot body came coiling out of the burned wag. Bleeding profusely from the stump, the serpent's body writhed on the ground, leaving black splatter patterns.

"Ryan!" Mildred called.

"I'm okay," he called back, scanning the wag for any further movement as the snake continued to flop around. Nothing else appeared. He took up point again, then noticed the shifting shadows under a series of forked branches from a fifteen-foot-tall spruce.

The back of Ryan's neck tightened, feeling eyes on him now. A gleam of metal flickered, picking up a purple and then a turquoise haze from the neon lights surrounding them. He reached down for the SIG-Sauer, moving sideways so his blaster hand was away from them.

Then branches cracked over Ryan's head. A massive feline head shook as the big animal regained purchase and leaped at him.

Clearing the blaster of leather, Ryan barely had time to yell a warning to the others before he was dodging, trying to get clear of the big mutie cat that was determined to drop on top of him.

DEAN GLANCED UP at the second story through the hole that had been chopped through the ceiling of the first-floor room he was in. Baron Vinge Connrad's sec teams poured liquid into the room from a fifty-five-gallon drum. It sloshed and sparkled in noisy glugs as it splashed against the wall and the floor.

The sharp, sweet odor told Dean what it was in a single drawn breath. "Gasoline!" he yelled to the other boys. They all retreated to the farthest wall.

Perry had drawn back, separating himself from the rest of the group even though he wore the same green armored vest as the rest of them.

Dean pressed against the double doors that would open onto the pit area. He was tired from seven days of travel, of constantly looking along their backtrail to see if his dad or some of Brody's sec people were following. In all that time he'd seen no one. Now his nerves were stretched tight as catgut on a bow. Adrenaline surged inside him again, though, as the gasoline pooled around their feet.

"Dirty fuckers!" Louis railed, his blond hair plastered to his skull by the heat that had stifled them in the room. "You brought us all this way just to set us on fire? That it?"

Dean felt like yelling, too, but he knew it would have been just out of fear, and he didn't want to give them that. He leveled his Browning Hi-Power. Solomon had stolen it out of Nicholas Brody's safe, proving that the phys-ed teacher hadn't planned on going back to the school after the transaction, and had given it to their captors with an explanation that it was Dean's personal weapon. Vinge Connrad had been pleased to discover that Dean had such a weapon, and had made returning the weapon a presentation just before the other boys were armed.

Squeezing the trigger, Dean fired at the sec boss now brandishing an unlighted torch. The bullet plunked into the see-through plas sheet on a tangent that would have put it squarely between his target's eyes.

The sec boss nearly fell over himself trying to get away,

then glared at the misshapen chunk of lead hanging in front of him.

"What the hell do you think you're doing?" Ethan Perry demanded. He pushed himself off the wall and came at Dean.

Shifting the blaster to cover Perry, Dean said, "Don't." One word, delivered hard, gave the implicit understanding there'd be no negotiations.

"Back off," Louis ordered, moving into position beside Dean, his pistol in both hands but not pointed at anyone.

Perry made a move to pull his own blaster.

"No," Louis said to Perry. "You do it and I'll put you down myself."

"Stupe fucker's going to set off the gasoline shooting that damn gun," Perry complained.

"He does, they do," Louis said, "you really give a shit which way it goes?"

Connrad's sec boss laughed. "You little boys got more sand in you than I'd have thought. Mebbe the baron did have the right idea."

"Ceiling up there is made of metal and concrete," Dean whispered to Louis. "Bullets'll bounce pretty damn good. Figure the angles right, that bulletproof glass won't do dick for them."

Louis gave him a tight nod. "Better than dying in here with nothing done." He raised his voice.

"Moxen?"

"Yeah?"

"Cover Perry. He moves, tries to pull his blaster, gun him down and be done with it."

"You got it." Moxen lifted his .45 and pointed it at Perry's chest. An evil grin tightened the big youth's round face.

Dean went one way, his boots slapping through the gaso-

line, leaving Louis circling around the other. When he had
the angle he wanted, Dean fired the Browning rapidly, zip-
ping rounds past the empty space not covered by the heavy
bulletproof plas.

The sec man laughed, pointing down at the boys. That
stopped when one of the sec men caught a flattened and
slowed bullet that cored through the side of his head and
tore his jaw off. The others were in shock, watching as the
dying man collapsed against the plas with blood spraying
from his ruined face. The man tore the plas sheet from the
grips of the men who were struggling to hold it stable.
Released, the plas came crashing down into the lower room,
sending up geysers from the inch-deep gasoline pool that
had gathered across the floor.

Dean continued firing, driving the sec men back, taking
down two more of them. The other boys joined them in
blasting the sec team.

Curses and screams of pain rewarded their combined efforts, the blasting and the voices almost covering over the
shrill buzz of the siren. The double doors abruptly jerked
open just as Vinge Connrad appeared behind the single
remaining plas sheet. He had his blaster in hand and was
scowling down into the room. His eyes locked with Dean's.

"You arrogant little whelp!" the baron snarled. "I might
have known you'd be ringleading this!"

Dean exchanged his empty clip for a fresh one, careful
to place the expended one in his pants pocket. His dad had
been a stickler about saving anything that could be used
again. Especially if it was hard to come by. He thumbed
the slide release and stripped the first round into the chamber.

The double doors gaped completely open. Gasoline
dripped over the edge, then began a cascade even though
the drum had emptied.

Raising his blaster, Dean put three rounds into the plas
sheet in front of Connrad's face.

The baron grinned, not worried at all that the bullets
might penetrate. "You do me proud, boy. Truly you do.
Now you haul ass out there and kill everything you can.
Don't let your guard down even for a moment, because
they're all going to be out to kill you."

Dean sidestepped, keeping up the Hi-Power, finding a
new angle to bounce bullets. He started firing as soon as
the muzzle cleared the plas sheet. Bullets skidded from the
walls and whizzed through the ranks of the sec men, driving
them to the ground again. Out of his peripheral vision,
Dean watched the hot brass drop into the gasoline, make
the liquid sizzle just a second, then sink.

"That's it, boy," Connrad said. "Keep that spirit." He
took out a self-light, scratched it to life on his jeans, then
applied it to a torch he got from one of his sec men. "Get
moving. Fly or fry."

The torch caught easily. The baron let it burn for a moment, giving the flames time to grow stronger.

"Dean," Louis said, "time to go." Some of the other
boys were already dropping over the side. Perry was among
them.

Stubbornly Dean tried to manage a new angle, reading
the way the walls and ceiling were set up.

Without another word, Connrad pitched the torch out
into the open. Sparks peeled back off it as it dropped,
smoke coiling in the trail it made through the empty air.

Dean turned and ran for the double doors. Louis was
waiting, his face pale with fear, eyes reflecting the falling
torch.

As Dean reached the double doors, blinking his eyes trying to get some of his night vision in place, he was aware
of the gasoline bursting into fiery movement behind him.

He turned his head only slightly, pounding his feet hard against the concrete floor and trying not to think about slipping and falling into the gasoline.

A wave of blue flames, turning yellow on the ends from the richness of the fuel, trailed him to the double doors.

Louis leaped from the edge out into the night.

Dean had a brief impression of buildings, concrete sidewalks and streets that seemed to be choking on underbrush. Then he launched himself out into space, fear causing his heart to bang against his ribs as if it were going to tear through his breastbone.

Gravity took over and he fell. Before he made it to the ground, the flames rushed through the double doors after him. Coiling, the fire followed the stream of gasoline from the doors down the fifteen feet to the ground. Along the way it ignited spatters in the air, turning them into fizzy comets. Most of them died out before hitting bottom.

The flames also set Dean's gasoline-saturated boots on fire. He felt the heat flare up around his calves, scorching his pant legs.

When the fire hit the ground, it instantly spread across the gasoline pooled at the base of the room at Bally's, lighting up the area at once.

Seeing his flaming boots, Dean landed hard and stamped them, trying to put out the fire. Ahead of him and a few yards to his right, he spotted a bowl of water nearly three yards across. He ran to the water, knowing it would be only seconds before the flames exhausted the gasoline clinging to his boots and started burning the footwear itself. There was no way he could do without boots.

He didn't stop running until he was almost knee-deep in the pool. White smoke curled up from the surface as the fire extinguished with hisses.

A bullet whizzed by Dean's head, sounding like a large

buzzing insect. A heartbeat later the sound of the initial shot cracked over them. By then the second bullet was already on its way. Enrique Green howled and went down on his butt, grabbing at his left leg.

Dean whirled, changing clips in his blaster. He hunkered down in the water, wanting to make sure there was no chance the fire on his boots would restart.

Green was on the ground holding his left leg, bright blood staining his left thigh while Moxen and Louis grabbed his arms. Together they dragged the boy to cover behind a stand of trees. Bobby Handley already had a strip of cloth torn from his own shirt ready to make a compress to cover the wound.

"Anybody see the son of a bitch did this?" Louis demanded.

"I got him," Jordie Ferguson announced calmly. The boy lay behind a wag lying on its side, a sniper rifle extended before him, snugged into his shoulder. "Tree out there. How far?"

Still low in the water, his backside almost touching the surface, Dean glanced at the tree Jordie was talking about. It was obvious, because a bright muzzle-flash blinked on and off again. The third round dug a hole in the muddy ground near Green's position.

"Hundred and twenty, hundred and forty yards," Dean called out.

"Which one?" Ferguson asked, working the range marking on his telescopic sight.

"Split the difference," Louis yelled, "and knock that guy's lights out before he kills one of us!"

Ferguson lifted the rifle, then squeezed off a shot, quickly working the bolt action and readying another round. The second bullet wasn't necessary. In the distance the sniper dropped from the tree without a sound.

Dean started to move from the water, but something rubbery and strong wrapped around his leg and wouldn't let him move. Glancing down, he heard a snuffling of loosed breath breaking through water, then a gray body rose up, pulled along by the arm-leg gripping Dean.

It was a mutie of some kind. That was all Dean knew for sure. The thing had five rubbery limbs nearly six feet in length at first glance. Then he realized one of the limbs had eyes, three of them, spaced in a triangular shape. In the center was an algae-covered shell that looked whole, then opened up into a teeth-filled mouth big enough for Dean to shove his head into.

Two more limbs roped around the boy's left arm and his neck, pulling the mouth toward his abdomen. Jaws extended, filled with razor-sharp ivory, reaching for Dean's flesh.

Raising his blaster, the boy felt his breath lock tight in his chest. He fired several rounds, blowing chunks of the shell away from the creature, sending the jaws retreating. As the limbs withdrew from their tight embrace, he put three more rounds through the appendage with the eyes.

The mutie beast screamed as it released Dean and slid back into the dark water. Blood floated on top of the water like an oil slick, throwing off patterns that picked up the garish neon lighting surrounding the pit.

"Hot pipe!" Dean said, backing out of the water with his blaster pointing at the pool. He was shaking, but tried to get over it quick. He wished he knew if the thing were still alive, then decided it didn't really matter, because he wasn't going close to any more basins. He joined the other boys.

Louis was staring intently at the terrain. "Remember how Solomon used to say that every battlefield was like a chessboard?" he asked.

Dean didn't remember, so he figured it was something the phys-ed teacher had talked about with the ten original members of the team. But the others nodded.

"Always said the best place to take was the high ground," Louis went on. He stabbed a finger through the darkness. "That, I figure, is about the highest ground we could take."

Following the direction the blond youth was pointing, Dean made out the red neon lights proclaiming The Mirage. More glittering sputtered in front of the immense building. He squinted his eyes, not daring to believe what he was seeing, then recognized that his eyes hadn't played tricks on him. Five, possibly six stories up on the building, water gushed out, creating falls that fell somewhere in front of it, lost in trees and foliage.

"Place is huge," Conor commented. "Be hard to hold."

Louis nodded. "We're not going to try to hold the whole thing. We'll just find a place inside it that we can hold, wait things out and make them come to us."

"Supposed to be chilling these people out here," Green said, his face showing the pain he was in.

Louis looked at him. "That what you want to do, Enrique? Start wandering around finding people and things to chill? This isn't a shooting gallery. Me, I'm just wanting to get out of here with as much of my own skin intact as I can."

"Said they'd chill us if we didn't fight." Green indicated the wound in his leg, then jerked a thumb back at the gasoline fire still coiling out of the room they'd been forced to evacuate. "I believe them."

Louis made his face hard, sweeping the faces of his friends with his gaze. "I don't figure they're planning on letting any of us out of here. And that's the truth. We never even heard about these Five Barons and their seven villes until a few days ago. Hell, we didn't know anything about Solomon, either. If they let us go, they'd know they were in for some trouble from mebbe our parents. Mebbe us on down the line. Safe jack's just to kill us and be done with it.''

"You got a mean way of putting things," Bobby Handley said.

"Mean world," Louis replied.

"Best way is like Louis said," Dean spoke up. "Chill anybody we have to, but keep an eye out for a chance to get out of this place."

Louis nodded. "Anybody want to do it another way, they're welcome to pick up and leave."

No one said anything, but most of them shuffled nervously, flinching when they heard a sudden spurt of gunfire to the east of them. For a moment Dean almost thought it was his dad's SIG-Sauer blaster. Then he shoved the idea away. It was just a hope that he had no business nursing along. His dad was a long way from this place.

Chapter Thirty-Two

Hayden LeMarck stood behind Baron Hardcoe's chair and stared out the bulletproof window. His hand rested on his Glock blaster, the restraining strap already popped open enough that a yank would have it in his hand. Wallis Thoroughgood stood at his side, eating a turkey drumstick from the kitchen that had been set up outside the room.

The other barons sat in chairs in front of the window, as well, two sec men allowed in with each of them.

The window gave a view of the pit that had been created of the quake-stricken area. LeMarck watched the sporadic gunfire dispassionately, making himself breathe regular enough to appear calm. For the past handful of years, he'd remained on watch in the room during the Big Game. No experience was ever the same as a previous one.

"Boys?" Baron Dettwyler drawled, pausing to glance at Vinge Connrad, who was safely out of arm's reach. "You sent boys into that pit, Vinge? Were you addled when you made that decision?"

Connrad hoisted a glass filled with a native beer Hardcoe had brought from the seven villes in weather-beaten casks. Though the barons had separate views on how rulership of the villes should be managed, they all kept the beer makers and wine presses moving right along, no matter in whose hands the villes were.

Taking a long drink, Connrad wiped the foam from his beard with the back of his hand and belched loudly. "You haven't seen those boys in action. Trying to get them out into the pit, they chilled four of my men in that room, injured seven others before we chased them out with burning gasoline.''

"They shot bullets through the plas sheets?'' Dettwyler asked. He was a huge, fat man with a bald head, and many people, LeMarck knew, made the mistake of thinking Dettwyler soft or simple. Neither was the truth. The fat disguised hard bands of muscle, and Dettwyler had a preference for biting out the throat of anyone he fought in hand-to-hand combat. A black silk half mask covered the right side of his face. Years back the baron's head had been forced up against a boiling-water container in a mutie encampment. The metal had contained some dangerous rad, hanging on from the nukecaust. The burn had opened Dettwyler's face, and the rad that seeped into it caused chronic cancers that had to be cut out, leaving a raw, bleeding area that never healed properly.

"Not through the plas,'' Connrad corrected. "Little bastards bounced bullets off the wall.''

"I've never seen or heard of that being done.'' Francis Giskard's youthful face broke into a delighted smile. He raised his glass. "I must compliment you on your choice of champions this year. They appear to be most industrious.''

Connrad lifted his glass and drank the rest of its contents.

"Where did you get them?'' Giskard asked.

LeMarck kept track of the conversations, but his eyes remained focused on the pit area. One of the wall sec men near the old Las Vegas Convention Center raised a flash with a purple lens cover, signaling twice. They had thermographic binoculars and could see a person's body heat through the walls of buildings. Special rad buttons inside the body armor, treated so they reflected different levels of light, announced the color of the person they looked at.

"It appears that you've lost a couple more men, Giskard," Deke Ramsey, the remaining baron, said. He was tall and ruddy, his rust red hair shot through with gray and thinning on the top. "That brings your total lost to what? Five?"

"Four," Giskard said easily. "And might I remind you, I need only one to win." He leaned forward and slid two more purple beads across the free-standing abacus on the low table in front of him. "Connrad, I await your answer."

"You can wait on it," Connrad growled. "It's my secret."

LeMarck flicked his eyes toward the pit, searching the valleys cut through the shadows by the strings of neon lights. He got only a glimpse of the boys in their green body armor, then they faded under the tree coverage. It was no great feat of intellect that they were on their way to the Mirage. He smiled to himself, knowing they would find plenty of surprises in the building. Connrad, who was the only baron among them who hadn't had to shift a bead yet, would be doing that in short order. Perhaps it would be a lot of beads. LeMarck waited in anticipation.

"Usually the mortality rate runs much higher at this point of the game," Dettwyler said. "Perhaps we didn't include enough beasts and muties this year."

"There's plenty," Hardcoe replied. "People we've got out there, they're better chillers than most."

All the barons nodded, then Dettwyler yelled out for more pitchers of beer to be brought.

"Something I want to ask you, Giskard," Connrad said.

"Ask away, my friend."

"Assuming that you by some freak of accident manage to win, what do you plan on doing with the seven villes?"

"I plan on living a life of luxury for a year," Giskard replied. "I'm painfully overdue, as you're well aware."

"Wasn't talking about that," Connrad said. "I was talking about the construction that Hardcoe's managed this year."

LeMarck felt a tremor of anxiety thrill through him. The statement confirmed that Connrad did have spies among their people at the seven villes. And he hadn't found all of them. He cursed silently.

"An intelligent man would take what I've started," Hardcoe said in a soft voice, "and keep on building."

Connrad whipped his head around. "That's what you think?"

"Yeah."

"You saying I'm not an intelligent man?" Connrad demanded.

LeMarck shifted in response to the new stances assumed by the sec men behind Connrad. His hand closed hard around the butt of the Glock.

"Didn't say that," Hardcoe said flatly.

"I think you did."

Hardcoe shrugged. His pistol was in his lap, LeMarck knew, barely covered by a red cloth napkin with white dice showing black pips on the faces. "Up to you what you think."

Connrad showed wolf's teeth, a rictus devoid of anything near human emotion, showing only cold calculation. Then he laughed raucously. "Better hope you win, Sparning, because I'm going to burn you out if you don't. And that's a promise."

Out on the wall, a sec man raised a flash with a red lens. It blinked on and off.

LeMarck surprised himself by holding his breath, waiting for the lens to flash again. But it was only the once. Hardcoe leaned forward and slid over another red bead on the abacus on the table in front of him.

"Your second casualty," Connrad stated.

"Only my first in this Mars Arena," Hardcoe acknowledged. "It's sure a fit place for that old god of war. But the Big Game is young yet. Don't count your victims before you see them stretched cold on the slabs in the morning."

Connrad laughed loudly, sure of himself.

LeMarck hated the sound, but his thoughts turned instantly to the red team out in the pit, wondering which among them had been lost. He hoped it wasn't the one-eyed man.

RYAN WENT TO GROUND, rolling over twice to put more yardage between himself and the big mutie cat.

The huge animal's shoulders stood almost as tall as Ryan's armpit. The eyes spit green fire, rolling in the weak moonlight, threaded with brilliant crimson blood lines burning in the yellowed whites. Its fur was night black, and white fangs stabbed free of purple-gray lips, drooling crystal-clear strings.

The cat landed with a loose thump in the area where Ryan had stood. Spitting out a wicked, irritated cough, the animal sprang after him.

J.B.'s Uzi ripped a spray of bullets against the trees and through the brush where it had been standing, but the mutie cat gave no pause at all.

Ryan squeezed off two rounds, faster than he'd wanted to because he knew he didn't have the shot he needed. Both bullets creased the raised muscle mass surrounding the cat's neck; neither did any permanent damage.

"Get back, Ryan!" Mildred yelled. "Get back and give me some room!"

Her last words got tangled up in the sudden screams and

yells of the stickies breaking out of the brush. Gunfire broke out in earnest as the other members of the group opened fire. Even with a number of them going down, the stickies rushed forward, waving clubs and stone-sharpened knives made of whatever metal scraps they could find.

The cat's shoulder smashed into Ryan. He barely managed to avoid the snapping jaws, but the impact knocked the SIG-Sauer from his hand. There was no time to bring up the Steyr because the mutie cat wheeled around instantly.

Whipping its head forward again, the cat tried to sink its fangs into Ryan's throat. Even focused on the animal as he was, he was aware of the stickies getting closer.

J.B. and Mildred raced forward to take away the no-man's-land that separated the stickies from Ryan and the cat, grabbing cover behind trees and rocks where they could. Spears sailed through the air, followed by a few stone axs and squared-off hammers that split or broke off pieces of the rocks they slammed against.

Ryan caught the cat by its dish-shaped ears, halting the wedge-shaped head. It howled in pain and surprise. Instantly changing tactics, the cat curled up backward and tried to bring its claw-studded hind legs into play.

Already expecting the move, Ryan wasn't there when the claws slashed through empty air. He moved to the right, feeling that he was moving in slow motion next to the cat's quickness.

Before the animal could come around, Ryan grabbed a fistful of the loose hide at its neck. With a lithe jump, he bounded onto the cat's shoulders, he gripped the fur-covered flesh he had hold of as tightly as he could, then locked his legs around in front of the cat's forward legs so it couldn't rip him to shreds with its hind claws.

The cat snarled and spit, twisting and turning to rid itself of its burden.

Ryan held on, putting his body on top of the cat's, weighing down the animal's head. Making the cat work the larger muscles of its body to support him and try to throw him off would cause the beast to use up oxygen more quickly, slowing and weakening it. Ryan still believed the creature could outlast his own strength. He leaned forward, biting into the animal's neck in an attempt to forge one more point of attachment.

He ripped the panga free and used his left hand to work the big knife. Reaching under the mutie cat's neck, he stabbed it in the chest. The beast quivered as though an electric shock had hit it.

Drawing the panga from its flesh sheath, Ryan stabbed again, burying the weapon as deep as he could, then twisting it to tear the wound open as wide as he was able. The cat snapped its jaws as he pulled the knife free again, barely missing sinking its ivory fangs into his arm.

The exertion of hanging on, avoiding the cat's snapping jaws and being on the offense took its toll. Ryan had difficulty breathing, choking on the wet, smelly fur in his mouth, the smell of fresh blood clogging his nostrils.

He took a fresh grip on the panga, shifting the blade. Knowing he couldn't hang on to the cat much longer, feeling the burning ache throbbing deep in his shoulder, his lungs working hard to suck in air he couldn't breathe, he drew the panga hard against the mutie cat's throat, pulling with everything he had left. The effort unseated him from the cat's back, but not before he felt the cascade of hot blood spill in waves across his knife arm.

Ryan sailed backward, flailing for something close to control of his fall. The cat had already turned, searching for its tormentor, scarlet frosting its purple-gray lips and black fur of its throat.

Landing hard on his side, Ryan felt the breath spurt out of his lungs. He forced himself to roll over and get to his feet as the big cat padded toward him. "Fireblast!" he cursed. He spotted the SIG-Sauer on the ground, but it was to the mutie cat's left. Getting it was impossible without coming too close to the injured animal.

"Ryan!" J.B. yelled from his position behind a young oak tree.

It was the only warning Ryan got about the stickie that exploded out of the brush with a spear held at waist level. Reacting to the attacker, Ryan shifted his body, letting the triangular spearhead slide past him, ripping along the scarlet armored vest. He chopped down with his hand and grabbed the forward haft of the spear, watching a look of surprise spread across the stickie's rad-burned features.

Continuing to use his weight and strength to push down the spear, Ryan buried it point first into the ground. He used the added leverage to flip the stickie toward the mutie cat.

The stickie shrieked as it flew upside down, smashing against the beast's snarling face. The cat closed its jaws over the stickie's head and shoulders. Bone crunched as it chewed. Breath rattled and made sucking noises as it passed through the animal's ravaged throat.

Still hanging on to the spear, Ryan ran to the mutie cat's side. It spit out the dead, nerve-quivering stickie and turned to face him. Before it had time to respond, Ryan moved in close, both hands gripping the spear. He chose his spot, then rammed it in behind the cat's foreleg, aiming for the heart.

The cat lifted a paw and swatted at Ryan, who was already in motion. The claws came close enough to shear his hair and break the skin along his forehead. Warm blood slipped across his face.

The paw slapped against the embedded spear, snapping the haft as if it was a straw. It took a step at Ryan, who'd moved off to recover his SIG-Sauer. By the time he'd scooped up the blaster and raised it, he saw death claim the cat.

The animal's hindquarters shivered, then dropped out from under it. The eyes were already glazing before its head slammed against the ground.

Breathing hard, his throat feeling as if it were on fire, Ryan raked a hand through his curly hair and moved it back out of his face. He kept his blaster pointed in the direction the stickies had attacked from.

Only a few of them were in view, and they were headed back into the brush, some of them limping or holding hands over bleeding wounds. The rest of them were dead, lying in all kinds of poses between the tree line and where J.B., Mildred and the others had held the line.

Waiting for his heart rate to slow to somewhere near normal, Ryan used the slack time to reload the partially spent magazine in his blaster, then do the same to the clips he'd used inside the holding area. "Everybody okay?"

"Not everybody," J.B. said quietly, nodding back and to the right where one of the Thompson twins lay on the ground, a short-hafted ax jutting from his cracked skull. The other twin knelt beside his dead brother, holding his sibling's bloody hand.

Ryan crossed to the younger man, making himself hard. He put a hand on Thompson's shoulder and shook it. "Got no time for grief. We need to be pushing on."

"Fuck you, mister," the twin said hoarsely, his eyes filled with tears. "My brother needs burying."

Ryan met the man's rage and sorrow head-on. "You plan on staying to bury him?"

"It's the Christian thing to do," Thompson replied. "I don't feel good about just leaving him here. Like this."

"You're not supposed to," Ryan said. "But it's got to be done if you're going to have a chance to tell your kids about their uncle. Only way he's going to live on."

Tenderly laying his dead brother's hands across his chest, Thompson stood. His jaw tightened, becoming a hard line as he gripped the haft of the ax and pulled it from the dead man's skull. The blade came free with a sucking noise. He tossed it away.

Ryan adjusted his gear. "Then let's get moving." He looked across the tops of the trees and brush. "See that building there, Mildred?" He studied the red neon lettering on its side.

"The Mirage," the woman said.

"You figure on making for the Mirage?" J.B. asked.

"Highest vantage point," Ryan answered. "We get inside there, mebbe we don't have to worry about the animals or the muties so much."

"We aren't going to be the only ones thinking like that," Mildred warned.

"Kind of planned on that," Ryan said, breaking into a ground-eating stride. "Some of the other groups will think of it eventually. Be best mebbe if we were already set up and waiting for them. I don't think any of the Five Barons have made any converts tonight. Could be we can offer to let them throw in their lot with us. The Mirage is close to the wall on that side."

"Mebbe," J.B. said. "Even if we made a way across the wall, chilled our way through the sec men keeping watch there, we'd still have to find a wag and get enough of a head start on the barons that they couldn't catch us."

"I know." Ryan nodded. "But Trader always said no matter how many beers you drink—"

"—you can only take one piss at a time," the Armorer finished.

Mentally Ryan plotted a course toward the Mirage that would take advantage of as much cover along the way as possible.

A FEATHERY WARNING brushed the back of Krysty's skull. She halted, Doc and Bernsen just behind her, ducking in the jagged crack they were using to creep up on the Las Vegas Convention Center. Her hand stayed tight around her .38 as she scanned the uneven terrain for any sign of Jak or whatever had tripped her psychic alert.

Jak had been less than twenty yards in front of them, but he'd disappeared as quick and traceless as morning mist getting hit by full sunlight.

Thirty yards away the convention center looked as if it had been through a war. Bullets and rockets from past encounters had left scars and gouges on the cracked exterior. If any of the windows had survived intact, Krysty wasn't able to see them.

The thing that made the convention center attractive was its proximity to the eastern wall surrounding the sunken center of the ville. She'd already spotted the men making the rounds on top of the wall, armed with blasters. The sounds of battle and dying, the crash of weapons and the growls of beasts, the smell of foliage thick and sweet with blossoms and otherworldly scents filled her physical senses.

Boots crunched on the rocky terrain only a few yards away.

Freezing into position, knowing sudden movement caught a person's peripheral vision faster than anything, Krysty waited, barely breathing. She saw the sec guard only a few heartbeats later, then he was gone, and the feathery touch inside her head disappeared with him.

She let out a tense breath, surveying the grounds in front of their position again. Three wags were parked near the entranceway to the convention center. She guessed that some of the sec men on top of the wall had driven over, then went up stairs on the inside.

Looking back over her shoulder, she waved on Doc and Bernsen. From the repeated scans she'd made of the sec men on the wall, their interest was primarily on what was going on in the pit.

Jak rose up out of the darkness by the first wag as Krysty reached it. Tense and nervous, she put the .38 on him before he realized who it was. Her finger had taken up the trigger slack.

"Me," the teenager said. "Was inside for a bit."

"What's it look like in there?" Krysty asked.

"Empty," Jak answered, coming closer and speaking in a whisper. "Most sec watching pit."

"Is there a way to get to the top?"

Jak nodded. "Way to get to top. Way underneath, too."

"Underneath?"

"Yeah. Place to park wags. Lots of dead wags already there."

"We'll take a look," Krysty said. "See what we have to work with. Let's check the wags out here first."

They split up. Doc and Bernsen went through one of them while Krysty and Jak took the other two. All of them held ammo and assault rifles, supplies and spare jerricans of fuel.

Jak's wag turned out to have something extra tucked away in a large red toolbox. "Krysty."

She crossed over to him, watching him drop the toolbox on the ground. Someone had put a lock on it, but the youth had gotten rid of it by simply slicing through the plastic grooves. When he opened it, she saw small grease-paper-wrapped blocks placed neatly inside.

"Plas ex?" Krysty asked.

"Yeah." Jak took out one of the small packages, juggling it easily in his hand. "Got detonators, too. Some timers, some distance. Batteries look okay."

"Help me put this stuff into the bags," Krysty said, kneeling quickly and beginning to shove it into her backpack. "Ryan and the others are going to need a back door. With this, I think we can make it."

Chapter Thirty-Three

Ryan took up a position behind an overturned truck nearly a hundred yards from the Mirage. Over the years trees had thrust insistent branches, trunks and roots through the wag's body, anchoring it to the ground while at the same time pushing it inches upward.

The Mirage was incredible. Small falls, probably less impressive than they were before the nukecaust had claimed the ville, jetted from the fifth floor, pouring into cracked basins that held some kind of return system that was only partially working. Lit by sporadic underwater neon lights, the white frothing overflow leaked out into the jungle.

It had taken the group long minutes to cover the distance. In that time they'd had three encounters and had lost Clingdon to a slimy, tentacled creature that had been wrapped up on a spit of land trailing from a broad pond on the east side of Las Vegas Boulevard. Fielding had died during an ambush by members of the blue team coming up from behind and to the side. The companions had dropped three enemy gunners before they'd managed an escape.

"How do you want to handle this?" J.B. asked. He slipped off his wire-rimmed glasses and cleaned them quickly on a handkerchief that looked miraculously dry.

Ryan mopped sweat from his brow and looked back over his ragtag army. Mildred, like the Armorer, was calm and collected, but the three remaining men appeared shaken, on the verge of spooking at every sound around them.

"Front door looks inviting," Ryan said, taking his binoculars from his gear, "but there're already some takers on it."

J.B. lifted an eyebrow. "Missed them. Damn, they must be good."

"Lots of other entertainment going on," Ryan commented dryly. "Missing them is understandable. And they are good."

Turning to face the building, J.B. put his glasses back on. "How good?"

"Good enough that I've only managed to lock on to their shadows a couple times."

"What's their color?"

"Green. Mebbe. They've made themselves hard to see."

"If they're green," J.B. said, "they've got no casualties that I've noticed."

Ryan nodded. The Armorer had been the first to notice the different-colored lenses used by the sec men on top of the wall. When they'd left the dead Thompson twin behind, a harsh, bright light had shone onto the area a few minutes later, splashing the corpse. Shortly after that, J.B. had pointed out the sec man waving the flash with the red lens, aiming the beam back at the big window in Bally's where the barons watched the game.

J.B. had been keeping count automatically. By his count, the purple team had taken the most damage with seven people gone. With four of their teammates dead, Ryan's red team was running a close second in casualties.

"Mebbe they're better than I was thinking." Ryan focused the binoculars and got a chance to watch the last three green-team members race into the Mirage. "They're boys."

"Boys?" J.B. echoed.

Ryan nodded. "From the looks of them. Saw some faces that time. Young. Mebbe early twenties, but I'm putting my jack on them being teens. No later."

"What are boys doing out here?" Mildred asked. "The blue team had some young among them, but they were all men."

"Don't know." Ryan kept careful watch over the entrance, but didn't see any of the green team again. "But they move like a unit. Solid. Working point, wings and slack, everybody keeping covering fire over everybody else."

"Just like Trader set up his operations," J.B. stated. "One of his commandments on War Wag One. 'Thou shalt cover thy neighbor's ass.'"

"Sec squad?" Mildred asked.

"From the look of them," Ryan answered.

"Don't see them as volunteers," Mildred replied. "Unless they got some kind of special arrangement that's going to get them out of here."

"We were promised," J.B. said. "Mebbe they got promised, too, and believed it."

"Stupid if they did," Mildred said. "But they're young. Maybe they just don't know any better."

Ryan put away the night glasses and took up the Steyr. "Two reasons that group went into the Mirage. One, they're hunting the high ground like us, mebbe going to take a chance at that wall if they can. Two, they've got something waiting for them that their baron set up."

"There's only one way to find out," J.B. said.

"Yeah." Ryan stood and pointed at a window on the second floor. "We go in from the side. Second floor. We've already seen some of these buildings are booby-trapped. That one's an obvious choice."

J.B. silently agreed. "What about those boys?"

Ryan kept his face hard. "If they get in our face and raise their weapons, blow them away. No other way about it. Them or us. Me, I'd prefer it be us." He stepped into the nearby shadows and moved toward the building.

DEAN FELT AS IF he'd stepped into another world. His clothing was still damp from the short run through the cascading falls spraying down from the fifth floor of the Mirage. He ran a hand through his hair and brushed it back in wet curls.

Conor still walked point, a rifle cradled in his arms. The boy craned his head, taking in the sights.

Dean knew it wasn't safe to be gawking, but he didn't blame the other boy for it, either. After walking through the entranceway, they were confronted by another jungle that had evidently overgrown its boundaries in the decades since the skydark.

Paths twisted in different directions between the trees and foliage. Some of them were just ruts made by small animals able to get under the lower branches of the trees. Others, though, were man-made, tall and cleared out, the ground pounded bare of grass in patches.

A few of the trails had been tramped down recently. Dean spotted the machete marks on the tree trunks and saw the amputated branches that still showed meat in places. The trees themselves weren't indigenous to the area. Dean recognized them as banana trees and palms. But they were mixed in now with spruce and oak.

The ceiling was eighty or ninety feet overhead, and it was hard to see through the darkness. Occasional brief movements let him know the branches held winged night predators.

"Tighten it up," Louis called out. "Conor, cut your lead

to about ten yards and hold up at corners. That way we can back you up if you need it.''

''Right.''

Dean kept his blaster before him in a two-handed grip. If someone or something jumped out from behind the trees, getting the pistol away from him would be harder with both hands on it.

A few yards farther on, they came in sight of the front desk. Dean had stayed in motels before, from honest-run little places operated by a family, to bigger establishments that held roomers in the second or third floor over the stage areas where gaudy sluts pandered their wares. He'd never seen a front desk as big as the one he gazed at.

Lazy tendrils from dozens of plants crawled across the pitted surface of the desk. Behind it, track lighting with subdued illumination played over the huge glass front of an aquarium. Dean was certain it measured over fifty feet.

Dean shivered as he stared into the cold, menacing eye of a small fish that coasted against the glass wall. Whether it was physically possible or not, he had the feeling the eye was staring right back at him, could see him in the dark and gazed with a chill and hungry limited intelligence.

''Bloodthirsty little bastards,'' Green said. ''Did you see the teeth on that one?''

Curiosity partially satiated, the group moved on under Louis's command. The hallway closed them in more tightly, and none of them saw the trip wire.

Conor's foot caught it. ''Hey,'' he started to protest, almost stumbling over the wire.

His next words were swallowed by a deafening blast. Dean struggled to maintain his balance, watching Conor fly through the air, the closest of them to the explosion that ripped the front desk to shreds and smashed the front of the aquarium.

Tons of water shot out of the broken glass wall, splashing over all the boys in a tidal wave of soaking force. Dean went down, losing traction and his footing at once. His hand slipped across the wet carpet, but he managed to get a finger hold on a hole that had been worn through the material down to the concrete foundation.

As he tried to shove himself up to his feet, a sharp agony started in the side of his neck, lighting a flame in his brain. He reached up to just above his collarbone, searching for the source of the pain. His fingers slid over a small, scaly body that wiggled fiercely in his hand.

Dean's stomach twisted in sudden sickness at the realization of what had him by the neck. He pulled, but the teeth were clamped on tight, making his flesh come with it. Blood spilled down the side of his neck, then tracked down onto his chest beneath the vest.

"Bastard biter's got me, Louis!" Moxen yelled. "Help me!" One of the carnivorous fish had fastened onto his face. Scarlet lines trailed down his cheek and across his lips. His eyes were wide, filled with fear.

Holding on to the fish with one hand, Dean holstered his blaster and reached for the knife he'd been given. One swipe, and he hacked the fish apart just behind its oversize jaws. The teeth remained embedded and fixed.

Louis crossed over to Moxen and sliced the fish off, inserting a knife blade just behind the bulging eye and twisting it. The jaws popped open, releasing Moxen's face. Louis tossed the dying fish away.

After removing the fish head from his neck, Dean surveyed the other boys. Many of them were screaming and cursing in fright. A chill ran through Dean as he realized how deadly the fish could have been if they'd remained in their own element.

Enrique Green shuddered on the floor as if he were having some kind of fit. The boy's mouth gaped open in a silent scream. The wound in his leg released a spreading pink stain into the inch-deep water littered with flopping fish.

Dean crossed over to Green, intending to help the boy to his feet. When he rolled him over, a sucking noise caught his attention. He glanced down and saw three fish working at the boy's side. They'd opened a large wound just below the rib cage.

Managing to grab one of the fish, Dean watched in horror as another one ate its way into Green's insides. "Oh, shit," Dean said, throwing the first fish away. He cut the second fish off, leaving the head and ignoring the sudden streams of blood squirting out that showed arterial flow.

He tightened his fingers and rammed them into Green's side, tearing the flesh with the pressure he exerted. He touched the sharp fins of the fish's tail, gained almost an inch on it as he watched the ridge of flesh that showed the fish's passage inside Enrique, moving across the boy's stomach. Another surge, and the fish was lost to him.

"Damn, Enrique," Dean cried in frustration. He felt a scaly body slip next to his leg and drew away. Tears filled his eyes, brought on by the helpless rage he felt.

The fleshy ridge turned abruptly, crawling up to Enrique's chest. It slowed when it reached his solar plexus.

"Dean," Green stammered, blood gushing from his mouth, spraying with his words, "it hurts. Hurts bad." Before he could utter another word, convulsions seized him. He died, choking and heaving, trying to get up. Then his head relaxed, and his eyes remained open wide.

"Fuck," Perry said.

Dean looked up and found the youth standing only a few feet away. The rest of the boys appeared bloodied but intact. Conor looked the worst, bleeding down the side of his face from a large gash across his forehead. Moxen and Handley were stomping fish still flopping in the shallow water.

"Dean," Louis said quietly, "he's dead."

"I know it," Dean said. "Fish got him."

"Got to go," Louis said. "No place for us to stay here."

Dean nodded. He picked up his strewed gear and arranged it for quick access, certain he was going to need it. He felt bad about leaving Green lying there, but it had to be done.

"Conor, do you feel up to taking point again?" Louis asked.

The boy hesitated just a moment. "Don't see how you could trust me after that. Got Enrique chilled, too."

"Did you see that trip wire?" Louis asked.

The boy shook his head.

"Neither did the rest of us. Shit happens. All we can do is our best. I don't think you'll get any complaints from us." He looked around the group meaningfully.

All the boys shook their heads.

"Can you do it?" Louis asked.

"I can try," Conor replied.

Louis nodded. "That's all we're asking. Ready when you are."

Conor took a deep breath, raked his gaze around the others looking for any last-minute changes of mind, then turned and took up his position.

Dean followed reluctantly, feeling that no matter where they went in the building, none of them were safe.

Chapter Thirty-Four

The convention center's underground parking garage was a sargasso of rusting and stripped wags. Remnants of the yellow lines that had once separated the vehicles lay along the dust-covered concrete floor, brought into sharp relief by the oil lantern Jak had stolen from farther down the hall.

The albino held up the lantern and turned up the wick. More of the shadows in the garage peeled away. "Wall," he said.

Krysty looked a few feet ahead of him and saw the solid concrete wall that ended their tangled journey through the steel husks. They'd gone down the emergency stairs on one side of the main lobby and followed them into the garage. The elevators didn't work, nor did any of the other lights in the building.

Evidently whatever the power source the Five Barons had tapped into to establish their private killing ground, hadn't been used to illuminate the convention center. Perhaps they didn't have the power to spare. In either event, the decision worked in the companions' favor.

"Doc?" Krysty said.

"This is the wall, dear lady," the old man replied. He came forward with the small notebook he'd liberated from Bernsen's pack.

On the sheets of paper, he'd carefully penciled in an utline of the building and the path they'd taken to get to e garage. Measurements—as close as he could approximate them by stepping off the distance—were tagged between marked arrowheads.

Doc tapped the paper. "I am sure this is it, Krysty, unless I am totally addled and cannot remember simple spatial and cartography skills. This building is not much of a challenge."

"This section," Krysty said, "overlooks the pit edge we spotted from the upstairs window?"

"A moment to confirm that, please." Doc left her briefly, sliding through the rows of overturned cars.

Sentient hair at the back of Krysty's neck coiled defensively. She turned, looking at Bernsen, who'd crept considerably closer while she'd presented her back to him.

"Don't even think about it," she warned, moving her hand to the butt of her blaster. "I'd kill you before you could touch me."

"I wasn't doing anything," Bernsen said with the most innocence he could muster, but his shoulders dropped in dejection. He stuck out his lower lip and backed off a few feet.

Doc returned a moment later. "This is definitely the location, dear lady."

Krysty approached the wall Doc had indicated and looked at the cinder blocks it was made of. Some of the mortar had cracked and worn away in places. Hunks and bits of it snapped and popped under her boots as she ran a hand along its surface to get a feel for it.

"Won't take much," Jak said. "Little plas ex probably make big hole." He came up behind her and stood at her side.

"Think you're right. Let's get to it."

Jak unhooked his backpack and started rummaging through its contents for the blocks of explosive.

Krysty kneaded the plas ex slightly before pushing it

against the rough, uneven surface of the wall. When she had enough little balls in place, she stabbed a remote detonator into each.

"You sure Ryan inside now?" Jak asked as they finished blocking out the circular patch of the wall they'd chosen.

"Yes," she said. Even though her mind swirled, threatening to conjure up all kinds of possibilities about what the near future might hold, she was convinced of her lover's presence.

"Know where?"

"Feeling I'm getting from him, I can track it."

"Dean there?"

"Him, too." She didn't even try to figure out what was going to happen between father and son out on the killing ground.

"Where?"

"I don't know, Jak. I just know they're close."

"Confusing in dark. Could be trouble seeing the other."

"I know. Dammit, I know." She inserted the last detonator, then walked back to the nearest empty wag.

Jak followed her. "Sorry. Stupe of me. You'd already thought that."

Krysty studied the wag. In the past someone had taken the engine and transmission, stripping other parts out of the inside. The windshield was cracked, two holes knocked into it big enough for her to fit her hand through. The tires were flat, but at least they were there.

"Give me a hand," she told Jak, "and let's see if we can move it." She grabbed the steering wheel while the teenager slipped in behind the wag.

The vehicle creaked and popped in protest, then grudgingly started to move. It took a lot of work to put the wag in front of the area they'd mined with the plas ex. Once they had it there, Krysty looked at the space, figuring it would only take one more wag and at most two more to block the brunt of the blasts against the wall. That way the explosion would be concentrated, hopefully opening up the wall.

If it didn't, escape would be even more difficult.

RYAN REACHED DOWN and gave J.B. a hand up into the window on the second floor of the Mirage. Mildred and the others were already behind him, lined up on both sides of the door.

The room had once been a storage area of some type. Racks that held barren clothes hangers shared space with cabinets, display counters and shelves.

Moosh Wandell, Thompson and Owen guarded the door, anxiously peering into the darkened hallway. The echoes of the explosion had died away less than two minutes earlier.

J.B. slithered in over the sill. "Saw a green light a minute ago."

"One of the boys is dead," Mildred commented.

The Armorer nodded. "Looks that way."

Ryan scratched his stubbled chin, thinking about it. "All the green team was inside the building. Means they've got a way of seeing through the walls."

"Unless they've got the windows staked out," Mildred said. "Maybe a sec man just looked in and saw the boy down."

"And confirmed him dead?" Ryan shook his head. "They've got buildings open all over the pit. Hadn't thought about it before, but they'd probably want a way to check on anybody inside them."

"Haven't seen any vid equipment," J.B. said. "Starlight scopes would take away the night, but they wouldn't allow the sec guards to see through the walls. Something else might, though."

Ryan looked at his friend.

"Thermographic sights," J.B. said. "They register body heat if things between them aren't too dense, or don't carry too much of a heat signature themselves. A barn would have to have serious jack to afford that kind of equipment. Hard to find."

Ryan didn't like the idea of the sec guards being able to spy on them at any time. "What about a heat signature?"

"Man," Owen whispered harshly, "we're sitting ducks standing in one place like this. That explosion, you know those green-team guys aren't going to stay put. They'll be moving. And with them moving, they're liable to run smack into us."

"With us moving," Mildred argued, "there's no less risk."

The man shifted nervously. "Moving around some would just feel better."

"When the time comes to move," Ryan said in a hard voice, "I'll let you know."

Owen's gaze burned for just a moment, then he looked back into the hallway.

"Heat signature of the human body is 98.6," the Armorer said. "Nothing else around us burns that hot."

"What about the neon lights?" Ryan asked.

"No."

"But if we got a good blaze going somewhere... "

J.B. nodded. "It'd blind the sec men's sights for a while, but when we moved from the fire, they'd find us again."

"It would buy us some time, though."

"Sure."

Ryan shouldered the Steyr. "Good to know. There'll come a time we may need to buy a few minutes." Drawing the SIG-Sauer, he started for the hallway. The skin across his neck and shoulders was tight. It wasn't pleasant thinking about the boys roaming around inside the building with them. But they were killers; they'd proved their ability. If it came to it, he'd put them down and walk over their bodies without a second thought if it would put him one step closer to his freedom.

PEERING THROUGH the thermographic sniper sights, Hayden LeMarck saw the human-shaped heat signatures of the green team walk away from the dying ember of the team member they'd left behind in the Mirage entrance. The dozens of piranha that had splashed across the floor after the explosion glowed steadily brighter as their body temperature escalated. Some of them still flopped weakly.

"Confirmed kill on one of the green team," LeMarck told Hardcoe. "His body temp's dropping." He looked at the baron.

"The green team is inside the building?" Hardcoe asked.

"Yes, sir."

Hardcoe smiled, then rubbed his hands together. "Wallis."

"Sir," Thoroughgood replied.

"Get a message to tell Phibes to let them go."

"Sir?" Thoroughgood looked confused.

LeMarck was confused himself. He'd known Hardcoe and Phibes had been working on the traps for this year's Big Game, but none of the details had been released. Phibes was renowned in the seven villes for his vicious, bloodthirsty ways and appetites.

"Just get him the message," the Baron said. "He'll know what I mean."

Thoroughgood left, moving quickly.

Hardcoe looked at Connrad. "It appears good fortune has turned the other cheek on you."

"One death," Connrad growled, reaching forward and sliding a bead across his abacus. "You've suffered four."

"Not as many as young Francis's team," Hardcoe answered good-naturedly.

Giskard made a mock woeful face, then reached for a fresh drink.

"What is it you sent your man for?" Connrad demanded.

"You're familiar with Phibes?" Hardcoe asked.

Connrad gave a short, impatient nod. "Calls himself a physician. A worse joke was never made."

"He is somewhat—coarse and ill-tempered," Hardcoe agreed.

"The man," Giskard said definitely, "is sick and perverted."

Dettwyler leaned forward. "Wasn't he the man who tried to bring life back into corpses, create some kind of army of the undead?"

"Yes," Deke Ramsey replied. "He was partially successful from what I was told."

LeMarck recalled the incident and shivered. The shambling monstrosities that Phibes had raised were mockeries of men, women and children, torn from the fresh womb of the grave and pieced together in various ways. Mercifully the things had only experienced near life for a matter of minutes and had appeared in no way under control of themselves, much less Phibes's control. They'd been burned so that no one would attempt to figure out what the man had done to raise them from the dead.

Hardcoe waved the comment away, not answering. "Phibes is a genius."

"The way I heard it," Connrad said, "he's got access to certain predark materials."

"I don't ask," Hardcoe responded.

"But neither do you deny knowledge of such a thing," Giskard countered.

"Forget that," Connrad said. "What is he loosing into the pit?"

Hardcoe smiled, a cold effort genuinely without humor. "In his travels in recent days, he came across an interesting strain of beasts created before the skydark. From somewhere along the upper Cific coastline."

"What kinds of beasts are they?" Dettwyler asked.

"Monkeys," Hardcoe answered.

"Monkeys," Connrad scoffed. He slapped his knee. "As a baron, you have a right to include whatever traps you deem necessary in the pit. How the hell can you expect monkeys to be a threat to armed men?"

"They've mutated," Hardcoe answered, "just as the big cats we found roaming this burg have."

"In what way?" Giskard asked.

LeMarck was interested, as well. He didn't like getting cut from the information loop, but he knew it was necessary at times.

"I didn't know this at the time," Hardcoe said, "but most primates are carnivorous to a degree."

"Primates?" Dettwyler asked.

LeMarck knew the term had come from Phibes, and Hardcoe had picked it up. Hardcoe liked appearing educated.

"Any kind of monkey or ape," Hardcoe replied. "These are meat eaters by choice. For the last seven months, Phibes has been working with them here—feeding them, making them angry and fearful, starving them sometimes until they almost went insane. Twice they started fighting among themselves, killing four of the weaker ones and devouring them. Over the years Phibes said they've been inbred until insanity is less than a stone's throw away for them.''

"Get to it," Connrad said.

"For the last two months the monkeys have had a constant feeding area," Hardcoe replied.

"The Mirage," Giskard guessed.

"Exactly." Hardcoe smiled. "They haven't been fed in the last four days and have been secured in a soundproof room near the top of the Mirage. Phibes has an electronic door opener. Those monkeys have been released into that building by now."

"They're still just monkeys," Dettwyler snorted. "Not much threat in that."

"I seem to recall that you weren't impressed with the piranha in the fish tank at the Mirage's entry," Hardcoe returned. "One of Connrad's prize team members is now dead because of it."

"Only one." Dettwyler still didn't appear impressed.

"True, but now that team is running scared. They thought to take the high ground, as other teams before them had planned on. Only now they're not as safe as they believed they were going to be. They're going to run into those monkeys." Hardcoe leaned forward in his chair and lowered his voice, drawing in the others to his story. "Those monkeys are meat eaters, as I've said, but they're also little more than a foot and a half tall, much stronger and faster than they appear, and have wings."

"Winged monkeys?"

LeMarck looked at Dettwyler. The baron definitely looked impressed now.

"Can they fly?" Giskard asked.

"Not fly," Hardcoe said. "However, they can glide pretty damn good. I've seen them do it myself."

A quick, covert glance at Connrad let LeMarck know the

baron wasn't receiving the news with the confidence he'd
had before.

"Something new, eh, Vinge? That's what we wanted for
the pit." Hardcoe grinned. "And no matter how well
drilled those boys you managed to gather up are, there's
no way they could have prepared for this."

Connrad didn't say anything; he just lifted his binoculars.

LeMarck raised the thermographic lenses to his eyes
again, scanning the topmost floors of the Mirage. In a matter of moments he managed to locate the monkeys, dimly
outlined by their shape as they scuttled across the floor.
They were a horde, their body temperatures considerably
elevated from a human's, and even slightly higher than a
mutie biped's. It was a certain sign of rad-influenced mu-
tation.

The monkeys moved quickly, seeking out the empty ele-
vator shafts and sliding down between the levels to the
bottom floor. Some of them unfurled wings almost twice
as broad as they were tall, and glided down, bouncing off
the walls.

"You've never said how many monkeys there were,"
Ramsey said.

"Dozens," Hardcoe replied. "The green team won't get
out of that building alive. I'm afraid, Vinge, that your sea-
soned troops—with their training and their intent to take
the high ground—are going to find that those tactics have
ultimately chilled them all."

Connrad paused for a moment before answering. "Getting down to the nut cutting, it's going to matter who's the
best chillers. Just like it always has."

"A man who's a believer until the bitter end," Giskard
said. "Very good of you, Vinge."

LeMarck moved the thermographic lenses around, picking up other hot spots. He felt better about the outcome.

The green team appeared the only ones who could give the one-eyed man and his party any serious competition.

Abruptly he ran the lenses across a heat signature that read human. He brought the lenses back slowly, finding what he was looking for on the second floor.

He leaned down to Hardcoe's ear. "Sir."

Hardcoe listened.

"Our team is in the building, as well."

"Where?"

"Second floor," LeMarck answered.

The muscles along the baron's jawline tightened. "I they've got the sense we've given them credit for, as soon as they hear the monkeys take the green team, they'll leave the building."

LeMarck straightened again, hoping it was true.

WITH JAK WATCHING her back, Krysty put the last plas-ex charge in place against the ceiling. On the top floor now she knew the sec men were only a few feet above her. The only things separating her from them were the crawl space ceiling, roof and whatever duct work was in place.

"Done," she said to Jak.

He stepped out of the shadows beside the room's door He nodded, then turned and led the way into the hall, fol lowed by Krysty.

They went down the emergency stairs in a matter o minutes, returning to the first floor. Doc remained in the underground garage with Bernsen, who'd become increas ingly nervous as he figured out what Krysty and the other were planning to do.

The man might become a problem. In Ryan's place Krysty thought she might have chilled the scientist then and there to protect the other companions. They owed Bernsen nothing; the man had even tried to kill them.

But she wasn't Ryan. So she'd taken the chance that Doc could handle the man.

On the first floor, Jak went through the double doors leading out into the main hall. Another two turns put them into a large meeting area. Rusted metal folding chairs were thrown haphazardly about, partially buried by the chunks of ceiling that had fallen over the decades.

They stopped at one of the large plate-glass windows overlooking the pit area.

Looking through the glass, Krysty saw intermittent gunfire flash yellow and white against the foliage and the neon burn spots.

"Ready?" Jak asked.

Krysty took a deep breath and nodded. The visions she'd had while in the airwag still made no sense, but her mutie powers told her definitely that Ryan was still in the Mirage and that Dean was probably in there, as well. Her power tweaked suddenly, and the sense of imminent danger for Ryan suddenly increased. "We need to go."

Jak removed the window. He'd loosened it earlier, working the dried putty from the framework with a knife. He spit on his hands, then rubbed them against each other.

The glass was a three-foot-by-four-foot rectangle. Jak placed his hands against it, using the friction of his moistened palms to draw the window back and prevent it from falling from his grasp when he drew it farther away.

Krysty caught the edge of the glass and helped him put it against the wall on the floor. She kept her ears cocked for the sound of a sec guard's shoe brushing against the carpet outside, but didn't think it would really happen. The sec men were too interested in the death being dealt in the pit.

Jak shook loose a length of climbing rope with a small

grapple already attached. He hooked it to the window's lip, then threw the rope outside.

When there was no immediate gunfire in response, he clambered out after it.

"Go," Krysty said. "I'll be right behind you."

Looking down, she spotted Jak already on the ground forty feet down. He looped the rope around his waist, bracing it for her descent.

Breathing a quiet prayer to Gaia, Krysty slid down into the waiting death arena.

Chapter Thirty-Five

The rope burned Krysty's hands and she bit her lip to endure the pain. Seconds later her boots hit the ground.

There was no choice but to leave the rope where it was and hope it wouldn't be spotted. If it was found later, it would be too late to matter. She hoped.

Jak turned and took the lead, running toward the foliage forty yards distant.

Krysty followed, drawing her weapon. If she had to use it, she'd only be one more shooter among the dozens left in the pit area. The only things she worried about were the bare places between the buildings, the forested areas and the wall. Care had been taken to keep them separated.

She ran, trusting Jak's woodcraft skills and her own persistent mutie powers to put her on the path to Ryan.

THE ONLY WARNING Dean and the other boys got was the heavy rustle of what sounded like leather on fabric behind them. They turned together, bringing up their weapons.

Dean's eyes burned, trying to sort out the shadows from reality over the sights of the Browning Hi-Power.

Several shadows were in motion, though. He peered at them intently as they approached. Then they started jabbering hostility.

"Monkeys!" Bobby Handley called out. "Just a bunch of monkeys! There's no reason to be scared!"

As the shadows went away and the moonlight leaking

through the building fell across the monkeys, Dean saw that they weren't ordinary beasts of their kind.

These monkeys looked leaner, their legs more proportioned with their arms and upper bodies. Their heads, however, were half again as large as they needed to be, and they were filled with teeth and bright, burning eyes. The lower jaws held more teeth than usual, and the bottom canines thrust belligerently upward, curving dangerously, fangs that almost reached the eyes.

At first Dean thought the monkeys were humpbacked. A moment later he saw that the abnormality on the creatures' backs was folded wings.

Louis stepped forward, dropping his rifle into position. "Monkeys or not, fuckers might be dangerous. Wouldn't put it past the people running this show to infect them with rabies." He burned a blast a couple feet in front of the advancing wave of monkeys.

Instead of retreating or coming to a stop, the monkeys instantly went on the attack. Some of them leaped into the air like ungainly birds, the wings flapping hard enough to crack the air.

"Shit!" Moxen cried out. "Chill them!" His weapon was already up and firing.

Dean joined in, trying to pick his targets to make sure of the kill. The monkeys were too densely packed to miss, but a wound would probably serve only to make them angrier than they obviously were.

The attempt to hold the line was over in seconds. The monkeys came on too fiercely, none of them appearing to be frightened by the gunfire exploding around them.

Dean backed away, the Browning's slide blowing back empty. He changed magazines, ducking under the gliding attack of one of the creatures. The fierce jaws snapped closed only inches from his left eye, hot drool splashing against his cheek.

"Run!" Louis yelled. "Break off and try to find a place to hole up!"

Slamming the fresh magazine home, Dean fought his way free of the clutches of three monkeys who'd seized his legs. To his right he saw Moxen go down under at least a half-dozen of them. Moxen screamed shrilly.

Dean started forward, wondering how he was going to help the other boy.

Abruptly Moxen stopped screaming. His body quivered, then relaxed. When it started to move again, it was due to the monkeys piled on top of him stripping the flesh from his bones in bloody gobbets.

Dean turned and ran, finding he was nearly the last of them to move out.

The monkeys continued to scream shrilly and raced after them, at a disadvantage because of their shorter legs. But the disadvantage wasn't much.

"Outside!" Handley yelled ahead of Dean. "We'd stand a better chance outside, Louis!"

"No way!" the youth called back. "We get outside in the open, these bastards would chew us to bits in no time!"

Without warning, something clipped Dean's shoulder and nearly toppled him from his feet. He managed to maintain his balance and watched in horror as a group of the winged monkeys flew into the boys.

Four of them landed on Handley, knocking the boy forward and to the ground, blood covering his features immediately. The monkeys clawed his back and buttocks, tearing through the clothing to get at his flesh.

"No!" Dean cried out hoarsely. He turned and brought up his blaster, so scared he had to fight to stay alive, fight to keep moving.

"Forget him!" Louis ordered, suddenly coming up hard against Dean. His momentum was enough to propel them both into a hallway splitting off the main corridor. "This hallway's smaller!" Louis helped Dean stay on his feet, kept him moving. "Mebbe we can cut down the number that come at us!"

More boys screamed out in the main corridor. Dean couldn't even recognize the voices. He got himself organized and started to match Louis's pace, not wanting to slow the boy and get them both chilled.

The hallway ended abruptly. Dean stared at the wooden door ahead of them. The plaque, its white letters barely visible against the black in the shadows, read Gentlemen.

"Bathroom," Dean said.

"Go through it," Louis ordered, looking over his shoulder. "We got no choice."

Looking back, Dean saw the monkeys approaching them, some of the mutie animals unfurling their wings to launch into a glide. He fumbled for the door and got it open. Louis followed him inside.

The only light falling into the room came from the weak illumination reflected from the hallway. Once Louis shut and bolted the door, even that went away.

Dean heard the monkeys' claws scratching against the door. The sound grew steadily louder, coming quicker and quicker.

"WE'VE GOT INTRUDERS inside the pit," Wallis Thoroughgood said as soon as he entered the room.

"Who?" LeMarck demanded before anyone else had time to react to the announcement.

"Don't know." Thoroughgood pointed through the glass down at the pit. "They came through the window of the old convention center, slid down a rope and are hauling ass.''

Connrad looked at one of his sec commanders. ''Get word out to the wall guards. Tell them I want these people killed.''

The man nodded and rushed out of the room.

Hardcoe gave the same order to Thoroughgood, who promptly vanished outside again.

LeMarck felt the tension in the room suddenly increase as all the barons leaned forward with their glasses in hand. He knew they were all thinking the same thing: if any of the barons had been behind the insertion of extra troops, that baron was a dead man.

The situation didn't make for casual conversation.

LeMarck trained his own glasses on the wall by the convention center and spotted the rope immediately, then he picked up the thermographic lenses and began to search for the intruders. In seconds he had their heat signatures. Neither of them showed the special ID buttons that were in the body armor of the team members.

He grew cold inside, because he figured he knew who the intruders were, and there was no way Hardcoe wouldn't be blamed for it. Death hovered over the room, waiting to be released. He dropped his hand to his Glock.

THE SHRILL SCREAMS and echoing thunder of blasters drew Ryan to a halt along the stairwell that led from the second floor to the first. Weak light dribbled in from the mesh windows in the doors to the emergency stairs.

''Not after us,'' J.B. said quietly behind him.

Ryan eased forward, the SIG-Sauer at the ready, hammer locked back so it would take only a two-pound squeeze to touch off the first round. He peered through the scarred, metal-ribbed glass, feeling the Armorer's breath light against the back of his neck.

The light was better outside. Scanning the scene before him, Ryan felt his hackles lift. Four of the green team were down, scattered along a couple corridors and almost buried under dozens of creatures that looked like things from a mat-trans chili nightmare.

"Dark night," J.B. breathed.

"Back," he told J.B. "Before these bastards get our scent." He signaled to Owen and Mildred, backing the group up the stairs. It had been Ryan's intention to identify the green team, isolate them from his group's own movements and chill them if it came to that.

"Looks like the green team's almost fresh out of members," J.B. stated.

Just as they started up the second set of steps, something smashed into the emergency door below.

At the tail of the line, Ryan peered back at the door. A monkey's face almost filled the rectangle, then two others popped into view, shoving the first beast away.

"Move!" Ryan ordered. "They're onto us!"

The door rattled, the knob turning slowly. Excited monkey screams filled the space.

"Bastards can work the knobs," Mildred said as she moved up the steps.

Ryan sighted along the length of his blaster, then put two rounds into the monkey's face. The screams of the animals increased, quickly reaching a frenzied stage. The bullets left holes in the glass, one of them snipping through the wire mesh. More monkeys suddenly clawed at the door.

Before Ryan reached the second landing, he heard the door below open, then the rapid padding of monkey feet against the steps.

"THEY'RE MAKING for the Mirage!"

LeMarck looked at Connrad's sec man. "Are you sure?"

"Yes, sir!" It was obvious the sec man was panicked, knowing it appeared that his own baron had at least a fifty percent chance of culpability in inserting extra champions. Otherwise, he'd have never responded to LeMarck's question.

Dettwyler pulled a blaster and pointed it in Hardcoe and Connrad's direction. "One of you two bastards is trying to pull a fast one on us. I want to know which one it is."

Quietly and quickly, LeMarck pulled his Glock and kept it out of sight by turning his body.

"You don't pull a blaster on me," Connrad warned, "unless you're going to use it."

"I'll use it, all right," Dettwyler said, "if I find out you're behind this."

"Then you'd better be fast enough to kill me, too," Hardcoe said. "Because I'll kill you right after you pull that trigger if you fuck around anymore."

Dettwyler grinned nervously. "Thought you and Connrad were enemies, Hardcoe."

"Hasn't changed a bit. If I had the chance out away from here and I thought I could take him, mebbe I'd find out if I could." He paused. "But not here. Not now. The truce between us will be honored in this place. It's the only thing that keeps the peace between us. I won't see it broken. By anyone."

Giskard calmly stretched out his hand. A small derringer popped into his palm. His fingers closed around the blaster as he shoved the blunt muzzle behind Dettwyler's ear. "I'm more of a gambling man," the young baron said cockily. "I think I can pull the trigger on this little pocket cannon before you manage to squeeze through that one. Want to see?"

"Get the blaster away from him," one of Dettwyler's sec men ordered, pulling his own weapon and pointing it at Giskard.

LeMarck took a step toward Hardcoe, intending to use himself as a shield to protect the baron if it proved necessary.

Giskard laughed. "And isn't this a fine how-do-you-do, Dettwyler?" He shook his head, moving the derringer slightly but keeping it in contact with the fat man's jawline. "As soon as you pull the trigger—or mebbe even only *look* like you're going to, why, mebbe all the people in this room are dead men."

Dettwyler didn't say anything.

"What I suggest," Giskard said, "is a moment of reason. You pulled the first blaster. By rights I think it should be you who first puts his away. Don't you agree?"

Face contorted with anger, Dettwyler complied.

With a sigh of relief, Giskard lowered the derringer's hammer. The barons ordered their men to follow suit.

LeMarck let out a long breath as quietly as he could, trying to appear indifferent to the whole situation. But his heart pounded inside him.

"Vinge," Hardcoe said, "I'll not see *you* make an attempt on Dettwyler, either, not while we're here."

"No man pulls a blaster on me and lives," Connrad said. The feathered earrings shivered with the fury moving the man.

"What you do away from here," Hardcoe said, "is none of my business. Here, I've had my say on."

"What we should all be doing," Giskard said, "is taking care of those interlopers, before they further interrupt the Big Game and we have to declare it a null effort. Then we'll be faced with leaving things as they are until next year and playing again."

Connrad eyed Hardcoe. "If that happens, it seems like things could turn out in your favor."

"I didn't put those people in there," Hardcoe stated.

"Mebbe we should go find out." Connrad turned to his nearest sec boss. "Pass the word along to those wall guards to get some people into the pit, track those two people down, kill them and identify them. I want their bodies brought out of there. And get some guards off the wall near the Mirage and into the building. Get some men in there with flame throwers. I don't want any of our people hurt by those monkeys before they have a chance to put down the interlopers."

"Yes, sir." The man left at once.

Hardcoe pushed himself out of his seat, his movements followed at once by Connrad. "I'm not going to stay in here and watch this. I want to be out there where I can see things for myself."

"Then so do I," Connrad said.

LeMarck took up his position and went with them. Never before during a Big Game had the barons left the security of the safe room. He didn't like the way the night was shaping up.

And if he was right about the identity of the two people out there in the pit, he was near to liking it even less.

"I DON'T KNOW what you're doing with these people," Bernsen said to Doc. "You're a man of science, hardly their ilk at all."

Doc sat against the opposite wall from the one Jak and Krysty had spent time salting with their explosives. He shook his head, listening to the frantic crack of weapons overhead, and offered a silent prayer to his Maker for his friends left so unprotected and outmanned in the pit.

"Are you acquainted with the works of the Bard?" Doc asked.

"William Shakespeare?" Bernsen looked puzzled.

"The very man," Doc agreed with a nod.

"He was no scientist."

"On the contrary," Doc said, "I believe he indeed was. And his spheres of investigation were the vagaries of the human heart versus the morality of civilization using power as a catalyst."

"Perhaps I'll look upon his works in time," Bernsen.

Doc wasn't fool enough to think the man was sincere. It was only an effort at placating him. "As the Bard said in his work *The Tempest,* 'Misery acquaints a man with strange bedfellows.' I've found that, in my years, to be a most apt statement."

"But we have a chance to get out of here," Bernsen said. "Those people are going to get caught. In the process they're going to get us caught, as well."

"You cannot say that. These people are very good at what they do. You have not seen even a fraction of the perils they've faced together during their travels."

"Fool's luck." The scientist shook his head. "You, my friend, are guilty of a most destructive false pride."

"That shall remain to be seen, and I shall have a front-row seat."

"THAT LOCK'S not going to hold them long."

Dean knew that, listening to the way the scratching of the monkeys filled the bathroom. "There's not going to be another way out of here, either. One way in, one way out."

"Got to be," Louis replied.

A self-light flared in the darkness, illuminating first Louis's features, then spreading across the interior of the bathroom.

It was a big room, perhaps the biggest of its kind that Dean had ever seen. His heart pounded in his chest, causing blood to rush through his ears.

Stalls lined the wall to his left, flanked by urinals. Shattered mirrors clung haphazardly to the tiled walls. Bugs fled across the tiled floor, retreating from skeletons that were decades old and corpses that may have only been weeks in decaying.

"Up," Louis said, holding the self-light toward the ceiling. "Mebbe some crawl space we can get through." He cursed when the self-light burned his fingers, and dropped the flaming stick to the floor.

Dean hated being left blind in the darkness. His skin crawled at the sound of the monkeys' nails scratching against the door.

Louis struck another self-light, then pushed his way through one of the stalls. He stood on the toilet and shoved one of the acoustic tiles out of the metal frame that formed the ceiling. Glancing down at Dean, he said, "I think we can get through here. Hurry."

Dean hauled himself up beside Louis and caught the lip of the metal frame. It took a lot of strength to pull his body up inside. The collection of dust and odor sent him into a sneezing fit as he lay against the top of the ceiling. The floor of the next level was scarcely more than two feet above him.

"Dean," Louis called.

Looking back, Dean saw the other boy struggling to pull himself up. Reaching down, Dean caught the vest of Louis's body armor and yanked him through. As he passed through, Louis dropped the flaming self-light to the floor.

"See anything?" Louis asked.

"There wasn't time," Dean replied, choking as the dust filled his lungs.

Another self-light flared into being. Perspiration dripped down Louis's face, glowing like pearls. "Over there."

Dean looked, seeing the access shaft in front of them. He started for it immediately. Before he reached it, Louis dropped the self-light, but finding the entranceway to the access shaft was no problem. Dean crawled inside, then found it shifted straight up within a few feet.

Louis lit another self-light. "Can we make it?"

"I think so," Dean said. "Be a hard climb."

"Beats the hell out of staying down here."

The sound of the door finally crashing inward filled the bathroom and echoed through the crawl space. An instant later brown hairy hands gripped the sides of the metal frame where Dean and Louis had come up through.

"Smell us," Dean said.

"Not for long," Louis promised. "Get moving." He retrieved a gren from his pack and pulled the pin. Turning, he lobbed the bomb back onto the acoustic tiles.

Dean went up the shaft, bracing his back against the side with his palms extended in front of him, shoving his way up with his feet. Louis was right below him.

When the gren blew, it sent a flash of light stabbing into Dean's eyes. Monkeys screamed in terror and in rage. Dean kept climbing, feeling the wave of heat pass over him. Wherever they were headed, it had to be better than where they were.

Chapter Thirty-Six

Ryan was the last man through the door on the second level. Monkeys filled the landing below, their eyes glowing ruby red. He paused for a moment, squeezing the SIG-Sauer's trigger as rapidly as he could until it was empty.

Monkeys flopped backward, chilled by the full-metal-jacket rounds.

He stepped back to reload, and J.B. stepped forward.

"Grens," the Armorer said, showing Ryan the spherical objects in his hands. J.B. pulled the pins with his teeth, then tossed the bombs into the stairwell.

When the explosion sounded so quickly after, Ryan thought for a moment that J.B. had miscalculated the time and blown them all to hell. Then he realized that the other explosion was farther off.

The two bombs the Armorer had launched erupted right after he pulled the stairwell door closed.

"Might have discouraged them some," J.B. said, adjusting his hat, "but they're still plenty interested."

Ryan took the lead. He sprinted down the hallway, past elevators with sagging doors torn from their tracks. Moonlight poured in through the windows at one end of the corridor and filtered out the set at the other end. They crossed two intersections before the monkeys came boiling out of the stairwell, screeches and blood-curdling howls reverberating throughout the corridor.

Taking the first left at the next intersection he came to,

Ryan slapped at doors, kicking them open. The locks had been broken or shot out over the years. All of the rooms were bedrooms of some type, though the furniture had been stolen or torn to pieces.

None of them offered any hope of escape.

"Those were winged monkeys," Mildred said, her words broken up by her struggle to breathe during the exertion of running.

"Yep," J.B. agreed. "Big teeth for monkeys, though."

"All we need," the woman said, "is for a green ball of fire to drop from the ceiling and suddenly proclaim, 'I am the great and powerful Oz!'"

Ryan didn't have a clue as to what Mildred was talking about. He sucked in air through his nose, keeping his lungs charged with fresh oxygen as he focused on surviving the trap that had been sprung inside the Mirage.

He took a right at the next intersection, spotting the huge plate-glass window at the end of the hallway. "J.B." He lifted the SIG-Sauer and started to fire rounds at the glass, which starred but didn't shatter.

"Take the glass out," Ryan ordered. "We'll go over the side, get back into the forest. Mebbe lose ourselves. We can't hold this building."

J.B. lifted the S&W scattergun to his shoulder and fired. The fléchettes struck the window already weakened by Ryan's rounds and blew out nearly the whole section.

Ryan stopped at the window, looking around warily for snipers posted outside. He knocked the ragged chunks of glass from the bottom track of the window with the barrel of the SIG-Sauer blaster.

Mildred touched his shoulder as she came up beside him. She pointed. "Look."

Ryan followed her line of direction and saw two figures dashing through the forest less than a quarter mile away.

He reached into his pack and took out his binoculars. Focusing them, he made out Jak and Krysty just as they slipped under low tree branches. He kept tracking them until he saw them come out on the other side only a few feet from a large pond surrounded by a raised bank.

Muzzle-flashes burned hot against the shadows and foliage behind them, marking the course of their pursuers.

"Fireblast!" Ryan snarled, watching his lover as bullets cut through the brush around her.

A dozen riders on horseback galloped toward Krysty and Jak's position, circling slightly to get through the tangled brush. Ryan lifted the SIG-Sauer and banged out a handful of rounds. At that distance the rounds weren't effective against the riders, but they did warn Jak and Krysty. Two rifle rounds struck fragments from the brickwork near Ryan's head, driving him to cover.

Spotting the riders, Jak and Krysty turned suddenly and headed for the pond. Bullets ripped into the ground where they'd been. Tracer rounds scattered sparks in their wake. In seconds they were gone from view.

"Go," Ryan told J.B.

The Armorer didn't wait to be told again, hoisting himself up immediately through the window and launching himself outward. Mildred followed, trailed by Moosh Wandell and Thompson.

Ryan wheeled in the direction of the approaching monkeys and started to fire. His bullets had little effect on the phalanx of hairy and winged bodies, as the beasts' anger kept them moving.

While the monkeys were still ten feet short of the final intersection that would bring them less than thirty feet from Ryan's position at the window, two men stepped out forward wearing some sort of sec uniform. Both men carried what appeared to be homemade flamethrowers.

Huge gouts of roiling black-and-orange liquid fire jetted from elongated tubes and flowed over the front line of monkeys. Gurgling hisses filled the corridor, followed immediately by the agonized dying cries of the animals. The smell of burned fur and feathers became an overpowering stench.

Ryan held his fire, hoping they'd escape unnoticed while the sec men were involved with the monkeys. Owen was now clambering through the broken window.

"There!" an armed sec man shouted, pointing at Ryan and Owen. A green armband marked him as belonging to one of the barons. Evidently someone was going to use the confusion to whittle down the odds on Hardcoe's team of warriors. Ryan grinned to himself, already in motion, knowing if it had been him, he'd have done the same thing. Why chance it when a victory can be made certain?

Instantly the men with the flamethrowers came around, both of them firing.

Ryan shouted a warning to Owen, then threw himself farther down the side corridor the companions hadn't traveled.

Orange-and-black fire coursed along the wall, blistering paint and peeling paper, which started to burn a heartbeat later when it reached flashpoint.

Owen was caught in the window by both flaming streams. He screamed the last few seconds of his life away as his body caught on fire. He fell from the window with flames wrapped around him, finally becoming mercifully silent.

With a last look at the fire-filled window, Ryan pushed himself to his feet and raced down the corridor. There was no way he could make it through the swirling inferno. Behind him he heard the shouts of the men who'd taken up the chase. He ran, searching for a way out of the maze, knowing there was little chance that Jak and Krysty could escape from the situation they'd been in unless J.B. and Mildred were able to get into position to help. Even at that, all of their lives might still become forfeit.

"CALL THEM OFF, dammit!" LeMarck yelled at Connrad. Through the binoculars he'd seen the men with flamethrowers attacking Hardcoe's champions. He knew he was stepping way past the boundaries that had been established regarding how underlings spoke to barons.

"Shut up, boy!" Connrad snarled. "Your team lost its immunity when they fired upon my sec guards!"

Atop the tall wall overlooking the pit, LeMarck turned to face Connrad. His hand dropped down to his pistol. Immediately two of Connrad's sec men lifted their own weapons. At least if he laid his life down taking out Connrad, maybe the blame wouldn't fall on Hardcoe.

"No," Hardcoe said, stepping in front of LeMarck, "not this way." He reached out and stilled his sec boss's hand.

His eyes remained locked on LeMarck's, he raised his voice. "Vinge."

"Yeah."

"Saying I agree with your view on that team of mine down in the pit," Hardcoe said, "and saying that I sit by and don't raise a hand while your sec men mow them down, let's also say that if your team joins mine and tries to win free of the pit, they're also forfeit and will be executed accordingly."

Peering over Hardcoe's shoulder, LeMarck saw Connrad run a big hand over his face.

"I said they're also forfeit," Hardcoe stated in a harsh voice. "Do you agree?" Satisfied that LeMarck wasn't going to move, the baron turned to face his foe.

"Yeah," Connrad answered, but LeMarck could tell it wasn't an answer he wanted to give.

LeMarck let out a tense breath. The die had been cast. Now it only remained to be seen who exactly came up with snake eyes.

THE AIR SHAFT BENT again another ten feet up. Dean followed it with difficulty, aided by the adrenaline surging through his body and urged on by Louis cursing at his heels.

He crawled another seven or eight feet, then his forward hand encountered a mesh screen tightly set into place. "It's blocked," he called back to Louis. The shaft had also narrowed, barely passable even if Dean flattened himself.

A self-light flared to life, throwing slashes of illumination over Dean's shoulder. The vent in front of him was about two feet wide by eighteen inches high. The self-light framed most of the rectangle on the carpeted floor on the other side of the vent.

Tables and chairs were scattered across the room, joined by a few skeletons dressed in the tatters. Rodents and insects scattered at the sudden illumination.

"Get the damn thing out of the way!" Louis ordered. "Those monkeys will be here any second!"

Now that he could see what was blocking the way, Dean slipped a long-bladed hunting knife free of his belt and shoved it under the vent frame next to one of the top screws. Once the knife was in place, he twisted with all his strength. The screw popped with a screech.

Before Dean could slide the knife beside the next screw, he heard the double *whumpf* of grens going off somewhere nearby in the building. He twisted the blade, popping off another screw. One more and he had the top of the vent loosened.

"Hurry, Dean!" Louis urged. "They're having trouble getting up the shaft, but I don't think it's going to hold them very long!"

When the two side screws had been popped free, Dean put the knife away, then rested his shoulder against the vent and put his weight into it. The self-light went out as the vent popped loose. It banged on the carpet below, lost in the darkness.

Dean slithered through, falling out on his head but managing to block the impact with his hands. Louis came out right behind him.

Monkey feet drummed against the sides of the shaft, the screeches and jabbering growing louder.

"Go!" Louis said, reaching out in the darkness and shoving his companion forward.

Dean made his way as quickly as he could across the debris-strewn floor, nearly tripping over unidentifiable objects. He caught himself four times before he made it to the opposite wall where he'd seen the door.

Light burned to life in Louis's cupped palms. The boy's blond locks were plastered to his head, his cheeks reddened by blood. "Damn door's got to be here somewhere."

"There," Dean said, spotting the door five feet from their position.

The first monkey dropped to the carpeted floor.

Dean spun and brought up the Hi-Power, banging out three shots. The bullets hit the monkey, and bounced it backward against the wall. "Go on," he yelled. "I'll follow you."

Louis didn't waste time arguing. He needed both hands to keep the self-light alive.

Shifting his aim, Dean pumped rounds into the vent area. A couple of the large eyes winked out. Two more monkeys dropped from the vent and charged forward. Dean heard Louis open the door behind him.

A third monkey launched itself from the vent, wings spread out to catch the air.

"Dean!"

Turning, the boy raced for the door.

Louis held it open. Weak illumination from the hallway windows took the place of the self-light Louis dropped at his feet. The boy had his pistol in hand and was firing over Dean's head and shoulders.

Once in the corridor, Dean helped Louis slam the door shut, both boys resting their weight against it as the flying monkey slammed against it hard enough to open it almost an inch. The monkey slid blunt, hairy fingers through the crack, angling to gain enough purchase to shove the door all the way open with its incredible strength.

"Bastard!" Louis growled, pressing against the wooden surface.

Dean unsheathed his knife, then ran it down the side of the door, neatly slicing off all five of the monkey's fingers. Blood squirted from the injured appendages as its hand disappeared back inside. Shifting his grip on the knife, Dean rammed the blade into the jamb near the top of the door. He slipped a second knife into the jamb near the bottom.

"Hold them for a little while, mebbe," Dean said.

Louis took the lead, trotting across the worn and stained carpet in the corridor.

Dean sucked in air, wishing his lungs weren't so empty because he knew he was making too much noise. The sounds of combat were all around him now, and the open spaces were filling up with the haze of smoke, as if the building had caught fire somehow. He wondered where the others were, how they were doing—if they were still alive.

Abruptly two bulky shadows stepped around the corner

of the intersection ahead of them, little more than twenty feet away.

Then Dean noticed the wavering fires captured in the barrels of the misshapen pistols they carried in their gloved hands. Hoses curled from the weapon and around the men's legs.

"Shit!" Louis said, backpedaling at once and streaking for the other end of the corridor. He bumped against Dean, pushing him back in that direction, as well.

Dean ran as hard as he could, understanding now where all the smoke had come from. He glanced over his shoulder and spotted the sudden mushrooms of orange-and-black flames suddenly gush from the spouts of the flamethrowers. A partially open door ahead of them only a couple steps on the left caught Dean's attention.

He slammed into Louis, knocking them both through the door as the boiling fire rushed through the corridor, filling it. The two boys fell to the floor.

Gazing around the empty boxes on the nearly depleted storage racks, the stainless steel gleaming in the sudden glare of the flames, Dean realized there was no other way out of the room.

"Back out," he told Louis. "It's the only way."

They got to their feet and poised by the door, checking their weapons as they waited for the flames to die down. When the flamethrowers ceased spitting fire, Louis took the lead around the doorway, breaking into a sprint at once across the corridor carpet. Fire pockets blazed on the walls and on the floor, some of them clinging precariously to the acoustic tile overhead.

Dean trailed after the other boy, sweating profusely, more scared now than at any time that he could ever remember. The corner of the next intersection was fifteen feet

away when the harsh crackle of blasterfire started behind
them.

Louis staggered abruptly, almost losing a step. Blood
spread in a widening pattern below the armored vest on his
left side, just above his hip.

As they turned the corner, Dean saw the other boy was
definitely losing his stride.

"Go on, Dean," Louis gasped, holding his side. His face
was white with pain. "I can't run much farther. Mebbe I
can give you some more time."

"No," Dean answered. He hooked the boy's arm over
his shoulders. "We're going to get out of this together."
Taking part of Louis's weight, he guided the boy toward a
door on the left.

Inside, the walls had been stripped to concrete. The low
ceiling held broken conduit pipes and shattered fluorescent
tubes. Overturned tables were in the center of the room,
broken chairs all around them. They were metal and
wouldn't burn, which was the only reason Dean could figure they hadn't been taken. It looked like a private gaming
room for small groups.

"Stay in here," Dean told Louis. "Try to find someplace
to hide. I'll see if I can't get them away from us."

Louis nodded, leaning against the back wall that dog-
legged and took it out of immediate view of the door. Blood
streamed out the side of his mouth. Wordlessly he offered
Dean his rifle, indicating he only had the strength to manage his handblaster.

"I'll be back," Dean said. "I promise. Just hold on."
Slinging the rifle, he sprinted back out of the room and into
the hallway, listening to Louis hack and cough until the
door closed and cut the sound off.

He also heard the running footsteps coming up the hallway they'd just turned off.

"I shot one of the sons of bitches," a man growled. "Know I did. Saw him stagger when the bullet took him."

"If you did," another man replied, "we'll find him soon enough."

"Not soon enough for me," a third man grunted. "Those bastard monkeys are dangerous. Did you see what they did to those boys below?"

In the distance Dean saw another intersection. With luck the sec men would think he and Louis had made it that far. Instead of racing in that direction, he holstered the Browning, then ran a few short steps and jumped for one of the metal crossbars in the ceiling overhead. A number of the acoustic tiles were missing, making a checkerboard of the ceiling.

Scrambling quickly, Dean hauled himself up into the darkness and lay along the crawl space. He positioned himself so he could see down into the corridor, then slipped the assault rifle over his shoulder and snapped the safety off. He pushed the selector to full-auto, snugged the rifle into his shoulder the way his dad and J.B. had taught him, and waited.

The sec team talked briefly below. Dean didn't look in their direction, not wanting to be a moving shadow above them. He'd gambled everything, his life and Louis's, on the play that was about to go down. His breath came forcibly.

"Must not have been hurt as bad as you thought, Clement," someone said. "Fuckers have already made the next corner."

The sec team went forward at a cautious jog.

Dean watched them come into view. He slid his finger over the rifle trigger, taking up slack. When the five men came into view, staggered out a little across the corridor, he dropped the rifle's open sights over the flamethrower tank on the back of the man on the left. He pulled the trigger, running through ten shots that struck the tank, then shifted to the other man with the flamethrower just now turning around to see where the shots had been fired from. Dean caressed the trigger, running the magazine dry.

Before the last shot cycled through the rifle, the fuel propellant in the flamethrower tanks blew up. Wet orange flames jetted everywhere from the explosion, curling against the windows on the opposite wall and filling them with a layer of soot. The wall on the interior caught fire in dozens of places, creating a stench that floated everywhere. Men screamed and writhed in agony until their lives ran out.

LeMarck WATCHED as the sudden flare of the propellant washed away the scene of the green-team member who'd gunned down the sec guards. He dropped the binoculars and glared at Connrad, whose face seemed to become carved of stone.

"They're forfeit," the sec boss said in a voice loud enough for them all to hear.

"Kill them," Connrad growled. "Kill them all."

Around them the sec men rushed toward the rope ladders that would allow them to get into the pit. Death was coming.

And this time LeMarck didn't think even the one-eyed man could escape.

BLINKING AGAINST the spots that suddenly dotted his vision from the exploding fuel tanks, Dean reloaded the rifle, then dropped through the roof to the corridor floor. He felt good, then, more certain that he and Louis would find a means of escape.

He returned to the room, pushing through the door.

Louis spun suddenly, more quickly than Dean would

have thought possible. The blaster in his hand went off, throwing out a foot-long muzzle-flash.

Dean jumped to one side of the doorway, the bullet barely missing him as it smacked into the door frame. "Shit, Louis, put that blaster down before you hurt somebody you're not supposed to." He walked into the room.

"What about the men behind us?" Louis asked. He held his hand to his side.

"All chilled," Dean said. "My dad always told me to take advantage of a situation if I could. Those flamethrower tanks strapped to their backs like they were, those bastards were just walking grens waiting to have their pins pulled. I pulled them."

"I don't think I'm going to make this one," Louis said. In the feeble light coming through the partially open door, his face was as pale as ivory, streaked with perspiration, and his eyes were starting to film over.

"You'll make it," Dean said confidently. "Come this far, I am not going to let you die on me now." His fingers worked the boy's armored vest, becoming bloody almost at first touch. When the body armor opened up, he peered under the armor and saw that Louis was right.

The bullet that had hit him in the lower back had passed through his groin, then deflected off the body armor covering his crotch and tore its way through his upper body, as well. The spent bullet lay a couple inches above his right nipple, a dark spot just below the freshly bruised skin that looked like a nest full of maggots.

"Those shitters!" Dean yelled in angry frustration and fear. "They shot you bad, Louis! They shot you real bad!"

Without another word, Louis toppled forward as if the bones had gone out of his legs. Blood leaked from his mouth below his sightless gaze.

Dean tried to catch the dead boy, but the sudden loose

weight was too much. He went down under Louis, panicked all over again. "Louis, you can't die! You can't leave me here alone! Louis!"

The absence of the boy's breathing seemed like an impossible vacuum to Dean. Then it was filled by the snuffling of some large beast just outside the door. Hooves rang on a concrete patch out in the corridor.

It felt as if cold talons suddenly pinched the skin on the back of Dean's neck, pulling it way too tight. Forcing himself up, the boy drew the Browning, barely breathing as he watched the door.

"Dean," someone said, and he couldn't believe how much it sounded like Krysty.

Something shimmered into being on his right. It was impossibly close, near enough to reach out and touch him. He'd have seen anyone or anything that had come that close to him.

Then he saw the face, made out the features. She was indistinct, as if he were seeing her through a heavy fog.

"Krysty?" he said, not believing it.

"Your father is coming for you. Look for him."

Her words sounded as though they were coming from a long distance, then she was gone, just like some kind of ghost. Before he could puzzle over her appearance and what it meant, the door burst open.

Framed in it was a nightmare figure that Dean remembered well: a giant mutie pig, its beady, merciless eyes nearly buried in wrinkles of scarred gristle. The wicked tusks curled up on either side of its mouth.

Before he could get the Browning, the beast started for him, squealing shrilly in anticipation of an easy kill.

Chapter Thirty-Seven

The corridor Ryan turned onto was filled with fire. A roiling ball of it wavered back and forth in front of him, seeking oxygen, threatening to collapse in on itself from the lack of fuel.

He had eluded his pursuers for the moment and was aware that the Mirage was showing potential for burning down around his ears. The sec men with the flamethrowers had been generous with their attentions, leaving burning areas and dead monkeys in their wake.

The group at the bottom of the inferno hadn't been so lucky.

Eyes stinging from the heat and the smoke, Ryan couldn't tell how many of them there were, or what exactly had killed them. With the way at least temporarily impassable, he turned back and took one of the other hallways that he'd passed up.

He sucked at the knuckles of his left hand, which he'd skinned badly when he'd thrown himself away from the flamethrower at the window. He spit out a mouthful of blood, hitting a small fire that clung tenaciously to fragments of the worn carpet in the hallway.

When he was halfway down the new corridor, glancing to the sides to check the doors of what turned out to be more hotel rooms, he felt a chill gust through him, and even thought he'd smelled Krysty's scent next to him. He didn't look; if Krysty was still alive, she was outside with the others.

Servos whined through the hall, but he didn't know what they came from. There were other men searching through the ruins of the Mirage, as well. He'd seen them. And he'd seen one more dead boy in green. At the most, only five of them remained.

Farther down the hallway, he found a door that had a short flight of stairs behind it. The brass plate on the door announced Hotel Staff Only. The lock had been shot through.

With the Steyr in his hands, his back and side pressing against the side of the stairwells for cover, he went up. His ears monitored all sounds. A slight whisper of movement came from the top of the stairs.

At the landing, he paused, looking back the way he'd come and wanting to make sure retreat was still open to him. Satisfied no one was closing the gap behind him, he put his hand on the doorknob and turned. It wasn't locked, and the door opened easily.

Inside the room, slashes of neon lights danced around carelessly. The wall to his left held only glass from top to bottom. A bed occupied a space to his right, tucked in beside a desk that held a comp. The broken mirror covering a big section of the wall on the other side reflected the furniture, making it look as if another room were just next door.

He looked for the source of the noise, his senses at full peak. He stepped into the room, then ducked under the attack of the winged monkey that had been clinging to the space between the door and the ceiling. Unable to get off a shot, he swung the Steyr and felt the meaty impact as he struck the monkey with the rifle's butt.

Shrilling in pain, the monkey scuttled under the bed.

Drawing the SIG-Sauer, Ryan touched off three rounds across the bed, trying to find the mutie creature.

With a scream of pain and rage, the monkey came out from under the bed in a rush. Its mouth was open, showing its deadly fangs, the black talons reaching for Ryan's throat.

"Fireblast!" Ryan shoved the blaster into the monkey's face and pulled the trigger. The 9 mm round punched a hole through the beast's mouth and exited through the back of its head. Some of the flying matter stuck to his armored vest, while the majority of the creature landed in a disjointed confusion of limbs and wings at his feet.

"Ryan."

He was moving, turning, lifting the blaster as he recognized the voice. His finger already rested on the trigger when he said her name. "Krysty." His voice came out hard, disbelieving. "I thought they chilled you." He reached a hand out to the one she had extended. Instead of flesh, he felt a chill similar to the one that had passed through him in the corridor down below.

"I'm not really here, lover," she said.

Ryan's mind whirled with the multiple meanings of that simple declaration. His heart suddenly felt like a stone, cold and as distant as her voice.

"Dean's here with you. Find him."

"Dean?" He shook his head, struggling with everything being dealt to him.

She started to fade, winking out of existence like a dying star.

Ryan reached for her again, called out her name, but felt even the chill of their contact melt away from him as she disappeared.

The only thing that remained was the pull he was suddenly aware of inside his head. "Dean," he breathed, walking over to the wall of glass.

He peered through it with difficulty. Soot grimed it over, layers deep from the fires burning below. At one time, judging from the way the room was laid out, it had been a sec office looking down over the casino below.

The main door held tropical plants Ryan recognized from the jump to Amazonia. They had overgrown boundaries previously established by the building's architects, and had even thrust branches and new growth through the wall.

Once, it looked like a ville had been built inside the gaming room. Tables, chairs and slot machines were toppled over, chaotic. Dead people littered the floor. Some of them were dressed in old-style clothing, while many of the others wore much cruder dress.

Sec guards moved below, as well, searching through the debris, shooting at the monkeys still living.

The pull didn't come from that direction, Ryan knew. He turned and went back down the stairs, getting more sure as he followed the sensation.

He couldn't keep his thoughts from Dean. He'd missed much of his son's younger years, but he didn't begrudge that happenstance. The things he'd done, the places he'd gone, Dean would have been dead.

But he was determined not to lose the boy now, not to the pit creatures, muties or other chill squads. Not to the barons.

He fed the anger inside him, working it until the fatigue dropped away and his nerve and reflexes were as sharp as they ever were.

Out in the second-floor corridor, he turned, going farther into unexplored territory. The pull grew weaker. Realizing his mistake, he turned and went in the other direction, the SIG-Sauer in his fist.

The pull in his mind led him around the corner where

the fire had been. It still burned, flames licking almost to the ceiling where acoustic tile smoldered.

A dark shape shoved at one of the doors on the other side of the fire. He squinted, peering through the heat wave given off by the flames, and recognized the shape as one of the wild pigs the companions had encountered before. There'd been plenty of them in the pit.

In the next second the wild pig thrust its way through the door.

Ryan took a few running steps and launched himself through the flames, covering his face with one arm. He felt the heat and smelled his hair singe. Then in the next moment he was through it, racing for the door as the pig disappeared into the room.

Reaching the entrance, Ryan threw himself to one side of it, the SIG-Sauer clutched firmly in both hands.

Shots rang out, changing the pitch of the wild pig's squeals. Impacts against flesh sounded wet and meaty.

Ryan peered around the door and watched as the pig bore down on a boy in green body armor who stood against the wall. Another boy, obviously dead, was at the feet of the first. The wild pig remained on its feet, running at the boy with the blaster flaming in his hand. The muzzle jumped with every rapid shot, but the boy brought it immediately back on target.

The pig careened against the wall as the boy adroitly shuffled out of the way. But its shoulder brushed against him hard enough to knock him to the floor. Recovering immediately, pushing himself one-handed into a sitting position, the boy stuck the blaster's muzzle into the pig's ear and pulled the trigger twice as the insane beast turned its head toward him, fangs snapping within inches of the boy's arm.

Then the pig shuddered, splaying out its legs, and died.

Ryan stepped part of the way around the doorway, knowing he was backlit by the flames in the corridor so that none of his face showed. The boy noticed him at once, lost in the darkness himself, and started to bring up his blaster.

"You make a move to pull that trigger," Ryan said, "and I'm going to chill you where you sit. Name's Ryan Cawdor. I'm looking for my son, Dean." He took up slack on the SIG-Sauer, knowing the boy might be too fearful to even hear him.

As he registered the words the man spoke, Dean recognized his stance, the way he held his head, the way he held the blaster.

His throat felt all closed up, but he forced his voice to work. "Dad?" He worked to shove the dead pig from his leg where it had him trapped, keeping his grip on his blaster. "Dad!"

The deadweight slid away, and Dean pushed himself to his feet, running toward his father with open arms.

Recognizing his son, Ryan rushed forward, grabbing the boy in his arms, his feelings running rampant. He couldn't remember a time when he and J.B. hadn't been friends, trusting each other with their lives. Opening up to Krysty had been hard after the experiences he'd had with most women.

And Dean—it had been a true puzzle to sort out exactly where to put his son in his life.

But in this instant, with death surrounding them and actively hunting them, Ryan was glad to hold the boy next to him, glad to see that none of the blood on him seemed to be coming from any serious wounds. Dean hugged him back, stronger than Ryan had remembered. For the moment this was the perfect place for Dean to be.

KRYSTY SWAM beneath the surface of the pond, trying not to leave a ripple in her wake, struggling not to imagine what might be in the water with them. Jak had her by the arm, and she had no choice but to trust his instinct for direction; the water was too murky to see through.

Just when she thought her lungs were going to burst from lack of oxygen, her hand encountered thick mud that felt greasy and cold. Jak guided them up a moment later.

"Breathe easy," he whispered in her ear as he gently guided her out of the water. "Hard not breathing fast, but got to. Otherwise get chilled."

Krysty started to turn her head, taking in her surroundings. Jak had brought them up in a nest of reeds and cattails. Some of them were broken off, stabbing uncomfortably into her neck and chin. At least, she hoped it was broken stems and not an insect or water creature. The pond was big, deep and cold, nestled into land that had been bermed at some point. One side of it still held chunks of pavement from a street, a stop sign and the rusted remains of a once colorfully painted trash container.

Jak put his hand on her head from behind. "Be still. They watch for us."

Krysty froze into position, noting the horses and their riders winding through the trees. All of the men had guns. Only a few of them carried bull's-eye lanterns, shining light across the surface of the pond and turning it almost mirror bright.

"What does that thermographic sight show?" they heard one of the riders demand.

"Nothing," another rider replied. "Bunch of water. What'd you expect?"

"What about the Mirage?" the first rider asked.

"Hard to say. The lower two stories are pretty much blazing. That much heat, hard to get any kind of reading at all."

"Did anyone see them jump into the pond?"

A chorus of negatives came back.

"There's a possibility they made it to the Mirage," someone said.

"Mebbe," the first rider agreed. "Let's stick it out here and see if we can turn up anything in the water. Beats the hell out of going up there and getting your nuts toasted."

Krysty freed her .38 from the soaked leather holster and set herself to move.

"Wait," Jak cautioned. "I go first. I kill silent. When shit hits fan, you move."

"Okay," she replied.

Jak reached into the shallow water and lifted up a fistful of black mud, which he smeared over his face, through his hair, then over his arms. When he finished, he was no longer as pale as milk. He looked like a black, wild-haired demon sprung whole from the night's shadows.

Jak crept out of the water as the riders went into motion, staying just outside the tall reeds and cattails. In less than a dozen steps, he'd disappeared soundlessly from Krysty's sight.

The riders split into two groups and went around the pond in both directions. The group to Krysty's left would reach her first. She kept the .38 in her hand, certain her skin was turning blue enough to match the water. Her sentient hair clung to her head.

Less than two minutes later, one of the riders directed his horse through the cattails and reeds toward where Krysty was hiding. His mount didn't like stepping through the mud and the water, shying away and nickering.

Krysty held the blaster, waiting, her heart thumping.

"Hey, Lloyd, what the hell's wrong with you?" someone demanded.

There was no answer.

The man in front of Krysty halted his horse and looked back over his shoulder, less than ten feet from her position. "You want to stop shouting like that?" the man asked.

Behind him a rider suddenly toppled to the ground, clawing at his throat.

"Hey!" the man in front of Krysty shouted. "Somebody just chilled Harris and Lloyd! Both of them are laying on the ground over there with knives through their throats!"

"I see him!" another man cried out.

Gunshots rang out.

Coming up out of the water just as the man in front of her tried to bring his mount around, Krysty grabbed the bridle.

The horse reared up in fear, its eyes rolling white.

Unprepared, the rider fell into the muddy water.

Krysty didn't hesitate about shooting the man twice in the back of the head before he could get to his feet. His body collapsed face forward into the murky water.

Knowing she wouldn't be able to calm the horse without letting it get out of the water, Krysty kept hold of the bridle and ran along at the animal's side, waiting for an opportunity to get into the saddle. The horse also served as a temporary shield, blocking sight of her from most of the other riders.

Up on the bank, her feet under her more solidly, she reached up for the pommel while never breaking stride. With a lithe leap, she pulled herself up into the saddle. Another moment spent taking up the slack in the reins, and she was in control of the fear-maddened horse.

She cut it in a tight half circle, searching the shadows for Jak.

He came up off the ground with no warning. One of the two horses that had belonged to the men he'd killed was tied to a tree, stamping its feet and fighting the bit in its mouth. Apparently one of the riders had gotten down to check out a suspicious area.

Racing across the ground, Jak approached the tethered horse from behind. Before it knew he was there, the albino placed his hands against the horse's rump and vaulted into the saddle. Bullets cut through branches and leaves above his head as he reached forward, staying low against the horse's neck, and untied the reins. He brought the animal around and kicked it lightly. The horse exploded into a gallop.

The other horse streaked for the trees, heading in a westerly direction that would take it toward the Mirage. Another horse was also free, galloping in the same direction.

"Get horses!" Jak called.

Krysty nodded, pulling her mount's head around and kicking it into motion. Bullets whizzed around her as gunfire split the night. Glancing ahead and to the right, she could see flames coming from the first and second floors of the Mirage.

Behind them the surviving sec-team members were already putting a posse together.

Cutting around a tree, Krysty halted her mount for a moment and looked back. Jak rode low in the saddle and fired his .357 Magnum blaster at the men less than forty yards behind him.

Krysty raised the .38 and thumbed back the hammer. The distance from herself to the first rider was less than seventy yards. She centered the muzzle over the man's chest, then squeezed away the slight pull. The .38 banged in her fist.

The lead rider slapped a hand to a spot where his throat joined his chest, then fell from the saddle.

Thumbing the hammer back again, Krysty lined up her second shot and emptied another saddle. Jak was almost on top of her when she fired her remaining round. The bullet went inches wide of its target. Krysty kicked her horse back into motion, barely taking a lead over her companion.

Seven men still remained in pursuit.

She swung the cylinder open and dumped the brass. Fishing shells from her shirt pocket, she tried to refill the cylinder and keep an eye on the frightened horse, as well. It took eight bullets to finally reload the blaster because she dropped three of them.

Jak was having the same problem.

Abruptly a shadow moved ahead of Krysty. Her horse noticed it before she did, sidestepping fast enough to almost throw her from the saddle. She pointed her pistol at the shadow, then saw that it wore J.B.'s beloved fedora and steel-rimmed glasses.

"Keep riding," the Armorer said. "Mildred and I will take care of the posse."

Krysty nodded, then kicked her horse in the sides again, closing on the animal in front of her. Jak drew abreast of her, pointing to the other one, then himself.

"I'LL TAKE THE ODD ONES," J.B. said, lifting his Uzi as the posse closed on their position. "Leaves you the even ones." He stood in the shelter of a blue spruce, the stiff needles scratching at his face.

"I got them," Mildred said calmly. She held the Czech target pistol balanced in both hands.

J.B. knew the wait wouldn't be long; the drumming sound of the horses' hooves grew louder. He was a patient stalker, but he knew the work would be bloody and quick.

Moosh Wandell and Thompson were farther back in the brush, set up to cover their retreat if any of the riders survived the ambush.

Listening to the hooves strike the ground, J.B. timed his move, stepping out when he knew they'd all be between the narrow defile leading through the brush. The rider didn't have a chance to register J.B.'s appearance before the Armorer caressed the Uzi's trigger and sent a 3-round burst into his face. The man's head came apart instantly, and he vanished under the hooves of the horses behind him.

The animals reacted badly, trying to avoid contact with the corpse tumbling under their feet.

Mildred remained in the brush, firing between the branches.

The next four riders dropped from their frightened mounts in quick succession. The woman worked to get the sixth rider, managing a hard shot uphill as the man took off in that direction.

The lone surviving rider retreated behind a row of trees, heading back to the area around the pond. A line of 9 mm bullets from the Uzi tore bark from the trees that he took cover behind.

"Gather up the horses that you can," J.B. told Mildred. He reached out with quick hands and grabbed the pommel of a horse passing by. "I'll be back."

"Be careful," Mildred called after him.

Hauling himself into the saddle, the Armorer reached for the reins, then took control of the animal. He brought it around sharply, almost causing the beast's legs to collapse under them. Then the horse recovered its footing, charging back down the trail when J.B. put his heels to it.

He stayed to the trail, his horse leaping over the corpses when it came to them. Through the brush he saw the last rider trying to wend his way among the trees and bushes to a clearing.

The sec man glanced at the Armorer through the forest, eyes going big with fear.

They came out into the clearing at the same time. J.B.

lifted the Uzi one-handed, guiding the horse with the reins in the other.

To the rider's credit, he wheeled his mount toward the Armorer and lifted his own blaster, firing immediately and screaming at the top of his voice.

J.B. cut his horse toward the man but held his finger poised over the Uzi's trigger until he was certain of the kill. By his own estimate, he had between two and eight rounds left in the 30-round magazine.

Less than twenty yards remained between them when the Armorer cut loose. The 9 mm rounds smashed the sec man out of his saddle, the riderless horse streaking past.

He went after it, catching the animal's reins in seconds and wrapping them around the pommel. Grinding engine noises drew his attention north. Through the trees and along the skyline in the distance, he saw the headlights of wags rolling through the pit toward the Mirage. Even the remnants of the streets that had once been Vegas were rough, causing the vehicles to jump and jar.

"Dark night," he said out loud. Reining his mount to the side, he kicked its ribs and sent it galloping back along the trail.

When he reached the spot where he'd left Mildred and the two surviving members of the red team, he saw that Jak and Krysty had returned, as well. Between them they'd captured nine of the horses. Moosh Wandell and Thompson were pulling themselves into the saddles.

Mildred saw his face and immediately knew something was wrong. "What is it?" she asked.

"Wags are coming," J.B. replied, "fast. And plenty of them!"

Chapter Thirty-Eight

"Where's the rest of your team?" a harsh voice demanded.

"Don't know," a boy replied. "Probably dead. Like everybody else."

"How many are dead?"

Ryan moved silently toward the voices, Dean at his heels. The boy showed more coordination and patience than Ryan could remember from past times. They walked along the corridors of the first floor trying to find a way out of the Mirage. The snipers along the perimeter walls of the pit had to have been put on the alert for any more window jumping. Ryan had nearly had his head taken off by a round while breaking out soot-covered glass along the second floor.

Coming around the corner opening onto the area by the front desk, Ryan saw dozens of big-toothed fish lying dead in the pools of water across the floor. One of the dead boys was there, as well, staring up at the black ceiling.

Farther back, near the line of foliage that had swept into the entranceway from the atrium, three sec guards stood over two boys wearing the green-armored vests.

The sec guards made no move to harm them, but they kept their rifles ready in their hands. The boys knelt on the floor, their hands tucked behind their backs.

"All of them are dead," one of the boys said.

"You know that for a fact?" The speaker was a grizzled man with a potbelly. His face bore the scars of past wars.

"No."

"How many do you know rightly for a fact, boy?"

"Six," the boy said. "Six for certain. Fish got one of them. Five others were killed by those damn monkeys."

"Hate those fucking monkeys," one of the other sec men said.

Not seeing anyone else around, Ryan lifted the SIG-Sauer and stepped out so he was in the clear. Without a word he shot the grizzled man through the side of the head, showering his brains over a broad-leafed fern of some type. Before the first man had time to drop, Ryan shifted his aim.

The second sec guard had his rifle up and was stitching a crooked pattern across the floor, leaving pockmarks where the bullets struck.

Shooting from instinct, Ryan put three rounds into the man's head. The third guard had a blaster in both hands and got off two shots before Ryan could pick him up.

Both rounds slammed into Ryan with bruising force despite the armored vest, but the bullets didn't penetrate. He shot the man four times across the crotch area. At least one of the rounds bounced off the bulletproof armor covering the man's cock, but the force was devastating. The other three bullets gouged into his thighs.

The sec man went down screaming. He tried to maintain enough presence of mind to keep his blaster on target.

Ryan walked over, squeezing the trigger as he neared the man, and put two rounds through the man's wide mouth.

The two boys in green body armor tried to go for the dropped weapons.

"No," Ryan cautioned in a hard voice. "Not until we reach an understanding about what's happening here."

The boys froze.

Dean came forward out of the shadows.

"You know these boys?" Ryan asked his son.

Dean nodded. "Ethan Perry and Conor. Don't remember his last name right now. If I ever knew it."

"Who the hell is this?" Perry demanded. His features were disheveled and bloodstained, carrying a multitude of scratches.

"My dad," Dean answered.

The smaller boy, Conor, looked up at Ryan. "You come here to get Dean out?"

"Didn't start out that way," Ryan replied, "but I'm aiming to see it done."

"What about us?" Perry asked.

"Free country," Ryan said. "If you can keep up, you can come along. If you don't carry your weight, you get left behind."

Both boys nodded.

"Arm yourselves," Ryan said. "We're pulling up stakes. Now." He strode toward the atrium, seeing the dark outline of the entranceway framed behind the trees and plants.

Dean stayed close behind him, and the other two boys fell in, as well.

"Louis?" Conor asked.

"Dead," Dean replied.

"Oh."

Senses alert for any sign of danger, Ryan came to a halt at the entranceway and peered around its edge. He saw the wags heading toward the Mirage, almost obscured in the white smoke drifting off the burning building. "Fireblast," he swore quietly.

He signaled to the boys and took off around the corner of the building, watchful of the snipers along the top of the wall on the other side. He skirted the edge of the outside swimming pool, counting on the falls streaming from the fifth floor to help cover them from easy view. He wondered where Mildred and J.B. had gone.

Hooves beat against the ground, the sound coming from the west.

Turning in that direction, Ryan watched a group of riders approach at a fast gallop, staying under the canopy of trees as much as possible. Then, under a bright shaft of moonlight, he spotted red hair on the rider of the lead horse.

Krysty brought the horse to a stop at the edge of the swimming pool, her eyes focused on him, guided more than by just her vision.

"Time to shake the dust of this place from us, lover," she called across the water.

Bullets from the guards on top of the wall suddenly sheared through the trees over the riders and horses. J.B. swung up a rifle he'd liberated from someone along the way. The Armorer cracked off expert shots, dropping two of the sec men from the top of the wall. One of them fell onto the top of the hotel, and the other took the forty-foot plunge into the swimming pool. The rest of the sec guards went into hiding as Jak, Mildred, Krysty, Moosh Wandell and Thompson added their fire to J.B.'s.

"Go," Ryan told Dean.

Without a word the boy dived into the water and began to swim briskly, followed by Conor and Perry.

Holstering the SIG-Sauer and pulling up the Steyr, Ryan picked off two snipers, further demoralizing the sec crew overhead. He dived into the water, staying under for a time to cut through it more swiftly. When he surfaced, he was barely two strokes behind Dean and ahead of the two other boys.

He reached the bank at the same time Dean did, then took the reins Krysty offered. "Good to see you again," he told her as he swung into the saddle. "After seeing you when I was in the Mirage, I wasn't counting on it."

"I know," Krysty replied. "Wasn't sure I'd be here my-self."

Puzzled by her words but knowing he didn't have the time to investigate them further, Ryan reached out briefly to touch her hand. He wanted to know for sure she was real, was there. Her fingers twined with his, strong, sure and permanent.

She leaned forward in her stirrups and brushed a kiss against his lips. "We get the time, lover, I'll show you how real I am."

Ryan smiled at her in spite of the situation and the rest-less horse tramping the ground beneath him. "I'll hold you to that." Then he reined the horse around. "Which way?"

"West," she replied. "There's a wall there separating the pit from the old convention center."

"I remember the convention center," Mildred said, "but I don't see how it's going to help us."

"It has an underground garage," Krysty said.

"Just another wall," Mildred replied.

The flame-haired woman pulled out two remote-control detonators. "Remember that old Christian story about the walls of Jericho? Well, I've got a couple of Gabriel's horns here."

The next few minutes were a hurried blur for Ryan. He stayed in the saddle, one hand filled with the SIG-Sauer as he kicked the horse's sides and kept it at a full gallop. He shot at everything that moved: muties, creatures and sur-viving members of the barons' teams.

They stayed within the trees as much as they could, tak-ing advantage of the cover offered. With the rough terrain the wags were struggling to close the distance, not able to gain much on the horses.

The horses, however, were only flesh and blood. All of them were sweat-flecked from their exertions, looking as if

they'd been dipped in soapy water. Ryan knew if they had
to run them much farther, they'd burst the animals' hearts.

As the group took a final sweep through the remaining
forest, Moosh Wandell caught a round in the side of his
head that dumped him from his saddle.

The others didn't slow their mounts for an instant. If the
man wasn't dead, he was certainly too wounded to keep up
with them.

Ryan fired a half-dozen shots at the tree less than a hundred yards away. He concentrated on where he'd seen the
muzzle-flash that had claimed Moosh. A few seconds after
the rolling thunder had died away, a body tumbled from
the branches.

"Good shooting," J.B. said.

"Lucky," Ryan growled.

Jak reached out and captured the riderless horse's reins.
"Doc has own mount now."

Another moment through the treacherous forest and uncertain footing of the terrain, and they were at the edge of
the brush in front of the wall that Krysty had guided them
to.

There was also a phalanx of sec men bunched together
on top of the wall. They fired at will, chipping branches
and bark from the surrounding trees.

"Fireblast," Ryan said, staring at the army assembled
before them. "We ride out into that, we're going to get
seriously chopped up."

"Mebbe not," Krysty said without explanation. "Could
be those sec men have picked the wrong place to be." She
took out one of the detonators, wincing slightly as a bullet
ricocheted from the elm tree just above her head. "Jak and
I didn't just mine the wall."

"Better do what you have to do," Ryan said, twisting

in the saddle and peering over his shoulder. "Those wags are getting closer."

She slid her thumb over the red detonator button, then pressed it.

DOC'S ATTENTION was focused primarily on the sudden and definite increase in shots cracking from the sec men's stations above him. He didn't hear Bernsen come up behind him until it was too late. Only the slight scuff of a shoe against concrete alerted him. He spun.

The scientist held a chunk of stone in either hand, turning both his arms into hammers that could crush Doc's skull. "You're a fool," he grunted, "and you're going to die a fool. I'm not going to die with you." He swung the rock in his right hand.

Pain exploded along Doc's jawline. As he went backward against the wall beside him, stars swam into the old man's vision, taking away the weak light coming from the lantern Krysty and Jak had left with him in the underground parking garage.

"With your background," Bernsen berated him, "you know you shouldn't let emotion get involved with your work." He swung the chunk of stone in the other hand, intending to smash Doc's skull.

By the time the blow arrived, Doc moved his head. The rock smacked into the wall, shattering and scarring the cinder blocks.

"I must insist, Doctor," Doc said, "that you control yourself. Otherwise, I fear your choice of actions will lead only to ill fortune."

White spittle framed Bernsen's mouth, and madness gleamed in his eyes. He swung again, this time succeeding in knocking the Le Mat blaster from Doc's grip.

"The only ill fortune will be yours," Bernsen said, "for

ever thinking you could hold me here against my will.'' He swung the stone again.

Senses still reeling, Doc dodged another blow and slid the sword stick from his belt. Without thinking, he twisted the lion's head and drew the concealed sword in a practiced and easy gesture.

Before Bernsen could avoid it, the tip of the steel blade flicked out and carved another mouth from one side of his neck to the other. He let go of the stones, reaching up to his throat and making drowning sounds. Crimson sprayed from his mouth and the slash across his throat.

"I will not be dissuaded from my post," Doc said vehemently. "Nor do I accept being killed while at it. May God have mercy on your soul."

Bernsen toppled forward, the light going out of his eyes.

Then the convention center shuddered like an arthritic dog being struck with cold shivers. The sound of the explosion hammered into the underground garage only a moment later.

"By the Three Kennedys!" Doc exclaimed as he glanced toward the section of wall that he expected to go flying, as well. Instead, a barrage of broken rock trembled from the ceiling. He braced himself against the wall behind him, wondering if the stories above might suddenly collapse and come crashing down on him, reducing him to a protein paste.

HAYDEN LeMARCK WATCHED as the center of the wall of the convention center blew apart. The explosives that ripped it to shreds were cunningly placed. The rooftop was ripped loose, then fell back in on itself, taking a thirty-foot section with it—as well as the sec guards trying to snipe the one-eyed man and his companions.

"Son of a bitch!" someone roared.

"Is someone inside the convention center?" Vinge Connrad demanded. The baron held his rifle in hand, his eyes wild and hot.

No one seemed to have an answer.

"Devil take all of you!" Connrad yelled. "I want a team down there now who can report the truth to me!"

LeMarck didn't figure anyone was inside the convention center. Whoever had entered the pit had mined it on their way in. Getting rid of the sec teams on top made sense, but he didn't know why the one-eyed man had returned to this site with his companions. There was no way out.

He peered through the scope, searching for his quarry. For a moment he thought he might have spotted the one-eyed man among the trees. His finger slid around the sniper rifle's trigger and took up slack. He let out half a breath, then held it. He thought he might have a shot, but also figured the bullet might have been deflected from the branches.

LeMarck also found himself of mixed emotions about killing the one-eyed man. Of all the champions in the Big Game, the one-eyed man and his group deserved most to live.

"Hayden."

The sec commander recognized Baron Hardcoe's voice at once. "Sir?"

"Do you see them?" The baron came to a stop beside them.

LeMarck hesitated only a moment. No matter what else the one-eyed man might represent, he was a danger to Hardcoe if he chose to follow a path of vengeance. "Not clearly, sir, but I'm hoping for a shot."

"Good man." Hardcoe set his Ameli 82 on the fence line. "Mebbe I can flush them out for you." He settled in behind the machine gun and opened it up.

"Dawson, Hughes!" Connrad roared. "You people are with me! Now move your asses!"

Out of his peripheral vision, LeMarck watched Connrad grab a home-built grenade launcher along with a small bag of bombs, slinging both over his shoulder.

"You can stay up here if you want," Connrad told Hardcoe, "but I'm going down to ground level and fuck those bastards over royally. You can sort through the pieces later."

"You've got men down there, too," Hardcoe said.

"Then mebbe we both lose," Connrad said. "Mebbe we'll do the Big Game over in the next few weeks, or mebbe Giskard just gets lucky this year. Either way, those skanks die in the next handful of minutes. You can take an ace on the line on that."

Connrad led his men down the metal staircase that had been welded together to reach the ground, their boots ringing against the steps.

LeMarck looked back through his scope, sorting out the blacks and the greens until he found part of a face. Memory told him the fedora and steel-rimmed glasses belonged to one of the men among One-Eye's group. He let out his breath and steadied for the shot as Hardcoe's machine gun howled in unrestrained carnage.

Then the building shuddered again, letting him know there had been a secondary set of explosives.

Peering over the edge, he saw the bottom of the convention center come spewing out. "Shit!" Glancing back up, he saw the line of riders gallop out of the trees. He turned and used the stairs Hardcoe and his sec crew had taken.

Chapter Thirty-Nine

Ryan fought his horse as the plas ex went off in the building, showering the trees with concrete chips and debris. Watching the wall fronting the underground garage, he saw the hole take shape, yawning open to a mouth of darkness almost twelve yards across and nearly as tall.

"Ride!" he told the others.

Krysty took the lead since she knew the interior of the garage, followed by Mildred.

J.B. held back, manhandling his frightened horse. Specks of blood glowed on the animal's muzzle, sprayed out through its nostrils. "These animals don't have much more to give."

Ryan nodded in agreement. "Mebbe they got enough, though."

When the last of the riders took off, Ryan kicked his mount in the sides. Bullets hit the ground in front of him and on both sides, striking sparks off rocks. The snipers on top of the wall were getting their nerve and the range back.

J.B. took a slight lead over him as they neared the rock-strewn incline leading to the hole in the underground garage.

Ryan stayed low over the saddle and the horse's neck as he passed through the hole. His eye had problems adjusting to the darkness in the underbelly of the convention center.

Wags had been blown haphazardly around, tumbling over one another. Even rusted ones showed new scratches and dents, whole patches of oxidized metal rubbed raw again.

On the other side of the garage, Jak had stopped the extra horse for Doc. The old man appeared shaken up but whole. Jak had to assist him in getting a boot into the stirrup, then reached down and grabbed Doc's waistband, helping pull him into the saddle.

Krysty navigated the stairway leading to the upper floors. The horses' hooves rang on the stone, echoing hollowly in the cavernous vault. Mildred was behind her, trailed by Thompson, Conor, Perry and Dean.

Coming up behind Doc, Ryan looked down and saw Bernsen's body nearly buried in refuse that had tumbled from the ceiling. His throat was cut, clots of crimson covering the front of his shirt.

"What happened to him?" Ryan asked.

Doc grabbed the reins from Jak. "Thank you, my dear boy. I fear I am somewhat shaken about, and my equestrian skills are not as sharp as we would prefer." He shifted his attention to Ryan. "He suggested, very strongly, that I be remiss in my friendship. I corrected his oversight."

"For once and for all, it looks to me," J.B. noted.

"Yes."

Ryan slapped Doc's mount on the flank and got it moving. Doc guided it up the stairs, the horse's breath blowing out in steamy clouds as it clopped up the steps.

Glancing out the hole made by the plas ex, Ryan spotted the sec wags only a few yards away.

"They might get them in here if they're lucky," J.B. said, clamping down his fedora more tightly. "But even if they get them through that maze of wrecked wags, there's no way they're going to get them up these stairs."

Ryan nodded, glancing up. Jak was already navigating

the landing. "Mebbe some waiting outside." He waited expectantly for blasterfire, but none came.

"Had wags outside," Jak called down. "Took coil wires." He held them up. "Got time, we make them ours."

Following J.B., Ryan urged his horse up the stairs. The saddle rocked violently under him as the animal found a gait that would allow it to climb the incline. Passing through the landing required a little more skill.

He caught the door at the top of the stairs as J.B. passed through, then the next one that opened up onto the main lobby. The horse's breath was loud in his ears, rasping back and forth like a bellows.

Dust filled the lobby, swirling in gusts that were lit up by the lanterns hanging on the walls. The horses' hooves striking the concrete under the tattered carpet made the building sound hollow, empty.

The smack of a bullet hitting flesh and the vibration under his thigh was the only warning Ryan had about snipers in the room. He wheeled his mount to the right, felt it stumble for a moment under him and spotted three men firing from entranceways across the foyer.

Over half the horses were already out the door. Ryan glimpsed the night sky beyond, filled with bright, dazzling stars.

Facing the men head-on to present a smaller target with the horse, Ryan lifted the SIG-Sauer and squeezed off rounds. Bullets plucked at his clothing, one of them burning a furrow across his temple above his left ear.

He put the sights over the lantern on the wall by the man on the right. Squeezing off a pair of rounds, he watched the lantern come apart, drenching the sec man in oil. The burning wick fell more slowly, but when it touched the man, it wreathed him in flames.

The man started to scream, distracting the other two gunners nearby.

Maintaining his stance, Ryan shot the next man in the head, then fired the blaster's magazine dry, hitting the last man in the chest and the throat, knocking him down.

J.B. held the door for him.

Ryan kicked his mount and ducked under the door frame. It was immediately cooler outside. In the moonlight he could see the blood dripping from his horse's nostrils, letting him know at least one of the bullets that had hit the animal had cored through one or both lungs. It was dying beneath him. He took the empty magazine from the SIG-Sauer and rammed a fresh one home, thumbing the slide release so it snapped closed.

The Armorer had his shotgun in his hand. "No time to make for the wags." He nodded upward. "They're already regrouping."

"Then we make do with the horses," Ryan said. "Get out into the forest as far as we can. Mebbe we can find a way to lose ourselves. They may be regrouping, but it looks like they're starting to fight among themselves, as well."

Across the top of the wall, some of the sec men had turned their fire on one another. One man fell from the side, screaming the whole way, until he crashed against the ground less than three yards away.

J.B.'s horse spooked. Wrestling with the reins, the Armorer headed the animal in the right direction. "See you on the other side."

Ryan nodded, wondering how much more his mount had to give. Before he could kick the horse in the sides to get it going, he saw an open-topped wag come around the side of the convention center, throwing out rooster tails of dust and rock behind it.

He squinted his eye to make out the men inside it. The

only one he recognized was Vinge Connrad. The baron's blue-jay earrings fluttered in the slipstream coming in over the wag's shield.

As Ryan watched, Connrad raised a tube to his shoulder and flipped up the sights. His target was J.B., but the others would follow. There was no way the horses could outrun the wag, and with the homemade rocket launcher, Connrad only had to get close to kill them all.

Ryan kicked his horse in the sides. At first it was sluggish, then gained speed rapidly. The animal didn't appear skittish about the wag. Ryan figured it was too far over the line of death to even realize where it was headed. Blood came from its nostrils in streams now, spraying across Ryan's pant legs.

Twenty-five feet from the wag, Ryan opened up with the SIG-Sauer, firing as rapidly as he could. Most of the rounds scored on the vehicle, and he managed to get the guy manning the heavy machine gun mounted on the rear deck.

As the gunner fell, Ryan rode out the end of his interception course just as Connrad turned the rocket launcher on him.

Five feet out, the horse plunging at breakneck speed toward the front of the wag from an angle, Ryan pulled his feet from the stirrups and crouched on the saddle.

A moment before impact, the horse suddenly realized where it was. But it was too late to avoid the collision. The horse gave a gurgling whinny of fear.

Ryan leaped forward, hoping he had enough momentum and strength to clear the wag. He tumbled over in midair, just as Connrad's rocket jetted free of the launcher to impact against the convention center. The warhead exploded a new hole in the side of the building.

As he continued to turn, seeing the ground coming up at him fast now, Ryan got a brief glimpse of the horse smashing into the wag. At the last moment it had tried to leap over the vehicle.

The horse never came close to clearing the vehicle. The front of the wag struck the horse at the legs, breaking all of them. Lifted by the low bumper, the horse bounced off the hood and crashed into the windshield. The driver had time for one short-lived scream before the horse's body smashed into him and killed him.

Then Ryan lost the wag briefly, going loose a moment before he struck the ground hard enough to knock the breath from his lungs. He made himself hang on to his blaster despite the pain of the sudden stop. He forced himself into motion, his reflexes working to get his lungs to function again, building a burning pressure in his chest.

He turned, getting his bearings, looking for the wag.

Connrad had kidnapped Dean and brought him to the Big Game. Ryan knew that from the brief conversation he'd had with his son back in the Mirage. He felt the anger work within his flesh and bone. His breath came back, and his legs worked just fine as he sprinted toward the wag.

Out of control, the vehicle had smashed against the bole of an ancient oak tree, gouging the bark. Steam sprayed from the broken radiator, throwing hissing puddles on the ground under the chassis. The horse was lying on the ground behind the wag, torn open and already dead, its intestines wrapped around the dead driver and the rear deck where the machine gun had been mounted.

For a moment Ryan thought Connrad might be dead, as well. Then the baron surged up from the passenger seat and got out.

The baron spun to face Ryan, his hand clawing for his blaster. The only thing he touched was an empty holster.

Ryan grinned coldly. "Looks like you lose the whole

hand this time. Guess they'll be talking about the four barons from now on.''

"Fuck you!" Connrad yelled. He reached into the back of the wag and took out a machete, then charged at Ryan.

Lifting the SIG-Sauer, Ryan squeezed the trigger, then noticed the slide had blown back empty. When he'd been shooting at the wag, he'd emptied the magazine and hadn't realized it.

"Got to have bullets for your blaster if you're going to kill me with it, stupe!" Connrad screamed, taking a two-handed grip on the machete handle. "I'm going to make you into twins!"

Tripping the slide release, Ryan closed the empty blaster and shoved it into his holster. Just as the baron started his swing with the machete, Ryan cleared leather with the panga. Knowing he couldn't stop the heavier blade without risking breaking his weapon, he used the smaller knife to parry the machete.

Metal screamed against metal and sparks flared when the keen edges met and slid against each other.

Ryan felt the anger burning in him.

Connrad closed on him, trying to use his greater weight to an advantage. "I'm going to break you, little man, but I'm not going to kill you. For that, I'm going to use a slow fire. Cut a piece of you off at a time and let you watch that piece burn. Then we'll move on to the next piece. Death's going to be a long time in coming."

"No," Ryan said calmly, "that's not going to happen." The one-eyed man whipped his free hand up suddenly, driving it into Connrad's unprotected chin.

The baron groaned in pain and shoved back, getting more distance between himself and his opponent. The big man swung the machete again, slashing sideways this time in an effort to shear his adversary's head from his shoulders.

Ryan ducked under the effort, but felt the keen edge shear a few dark curls from the top of his head. He kicked at Connrad's knee from a squatting position.

The kneecap shattering sounded like the crack of a gunshot. Even hurting as he was, Connrad tried to swing the machete again as Ryan came back up to a standing position.

Sweeping his left arm up to block the baron's weapon arm, Ryan rammed the panga's point into the underside of the bigger man's jaw. The blade slid home easily, gliding through flesh until it was stopped by the back of Connrad's skull.

The baron heaved convulsively, collapsing first on his broken knee as life left him. The machete dropped to the ground.

Ryan yanked his weapon free and let the corpse drop to the ground. He turned around and found himself confronted by Hayden LeMarck.

The sec boss had his rifle leveled, standing less than twenty feet away. "I hadn't counted on you killing Connrad. That's going to create problems, unless I shoot you myself and bring you in. Mebbe then the other barons will believe Hardcoe didn't have anything to do with Connrad's assassination."

Ryan breathed hard, giving in to his body's demand for oxygen. The panga was still clutched in his hand, and the empty SIG-Sauer was in its holster. The only chance he had was for the Steyr.

"Man come out here looking for trouble. I didn't go looking for it." Ryan paused. "Seems like you come out here hunting it, too."

LeMarck nodded back at the pit area. "You see all that fighting going on up there?"

"Yeah."

"You caused that. You and your friends. Thrown every-

thing that was balanced between the barons into a frenzy
Going to be a lot of chilling before things settle down
again.''

"With Connrad dead, Hardcoe should have an easier
time of claiming the villes.''

"Mebbe. Be easier to do if I chill you here and take your
body back.''

"Be difficult to drag a man when you're dead yourself,''
a hard voice said.

Looking over LeMarck's shoulder, Ryan saw J.B. on his
horse in the shadows, his shotgun raised to his shoulder.

"Your friend with the hat?'' LeMarck asked. He didn't
move the rifle's sights from Ryan's head.

"Yeah.''

"I'll tell you something,'' the sec boss said, raising his
voice, "if you thought you could have taken me without
getting your friend chilled, you'd have already done it.''

"True enough,'' J.B. admitted.

"But you don't think you can shoot me and keep me
from shooting your buddy.''

"Got a better than average chance,'' J.B. replied. "shot
gun's loaded with twenty razor-edged fléchettes. The im
pact of them shredding flesh from bone is going to stagger
you some.''

"But will it be enough?'' LeMarck was smiling.

"I guess that remains to be seen, doesn't it?'' Ryan
asked. "One thing's for certain—we can't hang around
here to think about it much.''

"Agreed,'' LeMarck said. "I get myself chilled, I figure
Hardcoe's going to have an even harder time hanging on
to the seven villes. How do you want to handle this?''

"Start walking backward,'' Ryan said, "toward the wag
You can keep the rifle on me. Before you get behind it

you throw out the rifle or my friend takes your head off with the shotgun. Sound fair enough?''

"Fair enough," LeMarck said. "But I'd rather see you dead. Don't want to have to get sleepless at night wondering when you're going to be coming back our way."

"Revenge isn't all that high on my list," Ryan told him truthfully. "I see a chance to get it, walk away clean, I'll do it. I'm more interested in a whole skin. Cut my losses here. But I will tell you one thing—if I see you anywhere around me again, I'll chill you on the spot. No questions asked, no warning given."

"I'll keep that in mind." LeMarck started to back up, reaching the corner of the wrecked wag.

"Far enough," J.B. called. "Throw out the rifle."

After only a moment of hesitation, the sec boss did as he'd been told, moving swiftly behind the wag.

Ryan ran toward J.B. The Armorer kicked a foot out of the stirrup on Ryan's side. Hooking his boot in the stirrup, Ryan hauled himself up behind his friend. The horse jostled around, adjusting to the weight.

Pulling on the reins, J.B. backed the horse to the trail leading into the forest. Ryan rammed a fresh magazine into the SIG-Sauer, then pointed it at LeMarck's position.

"Okay," Ryan said. "I've got him covered."

J.B. wheeled the horse and kicked it into a full gallop.

LeMarck moved at once, coming up over the edge of the wag with a blaster in his fist.

Ryan fired, scattering bullets all around the sec boss and sending the man to cover again. In a heartbeat the wag and the convention center were out of sight.

Less than two hundred yards farther on, with the horse giving out beneath their combined weight, Ryan saw the clearing up ahead where an armawag sat like a mythical beast, its ugly cannon snout pointed toward the ruins of the ville.

Remains of Vegas's former glory still thrust above the trees and grass around and behind the wag, letting Ryan know they hadn't yet cleared the area where the ville had once stood. Most of the buildings were smaller now, mainly private dwellings and scaled-down shops. A lot of the area hadn't had much in the way of development. A sign nearly hidden by a blackberry bush read Las Vegas Country Club.

Saddles and bridles littered the ground in front of the armawag.

"What the hell?" J.B. said, pulling the horse up short and guiding it behind a stand of trees.

Ryan slid down, refilling the hand blaster and holstering it so he could take up the Steyr.

Abruptly the armawag's hatch opened, and a man pushed himself into view.

Ryan recognized the weathered features of Jake, one of Nicholas Brody's chief sec men.

Jake touched the brim of his hat. "Cawdor, you know me?"

"I know you," Ryan replied. "Just don't know what you're doing here." He put the telescopic sights over the man's heart.

"Brody sent me for the missing boys," Jake replied. "Took me a while to round up some able-bodied men and come running, but we're here now. Dean told me him Conor and Perry are all that's left."

"Yeah."

Jake let out a breath. "Don't reckon Mr. Brody's going to be overly fond of hearing that."

"Probably not."

"I got the rest of your people aboard this wag and others," Jake said. "I'm offering you a ride back to the school if you want. Don't figure on anybody back there bothering us too much if we come outfitted like this."

"I'd say you're right," Ryan replied with a grin.

"So I'm asking you now. You want to ride back or you want to fight your way out of this forest?"

Ryan slung his rifle. "If it's all the same to you, I'd rather ride."

Epilogue

Days later, rested from sleeping in beds for two nights and their wounds cleaned and tended, Ryan and Krysty sat at one of the patio tables sharing a breakfast that had been made in the Nicholas Brody School. There were melons and hash browns, fresh-cured bacon and breakfast steak, eggs any way a person wanted them, warm biscuits and coffee that was real coffee and not coffee sub.

During their stay, Ryan had found the headmaster to be reclusive, suffering more from the sickness that plagued him. Mildred had spent some time with the man, offering a treatment plan and some of the medicine Krysty had recovered from the airwag in the mountains.

Even with the deaths of seven children hanging over the school, evidenced by the flag in the center courtyard flying at half-mast and the black armbands on the student body and teachers, the situation Nicholas Brody had created with his dream seemed idyllic.

Farther down the hill, Mildred and J.B. stood side by side in a field, getting the companions' weapons travel ready again. Doc had spent some time lecturing in a few of the science classes, much to the chagrin and irritation of the teachers, and Ryan figured the old man was there now talking elegantly of how important knowledge was. Jak spent his time in the woods with Jake, tracking down venison and other meats for the school's larder.

"I figure on moving out tomorrow morning," Ryan said

pushing his plate away, finally unable to handle anything more to eat. He was still sore in a few places, but the level of pain was a comfortable, familiar one.

"This is a nice place," Krysty said wistfully. "Mebbe we could spend a few more days here."

He reached out and took her hand. "But it's not our place. Me, Jak and J.B., we fly in the face of everything Brody's trying to teach these young people. Death sits down at the table with us, and they know it. You and Mildred and Doc, you're not so far gone that you can't fit in with these surroundings. They look at us, they know we're one step out of the grave."

"I know, lover. What about Dean? Is he going with us?"

Ryan glanced back toward the picnic area where Dean and Phaedra Lemon sat at one of the wooden tables. "I'll have to ask him."

"He seems to be quite smitten with Phaedra, lover."

"She's a cute girl," Ryan allowed. "Seems to like him, too."

"I'd say so," Krysty replied with a small smile. "Wouldn't it have been nice if we could have met like that? Shared some of our innocence awhile?"

Ryan looked at her grimly and told her the truth. "I don't remember ever being innocent. And if we had met, mebbe we wouldn't have cared at all for each other. It's the travels we've had this far that's brought us together and kept us that way."

"Gaia's will that it'll always be so. My heart has never been bound to anyone the way it has been to you, Ryan Cawdor."

He tried to say something, but the words refused to find their way into his head.

Krysty touched his lips with her fingers. "Shh. I know what's in your heart. It's enough for me."

Leaning forward, Ryan kissed her. When they parted, he glanced at Dean and saw his son was getting kissed by Phaedra.

"Like father, like son." Krysty laughed.

And the sound was pleasant enough to Ryan that he didn't feel any embarrassment at all.

IT WAS A FEW HOURS LATER when Ryan caught his son alone. They'd spent quite a bit of time together over the past few days, but Dean had made time for Phaedra, as well.

The boy was standing on the catwalk around the inner palisade wall, a piece of straw between his teeth as he gazed out over the land spread before him.

"Mind if I come up?" Ryan called.

Dean looked down, startled. "I can come down."

"Rather come up if you don't mind," Ryan said. "Been inside these walls all day. Be good to look out some."

Dean nodded.

Ryan scaled the ladder easily and clambered up beside his son. "See anything you like?"

"Everything. I haven't gotten out much in the time I've been here. Field trips occasionally, camp-outs overnight even less. Still not used to having walls around me all the time."

Ryan grinned and tousled his son's hair. "Know how you feel." He stood beside Dean and looked out over the world, feeling the wanderlust calling to him, making him want to roll on to see what he could see. "We're clearing out of here tomorrow morning."

"I thought it would be sooner."

"If we hadn't been through everything like we were might have been sooner." He looked at Dean. "Got to ask you what you want to do, though."

Dean returned his gaze, eyes wide. "What do you mean?"

"I talked it over with Brody. He says you're welcome to stay here if you want. Instead of kicking you out of school for prowling, he's willing to work out some other punishment that'll allow you to stay in your classes if you'd rather."

Dean looked a little disappointed. "Good to know."

"He says you're a good student, showing some real potential."

"I've been studying hard."

"I know that, too."

Dean looked deep into Ryan's eyes. "What if I asked to come with you?"

"Then you'd have to have all your gear packed and be ready to move out at daybreak."

It took a moment for the words to penetrate, then a broad smile lit Dean's face. "You mean it?"

"Yeah."

"I didn't do the whole year."

"You did enough," Ryan said, "for now. You want to come back later, we'll see about that, too. I just thought right now it might be difficult for you to leave with Phaedra hanging around and such."

Dean shook his head. "She knows, Dad. She told me that I'd be leaving soon as I could. Said she could see it in my eyes. Went on to tell me I'm not a domesticated bird. I'm born to the wild. But that doesn't mean I can't come see her if I get back this way."

"Sometimes a woman knows a man's heart more than he knows it himself, son. Man gets too used to living by his wits, and stopping to feel things slows that down."

"I guess so," Dean agreed. "You mind if I go tell Phaedra?"

"Go ahead," Ryan said.

Dean grabbed the sides of the ladder and wrapped his feet around them, creating just enough friction to let himself slide safely down the ladder. When he hit the ground, he took off running.

"Dean!" Ryan called.

The boy turned around, eyes full of mischief and a big grin on his face.

"One other thing."

"What's that, Dad?"

"When I get up in the morning," Ryan said, "I don't want to hear about you being caught on top of the dorm in the middle of the night again."

"Don't worry about that," Dean called back. "Nobody's going to catch me."

Ryan turned quickly, before his son could see him start to laugh. He saw Krysty out in the vegetable gardens, going through plants and vines with students, her hair flame red in the bright sunlight.

He thought about her and him, and how things might be if they had a place of their own. Krysty would love the children they had, bring them up in gardens like the one out there, be content in a small house.

Ryan couldn't see it happening any time soon. But the thought was pleasant enough. After a few more minutes, he went down to join Krysty, to share in one more peaceful afternoon before they once again took up their journey through Deathlands.

James Axler

OUTLANDERS™

Trained by the ruling elite of post-holocaust
America as a pureheart warrior, Kane is an
enemy of the order he once served. He knows
of his father's fate, he's seen firsthand the
penalties, and yet a deep-rooted instinct drives
him on to search for the truth. An exile to the
hellzones, an outcast, Kane is the focus of a
deadly hunt. But with brother-in-arms Grant,
and Brigid Baptiste, keeper of the archives, he's
sworn to light the dark past...and the world's
fate. New clues hint that a terrifying piece of
the puzzle is buried in the heart of Asia, where
a descendant of the Great Khan wields
awesome powers....

Available September 1997,
wherever Gold Eagle books are sold.

TAKE 'EM FREE
4 action-packed novels plus a mystery bonus
NO RISK
NO OBLIGATION TO BUY

**When terror goes high-tech,
Stony Man is ready**

STONY MAN™ 30

VIRTUAL PERIL

When North Korea captures a SEAL team, the world is flooded with media images and film footage of American aggression on the seas. International outrage and condemnation follow, and for the U.S. there is only one option: a covert probe to recover personnel and the illegal arms shipment the SEALs had pursued. Stony Man's initial breach of the Korean border ends in capture for one, betrayal for all. For even as they are lured into battle, an unknown enemy strikes deep at the heart of Stony Man.

Available in September at your favorite retail outlet.